# Unbound

## THE GUARDIANS OF THE WELDAFIRE STONE

### TRINITY CUNNINGHAM

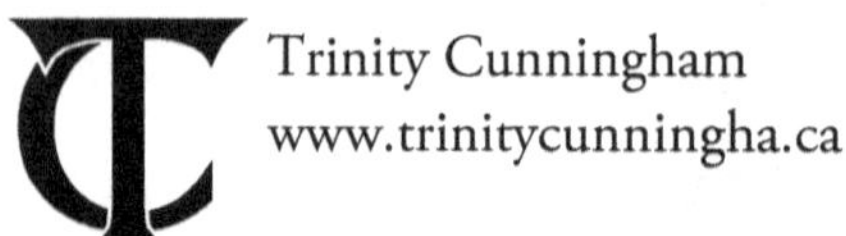




ISBN
978-1-0689558-0-8 (PAPERBACK)
978-1-0689558-1-5 (EBOOK)
978-1-0689558-2-2 (HARDCOVER)

*I.*     *FICTION, FANTASY, ACTION & ADVNTURE*

Those dreams you began to pursue . . .

Don't give up on them.

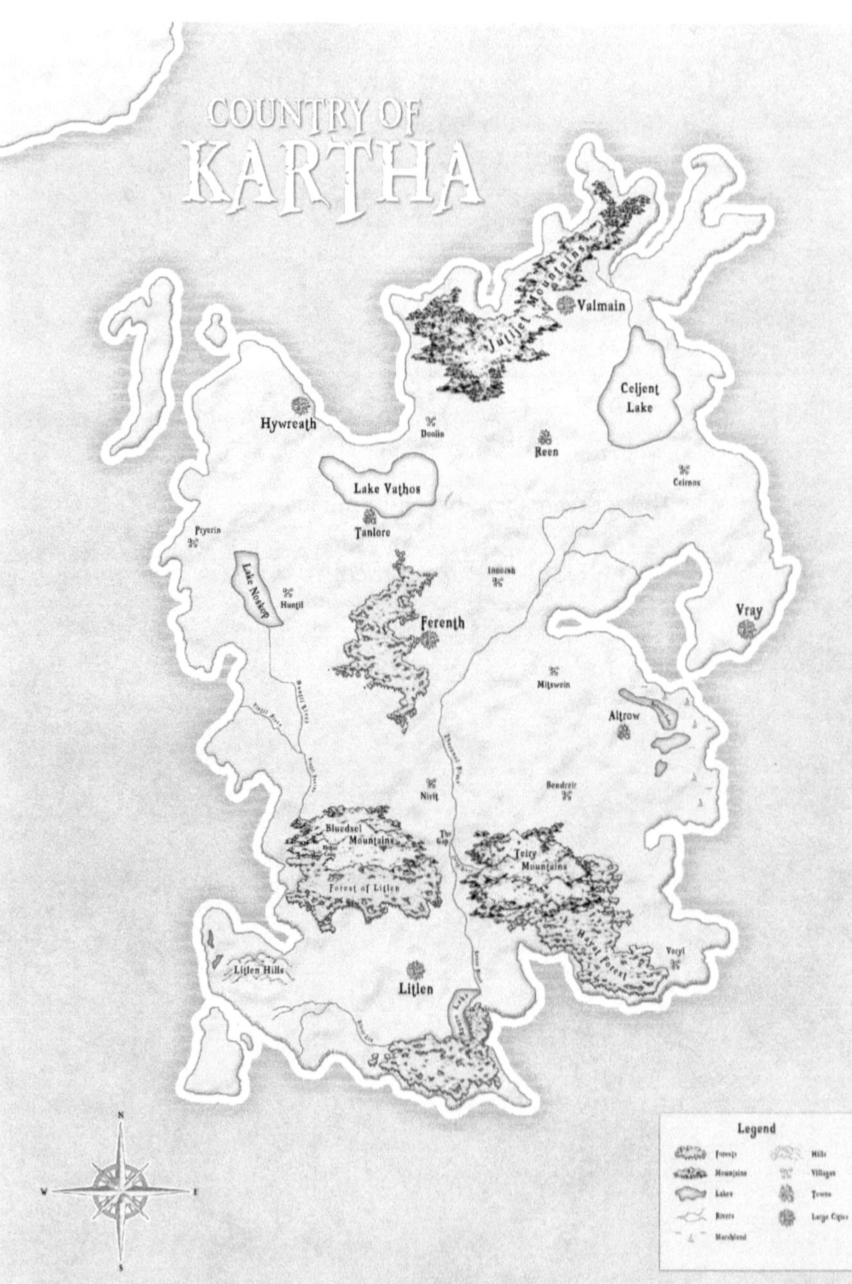

COUNTRY OF
KARTHA
Juljiet Mountains
Valmain
Celjent Lake
Hywreath
Doolin
Reen
Celrnox
Lake Vathos
Tanlore
Ptyerin
Innorsh
Lake Noskop
Huntjil
Vray
Ferenth
Mitswein
Altrow
Bendreir
Nivit
Bluedsel Mountains
The Gap
Teiry Mountains
Forest of Litlen
Hazel Forest
Voryl
Litlen Hills
Litlen
Legend
Forests
Hills
Mountains
Villages
Lakes
Towns
Rivers
Large Cities
Marshland
N
S
E
W

IPTIN
"FORMERLY IPTIN PROVINCE"
KARTHA
ECTARIN
Dunae Lake
Legend
Forests
Villages
Boreal Forests
Towns
Mountains
Large Cities
Lakes
Rivers
Prairie/Grasslands
Bevay/Cliffs
Beaches
N
E
S
W

# Chapter 1

Nothing hurt Mick. Not really.

His knife slipped from his hand, and he nicked his finger. He winced and clenched his fist as if he could tame the trembling beneath his skin. He'd blame his distracted thoughts, except he couldn't deny that the trembling had been worsening. At this rate, he'd not be able to perform these simple tasks in his work anymore. He'd have thought that after twenty-two years of having to deal with the shakes, as he called them, he'd at least have had better control of his reaction when things like this happened. He'd not been too subtle.

Aira, his assistant, glanced his way. She raised a brow. "Everything all right?" Her dark hair showed under her cap, which kept it all neatly together. The way she wore it in her typical tight bun accentuated her clear, flawless skin. In their line of work, Mick opted to keep his face cleanshaven, but it always had the rough feel of stubble by the end of the day. And he could never get his loose curls to stay under his cap the way Aira could.

A thin line of crimson traced along his skin, down his thumb. Mick twisted his body so he had his back to Aira while she stood over the sink, washing the potatoes that were to accompany the meal they were preparing. He'd been chopping carrots before his knife slipped and left its mark. The cut healed, tingling like tiny pinpricks weaving the wound back together just beneath his skin, creating a deep itch he couldn't scratch. And then it was gone. It never took long. But this wasn't the first time the shakes caused him to cut himself, and considering much of his work involved using a knife, he really should be more careful.

A small window looked out into the grassy knoll on the western side of the manor and a sliver of the sun peeked out from clouds, brightening the kitchen.

Mick wiped blood from his thumb and wrist and removed any trace of the now non-existent cut. "I'm all right. Just a little distracted."

Aira's lip quirked up and she gestured to his hands. "You do that a lot you know—get distracted." She resumed her peeling without mentioning the cut. "Where do you go inside that head of yours?"

Scooting in beside her, Mick got a whiff of her honey scent as he poured water from the jug into the sink. He cleaned the knife and his hands before getting back to chopping. Using more caution this time, he started on the next carrot.

"To a bigger kitchen." He smirked. "It's got a massive fireplace and stove; a whole wall of counter-space, an open window that takes up the wall and looks out over the sea from a hilltop. I imagine it every time I close my eyes." He waved his hand in a dreamy kind of way. "Can't you see it, Aira?"

Although this kitchen was modest, it wasn't his own. The idea was nice, but Mick knew better than to hope for so much. Iptin Province was but a speck on the map. In comparison to the neighbouring country of Ectarin, it was nothing. Acquiring the position as head cook in the Governor's manor in the country's capital was about as good as it would get for him here. To achieve anything higher, he'd have to cross the Scedni`j Sea and sail to the country of Reij, where he might seek out a position at the king's Palace.

When Mick first applied for this job, he wished he'd known what he knew now. He wouldn't have been so eager. He thought an opportunity to work for the Governor would allow him a chance to cook for the most esteemed guests—those of the nobility who sought to do good by the people; who hoped to make a difference for the better. The guests who visited the manor were of no such kind. Aira's companionship was the only saving grace to remaining and continuing to work for a man like Governor Riggs.

Maybe one day he'd convince her to leave with him to find work elsewhere.

Aira grinned, showing off a dimple on either cheek. "Oh yes, I can imagine it now," Aira said with an air of whimsy. She chuckled and raised her shoulder to the side of her face, wiping the perspiration there. "This dream place of yours, does it happen to be in Kartha?"

Mick slowed his cutting. *Yes* was his immediate response, but he took a second to think it through. He'd been born in Kartha. His mother and father had moved him to Iptin Province when he was a baby, and they never returned to their homeland. Despite the fact that he grew up here, and the bonds he had with the people in his life, this place never felt like home.

He finished cutting the carrots and transferred them into a pot of boiling water. "Maybe," he said, answering Aira's question. He dried his hands on the apron that draped over his legs. "No, actually. Probably not. I'd never hear the end of it from my parents."

Aira paused her chopping to cock her head at Mick. She said nothing, but her silence made her thoughts clear enough.

"What are you looking at me like that for?" Mick asked.

Aira shrugged, then returned her attention back to the potato in her hand. "It's nothing."

*Nothing* was never nothing. Mick rolled his eyes as he stepped around Aira to check on the lamb roast cooking over the fireplace. He lifted the lid of the pot, and the scent of thyme overwhelmed his senses. The fresh herb mingling with the rosemary filled the kitchen with a delightful aroma. Mick breathed it in and his muscles relaxed. Cooking was about the only thing that ever made him feel like things were right in the world. Smelling the savoury herbs and various spices brought a sense of calm to his otherwise agitated mind.

If only it did the same for the trembling under his skin that irritated him constantly. He wished he knew how to make it stop. Not even cooking helped these days.

The kitchen door opened from the hall and Rugio popped his head in. The mop of hair on the governor's butler couldn't be tamed, though the man did make his attempts at keeping it back by tying it in a low tail behind his head.

"Mr. Dairner, someone to see you," Rugio said through clenched teeth. He stepped fully into the kitchen and lifted a finger. "In the future, please inform your guests that they are to come after regular work hours and they must come to the back entrance *only*. The Governor does not appreciate people coming in through the front entrance to call on his staff."

Mick gave his hands a quick wipe with his apron. He then removed the apron, rolled it up in a ball, and placed it on the counter, laying his cap next to it. "But you must admit," he said, "the guests who call on the staff probably have better manners than the Governor's guests, wouldn't you say?" He offered a sly smile.

Rugio's scowl deepened, so Mick dropped the humour. "Apologies, Rugio. I'll be sure to pass along the message." He was certain that anyone who visited him already knew that—not that he had many guests in the first place. So just who might this be?

Aira kept her head down and focused on her task. She'd be the first to know about this mystery guest of his.

Rugio opened the door and allowed Mick to step through first. "Right this way."

Mick got the impression that Rugio didn't like him very much. But then again, he got the impression that Rugio didn't like a whole lot of people.

Rugio led him through the blinding stark-white walls of the hallway, void of any colour or adornments. Mick suspected the Governor's lack of creating a warm space for employees was just a strange kind of torture he liked to inflict. It wouldn't be so unlike the man. From time to time, Mick thought he could hear cries of terror and pain echoing through the corridors. He couldn't be sure if it were his imagination or if Governor Riggs had yet another poor victim to torment, tied up in his study like the one Mick had stumbled upon a year ago. How did one work up the courage to quit a job at an establishment when he knew what secret things went on within its walls?

Rugio led Mick to the manor's front entrance and to an overly large wooden door, where a broad-shouldered man turned around to face them. His brown eyes and hair matched Mick's own chestnut features. He was dressed nicely in his charcoal wool overcoat and navy trousers. And his hair, though longer than Mick's, was tidy and neatly combed. It wasn't as if the handsome figure at the door harmed the Governor's reputation by being seen here.

Mick approached his great-uncle, wearing a wide grin. It took everything in him not to bound over to Dimitri and wrestle him down, as had become their traditional form of greeting. By the time Mick was seventeen, he could nearly pin Dimitri, which Mick always thought was pretty good since his great-uncle was nearly six inches taller and had a wider breadth all around. Now, five years later, he'd learned some new tricks and was still familiar with the bigger man's signature moves.

But something told him that behaving in such a manner here might not be the most appropriate way to say hello. Especially since there were *so many* people watching to see who came to visit the Governor's manor. Mick noted the otherwise empty hall.

"Make it quick, Dairner. The governor is expecting a guest shortly and I expect you to wrap up your business by the time I return." Rugio turned on his heel and exited down the long corridor, leaving them alone.

"Uncle Dimi." Mick settled for a simple handshake, which felt too formal. Dimitri mustn't have cared about formalities because he reeled Mick in and wrapped his arms around him in a great big bear hug. He patted Mick's back.

"Mickey, it's good to see you. It seems every time I visit, I've missed something. Look at you. You're growing up too fast."

"That's what happens. Maybe when I get older you can share your secret as to how you've managed to maintain your youthful looks well into your seventies."

Something to do with the magic of Kartha, Mick suspected.

"But until then," he added, "I'll just have to keep aging like the normal folk.

"What are you doing here? Do my parents know you're visiting?" Mick's grandparents and Uncle Dimi had visited often in the early days of his childhood, but then the visits became less frequent. Sometimes they'd come together, but other times only his adefa would come. Raidan didn't do well with the journey, and he limited his time at sea. As for his adema, Ida, she'd come to visit a few months ago, but even after Mick had healed her aching joints, old age took its toll on his grandmother's body faster than he could keep up with at this distance. Unlike Adefa and Uncle Dimi, she'd aged as might be expected.

"No. I came only to see you this time." Dimitri gestured in the direction Rugio had taken off in. "I'm sorry if my visit got you into trouble. That one didn't seem too happy when I said I was looking for you. I guess having a foreign diplomat visit the Governor's house to see someone other than the Governor isn't the best look."

Mick shrugged, waving away the apology. "I'm sure it will be all right. Rugio will get over it. But I'm supposed to tell you to come to the back entrance next time, should you visit again. Are you going to be here long?"

"Not this time. I came to give you something." Dimitri dug a hand into his inner coat pocket. Then his hand reappeared, holding a small leather pouch closed off at the top with a drawstring. "This belongs to you. From the moment you were born, your grandfather and I both knew it. We've held onto it for now, but we've agreed that the time has come for you to have it."

Mick put his hand out and accepted the simple tan leather pouch Dimitri offered. It didn't look like anything special, but as soon as it fell into his hand, the trembling beneath his skin ceased. Mick gasped and nearly dropped it.

Dimitri wrapped Mick's hands in his own.

"Do not lose this. Don't show it to anyone. I want to tell you more, but this is neither the time nor place to speak of these things. As it is, I'd rather have given this to you someplace more private." He glanced around.

"Then why are you giving it to me here?"

"I'm in a bit of a hurry." Again, his eyes flitted to the hall.

With the pouch in his hand, Mick experienced a stillness like never before. It did the opposite for his mind, as his thoughts raced.

Dimitri removed his hands from Mick's and placed one on his shoulder. "It's time for you to come back to Kartha, Mick."

Mick's stomach fluttered. But before the excitement could take root, he shut down the idea. Going to Kartha was a dream. But it was one he couldn't pursue. "Uncle, I can't. I promised my dad." It was out of respect that Mick had agreed to his parents' wish for him to stay away from Kartha. They feared his ability would be discovered and that he'd be taken advantage of by the people there. Having supposed magic of their own, Mick would have thought they'd be more accepting of him. Apparently it was not so.

Dimitri lowered his hand. "That's not a realistic promise for you to make. Kartha is where you belong, and you know it as much as I do. Make the arrangements. You'll find us in Litlen. When you arrive, we can further discuss *that*." He pointed to the simple pouch in Mick's hand, which remained closed.

Mick held it in his open palm and stared at it without properly focusing on it. Realizing himself, he blinked twice. His hand closed around the pouch, and he offered it back to Dimitri. "I can't take this. I'm sorry, Uncle." As much as it pained him to give up such a token that dulled the shakes, he couldn't hold onto the gift if it meant making promises he couldn't keep.

Dimitri took a step back and threw his hands up. "It's yours. I came here to give it to you. All I ask is that you take care of it as if your life depended on it."

What was so special about this that he'd have to guard it with his life? Curious, Mick pulled open the top of the pouch. He dropped the item into his palm. The blue-green stone was about the size of a strawberry and appeared to change hues when he looked at it from different angles. It shimmered in the light shining through a nearby tall window. Its colours stood out, contrasted against the white tiled floor of the entrance. "What is it?" he asked.

"A piece of home."

"It's more than that." Mick didn't understand how he knew, but he could sense that there was more to the stone than Dimitri let on. Nothing had ever made the shakes stop before. There had been moments in the past when contact with his adefa or Uncle Dimi could help lessen the intensity of it, but never to this extent.

"I don't feel the shaking anymore."

A knock on the door startled Mick as it echoed throughout the high-ceilinged entrance. He'd nearly forgotten where they were. Dimitri closed Mick's hand over the stone. His forehead creased in the serious look he gave him.

Mick understood his meaning, and he put the stone away in its pouch, tucking it into his pocket just as Rugio walked back up the corridor with purpose.

"Still here, are we?" He walked past them and reached for the handle to open the door and welcome the new guest.

A man in a ridiculous-looking frazzled blond wig entered. Mick looked the man up and down, then tilted his gaze to meet Rugio's. He nodded his head in the man's direction. This guest just proved his point he'd made earlier. "You see what I mean, Ruje?"

Rugio's face flushed. Mick didn't think he'd ever seen that shade of red before.

The guest's eyes flitted from Mick to Dimitri, then finally to Rugio. "What is this? I was told Governor Riggs would see me today with no interruptions. Who are these two?"

Dimitri turned and gave a slight bow to the abnormally round newcomer. "Forgive me; I came only to deliver a message. I've taken enough time here and will see myself out." He turned to Mick. "I'll see you soon, Mickey." He winked. "Remember what I told you."

Mick had no time to ask any more questions. Dimitri tipped an imaginary hat and slipped through the open doorway.

# Chapter 2



Billions of stars shone over the prairie, where no moon was visible in the night sky. Mick stood at the end of the drive to his childhood home. It wasn't very late, but the sun went down earlier in the autumn.

He'd left the manor after his work was done for the day. The journey by horse to his parents' place in Caymre was a little over an hour's ride. By now, it had to be nearly eight in the evening. The lamps were lit inside, and shadows moved behind the closed curtain of the front window. A light shone in the shed nearby, where his father was likely building or fixing something. Try as he might to convince his son to apprentice him in his trade of carpentry, Mick had fought hard against it. If he didn't have his cooking, Mick was certain he'd be completely miserable for the rest of his life.

He let out a long breath and released the stiffness from the journey, though it did little to relieve the tension he often felt when visiting his parents. Coming here had a way of draining him before he'd even set foot inside. Only after he'd moved out did he notice the heaviness in the air that loomed in every nook and cranny of their home. The foundations were built on loss and restraint, and now it was as if these were the very things holding the place together. Loss of a home, a country, relationships, a child. Restraint in that Mick could never explore his power and use it freely.

Strangely, the stone in his pocket had a sort of calming effect on Mick. Considering what he'd come here to discuss, he didn't feel nearly as anxious as he'd expected to.

Mick led his borrowed horse, Maroon, to a post and tethered him there, then made his way up the stairs of the porch and knocked on the front door. He'd lived here—grown up here—and knew he didn't have to knock, but oftentimes he felt he should. Tonight was one of those times.

The door opened, and his mother's bright grey-green eyes shone as she smiled up at him. For as long as Mick could remember, her eyes displayed a weariness that made him suspect she wasn't well.

"Mckal!" Willa waved him inside. "How many times have I told you not to knock? Just because you live in that fancy city manor doesn't mean you've lost your place here. Come inside, come in."

Mick entered the house and greeted his mother with a hug. Ever since he was sixteen, he'd had to bend down to hug her.

The small landing extended straight to the stairs ahead. An open threshold to the right led to the sitting room, and the door on the left led to the kitchen. Glass ornaments adorned the walls in every room—gifts from Adema.

Willa showed Mick into the sitting room. "Your father is in the shed. He'll have heard you coming, I'm sure." She invited him to sit. "Are you hungry? Do you want something to eat or drink? How was the road coming out here? You shouldn't travel past dark. We've heard reports of trouble in the area with horse thieves lately, and I'd hate for you to be in the wrong place at the wrong time and get yourself hurt."

"Horse thieves? Hurt me? I'd like to see them try." Mick cackled, trying for some light humour, but the atmosphere snuffed it. That and his mother, with her lips pressed tight. Mick raised a brow and gave a reassuring smile.

"I'm fine, Mom. And I don't need anything right now, thanks." He took a seat on the two-seater sofa and leaned forward over his knees.

Willa stood at the threshold, watching him with a frown. Mick learned a long time ago that nothing he could say or do would stop her from worrying about him. He'd come to terms with that fact and stopped trying to convince her of his well-being. For someone whose body could physically heal—literally in seconds—he had parents who sure fretted a lot about him getting hurt.

"Will you stay the night?" his mother asked. "The bed is made up, and it's already getting late."

"Thanks." Mick hadn't decided yet what he was going to do about his sleeping arrangement. A lot depended on how this conversation went tonight. "I'll think about it."

Cassian entered the house and came into view around the corner. Mick rose to greet his father, meeting him halfway and embracing him in a tight squeeze, which momentarily cut his breath short. His father it seemed, didn't know his own strength. He released Mick and held him at arm's length, taking a good look at him.

"Not that I'm complaining," Cassian said, "but isn't it a bit late for a visit? Is everything all right in Balmell?"

"It is. Does something need to be wrong in order for me to visit?"

"No." Cassian dropped his arms to his sides. "You don't usually come this late, is all."

"No, not usually. But I need to speak with you about something."

Cassian took a seat in the chair by the window. He'd built it himself years ago and cozied it up with cushions that were starting to look weathered and in need of replacing. He scratched his chin through his short beard. "Right," he said. "We can talk. What's on your mind?"

All along the way here, Mick had played out at least a thousand scenarios as to how this conversation might go. Each time, he'd started it differently in his head. He'd guessed how his parents might respond and tried to gauge what the best outcome would be from each starting point. None were good.

Mick sank into the couch. He casually leaned back and rested his hand over his thigh, where he could feel the bulge of the stone through his trousers pocket. This was a bad idea. Why did he ever think this would go any differently from the many other times they'd sat down to have this talk?

While he sat there, deciding the best way to begin, his mother came fully into the room and took the seat beside him. She rested her hand on his. "Is this about Aira? Have you…decided to go ahead and ask to court her?"

If he weren't so nervous about bringing up the forbidden topic, he might have laughed. She would ask this question every time he visited, and Mick suspected it was her wish for them to marry one day.

"No. I haven't asked her. Aira deserves to be with someone who shares the same goal for her future. And what she has in mind is not what I want right now."

"What is it you want?" Willa asked.

Rather than look at his mother, Mick locked eyes with his father. "You know what I want. It's the same thing I've always wanted."

Cassian sat forward in his chair as though he were about to stand up. "Mick, let's not do this tonight, please. Why don't you settle in for the night, and we'll talk tomorrow after breakfast? I'm going into town for work in the morning. You can accompany me, and we'll talk on the road."

*Typical.* He was ending the conversation before it had even begun. But Mick had done it now. The ice had been broken, and the defences were already up. He may as well say his piece.

Willa gave his hand a squeeze, and Mick broke their contact.

"Why do you do that?" he asked his father. "Why do you shut me down before letting me say anything? I've been patient and have respected your wishes. I've kept my promise and have been waiting for your blessing. It's been years, and I'm starting to think I'm never going to get it. I don't think you understand how much I need this."

The room fell silent, with his last words lingering in the air. The fire popped in the fireplace.

"Mick." Willa put a gentle hand on his shoulder. "We've told you why. We're just trying to keep you from getting hurt."

"Not much can hurt me, Mom. I don't know if you've noticed, but all my injuries disappear in a matter of seconds."

Cassian clasped his hands together in front of himself and hung his head. "That's the problem, Mickey. Your ability is *exactly* why you shouldn't go." He raised his head, and his brown eyes, which matched Mick's own, bore into him. "They'll tear you apart in Kartha."

"You make it sound as though everyone there is so awful. They can't all be."

"There's enough to warrant taking the risk."

"Why don't you let me decide if it's worth the risk?"

"No." Cassian stood and approached Mick. He looked him dead in the eye. "The answer is no. It's too dangerous for you. If you came here to ask for my blessing, you don't have it. I'm going out to the shed. You're welcome to stay." He walked past him, making it known the conversation was over.

But Mick wasn't finished yet. His father was about to round the corner of the threshold into the hall.

"Uncle Dimi came to see me today," Mick said.

Cassian stopped. He turned around to face Mick, who rose from the couch.

Mick hovered his hand near his pocket, contemplating whether or not he'd show them the stone.

"He told me that I need to come to Kartha."

Cassian crossed his arms and dropped his chin. "What else did he tell you?"

"That it's time I know everything. What is he talking about, Dad? Know everything about what?"

"I can't believe he'd go behind my back like that" Cassian scoffed, shaking his head. "Dimitri needs to know when to back off."

Mick stuffed his hand into his pocket and wrapped it around the pouch with the stone inside. He weighed the likelihood of them taking Dimitri's gift from him against the possibility they'd tell him more. If they knew it came from him, would they refuse to elaborate on its importance? Or about why it was the only thing to ever stop the trembling under his skin?

He removed the pouch from his pocket but kept his fingers wrapped around it. "I want answers," he said, "and if you're not going to give me any, I'll go to Kartha and find them." He emptied the pouch, dropping the stone into his hand.

His mother gasped and covered her mouth.

Mick didn't tear his gaze from his father. "Uncle Dimi gave me this today. He told me it's mine."

Cassian's jaw twitched.

"The strange thing is," Mick said before either of them could speak, "I know it's mine, but I can't explain why. When I hold it, for whatever reason, I get a sense of belonging. Like it's… calling me or trying to communicate with me. I can't make any sense of it, but I want to. I need to know what this means. Why do I have this ability to heal? Why do I feel like I've been missing something all my life?" He swallowed past the lump in his throat. "And why does this stone affect me the way it does?"

Embarrassed, he tried to avoid a total loss of control over himself. He lowered his eyes and stared at the well-worn rug. The dull, matted wool had seen better days. He bit his cheek until the quiver in his chin subsided.

Willa rose. She placed a cold hand on his cheek and turned his face to look at her. "Why don't you have a seat, Mick? Take a deep breath. It was reckless of Dimitri to give that to you."

"Reckless is right," Cassian said. "What did he hope would happen by giving it to you anyway? Put it away, Mick. Keep it hidden, and show it to no one." He turned his gaze to the window, though the flickering light of the fire reflected in it prevented anyone from seeing outside. "The next time Uncle Dimi visits, he's taking it back."

Mick dropped the stone back into its pouch and stuffed it into his pocket. He wished he knew why Uncle Dimi had given it to him, but now that he had it, letting it go wouldn't be easy.

He slumped onto the couch and ran both hands through his hair. "I need answers. If neither of you are going to give me any, I'm going to find them elsewhere."

"Mick." Willa crouched, facing him. "People in Kartha think differently than they do here. Magic is real. You know that better than most. People who have seen magic and know its power have certain beliefs, erroneous or not, and those beliefs could put you in danger."

"Willa," Cassian interjected. "Don't."

Willa waved off Cassian's concern. "You want to know why we left Kartha? It's because of people who believed the word of an old misguided woman and sought to harm a baby just because he's different."

Cassian strode over to Willa and put a hand on her shoulder. "Willa. This isn't going to help."

"What are you talking about?" Mick asked his mother.

"There was a prophecy. Long before you were born. It spoke of one called the Healer, one who would bring a sickness upon Kartha that would destroy all the land. When you were born, it became obvious that you could heal. It was only a matter of time before someone else figured it out. And then…" Willa bowed her head and pressed her fingers to her brows. She let out a sob. Cassian bent down and wrapped his arms around her.

Willa sniffed and took a deep breath. "My mother. My own mother!" She wiped her face and met Mick's gaze. "She spoke to others about you. Tried to have you taken from me. One night, we arrived back from Adema and Adefa's, and there was a mob outside our home. That was the night we left Kartha. I don't know what they would have done to you." She wiped more tears away.

"And it's why we won't let you go back." Cassian stood and eased Willa up gently by her elbow. He held her in his arms, and she buried her face into him.

*Destroy a country?* How was that even possible? Mick had never heard anything so ridiculous.

He breathed deeply. "I would never do anything to bring harm to Kartha." *Not intentionally anyway.*

"It doesn't matter," Cassian said. "We know this, but it doesn't matter what we believe. It's what they think and what they'd do to you to protect their country. You have to realize that many of them lived for years in isolation because their home had been destroyed. Those same people remember what it was like. It's them that make us afraid for you, Mick. And why you can't go back there."

Mick closed his eyes and massaged his temples. That explained why he'd never met his grandparents on his mother's side. Or any other relatives for that matter.

"Dad, that was a long time ago. They won't even know who I am."

"Mickey, if you show up in Litlen, people will know. They'll take one look at you, and it won't take them long to realize you're a Dairner."

The room was quiet, with only Willa's sniffles and the crackling fire to dispel the silence.

Cassian filled his lungs with a deep breath and stood tall. He let an arm fall to his side while the other remained around Willa, drawing her close. "This is where you belong, Mick. Just—leave it be and move on with your life."

Now more conflicted than ever, Mick clenched and unclenched his fists. Everything within him screamed for him to go to Kartha. It was as if Kartha itself called to him from across the way, bidding him to come. And now with this stone, it was going to be so much more difficult to push the thought from his mind like he used to be able to do. Something felt different now.

Consumed by this desire, he made no promises to stay away. But would he stand by his word on his previous promise? He could only suppress this longing for so long.

Cassian kissed Willa on the side of the head. "I'm going to put away my tools." He turned toward Mick. "Stay tonight. We can head into town tomorrow morning together. It'll be nice to catch up."

And just like that, the conversation was over.

# Chapter 3

"How did it go last night?" Aira ladled a small amount of stew onto a plate to taste it.

Mick sat—slumped was more like it—in one of the two kitchen chairs. Lunch would be served soon, and there wasn't much left to prepare for the Governor's meal. The bread was baked, and the stew simmered over the fire. Aira replaced the lid and took the seat across from him, resting her chin on her fist.

"That bad, huh?" She gestured to his sunken posture.

"Well, let's just say it wasn't good."

"Did you tell them about your uncle coming to see you?"

"I did. They weren't too happy about it. Hey, can I ask you something, Aira?"

"You know you can."

Mick sat up straight. He then leaned across the table, brought his face closer to hers, and peered into her eyes. They were like dark pools of wisdom. To stare into them, one could become lost there and have a hard time finding their way back to reality. A strand of her black hair fell loose from her cap and draped in front of her face.

"What is it, Mick?" Her nose wrinkled when she smiled as she tucked a lock behind her ear.

"Do you think you—?"

The kitchen door swung open, and Rugio stepped in. He jutted his chin out. "Governor Riggs wishes to see you, Mr. Dairner. Allow your assistant to finish the meal preparations."

The words on the tip of Mick's tongue vanished. He closed his mouth, and the corners of his lips pulled toward his cheeks. He'd wager Rugio had planned the timing of his entry like that on purpose. Or maybe it was just bad luck for Mick. But nothing pleased Rugio more than the demise of others. It wouldn't have surprised him. Unless Rugio's smug expression was because of something else. Something Mick suspected he wasn't going to like.

Aira straightened her posture and fixed any stray hairs. Mick stood up from the small table. To Aira, he said, "I guess we'll pick this up later." He removed his apron and followed Rugio into the hall.

The whole manor was built with natural white brick from Xihngrahv. Either the lack of accents was indeed a tactic to invoke a depressing atmosphere, or Governor Riggs truly liked the natural look so much, that he chose to omit adding any warm accents to counter the stark white. The only decorations to hang from the walls—if they could even be called decorations—were yellow banners, bright as sunlight, which nearly blended into the white. Each banner bore the Ectarin coat of arms at the top left corner—a ship sailing over the horizon in a sea of sparkling red. A crown sat perched atop the mainmast of the ship. In the middle of the banner, a horned grey bear stood on its hind legs, claws sticking out as it pawed at the empty space in front of it.

The Governor's parlour was on the west end of the manor, opposite the kitchen. Rugio walked with his head held high. Mick could not think of what had him in such high spirits.

He was shown into the room, which was, even in its grandness, the smallest of the rooms in the manor. Mick tried to shake the fear he felt whenever he was in the presence of his employer. His stomach churned, but even so, he walked in with his shoulders back, masking his apprehension.

Natural light spilled in through the two tall windows, and between them was a thin table that held a book and an unlit lamp. The dull sky. The white walls. The equally bland furniture. The entire room practically glowed. Mick tried to ignore the lack of décor. With his face neutral, he stopped next to Rugio, just inside the room.

"The cook for you, Governor," Rugio announced. Then he left.

Governor Riggs, a few decades older than Mick, had subtle crow's feet framing his eyes. His perfectly groomed eyebrows gave him a look of sophistication. And while his smile was welcoming and friendly, Mick knew it to be anything but. He'd seen the man's crueller side and wasn't fooled by the façade.

Riggs waved a hand from his chaise longue. Mick obeyed his bidding and, calming his nerves with a deep breath, strolled over to him.

Governor Riggs leaned all the way back into the corner of the chair. His feet rested upon a wooden coffee table. Without looking at Mick, he swirled blue liquid around in a glass. Eterras—an alcoholic beverage he'd had imported from Reij.

Mick stuffed his hands into his pockets, clutching the stone. "This room hasn't changed a bit since the last time I was here. Stark, blank, and blinding." *What was that about trying not to notice?* "You know what would go really nice in here?" He removed a hand from his pocket to point at the walls. "Some colour. Maybe a little bit of green. A couple of cushions here, a curtain over there." He pointed to the windows. "A plant or two, or five."

"Enough babble. I didn't call you in here for decorating advice. Care for a drink?"

"I'm working," Mick said. And to not come across as rude, he added, "But thank you anyway."

Riggs waved a hand again in a nonchalant kind of way. "Rugio tells me you had a guest yesterday."

Mick refrained from rolling his eyes. *Of course he did.*

"I did, sir. A relative. And I assure you, he has been informed to use the back entrance, should he visit again."

"Right." Riggs put his feet on the floor, set his glass down, and leaned forward. "I hear he's a ruler in Kartha. Is it true?"

*So* that's *what this is about.* Mick glanced out the window. The sky was overcast and still somehow had more vibrancy than this room.

Mick scratched the back of his head. "He and his brother have roles of leadership in Kartha. As I understand it, they have a spokesperson from each region who gathers frequently to discuss matters of governance. Decisions are not made by them alone."

"Kartha." Riggs said it like it was a mystery to solve. "There are stories, you know? That's where everyone reckons the Witch is from. And they say that the country itself has life. That it feeds the people's magic, allowing them to live for centuries. Magic… Ha! As if there were such a thing."

Mick nodded but said nothing. His understanding was that only people from one particular region were magical. Whether they lived for centuries, he didn't know. He never got straight answers from his family. Whatever Mick knew, he'd had to learn for himself.

"I've never heard of the Witch," Mick said. "But I've heard much of the same otherwise."

"Who is he? Your guest."

"A relative."

Riggs glared up at Mick, his eyebrows arching high. "Yes, you said that. Give me a name. Who is he? I should like to arrange a meeting with him. Tell me so I may have my letter delivered to the right person."

Mick's heart sank. Riggs was not the kind of person that good men did business with. Putting Dimitri in a room with this man would not go well—for Riggs. Mick would be out of a job, and Dimitri— He might have other consequences to face. It all boiled down to what Dimitri determined would be the best way to deal with Riggs when he learned of his other name. The one he was known as all over the Zareff Continent, and yet somehow remained anonymous. Mick considered it more likely that people knew who he was, but what could they do to stop him? Riggs had everyone in his pocket. Few could stand in the way of the Tax Collector. No way would Mick subject his uncle to any involvement with a prominent slave trader.

"I'm sure I can pass along a message when I see him again," Mick said, with no real intention of doing so. "I'll tell him you're interested in having a conversation."

Riggs stood and walked to the window. "Rugio tells me he witnessed him give you something. What did he give you?"

Mick tensed and became aware of the warmth radiating against his leg. Leave it to Rugio to act as Riggs's spy. If Mick were a better liar, he'd have denied that Dimitri had given him anything at all. Instead, he settled for a half-truth. "There's a spice I like to use that comes from Kartha. He thought I might need to replenish my stock."

Riggs rubbed his chin and studied Mick.

"If you'd like, I can grab it and show you," Mick added, throwing his thumb over his shoulder and pointing toward the door.

After a long moment, Riggs waved his hand in the air as though he didn't care to hear more. "Never mind that. I need a contact within Kartha. Someone I can count on. Someone who has the means to get me what I want without questions asked."

Mick withheld an exhale, glad for now that they had dropped the topic of the gift.

Riggs continued, no longer looking at him as he gazed out the window. "The place is a xanteén mine waiting to be discovered. No one touches them for fear of their supposed magic, but it's high time that changes. That magic is just the thing I need to grow my business and provide products that none of my competitors have access to." He turned and faced Mick. "Well, come now. How can I get in touch with him?"

"Governor Riggs, I don't think he's the man you want for this. He won't—"

"You don't think? I didn't ask what you think. Are you going to tell me how to reach him or not?"

"No, sir. All due respect, sir, he won't take any offer you make."

"And now you speak on his behalf? I was under the impression you valued your job here. Perhaps I was wrong."

Mick clenched his jaw. "Unless Rugio has some hidden talent, I doubt you're prepared to let your cook go."

"Cooks are not hard to come by."

"The best ones are. I'm the best there is in Iptin Province. You can replace me, but good luck finding someone who can imitate my criyun glaze you like so much on your poultry." Mick clamped his mouth shut. He really needed to stop talking. Why should he care if Riggs let him go? Relieving Mick of his work would save him from having to find an out himself.

Riggs walked back over to the chaise and plunked himself down. He reached for his drink, swirled it around, and sucked back the rest in one swig. When he put the glass down, it clinked against the half-full decanter next to it. "Mind yourself, Dairner. One would think that a cook values his tongue." He sat back and linked his hands behind his head.

"What's this I hear about your late-night outings?" Riggs asked. He said outings as if they were a frequent thing. Going to his parents' home last night had been the first time in a month that Mick had left the manor for any length of time.

"I had something personal to attend to."

"Those who linger in the dark are usually up to no good. And when I hear that you're returning first thing in the morning after being away all through the night, I tend to think that you're up to no good."

*Says the slave trader.* Mick bit his cheek to keep himself from opening his mouth to say so.

Riggs raised his chin. "I can't have people seeing my staff doing shady business at night. It's highly unprofessional. What will people think? Keep your personal errands to the daytime. To a time when people will not assume that you do dark deeds in the shadows."

With Mick's schedule, there wasn't any time in the day for him to do anything other than run one or two errands in town. But saying so was pointless and would only encourage Riggs to make a more obvious display of his power.

"Of course, Governor. Anything else?"

"That is all." Riggs sat up again and poured himself another drink. He waved Mick off in his flippant way. "You may go now."

Mick excused himself. Rugio stood on the other side of the door, smirking. He said nothing while Mick passed him by.

Mick took his time to return to the kitchen. He just had to go and open his big mouth. The fact alone that he was aware of Riggs's business was enough reason to shut up and keep his head down. It'd been about a year since he'd stumbled upon that horrible scene in the very room he'd just left. Since then, Mick had planned multiple ways in which he might resign. He'd nearly done so twice, but something held him back. Was it Aira who kept him here? Or was he really afraid of the fallout from trying to leave the Governor's service? Riggs hadn't acted upon seeing Mick outside the hall that night, and Mick dreaded the conversation he'd expected to have the following day, but there wasn't one. He supposed it was only a matter of time before it all caught up to him.

He pushed open the kitchen door and was met with the scent of freshly baked bread and a blend of earthy herbs. The pot of stew had been removed from the heat. Aira was busy transferring a portion into the serving pot for the servants to take to the Governor's table. Another portion would be set aside for the staff, including Mick and Aira.

Wasting no time, Mick took a loaf of bread, picked up a knife, and began slicing.

Aira was kind enough to give him a moment to get a few slices cut before saying what was on her mind. "I'd say things didn't go well, but you've done this thing before where you pretend it's gone horribly bad and then tell me something like your pay has been raised."

Mick wrinkled his nose. "I've never done that."

"I know. But you know what I'm saying. How did it go?"

"Well, I'm not out of a job yet." Mick chuckled. "Can't get rid of me that easily."

Aira did not share in his humour. She peered over her shoulder. She furrowed her brows when she caught his eye, then returned her attention to her work before changing the subject. "Anyway, what were you going to say earlier before we were so rudely interrupted?"

Mick nearly cut his finger again. He'd almost forgotten. Before Rugio had sent for him, he'd been considering what his mother had said about a future with Aira, if that were even possible. But the moment came and went, and he didn't know if he had enough emotional energy to go there now. "It was nothing," he lied. "Forget about it."

"Want my advice?"

With the bread all sliced, Mick began laying it out on a platter.

Aira stopped what she was doing and faced him. "Go to Kartha, Mick. What's holding you back? Since I've known you, that's all you've wanted. This isn't where you want to be for the rest of your life." She gestured to the room.

"What's wrong with this?" Mick grinned.

Aira crossed her arms.

Mick got serious. "What about you?"

"What about me? You think I can't work without you?"

"No, not that. I mean, we've hardly been apart since we started working together. I don't want to just leave you on your own."

Aira's lips twitched. She turned around and picked up the serving pot, carrying it over to the platter of sliced bread. "It's not like we're married. Besides, maybe with you gone, I can actually find myself a husband. I hang around with you all the time, and I'm certain men stay away because they think I'm spoken for."

"Would you like to be married to me?" Mick blurted the words before he could stop himself. "I'm sorry. That came out wrong." Of all the dumb things he'd said, this topped them all.

Aira didn't bat an eye. "Mick, I'm sure you would make a wonderful husband…"

"But…" There was more. Mick sensed it. He shouldn't have brought it up. "Aira, forget I said anything. It was—I was—I'm not—" *Was what? Not serious?* Was he? He didn't know what he was saying. Did he really want to marry her, or had he only said that because of his mother's influence?

Aira's cheeks turned pink. She reached her hand across herself and rubbed her arm. "Mick, I like you. Truly, I do. But I want to be with someone who can give me all of their heart. Your heart isn't here, and I don't think it ever will be. My place is in Iptin, not sailing the sea or going on big adventures. I want a quiet life, to raise a family. I don't think you know what you want, but I don't think you'll settle until you find out what it is. And as long as you don't know, you're not going to find joy with me."

Mick had grown accustomed to the way Aira cut to the core of a matter.

Inasmuch as she was right, the rejection still hurt. He rubbed the back of his neck. "I'm happy."

"I didn't say you weren't. But joy and happiness are not the same thing. I've been your friend for a long time, and I know you well enough to know that you'll never be content until you chase after that longing in your heart. You may not know what you're searching for, but you know where you think you'll find answers." Aira pressed a hand to Mick's cheek, grazing her thumb over his rough skin. "Stop wasting time and go after it, whatever *it* is." When she removed her hand, his face felt cold without it there. Only nineteen, and she was already an old soul. And he, two years older, often felt like a fool. She'd said everything he'd wanted to hear, and yet he still doubted.

"I'd have to tell Governor Riggs. I don't imagine he'll be too pleased."

"So what if he isn't? It's not like he sponsored your apprenticeship. You owe him nothing."

Mick nodded. He'd apprenticed with his friend Ollie's father and had later convinced Governor Riggs to take him on as his cook. He owed the Governor nothing, it was true. But knowing what he knew made him uneasy. Would Riggs so easily let him go?

# Chapter 4

The manor housed eight live-in employees. Mick shared quarters with Riggs's personal messenger, Jury, and the coachman, Morris. Rugio had a room to himself, and Aira and three maidservants shared the larger room at the other end of the manor. The beds in Mick's room were spread out, one in each corner. Mick lied in his. He and his roommates each had their own shelf for storage and hanging space in the modest accommodations.

On the north wall, facing the grounds outside, a window stretched from halfway up the wall, to the ceiling. The moonlight shone in and glinted off the stone in his hand. He twirled it in his fingers, admiring the way it changed from green to blue. It never stayed just one colour between the two.

Jury had taken a temporary leave to deal with a family matter—or so Mick had been told. But he'd been gone for nearly two weeks now, and Mick wondered what kind of situation might require so much of his time.

Morris—a thin, grey old man who always smelled of horses, snored loudly from his side of the room, even though it was only half-eight in the evening.

The room was uncharacteristically quiet without Jury. Most nights, he'd play music on his drigyn, a stringed instrument similar to a lute but with a flat hollow part on the body meant to be drummed. The way the instrument curved allowed for the sound to resonate at different pitches depending on where the player drummed, and the way Jury played it, it took on a melancholy sound that would have echoed Mick's mood right then.

A rap at the door made Mick jump, and he nearly dropped the stone. Morris snorted in his sleep and turned onto his side, facing the wall. Mick hopped to his feet and shoved the stone into his pocket. He took long strides to get to the door before another knock could come.

Rugio stood in the hallway with his hand poised to knock again. His eyes widened as though he were surprised to receive an answer. He quickly stuck his nose in the air and reverted to his usual pompous manner. "Dairner, the Governor wishes to have a word with you in the parlour."

"Now?"

Rugio's reddened face turned a deeper shade. "Of course now! Why else would I be here?"

Mick stepped into the hall and closed the door so as not to disturb Morris, what with Rugio's noise. "All right, all right, keep your voice down." The door clicked shut. "Take me to him."

Rugio stood there, narrowing his eyes at Mick. In his *very* important position, the only one to speak to him with such a tone was the Governor. The vein in his neck pulsed. He turned on his heel and tromped down the hall. Mick kept up, taking pleasure in the way the man got so easily worked up.

They arrived at the parlour door, and Rugio knocked twice. Governor Riggs called for them to enter. Rugio went in first, his back straight. "As requested: Mr. Dairner. Is there anything else I can do for you, Governor?"

Governor Riggs stood at the window and gazed out at the clear night sky. The decanter on the coffee table had been refilled with a new type of drink since Mick was here last.

Riggs held out his nearly empty glass. "That will be all, Rugio. You've done well. Come in, Mckal. Take a seat."

*Uh oh, this can't be good.* He'd used Mick's given name.

While Rugio saw himself out, Mick sat on the edge of the chair across from the chaise. Not knowing where his mouth would lead him, he thought better of opening it.

Riggs walked over to the end of the table and took the seat across from Mick. Next to the decanter was a set of glasses turned upside down. He retrieved one and poured Mick a drink. Judging by the sweet fragrance of adleberi, with a hint of lime, plus the bright red hues, Mick guessed the decanter had been filled with crimag'd, a stronger and more expensive liquor compared to the Governor's earlier drink.

"I was thinking about our meeting earlier and didn't like the way it ended," Riggs said. "I spent some time contemplating how to fix things between us and came up with an idea. You made some good points, and you're right; there's been a fair share of cooks who've come and gone in this manor, and there is no doubt that you are the best. Even that other cook here can't get the flavours just right like you do." He offered the drink to Mick, who accepted but didn't drink.

Riggs downed the last bit of his. "It would do me no good to lose you." He sat and licked his lips, then leaned forward. "I'd like to make you an offer. You agree to sign a contract and stay on for another ten years, at the end of which we'll revisit our agreement to potentially extend it further. During the ten-year contract, I will double your income. What say you?"

Mick's breath caught. His position in the Governor's household already paid him handsomely—nearly thirteen pounds of cruclum a month. He frequently traded up for xanteēn and had been putting it away for something—he didn't know what yet. If he accepted Riggs's offer, he could almost be mistaken for nobility with that amount of money. As it was, he already had more than he knew what to do with.

His head swam with all that he could put it towards. The grand kitchen of his dreams no longer sounded so impossible. And why not go to Kartha?

Or he could put the money to better use.

However, his initial excitement at the prospect plummeted. The bloody scene he'd walked in on in this very room the night he'd learned of Riggs's private dealings would forever be etched in his mind. A man—a stranger to Mick—knelt, his body bent so his face nearly touched the floor, blood dripping from his hair and face, hands bound at his back. And Riggs. Standing over him with his fists clenched and bloodied. At a guess, the man was one of his slaves. Perhaps he'd tried to run, and Riggs thought to make an example of him.

At the time, Mick couldn't have known this, nor was he aware of the Governor's private dealings, but he'd done his own digging and later learned. The man hadn't been a slave, but he'd been sneaking through Riggs's warehouses and had managed to rescue a handful of others before getting caught. Mick began listening and paying attention to the manor guests and staff, and eventually he'd learned more than he cared to know. And no matter how spotless this room looked the following morning after seeing what he saw—those stains could never be forgotten.

He'd seen; the door had been closed. Riggs had said nothing, and Mick felt trapped ever since. If he knew any amount of money could put Riggs out of business, he might have considered taking the offer.

Imagine that—Riggs paying Mick to put himself out of business.

Riggs poured more drink into his glass. Mick remembered the one in his hand and took a swig, scrunching his face when the liquid burned his throat on the way down.

To agree to the arrangement would mean committing to another ten years here. Ten more years of thinking about every guest who came and went. The kind of business being done in these rooms.

Then there was Kartha. When it came down to it, could he really wait so long to go?

The stone radiated heat onto his leg from the pocket in his trousers.

No, his place wasn't here. Dimitri had said it. Aira had echoed it. He couldn't keep putting off going to Kartha. Not by ten years.

Mick shook his head. "Your offer is more than generous, Governor Riggs. But I can't accept. Ten years is more than I can commit to."

Riggs set his drink down on the table and linked his fingers in his lap. "Then I'll sweeten the deal and triple your pay."

It was a good thing Mick had no drink in his mouth because he would have spewed it.

He swirled the liquid in his glass, knocked back the rest, and said nothing for a minute. Part of him didn't want to pass up such an offer. Who would? The rational part of his mind was trying to make sense of why Riggs would be willing to pay such a high wage to a cook. Sure, Mick had a knack for creating unique and wonderful flavours, but he wasn't worth as much as Riggs was willing to pay. Just to what? Keep him here? Ensure his silence?

Mick's heart sank. He knew what this was. He set his glass down next to Riggs's. "I'm flattered, truly. But I—"

"Sleep on it," Riggs said. "Take time to consider. Whatever your decision, the offer will not be made again. I'd hate for you to regret making the wrong choice." His voice deepened, emphasizing the subtle threat.

With an offer like that, Mick didn't think he'd get any sleep at all tonight. He would have preferred to give his answer here and now rather than have time to reconsider. Or be given more time to imagine what the alternative was to turning him down. Besides, that kind of money was hard to pass up. The longer he had time to think, the harder it would be to stick with his choice. Unless Riggs was willing to negotiate the terms…

Would it be too bold to request a leave and ask to work something out upon his return?

Riggs stood. "I'll send for your answer in the morning."

Mick wiped his clammy hands on his trousers and rose. For once, he struggled with what to say. Something had changed in Riggs from the time Dimitri had visited until now. The Governor had never been so overtly menacing toward Mick. He'd generally been amicable. This deal wasn't as simple as it seemed, and Mick suspected that requesting any time away was out of the question.

He nodded and excused himself, his mind a whirlwind. The offer itself was one thing, but what might the consequence be if he declined? He had a feeling that doing so wasn't going to be a matter of simply saying no. But accepting may as well be the same as signing himself up for the rest of his life. Who was to say it would be only ten years? Riggs had said they'd reevaluate in ten years. What was that supposed to mean?

In any case, Mick was sure that whatever answer he gave, none would be good for him.

# Chapter 5

MICK WAS AWAKE BEFORE THE KNOCK CAME. HEAVY DRAPES BLOCKED THE twilit sky. Morris's bed was empty and neatly made, so Mick didn't have to worry about waking the coachman.

He slipped out of bed, donned some clothes, and scurried across the room to open the door. Expecting Rugio, he opened it only a crack to peek out. But standing in the hall were two burly men clad in padded black leather vests. One of them had thick biceps with tattoos around their circumferences. The markings on his sun-weathered skin looked to be foreign script. The other man had a dark complexion, and small silver hoops pierced through the outer part of each eyebrow. He placed a hand flat on the door and pushed it open the rest of the way. His gaze scanned the otherwise empty room before falling on Mick.

"Gentlemen, can I help you?" Mick asked, trying to sound unaffected by their frightening appearance here and now.

"You're Mckal?" the tattooed man said with a deep voice.

"I am."

"We're to deliver your response to the Governor."

Mick glanced between the two men. They were probably Riggs's private guard, sent with the intent to intimidate.

In an attempt to come across as relaxed, Mick leaned against the doorframe and crossed his arms. His nerves were on edge. What he wanted to do was slam the door in their faces, but that might prompt undesired action on their part.

Mick made direct eye-contact with the tattooed man. "Where's Rugio? He must be distraught. He lives for this job—running the Governor's errands and all. Must have been heartbroken he didn't get this one."

Both men remained straight-faced. Not a muscle twitched on either of them. Mick, in turn, matched their impassiveness. His throat dry, he ignored the need to swallow.

The dark-skinned guard broke the silence. "Governor Riggs made you an offer last night. He wishes to know. What is your answer?" His thick Ectarin accent made his words sound sharp.

Mick couldn't keep stalling. He straightened, stepping away from the door-frame while rubbing his nose. "Please inform Governor Riggs that I must decline."

The guards didn't move right away. Then together, and without further questions, they turned and walked off. Mick stood between the hallway and the room, staring in disbelief.

*That's it?* He'd half expected them to beat him, or haul him to face the Governor and demand an explanation for his refusal.

Now what? Did he carry on as normal, or would Riggs make another offer? Would he tell him what he actually wanted or what this was really about?

Did it make a difference? Mick had made his decision. All he could do now was wait and see what came of it.

Having everything he needed to be on his way, he exited the room, closing the door behind him, then stalked off toward the kitchen to begin work.

He entered the kitchen, and the low sun blinded him through the window. He turned his gaze away from the light.

Aira hadn't arrived yet. It was still early. Typically, he'd have slept until the last minute before having to begin work, but as he'd predicted, he hadn't gotten any sleep with Riggs's offer buzzing around in his head.

He lit a fire in the fireplace and gathered what he'd need to begin preparing breakfast: a pan, a spatula, the wrapped leftover bread from yesterday's dinner, and two baskets—one for berries, the other for eggs.

Aira entered the kitchen, wrapping her hair up under her cap. She mumbled a greeting.

"Morning," Mick said, sounding a lot more chipper than he felt. "Could you get the eggs and berries? I'll check on the yogurt and see if it's ready."

Without a word and with eyes half closed, Aira snatched the baskets and dragged herself outside to collect the food from the gardens and chicken coop. When she returned, they prepped and cooked the Governor's breakfast of boiled eggs with salt, toasted bread, and raspberry jam, to be served with yogurt and berries.

The serving staff arrived, and with them were the two guards from earlier. The guards stood at the door with their hands clasped at their fronts. The serving crew each grabbed an item to bring to the dining room, where Riggs awaited his meal. One took the tray of food, another picked up utensils and serving dishes. Lively—one of the maids—grabbed the pitcher of freshly made orange juice. Her neck had the unmistakable tint of bruising around its circumference. Mick met her eyes, and she quickly lowered hers.

As they all exited, the tattooed guard gestured to Mick. "You're to accompany the meal to the Governor's table."

Mick looked at Aira, who'd become more alert and awake since first arriving. Her wide eyes held concern, though he didn't know why she would think to expect any trouble. He'd not had a chance to share with her about his visit to the parlour last night and Riggs's offer. This summoning from the Governor was expected, but Mick thought Riggs would have waited until after breakfast. This was also the time he and Aira would normally eat. Mick's own meal sat on the table next to Aira's.

He nodded at the food. "Go ahead without me, Aira. I'll eat when I return."

He then followed the guards out of the kitchen, down the bland hallways, and into the dining room. Riggs sat at a round table large enough to seat a dozen people. With its hollowed centre, chairs could be placed within the inner circle as well as on the outside. There were no other chairs, though Lively stood in the middle, filling Riggs's cup with juice. She kept her eyes down.

Riggs's food was set on the table before him. Rugio lingered near the door. Even he kept his gaze on the floor. Everyone was silent as Mick entered with the guards.

"Mckal," Riggs said. "Good, good, you're here. Come." He waved his hand for Mick to approach the table. His food remained untouched.

Riggs slid the dish with the yogurt and berries in front of Mick. He twisted in his chair to face him, looking up. "If you will, please?"

Mick hesitated, unsure of what he was meant to do. Rather than wait to have it explained, he bent down and said, "Right, yes, here we have yogurt, incubated since last night, made from the milk of…" He paused. "Would you like to know which cow?"

"Taste it," Riggs said.

Mick straightened, standing upright. "Apologies, Governor, but that isn't my job."

"It is now. Taste it."

Mick glanced around the room. Had this all been set up to humiliate him?

Rugio kept his gaze averted, occasionally looking up. Lively's eyes peered up, though her head remained bowed. The two guards hovered within arm's reach, watching.

"Governor Riggs, I—"

"I said. Taste it."

Mick scoffed. "Sir, is this because I turned down—?"

"How am I supposed to trust a man I can't buy?" Governor Riggs turned his chair to face Mick fully. Even from his seated position, looking up, he was intimidating. "You've worked for me for, what, three…four years?"

Mick nodded. Something like that.

"And you're aware of what I do?" Riggs said.

*Is this a trick question?*

Mick found it difficult to keep still. "You're the governor. Everyone knows—"

"Don't play me for a fool."

Mick sighed. What was the point in speaking when he couldn't get a full sentence out? He nodded. "I'm aware."

"You don't fear me as others do. You won't accept my offer to increase your wage, and you take off at night and don't return until the next morning. What am I supposed to make of all that? How am I to know you're not secretly trying to destroy what I've built? Or plotting to assassinate me?"

"I would never—"

Riggs raised a hand, palm out, to silence him. "You are an excellent cook, Mick; you said so yourself. It would be unfortunate if I had to let you go."

His words hung in the air.

Mick wasn't sure what Riggs was saying. Was he being fired?

He let his shoulders fall. "I don't understand what you want from me."

"You may continue to work for me, provided you accompany each meal and taste it first. All of your work will be supervised by Ighur and Theérl." Riggs gestured to the two burly men. "You'll be restricted to the manor and not permitted to leave the grounds. If you refuse these terms… Well… attempting to kill the governor by poisoning his food will earn you a death sentence. I have witnesses who can confirm you were seen slipping nilothran into my meal."

The sun shining outside suggested it was a hot day. In here, Mick's arms prickled with goosebumps, and his blood ran cold.

"Of course," Riggs went on, "you might escape jail, and wind up lost and in the company of the wrong kinds of people. There are all sorts of shady folk around who'd take advantage of you in whatever ways they deem fitting. You're young and strong. I'm sure there's someone out there who'd love to break your strong will and put you to work."

Riggs sat back and raised his hand to his chin as if actually considering Mick as a product to be sold.

Mick's knees shook. His mind reeled with shock from this ultimatum, and he couldn't think of anything to help him out of this situation.

"Well, Mick, what's it to be?"

"Have I done something to offend you?" Mick scratched his head. He couldn't think of why Riggs was doing this now when he'd had plenty of opportunity in the year since Mick had found him out.

"In all your time here, I've been watching you," Riggs said. "This past year, you've shown little enthusiasm and no desire to be here, yet when I met you, you were adamant that this was the job for you. So one does wonder why. Who are you really, Mckal? Because I don't believe you're just a carpenter's son from the countryside who lives to cook. So, who are you? What are you here for?"

Aware of everyone watching, Mick considered his words carefully—something he struggled with. "I'm no one. I'm exactly who you said: a carpenter's son. I grew up in Caymre. That's all there is to know."

Riggs nodded, his forehead wrinkling. "Mm-hmm. Yes, well, forgive me if I don't take your word for it. You have a choice to make. Refusal to choose will be your decision made."

Mick wasn't sure if his shaking was out of anger or fear or if it was because his jitters had come back, despite the stone in his pocket. His choices were jail and potentially being sold into slavery or confinement to the manor as the Governor's personal dog. The manor option would be easier for him to slip away unseen compared to the other option. But being under constant watch would make things more difficult, regardless. Sweat trickled down the side of his face.

"Very well!" Riggs snapped. "I'm sorry to see you go."

The guards approached. Mick couldn't think fast enough. What should he do?

The dark-skinned guard grasped Mick's arm and tugged.

"No, wait, wait!" Mick said, panicking. "I'll stay. I'll… I'll continue to work here."

Riggs raised a hand to stop the guards from taking him. He cocked his head at Mick. "According to my terms?"

The guard's grip squeezed tighter.

"Yes," Mick said. "According to your terms."

"Excellent." Riggs clapped. "I'll have a contract drafted."

"A contract?"

"Of course! Confirmation of our agreement. You'll remain in my employ as my cook and personal taster, agreeing to be under constant supervision. You will carry out this work for the next twenty years on your current income."

Twenty years? Mick swallowed. He couldn't adhere to those conditions.

But what else could he do?

The guard released Mick's arm and took a step back.

Riggs turned his chair to face the table. "If I can't buy you, then I'll just have to own you. My eggs are cold now. Ighur will escort you back to the kitchen so you may cook up fresh ones. But first…" He pushed the yogurt bowl toward Mick. "Taste."

# Chapter 6

Embers burned in the fireplace. Riggs's guard, Ighur, stood at the door to the kitchen with his arms crossed, his biceps bulging, showing off his tanned tattooed arms. He'd not moved since Mick came to sit with his thoughts. He sat, hidden from Ighur, with his back against the counter, facing what remained of the fire. The warmth had left him long ago.

Aira had gone into town. She'd asked Mick to join her, unaware of his situation. With Ighur never leaving his side, he'd not had a chance to speak to her alone. It was going to be a challenge to convey to her to get out while she still had the chance.

A shiver came over him, and he rubbed his arms. The only warmth he felt came from his pocket, where the stone was. Before taking it out, he tilted his head sideways, listening for Ighur to ensure he wouldn't disturb him. No sounds came from his direction. Mick retrieved the stone and dumped it from its pouch into his palm.

*Twenty years in this place?* He couldn't agree to that, even if he had no intentions of honouring his word to stay.

The stone offered a sense of peace to his distressed spirit. He closed his fingers around it and rested his forehead on his knuckles. Riggs was being unreasonable. There had to be something Mick could do to make him change his mind.

He tucked the stone away into its pouch, then dropped it back into his pocket. Slowly, he got to his feet, shaking out his muscles as he rose. He swiped dust from his clothes. There had to be something he could say to make Riggs reconsider. What was the point of a contract if he was just going to enslave him anyway?

As Mick left the kitchen, Ighur met his gaze with stern eyes. The guard's multiple earrings ascending around the lobes of both ears shimmered in the light of the dimmed lamp.

Mick had no chance of swaying him to help. If Riggs was offering to pay Mick such a substantial income as a cook, Ighur was sure to be getting paid a lot more to put his muscle behind the Governor's whims.

Ighur followed closely as Mick strode through the corridors and arrived at the parlour door. Mick raised his fist, ready to knock, then hesitated, slumping his shoulders while his hand remained poised.

*But what to say?*

Now wasn't the time to second-guess himself. He straightened his posture. He'd come up with something.

Before he could talk himself out of it, he rapped on the door twice.

"Come in," Riggs's voice called.

Mick entered.

Riggs leaned forward in his chaise, bent over the table with the tip of a quill hovering over a sheet of parchment. An older man with a curly, dark-haired wig stood across from him with his arms full of books. The hair colour didn't match his scraggly grey eyebrows that stuck out from behind small, round spectacles.

Riggs peered up. "Ah, Mick, good timing. I was just about to send for you. The contract is ready for signing." He gestured to the old man. "Ferind, my lawyer. He's here to act as a witness. Come, come."

*So much for talking him out of this.*

Mick approached the two men slowly. Ighur closed the door and assumed his place, standing on the opposite side of the frame from Theérl, who, it seemed, never ventured far from the Governor.

"There's no need for this, Governor," Mick said. "Hasn't this gone far enough?"

Ferind took two steps back as Riggs set the quill down and rose.

Riggs stroked his smooth face and narrowed his scheming eyes at Mick. "When I say I'm going to do something, I'm going to do it. I never say anything I don't mean." He closed the distance between them until they were nearly nose-to-nose. "Do you, Mick?" His breath smelled like his drink—sweet with a hint of lime.

Against everything in him, Mick lowered his eyes, submitting. His jaw twitched as he refrained from saying anything, lest he make things worse.

Riggs leaned forward to speak directly into Mick's ear. "The contract states that if you break any of the terms in our agreement, your years of service will be increased. You'll be my cook for the remainder of your life."

Given the kind of man Riggs was, Mick could only guess just how long it would take for some imaginary breach of contract to emerge. He clenched his fists.

What was he doing? Entering into a binding contract, signing away his life.

"Your terms are unrealistic." Mick shook his head. "I won't sign."

This didn't faze Riggs. "You understand what it means to reject the contract?"

Mick nodded. At least in jail, he'd belong to no one. Under the circumstances, it sounded like he'd have a better chance at escaping and disappearing from there than if he stayed here. All provided he could do so before Riggs's Collectors came for him.

"I understand," he said.

Riggs raised his chin. "I'm disappointed in you, Mick." He took a step back and summoned Ighur and Theérl to come. "I can't believe you would do something like this. Trying to poison me?" He raised his voice. "I wouldn't have thought it of you. Guards, arrest this man for attempted murder."

Ighur grabbed Mick's arms and yanked them behind his back. He was rough while he clasped irons around Mick's wrists.

Riggs went on. "Mckal Dairner, you will be tried and condemned for your crimes. Is there anyone I should notify? Someone you'd like to be present? Any family or friends? *Relatives*?" His voice went up a notch on the last word.

Mick's eyes grew. Was all of this about Dimitri? Because Mick wouldn't give Riggs his name?

Ighur, the guard who'd been Mick's personal babysitter all afternoon, dragged Mick toward the door to leave.

Mick scrambled to think of something to say before his last hope slipped away.

He tried to twist himself around so he could see Riggs past Ighur. "Governor Riggs, I have a proposal! Wait, please!"

Ighur shoved him forward while guiding him to the door where Theérl stood on standby, his dark, muscled body tense and ready to assist.

"Please, Governor, let me speak!" Mick dug his heels into the white carpet. Theérl reached over and grasped Mick's arm, taking over from Ighur. His fingers pinched Mick's skin as he pulled him forward.

Governor Riggs's voice commanded the room. "Hold up, gentlemen. I will hear what he has to say."

Both guards let go of Mick. If this plan didn't work, Mick would never make it to Kartha. With his hands bound behind him, he faced Riggs.

"Let me find you a contact. Allow me to go to Kartha and find someone you can do business with. Believe me when I say that my uncle is not your man. But he has contacts and knows all kinds of people in his line of work. Let me go meet some of them and set something up."

Riggs smirked. "I have plenty of people I could send for that job."

"But none can gain the trust of government officials there like I can. I can go to my uncle and have him introduce me to his friends and acquaintances.

After a few months, when I've found someone who I think will be a good fit, you can set up an interview to meet them."

The room became quiet enough to hear the wind gusting against the windows. Riggs gave Mick a hard stare. "All right, Mick. I can go along with this idea. But you'll have only three weeks to complete your task."

Mick's jaw dropped. "Three weeks? Governor, I've never been to Kartha. That won't be enough time. I—"

"This isn't a holiday you're going on." Riggs waved his hand in the air. "You'll be there on business. You'll have three weeks to arrive, get to know some people, set something up, and then return with a potential contact for an interview. If I don't think you've made a good match, you'll be mine to do with as I see fit. That's the arrangement."

Mick glanced at the others who stood watching. Ferind transferred his books to one arm so he could adjust his spectacles. Ighur hovered nearby, and Theérl remained at the door with his wide shoulders pulled back.

"And if I find a good match?" Mick said.

Riggs scratched his head, and flakes of dandruff fell through the last rays of the day's sun. "What do you think?"

Sweat tickled Mick's brow. Without the use of his hands, he couldn't wipe it away. *What* did *he think?* He considered his response. Riggs demanded much. His gain would be substantial. And so Mick would match his boldness.

"We're done with each other, you and I. If the match is good, you accept my resignation, and we will never see each other again."

Helping Riggs find a contact to do his dirty business with in Kartha was the last thing Mick wanted to do. What kind of message would he be sending to the people there about who he was? He already had his work cut out for him in trying to persuade the citizens there to accept him, being the supposed foretold destroyer of the land.

But for now, he needed to be free of this place. The rest, he could figure out later.

Riggs nodded once and signalled for Ighur to release Mick from the irons. Mick hadn't realized how tight they were until the air hit his tender wrists.

The Governor thrust his hand out for Mick to shake. "Very well. Three weeks. You leave at dawn, and Ighur will escort you."

Mick glanced at Ighur, who barely moved, save for a slight shift of his weight. Mick couldn't tell who was less pleased with this arrangement. Him or Ighur.

Ignoring the voice of reason within, Mick shook Riggs's hand. When their hands clasped, Riggs squeezed Mick's and reeled him in close. "Double cross me, and I'll take everything from you." He gave his hand a hard squeeze, then released him.

That was going to be a problem. Did Riggs know exactly what *everything* meant to Mick?

It wouldn't be difficult for him to discover.

Mick exited the parlour, followed by Ighur and Theérl. He left with a tinge of excitement, but this growing dread overpowered it. After all this time, he was going to Kartha, but under these conditions, he didn't want to think about how things would go when he got there. What would Dimitri say when he showed up with Riggs's man? What would he do once he knew what his purpose was?

One thing Mick knew for sure: It wouldn't be good.

His cooking was done for the day, and Aira had probably gone back to her quarters for the evening. He needed to tell her everything. Somehow, he had to make her see the heightened danger she was in. If Riggs paid attention, he'd know Aira was a part of that *everything* he threatened.

Mick turned the corner that would lead him to his room. Theérl thrust his arm across his chest, stopping him in his tracks. "Not that way," he said in his thick Ectarin accent. "The manor staff lodgings are for employees only. You are no longer employed as the Governor's head cook. You will have other accommodations this evening."

Other accommodations? Mick tried not to let his imagination run wild. "Ah, yes. Of course. I'm an ambassador now, aren't I? Can't have an ambassador in the servants's quarters now. That wouldn't be fitting."

"Right." Ighur grinned. His eyes gleamed with sadistic pleasure. "We're to take you to the Governor's guesthouse. You should be more comfortable there."

The guesthouse didn't sound so bad. It beat the warehouses.

"Someone will see to your bags in the morning." Theérl directed Mick down the opposite hall. "This way."

What guesthouse could they be referring to? Mick's legs took him foreward, though he didn't know how they could still carry him with all their shaking.

He licked his dry lips. "Before retiring for the evening, I'll need to see the other cook. She needs to know she'll be on her own for a while."

"She'll be informed," Ighur said as he guided Mick by placing a hand behind his back.

Mick bit his lip, trying to keep himself calm. "It's about cooking. I need to tell her a few items to remember for certain dishes. Will you inform her of those too?"

Theérl led the way down another hallway and out of the manor, toward the woodshed atop the same hill the manor was built upon.

He looked back and grinned. "Write a note. I will ensure she gets it."

Ighur kept a hand hovering close, as though he thought Mick might try to run. *Should he?* What kind of repercussions might he face if he tried and failed?

The man Mick had seen beaten a year ago came to mind and he decided not to take his chances. Not here, when the perimeter was likely to be well guarded and he had little hope of getting off the grounds. He'd have a better chance as soon as they were out of Iptin. Maybe he could slip away while they layover in Ectarin. Not that Riggs didn't have an army of Collectors there. Kartha might be his best bet, where, as Mick hoped, the Governor's influence wasn't as prevalent.

His constant jitters were held at bay thanks to the stone, but these tremors beneath his skin were something else. Anger? Fear? Frustration? Probably a bit of them all. Would Aira wonder what happened to him? Or would Morris note his absence? One night was just one night, but he'd be gone for three weeks. Jury had already been gone for almost two weeks, and no one seemed too alarmed. Was there even a family matter he'd been called to, or was that a lie? Had he been sent away to one of Riggs's warehouses? Did Morris suspect anything? Or did he know of this deal too? Had he been given the option to accept an offer of raised pay in exchange for years of service? If so, how could Mick have been so blind?

They arrived at the shed, and Ighur unlocked the door.

Theérl crossed his arms, tilted his head down, and jutted his chin at the door. "In."

With Ighur at his heels, Mick stepped inside and paused. A cot sat in one corner of the plain room. The wooden floor bubbled and bulged in places, and he'd be susceptible to getting splinters if he weren't careful. At the foot of the cot sat a small table whose purpose seemed to be to serve as a lampstand but without the lamp. As night grew darker, shadows lengthened along the floor. It took less than a second to take in the windowless room. How was he supposed to write a note for Aira?

Mick turned to Ighur. "You mustn't know how writing works, and one could hardly blame you for your lack of education. However typically, when writing, one generally needs to see to put words on a page. And one can see only when there is light."

Ighur grasped Mick by the throat and squeezed, cutting off his airflow. He lifted Mick until his toes wriggled, hovering above the floor. Mick clawed at Ighur's hand. He clutched his forearm, scratching through his arm hair and trying to break his thick skin.

Theérl's voice spoke from just outside the door. "Stop playing games, Ig. He's not your toy to play with."

Mick's body slackened against Ighur's, and only then did the guard release him. Mick coughed and tried to get air back into his lungs.

Ighur bent over him on the floor. "Just wait, Cook. This little trip we're taking is only delaying the inevitable. You'll come back. They always do. And believe me, you'll break sooner than you think." He stopped at the door and added, "They always do." With that, he left the shed, closing the door and leaving Mick in complete darkness, still gasping for air.

When he finally managed to suck in a full breath, Mick hopped up and tried the door. Of course it'd be locked. Why else would he have been brought to a windowless shed? If he was thinking of making a run for it before dawn, he had no hope of it now.

Not only was that problematic for his own situation, but now how was he supposed to warn Aira?

# Chapter 7

THE SHIP'S BOW CUT THROUGH THE WAVES. IT WAS HIS FIRST TIME AT SEA, AND Mick had so far managed not to release the contents of his stomach. Iptin was a small island off the coast of Ectarin, and no ships went directly from there to Kartha, so they'd switched ships in Ectarin and now made the long stretch across the Pinbei Ocean.

As promised, Ighur served as Mick's escort for this trip, while Theérl remained behind to carry out his usual work and all that entailed. Mick didn't know if the extra dozen men were for him or if they had other instructions upon arrival. He'd been successfully avoiding them for the duration of the journey, but Ighur stuck close, never taking his eyes off him. Where did he think Mick would go? Into the sea? He supposed it could have been worse, though. He could have been confined to a cabin for the whole trip.

A gust of wind blew, misting Mick's face. He closed his eyes, glad to be on deck among the other passengers roaming about the ship, rather than locked away down below and not having the chance to catch his first glimpse of Kartha.

When they'd first set out, Mick could think of nothing else except Aira. He never did get to write her a note or find some way to warn her about Riggs. If he could somehow send her a message from Kartha, he could tell her to flee. Run, and never return to the Governor's manor. She had to know something was wrong and that he would never just leave without saying goodbye.

With Ectarin behind them, what lay ahead consumed Mick's thoughts. And as the sun sank lower in the sky and he got nearer to Kartha by the second, he couldn't still his anxiety. He was so close to reaching the place he'd dreamt about his whole life, yet for all his excitement, his mother's words about the prophecy burrowed into his thoughts.

What if the people of Kartha discovered who he was? Or, rather, who they thought him to be? Maybe the sickness referred to in the prophecy wasn't a literal kind. Maybe this task—finding Riggs a contact—was the sickness, and Mick was about to set into motion the very thing that could destroy the country. It didn't matter that it didn't make sense or that he was overthinking it. The point was that if Riggs had a contact to work with in Kartha, he would have his Collectors swarming the place. No one would be safe. Especially if those Riggs intended to abduct and sell had magic. As far as Mick knew, that would make him the only trader in all of the eight countries of Ecstein providing his clients with magical people. Wasn't that the main appeal of his coming here at all?

Mick looked ahead. Dark shadows of land came into view on the horizon. Wind whipped his curls over his forehead and all over the place.

Ighur approached and stood at Mick's side, gazing out to where the land grew closer. His biceps bulged from under his coat sleeves. "We're nearly to the port at Hywreath. Once we've disembarked, we'll hire a coach to take us to your uncle. Upon our arrival, arrange to meet some people and narrow down the potential contacts to two or three. I'll assess your choices, then we'll board a ship and set sail for home. The sooner we leave this place, the better."

Mick licked his lips, which had been salted by the sea spray. As Kartha became distinguishable, the unsettled feeling worsened. Wasn't his coming to Kartha supposed to feel good? After all this time, he was getting what he'd always wanted. So why did it feel wrong? Was this a mistake?

The ship slowed, and crewmen tossed ropes over the sides, to where men caught them and reeled them in toward the docks. Water lapped against the side of the ship as it came to a full stop. The captain stood at the helm to announce they'd arrived at Hywreath and that the local time was a quarter past three in the afternoon. He barked out a few instructions regarding disembarking in an orderly fashion, then waved his arm in a grand gesture, dismissing the passengers.

Mick adjusted the strap of his bag over his shoulder and fell in line behind a woman with her two young sons. She clasped the back collars of each boy's shirt, guiding them across the gangplank. Ighur cut off the man behind Mick and took his place, while Riggs's other hired men hauled their belongings and joined the queue behind them.

Within the harbour, a clock tower stood beside the wide gate, welcoming travellers to Kartha. Beyond that, a bell tower in the middle of the city rose taller than every other building. Mick froze, overwhelmed. Hywreath bustled with people and horse-drawn coaches. The scent of seaweed and fish filled the air, masking the fragrance of manure from the horses. Streets zigzagged in all directions, extending every which way and disappearing around tall buildings. The traffic hustled at a much quicker pace than that of Iptin.

Ighur nudged him from behind to move with the crowd. Mick's feet carried him along, moving synchronously with the others. He stepped off the gangplank onto the pier and followed the mother and her children toward the gate.

While he tried to soak everything in at once—the scent of sea and smoke and something floral; the busy bustle of people coming and going, walking the streets or sightseeing in the harbour; and traffic moving in a constant flow—the harbourmaster walked past Mick and put a hand up to halt Ighur.

"Excuse me, sir," the harbourmaster said. "You're going to have to fill out some papers declaring your weapons before coming any farther. Is this lot with you?"

Mick peered over his shoulder. The man indicated Riggs's men but paid no mind to Mick. It served them right for walking around and flashing their custom-made guns on their hips so freely. Riggs often boasted of his weapon, imported from Nuwnot, that would pave the way for the future. With guns designed to rapid-fire, eliminating the need to reload after every shot, he declared himself "the most dangerous and feared businessman in all the Zareff Continent." Mick wasn't sure how vast his fame truly was, but he had no doubt about the Governor's authority in certain circles. Evidently, the harbourmaster here didn't fear repercussions for calling out Riggs's men.

Mick caught Ighur's warning in his eyes, but he didn't stop. Or he couldn't, rather, as the flow of disembarking passengers carried him along.

The harbourmaster continued speaking to Ighur. "And I should like to know your business here in Kartha." He lectured Ighur, his voice fading as Mick walked farther away.

The pier ended, and as soon as Mick's feet touched solid ground, warmth radiated from his pocket, where he kept the stone. He slowed his steps. Everyone who'd just disembarked had joined the foot traffic on the pathway, and people bumped into him. He integrated into the flow of the movement.

In a slow, dazed manner, he turned his face skyward, and a gust of wind swept through, whipping his clothes about his body. It was as if the wind spoke to him. Whispers of breathy, incomprehensible words brushed past his ears.

With his eyes on the sky, he wasn't paying attention to where he was or to the people around him. He came to a full stop in the middle of a sidewalk, where the crowd strode past on either side, nudging shoulders with him. A man carrying a cane shoved into him. Another wearing a red scarf ran into him as he passed in a hurry. If Mick weren't so enthralled with everything in sight, he might have been quicker to get out of the way.

The stone in his pocket burned, infusing him with an urgency to do something. What exactly he didn't know. But whatever it was, he intended to find out. He was here for a reason, and it wasn't for Riggs. This was for him. And for Kartha.

From shuffling about to get off the ship to getting to where he now stood, he'd lost sight of Ighur and the others. He circled in place, scanning the faces of those around him. Had it really been that easy? Ighur's thin, pale hair was nowhere in sight above all the heads. Mick tried to remember if he'd told him where Dimitri lived. He didn't think he had. If Mick could get to Dimitri without his escort, he could enlist the help of his family to figure out how to send a message to Aira and to his parents,—and to get out of this situation with Governor Riggs.

He started walking slowly, making himself inconspicuous as he joined the crowd. A large group crossed a street, and Mick fell in step with them.

Ahead, a man shouted. At the same time, people scattered sideways in front of where he walked, and a woman came sprinting toward him. She toppled over a lady, who screamed and nearly fell but was caught by the man at her side.

"Hey!" A boy threw his arms up when the woman charged past.

She sped toward Mick. He couldn't gauge which direction to dive out of the way. He'd not decided fast enough and was thrown back by the impact of her crashing into him. He fell and landed on his knees, scraping his forearm in the fall. There was a lack of warmth from where he'd put the stone.

His heart lurched. *No.* He panicked as he scrambled on his hands and knees through the parted crowd, scouring the ground. He patted his pockets. Empty. Sweat glazed the back of his neck, and he crawled on all fours, searching. *Please be here.*

He sensed that people were watching. *Let them.* All the noise and activity around him faded while he searched. He didn't even care if Ighur found him now.

His bag lay near where he'd fallen. He picked it up and checked to see if the stone had fallen underneath it. Someone grasped his arm and yanked him to his feet, pulling him out of the street just as a coach swerved past—right where he'd been kneeling. Mick glanced up and was met with bright, doe-like green eyes, staring at him. The eyes of the woman who'd toppled over him. She pulled his arm, urging him to get off the street and into the shadow of a cluster of buildings. Her gaze darted around as though she were trying not to be seen.

Mick was taken by surprise by her stunning appearance and he almost allowed himself to stare a little longer.

*But the stone.*

His eyes grew. He threw his bag over his shoulder and turned around to scan the ground, his heart racing.

The woman tapped his shoulder. "Did you lose something?" She held in her palm the stone, still secured in its pouch.

Mick's eyes flitted to hers. He waited for her to snatch it away. Did she know what she held in her hand? What was tucked away within the pouch? How important it was?

Did *he* know?

She held it out, offering it for him to take. Mick wasn't prone to getting emotional, but right then, he could have cried. He grabbed it and wrapped his fingers around it, clutching it close to his heart. That had been too close.

# Chapter 8

Tight, dark blonde curls hung loosely, framing the woman's petite, narrow chin. She caught sight of Mick's forearm where he'd been injured in his fall, and she reached for his arm. "You're bleeding."

Mick jerked his arm from her touch. "I'm not. I'm all right." He covered the place where a small amount of blood had dried, but no marks remained. He'd not even noticed the usual itchy sensation he'd get when his healing kicked in.

People hollered in the streets. "She came this way! Over here!" The woman took a step back, deeper into the shadows. The three men who stood shouting by the gate wore plain clothes, but each of them had a sword on one side of their belt and a dagger on the other. One man waved his arms about, directing the others in various directions.

"Are you in some kind of trouble?" Mick asked.

The woman's eyes darted from the streets to Mick. "That depends on your definition of *trouble*. If exerting my will not to marry a man chosen for me is trouble, then, yes, I am."

Had her parents sent people after her over an arranged marriage?

"What are you, a princess?" Mick half-joked. He glanced over his shoulder, aware that Ighur would be looking for him.

"There's no royalty in Kartha." The woman looked him up and down. Royalty or not, she must be high-born.

She crept back against the wall, hiding herself further in shadow but she looked in no hurry to move from this spot. "What is that thing anyway? In the pouch? I sure hope it was worth almost dying over. You really should pay closer attention."

Mick clutched the stone and glanced back at the place where he'd nearly been run over. He could just imagine what people would say upon seeing a dead man rise up in the streets as if he'd not just been killed. That would have been a bad start to his time in Kartha.

"It's a gift from my uncle," he told her. "And I guess you can say it's worth dying over." According to Uncle Dimi, it was.

"That's some gift. I'm Vidia, by the way." The woman offered her hand. "Did you just arrive on a ship from Ectarin?"

Mick shook her hand. His pulse thumped in his ears. How could she know that?

"It's the accent," Vidia said, smiling.

"Of course. Right. I'm Mick." He dropped his hand to his side and inched into the alley with her so he'd be hidden too. "Are you really running away from an arranged marriage?"

"Well, it's not just the marriage. It's a bit more complicated than that, but, yes, that's one reason."

Mick thought he understood, confusing as it was. Family was never not complicated. He took another glance behind him, looking for Ighur or any sign of Riggs's men. They were probably still held up by the harbourmaster. This would be the perfect time to make a good headstart, but he had no idea which way to go. For all the maps he'd memorized of Kartha, it did him little good now that he was here and lost in a maze of streets that went in circles and not-so-straight lines. Tall buildings towered, casting shadows around every corner. Having been raised in a small town, he worried the bustle of the city would swallow him whole. Not even Balmell at its busiest was this overwhelming. If he could figure out which way was south, he'd at least have some idea of which way to head. Hywreath, the northernmost point of Kartha, happened to be the only city with a major port, while Litlen, where he needed to get to, was the southernmost point. It'd be a long time before he'd arrive, especially if he needed to travel on foot. Mick refrained from bouncing on his heels and looking too eager to go. How soon could Ighur get word to Riggs of his desertion?

Vidia's beauty drew his gaze back to her. She chuckled softly and moved a lock of hair behind her ear, where just beneath it lay a birthmark in the shape of a downturned crescent. Her unruly curls fell right back in front of her face.

Mick blinked. He'd been staring. Had she asked him something? He cleared his throat. "I'm from Iptin Province."

"Iptin Province? Never heard of it."

"It's small."

"Kartha's small."

"True, but Kartha is different. It's…" Mick searched for the right word. "Alive." The stone emitted a wave of warmth into his hand. *Alive* was the right word. He tucked the stone back into his pocket and made a mental note to take better care of it from now on.

As he thought about taking better care, he remembered that he was supposed to be on high alert. He couldn't afford to let his guard down. In the time they'd been speaking, he'd slowly shuffled out of the shadows of the alley. He slipped back into the shelter that the two walls provided on either side. The crowds going to and from and bustling within the harbour never seemed to diminish. Was it always this busy?

Vidia snuck a peek at the crowds. She stared at the same spot at the harbour gate for a full minute. When she faced Mick again, she said, "Those men look like they're searching for someone, but they're not my uncle's men."

Mick glanced out to see who she was looking at. Ighur stood with Riggs's dozen other men. They were dispersing into the crowd, spreading out. Mick tucked himself farther into the shadows.

Vidia's eyes searched him. "Are *you* in some kind of trouble?"

It wasn't like Mick could hide it for long if he were going to have to make a run for it right away. "If exerting my will not to be made into a slave is trouble, then, yes, I suppose I am."

Vidia's eyes bulged. "Are you serious?" Her head whipped toward the street. A woman glanced their way, but besides her, no one paid them any mind, even though Vidia had practically shouted. She lowered her voice. "You're not serious…?"

"Not usually, but in this case, unfortunately, I am."

"Oh." Vidia slumped her shoulders. "So, you've come to Kartha to run away?"

Fully aware that Ighur could find him at any moment, Mick shifted on his feet. "It's complicated." He tried for a smile, but it didn't reach his eyes. "Long story short, I have family here who I hope can help me."

Vidia nodded her head in the direction down the alley and away from the harbour. "Want to walk this way and get out of here?"

"Yes," Mick said a little too enthusiastically.

They kept to the shadows and walked the length of the alley. When they reached the end, it opened up onto another street that was just as busy as the last. Mick turned his head from side to side, checking around for any of Riggs's men. How far had they spread out? Vidia, too, checked around. Mick tried to recall what any of Riggs's men looked like. Most of them had remained below decks for the duration of the journey, but still, Mick was pretty sure he'd seen each of them at least once before they'd arrived. He should have paid better attention.

"How did you know those men don't work for your uncle?" he asked.

As though his question might have caused her uncle's men to flock to them, Vidia tensed. She spoke a little over a whisper, and Mick had to lean toward her to better hear.

"Those who work for my uncle wear red as a show of loyalty to my family. It has some significance in our history. I think it's ridiculous, but it does make it easy to tell them apart. If you see anyone sporting a red hat, bandanna, scarf, shirt, you name it, chances are they'll answer to my uncle."

Now that she'd said it, Mick recalled a few people wearing red he'd passed. They seemed to be everywhere. "Were you trying to get onto one of those ships?"

Vidia's tan cheeks turned a dark shade of red. "No." She bit her lip and grimaced. "Yes. Don't laugh, but I was going to stowaway and go looking for my parents. They went missing ten years ago, and my brothers and I went to live with my uncle. Supposedly, their ship went down and everyone was declared lost at sea, but I don't buy it. They can't just be gone without any explanation. Besides, they found the wreck, but I heard there weren't any bodies discovered anywhere near it. That's weird, right? If everyone died in the incident, shouldn't there have been at least a few bodies?" She didn't let him respond. "Anyway, it doesn't sound likely. I think they're still out there but can't come home for whatever reason. Maybe they got stranded on an island. Who knows?"

A flash of red caught Mick's eye and he placed himself on Vidia's side, where she'd be obscured from the view of the men in red. He steered her in the opposite direction and crossed a street with a handful of other pedestrians. The buildings rose tall here, but they became less grand the farther they got from the harbour. Without drawing attention to himself, Mick peered around, keeping a sharp eye out for Ighur. At least he'd be easier to spot than the others. As far as Mick could see, he wasn't going to have to make a quick getaway just yet. If his luck continued like this, he could make it to Litlen without incident.

A man's voice shouted from nearby. "Over there!" The man pointed at Vidia. He wore a red sash wrapped across his body from shoulder to hip.

Mick leapt and took Vidia's hand, acting without thinking. He tugged her along, across the street and toward another alley. This one was shorter than the last, and he could see straight across to the other side. It looked like it came out onto another street at the end.

"Come on, this way."

They ran through the narrow space—Vidia behind, while he led. He didn't know where they were going, but didn't care so long as they weren't caught. They exited the alley and rushed down the walking path, crossed a street, ran into another alley, rounded a bend, and came out the other side onto a less busy street with no carriages or wagons. It was lined with vendor stalls and foot traffic only. And as everywhere else seemed to be, it was busy. This whole city buzzed with life.

For now, it looked like they'd lost their tail. Mick slowed to a walk and caught his breath.

Vidia wrapped an arm around her torso, breathing heavily. "Thanks." She laughed. "That was close."

# Chapter 9

MICK GLANCED AROUND FOR IGHUR AND THE OTHERS. THEY'D DRAWN attention to themselves but no more than the odd glance in their direction or a shake of the head from an elderly man. They'd lost the red-clad soldiers for now, but Mick wasn't about to let his guard down.

Vidia exhaled heavily. "Let's not do that—"

"Vidia?" A red-headed woman stood at a vending cart where an old woman sold healing potions and ointments. The redhead smiled at Vidia, making her bright green eyes sparkle in the low red sun that shone between buildings and intensified the brightness of her hair. She couldn't have been much older than Mick's mother.

Vidia's smile faltered. "Miss Madx." Her voice held uncertainty.

The woman Vidia addressed accepted a jingling pouch from the vendor. She handed the old woman a small wooden box, thanked her for her business, then stepped away from the cart, giving her full attention to Mick and Vidia. "Please, call me Laila. I'm just on my way to see your uncle. I've seen quite a few of his men rushing around here today." Laila dipped her chin. "That wouldn't have anything to do with you now, would it?"

Vidia glanced sideways at Mick, then turned her eyes down.

Laila smiled. "It's all right. You have nothing to fear from me. It's none of my business. Who's your friend?"

Mick extended his hand for a handshake, saving Vidia the introduction. "I'm Mick."

Laila shook his hand and stared at him. "Have we met before? You seem very familiar."

Mick was reminded of what his father had told him: *They'll take one look at you, and it won't take them long to realize you're a Dairner*. In all the trouble with Ighur, he'd almost forgotten. He'd hoped his father had been exaggerating.

He shook his head and released Laila's hand. She looked at him a moment longer, her expression unreadable. Her lip quirked up. "Oh well, you remind me of someone I know." She hesitated, and Mick thought she might say more. But then her eyes flitted back to Vidia. "I should be on my way. I'm sure I'll see you around, Vidia. It was nice meeting you, Mick." She excused herself and walked in the opposite direction.

Vidia let out another sigh. "For a second, I thought she was going to call for my uncle's men."

The way Laila had looked at him, Mick thought she could read his mind. Or that she knew a secret but was keeping it to herself. "How do you know her?" he asked.

Vidia started walking, and Mick followed suit, glancing over his shoulder every few steps. Ighur and his men hadn't found their way down this street yet, as far as he could tell.

"She sells fancy trinkets to my uncle. Oh! Actually, I didn't even think of it, but she might be someone who can help you. I've heard my uncle call her the Witch before, and if the stories are true, she's supposed to be some kind of slave freer."

The Witch? Hadn't Riggs mentioned something about a witch in Kartha? "She sells trinkets and rescues slaves? And she's called a witch?"

"She's more like a privateer or an apothecary, I think. I'm pretty sure she got that name because of her magic."

Mick stopped walking. "Magic?"

"Supposedly. I've never seen her use any, but if rumours are to be believed, then she's very powerful." Vidia stopped beside him. "Do you want to go talk to her?"

Mick looked back in the direction where Laila had disappeared and saw no sign of her.

A vendor had a display of candles and incense, and the fragrance of vanilla wafted in the air as Mick and Vidia stood there. Children ran in circles around a fountain at the centre of intersecting streets. Mick envied their carefree spirits.

Since stepping off the ship, a heaviness weighed on him, carrying an urgency that he needed to fix something. But he couldn't think of what that might be, apart from his dilemma with Riggs. He'd take whatever help he could get, but why would Laila help him if she even could? He was just one man. He searched the crowd, looking for her bright red hair, but she was gone. Probably for the better. He already had a sense that Laila could see right through him. He didn't like the way she made him feel so exposed.

"It's all right," he said. "I should try to get to Litlen to find my family before anything else."

Vidia led them down a walkway that took them onto another street designated for foot traffic only. This one looked just like the last, with lines of carts set up, couples and families meandering at a leisurely pace—unlike the hurried flow at the harbour—and still no sign of Ighur. For now.

Mick circled in place. "How does anyone know where they're going around here?" If he couldn't find his way out of this city, how was he ever going to find his way to Litlen?

Vidia smirked. "You came at a busy time. The Amifildel festival is on all week and the whole country makes a big fuss about it. These streets have all been blocked for vendors and performers."

Mick recalled reading about the holiday once before, but he hadn't realized his arrival aligned with it. If he weren't in such a predicament, he'd leap at the chance to take in all the festivities. But the longer it took him to deliver a message to Aira and his parents, the more danger they were in.

With evening upon them, Mick followed a line in the sky in the direction which the sun gradually descended. Some of the buildings were so tall here that the sun was already partly blocked.

Vidia stuck a hand on her jutted hip. "A little lost, are we?"

Orienting himself was one thing, but it didn't help him with knowing the terrain and which roads to take and which ones to avoid. He looked over his shoulder, then all around. "If I admit that I am, will you help me find my way?"

"I might. But if you're looking for a guide, I'll tell you right now that I'm not familiar with the east of Kartha, and I'm not going back to Valmain anytime soon. But I know my way around Ferenth and a bit of the south. You mentioned Litlen is your destination, so in that case, I may even be able to take you as far as the Bludesel Mountains."

Mick tried to remember where the Bludesel Mountains were on the map. There were two major mountain ranges, if he recalled correctly. Both were south, and heading in that direction would put him on the right track.

He tightened the strap of his bag over his shoulder "In that case, I'm very lost."

"I knew it. I'll tell you what," Vidia said. "Why don't we travel together? Then, when we get to the Bludesel Mountains, we'll part ways. I'll go on to the village where I lived before moving in with my uncle, and you can continue south to Litlen. From there, I'd be impressed if you managed to lose your way."

Could it really be that simple? Losing Ighur so fast, then finding a guide to take him as far as the mountains? It was as if the country itself shifted pieces into place in his favour. Mick scanned the faces of those walking by—vendors and shoppers. Even the red-clad men seemed to have given up looking for Vidia in this corner of the city. There was no telling how long it would take Ighur to discover where to go to look for Mick. And if Mick was going to make it to Litlen before Ighur could get there, a guide would certainly help. Especially one as beautiful as Vidia.

"What about your getaway ship? Are you still planning on leaving Kartha?" Only a few minutes ago, she'd been ready to flee the country. Now she would change her entire plan just for him? He didn't want to suspect her of being anything but friendly, but his father's warnings latched onto his thoughts.

Vidia led the way while they walked. She took them around a corner and onto another street, this one wider than the last. There were fewer shops here and no more carts and vendors. Horse-drawn carriages travelled up the road, which ascended at a gentle incline.

"It may have been a bit irrational of me to try to hop aboard a ship and leave Kartha without a real plan." Vidia lifted a finger and pointed it skyward. "Make no mistake, I did have a plan. It just… wasn't a very good one. Now I've got a better one. I have a brother who lives in our old village in the mountains. He left my uncle years ago after they had a big fight. I was too young for him to take me with him then, but I wonder if he might help me leave my uncle's Keep now that I'm older."

Vidia didn't look much older than Aira, though her mannerisms were less sophisticated and more playful.

Mick glanced up and down this new street for any signs of a threat to either  him or Vidia. Days on the road and both of them on the run. What could go wrong?

He stuck his hand into his pocket and held the stone, taking comfort in its calming effect. That sense of some unknown purpose tugged at his heart, but whatever lay ahead, he was here now.

"That's settled then." He waved his hand, palm out, giving it extra flair. "Lead the way."

# Chapter 10

Laila closed the door behind her as she walked into the Valca Keep. Hallways branched in three directions, and the staircase in the foyer trailed up the wall to the left.

This place had become a regular stop whenever she returned to Kartha, and it no longer felt strange to enter. And while most people would have knocked and waited to be welcomed in, she couldn't recall ever having done so. Walking into places unannounced and unexpected was something others had come to expect of her.

And she would not disappoint.

Among the stairs and hallways, a chandelier hung high from the centre of the foyer ceiling. Since Daegan had inherited the Keep, he'd made a few improvements to the décor, including adding the long, deep green rugs that ran down each hallway and the potted plants that took up a corner or two. A sculpture of a nude woman with a long scarf of stone draping from her shoulders down to her feet rested on a pedestal by one hallway. Her body twisted in ways to accentuate her curvy figure. The piece was one Laila had acquired years ago upon first learning of Daegan's fixation with collecting rare and beautiful items. His expensive tastes suited her, both for the business it brought her and the fact that it made this place look less like the home of his ancestors. Now it was something that could be considered a comfortable abode.

A hulking figure came up the hallway from behind the stairs. His hair fell past his shoulders and was not nearly as bright red as her own hair. His face lit up. "Laila!" He extended his arms out and approached her.

Laila smiled and welcomed his embrace. "Win." Her old friend must have been delivering a crate of his finest catch. Win liked to cast his nets in places where no other fishermen dared to venture. It paid off with the exotic fish he caught and sold.

"You show up in the most unusual of places," Win said. "Where was it we last ran into each other? Was it the Marked Masquerade in Xihngrahv?"

Laila tapped a finger on her temple. "It was aboard the *Whisp of Seas*, but only for a moment in passing. The Masquerade was the time before."

"Yes, that's right. I do remember catching a fleeting glance of you before you vanished, as you do. Good memory you have. I've never seen you in Kartha. Do you come often? I can't say I'm surprised you venture here to do business. Fearless Laila."

Laila wrinkled her nose. "I've been called many things in my life, Win. But fearless is inaccurate. I've had my share."

"I didn't see Judwin's ship at the port. Did you come alone? And are you still running that apothecary with Finnig? How is the old man?"

"He's well. Carrying on business as usual in Tsein." Her business partner never ventured far from his home. Neither did Judwin, her colleague. But it just so happened that his home was the *Gypsy Lady*, his beloved ship. "Jude took the crew to settle a job in Reij. Even I'm allowed to take a break every now and then." Could this trip home count as a break if she was still technically working?

The young man who entered the foyer glanced up and startled. His dark hair was so unlike the light blond hair his father, grandfather, and great-grandfather shared, yet so like his uncle's. If Laila didn't know better, she'd have thought Preston could pass for Daegan's son rather than his nephew. Preston's gaze landed on Laila, then on Win, then back on Laila. "Miss Madx, I didn't know my uncle was expecting you today."

"He's not. Would you tell him I'm here? And remind him I don't like to be made to wait."

Preston paused with his mouth agape. "I'm—He's with someone."

Laila shifted her weight as if to go. "Oh. All right, so I'll just take what I have and go then. I'm sure your uncle won't mind that he missed me." She turned to Win and bowed her head, bidding him farewell.

"No, wait!" Preston jumped. "I'll let him know you're here. Please, don't go. He'll want to see you." He turned back down the hall, toward the study to inform Daegan.

Laila winked at Win, who smirked.

"Cheeky, as always," Win said. "I better go. My ship awaits. It was good seeing you, Laila. Don't be a stranger. Come visit me sometime."

"You're about as difficult to find in any one place as I am. But that won't stop me. I'll see you around."

Win leaned in and kissed her cheek before going.

Preston reemerged. "My uncle will see you. Come this way." He showed her to the door of the study. "He'll just be a minute."

Laila raised a brow. "I thought I told you I don't like to wait."

"He's almost done. Just…go in when his guest comes out." Preston dismissed himself and left Laila standing at the door. He wasn't the friendliest kid, but being raised by Daegan for most of his life might have had something to do with his harsh mannerisms. If Laila remembered correctly, Preston was the second of the three Valca kids. He took the most after Daegan, though Laila knew enough Valcas to recognize similar traits in them all. Each of them was strong-willed in their own way. Even Vidia had a strength in her, hidden beneath those timid eyes.

Voices spoke from within the study. The solid wood of the door might have kept sound from carrying into the hall, but the latch hadn't been closed properly, and Laila's natural curiosity piqued as she overheard Daegan. Listening was part of her job, after all. It was one of the reasons she did business with him in the first place.

She rested her back against the wall in the hallway, arms crossed, while she listened.

"You let me worry about my niece. I can make her understand." Daegan's voice was low and nearly inaudible from within.

The second voice was husky and calm. Whoever he was, he was even more difficult to hear. "She's out of control. If you can't rein her in, you won't have their loyalty. How are you to gain their trust when you can't control your own niece?"

"I'm not her father, Damien. She still believes her parents are coming home. She won't listen to me."

"Then make her."

Silence stretched between their words. Daegan sighed loudly. "There has to be something else we can do. We just haven't come up with it yet. But I'll have to think of something later. I have a guest waiting. Let's continue this discussion another time."

"I'll be in this region for a few days more." The guest's voice sounded closer to the door. "Daegan, if you're serious about this, then take it seriously."

The door opened, and Daegan's guest stopped short, facing Laila.

Laila pushed off from the wall and straightened. She moved aside so he could pass. The guest—what had Daegan called him? Damien? —made no move to pass her. His eyes lingered on her, taking in all of her from top to bottom. He licked his lips.

In Laila's field of work, she'd dealt with all kinds of people, and had received leers like this a million times. But there hadn't been too many of them that made her feel like shrinking back from their gaze like this man's did. Not because he intimidated her. No, that wasn't it. Sure, he stood taller than her and was quite broad, but there was something about him that gave her a bad feeling. He carried a darkness that reminded her of her father. She hardened her eyes and tried not to show any sign of discomfort.

Damien's upper lip curled back in a sneer that was possibly meant to be a smile. He cocked his head as if tipping a hat, then passed her.

Daegan appeared in the doorway. "Laila, come in, come in." He extended his arms out wide in greeting. She entered, and he closed the door. The light of the afternoon sun shone through the tall window behind him. "Take a seat. I wasn't expecting you today."

Laila strode past the chair intended for guests. "That's because I didn't tell you I was coming." She dropped her bag on the floor by her feet and settled into Daegan's throne of a chair behind his unique desk. He'd had it specially crafted from the thrinduk tree. Engraved on one side was the Valca crescent, and on the other, a tree was carved with the names of the Valca family members written over the extending branches. Laila had met a few of them. Earlier generations of the family had dedicated their resources and power to trying to destroy her people. Daegan's father, Ilan, had put a stop to the dissension between the Elderace and mayanon. It was he who ended The Valca Order's reign. Before Ilan's disappearance ten years ago, Daegan had been known to argue often with his father about their differing opinions regarding how Ilan handled that time. Since then, the country was on its way to unity. But there were those who longed to see The Order returned to power if it meant they held supremacy over the Elderace. Something about their magic sparked fear in people, though Daegan himself never expressed any, having been raised among them. From what Laila deduced, he couldn't care less about politics and cared only about maintaining this lifestyle his inheritance bought him. And if his wealth dwindled, it was all the motivation he'd need to try and take up his grandfather's mantle.

It seemed Laila was going to have to pay extra close attention to whatever Daegan was up to after overhearing his private conversation with Damien.

Daegan lowered himself into the guest chair, biting his lip. He loved his chair, but he'd keep his remarks to himself when it came to her. He wore a deep blue shirt over black trousers. His black leather boots went up to his knees and had intricate lace woven along the top edge. He had on a ring that shone with a single pretishfire on it—a glimmering black diamond—a piece she'd acquired in Morrovac, mined from the Mrindilin Mountains. Everything about him boasted extravagance.

Daegan swept his dark hair from his face. "As much as I like to flatter myself, thinking you've come only for my company, I know you better than that. You've got something for me."

That she did.

Laila leaned forward. She reached into her bag and withdrew the dagger she'd bought, knowing it would suit his tastes. He had a thing for anything that glittered. Particularly sharp things. The sparkle of the single rounded crystal on the end of the hilt caught in the light, and Daegan's jaw dropped. He stood and skirted around the desk. He reached both of his hands out to gently lift it from hers.

"I don't know where you get these beauties, Laila. This is even more exquisite than the last item you brought me." He removed the dagger from the scabbard and gazed upon the dark cluvasil steel. The deep red colour of the handle complemented the black blade nicely.

"This particular piece was originally from Reij," Laila told him. "I stole it off a pirate when returning from one of my runs from Xihngrahv." *Stole* wasn't quite the right word. *Bought* would be a more appropriate one. She'd bought the dagger, but it was such a good price that she may as well have stolen it. And Daegan liked it whenever she added a bit of thrill to her stories of how she'd attained her items.

"You know," Daegan said, peering past the dagger to look at her. "You spoil me."

"Well, you pay well. Speaking of…" She rose from his chair.

Daegan lowered the dagger. He tilted his head so the corner of his eye caught Laila's. "It's always straight to business with you." He wound his arm around her waist and drew her closer to him. He smelled of peppermint. "I would drop everything on my schedule for the day if you would stay. I can have the kitchen prepare something. I'd be happy to show you around Valmain if you'd like."

This again. Laila had to hand it to him; the man did not give up easily. Of the few men she could see herself with, Daegan was not one of them. She placed her hand flat on his chest and gave him a gentle push. Unless he became a true threat and tried something, she had no need to show him the power that had saved her from trouble on so many occasions. If that failed, she always had her knife, sheathed at her ankle and hidden beneath her trousers.

Daegan resisted her push and pulled her in closer. His breath touched her ear. "You truly are a wonder, Laila."

Laila leaned into him. She breathed in his minty scent. Then with a little more force than before, she pushed his chest again. This time, she added a touch of magic to give him a slight shock. He drew his arm away and stepped back. The shock wasn't an obvious show of her magic, but he did look her up and down with his eyebrows drawn together.

"And you are persistent, Daegan Valca. But your attempts to seduce me will get you nowhere." Laila put her hand out expectantly. He would either pay her or return the dagger, and their business for the day would be done. "Come now. I've got places to be. I'm a busy woman, as you know."

"And I a busy man. Yet here we are."

Laila hummed and smiled. "Yes, here we are. And if you don't want the dagger, then I'll take it and be on my way."

"Oh, you're too cold, Laila." He twirled a lock of her red curls between his fingers. "I can see why you're called a witch."

Laila took his fingers gently from her hair. She laced them between her own while stretching her neck so her face was close to his—so close that her lips barely touched his. "You think I'm cold?" She teased a moment longer. He took the bait and reached his lips toward hers. She backed away and removed her hands from his. His lips met nothing but air.

"You have no idea." She snatched the dagger from his hands in a smooth motion. "Goodbye, Daegan." She gave a small curtsy, which still felt odd to do in trousers.

Picking up her bag, she turned to go. Daegan grasped her arm. "Laila, wait. I'll buy it. Please, don't go. You can't blame a man for trying."

"I can, actually. But I'm willing to let it go." She shrugged her shoulder to remove Daegan's hand from her arm. "But only because you're such a good customer. So let's do business."

# Chapter 11

The buildings in the city of Ferenth obscured Mick's view of the sunset as it rested low on the western horizon. He and Vidia had managed to hitch a lift on an oxcart that took them most of the way to Ferenth. During the journey, they'd been lucky and didn't have any encounters with Ighur or Vidia's uncle's men, and Mick could almost convince himself it would be smooth sailing from here on out. But that kind of thinking was reckless.

He continued to keep a watchful eye. Just because he didn't see Ighur, didn't mean Ighur wasn't around. And even if Mick refused to play his part in Riggs's dealings, Riggs wouldn't give up his goal of setting up his trade in Kartha. If he succeeded and got his foot in the door, it wouldn't be long before he'd have the country in his pocket just like all the other countries in the Zareff Continent.

Much like Hywreath, Ferenth teemed with people all setting up for the week-long festivities. Here, the air smelled of grass and livestock rather than the sea as it'd been in Hywreath. Shops and homes were crammed along the sides of hilly, cobbled streets, where torches were lit for the approaching night.

Vendors were set up around every corner of every street, and each street held its own entertainment. People wandered up and down to see all that there was to see. Vidia and Mick had already passed a puppet performance being put on for the children. Down another street, there had been a juggler. Another had a contortionist who'd hooked his feet together while his rump sat perched on the ground. His head stuck between his legs, and his arms twisted behind his back in such a way that he mustn't have had any bones in his body at all. It seemed everyone here took the opportunity to show off their strange talents and sell their goods.

A woman wearing a big hat stood at her cart. She had multiple scarves draped up her arm and flowing behind her as she rushed over to Mick and Vidia, holding them out. "Feel them," she said.

Mick encouraged Vidia to keep walking. The woman followed. "Softest you'll ever touch. Straight from the kingdom of Reij. The Queen herself wears these. Only four belds, and that's a deal."

Vidia shook her head, politely declining the woman's offer. Another lady walked past, and the scarf saleswoman ran to her next. Mick took Vidia's hand in his, tugging her away from there before another salesperson could get to them. Vidia made no attempt to take her hand back; rather, she accepted his direction and allowed him to lead her down a narrow street. Mick wasn't in any hurry to break their contact.

Although Vidia was nothing like Aira, Mick took comfort in her company. He could just imagine his father reprimanding him for being too trusting. Maybe he *was* being too trusting, but he needed a friend right now, and all during the journey here, Vidia had shown him nothing but kindness. Would that change if she knew who he was?

They turned down another street, always watching around each corner. They'd travelled a great distance from Hywreath. It wasn't likely Ighur would stumble upon them here, but Mick remained vigilant.

Music resonated, coming from close by. Lively music on stringed instruments played. They passed a man who balanced knives and swords from his fingers, nose, and forehead. Another man lifted a short, narrow sword over his head, turned his face upward, and glided the blade down his throat. Vidia raised a hand to her mouth. "Oh my. What inspires a person to try such things?" When the man did a handstand with the sword's hilt sticking out of his mouth, Vidia, along with other onlookers, gasped. She turned her face away. Mick couldn't tear his wide-eyed gaze away from the act. The sword swallower landed a backflip, then pulled the sword out of his mouth. A unified sigh of relief drew Vidia's eyes back to the scene.

She tugged on Mick's arm, urging him away from there. "That man has a death wish."

Mick chuckled. It felt good to smile and forget about his worries.

They rounded a corner, and Vidia gasped. Mick's stomach somersaulted at her surprise, but she grinned and pointed ahead. "Look, there's going to be a light show!"

"A light show?"

Three men and two women looked to be practicing for a performance with odd blue lights that hovered over their hands. One man shaped his light into different animals, such as cats and birds. A woman sprinkled something over her light, and it changed colour from blue to purple. She did this a few times, going through a variety of colours.

"The Elderace sometimes put on performances where they manipulate their light magic for entertainment. It's hypnotizing to watch the way the bright colours and shapes move. I would have thought that, even abroad, Kartha's light shows would be well known. I can't believe you've never heard of them.

"Oh, Mick, we have to stay for it. You must experience a light show while you're in Kartha."

That did sound amazing. But they'd been on the road for days and still had farther to go before they arrived in Litlen. He felt they should keep moving as long as there was still daylight. Last night, they'd found a small inn and had spent the night just within the town of Tanlore. He suspected they wouldn't have such luck finding a place to stay in this city, where it appeared most of the festivities took place. It'd be a miracle if any inn had rooms available.

Mick scratched his ear. "How far is it to the next town from here?"

Vidia squinted and pinched her lip as though she needed all her focus to think. Then she pointed down the street at no particular place. "There's a long stretch of plains from here until we get to Nivit, then the foothills. It could take us until morning, but I'd really like to be off the road by nightfall."

Travelling through the night in unfamiliar territory didn't sound appealing to Mick either. "If we stayed the night here, where would we sleep? I can't imagine a noblewoman such as yourself is accustomed to roughing it."

The gleam in Vidia's eyes was a mixture of offence and amusement. "I can't tell if you're messing with me."

"I'm neither messing with you nor being serious." Mick tapped his temple, then laughed at the way Vidia squinted at him.

She let his remark slide and shook her head. "You're right. We'll probably have no luck finding a place tonight. But my grandfather owned a cottage just on the outskirts of the city, and my uncle never goes there. He may have even forgotten about it. We could spend the night there."

A man and woman cycled by on a tandem bicycle. Streamers tied to the handlebars blew behind them as they rode. A handful of older children giggled and tried to chase the streamers. Pedestrians stayed on the opposite side to keep the path clear for them. A few of the light-bearers continued to practice their magic, while two chatted with each other. Mick hadn't realized how exciting it would be to see others who could do magic. He had so many questions to ask anyone who would give him answers. He may as well make the most of his time here. Staying might not be such a bad idea.

"Would any of your uncle's men think to look for you at the cottage?" As Mick entertained the idea of spending the night here, he felt relieved about potentially not having to go any farther tonight.

"I don't think so. We can head there after a few performances, then be out first thing in the morning. It'll be like we were never there."

As night approached, much of the crowd seemed to be heading in the same direction, toward an opening between the three- and four-storey buildings. Mick supposed that if they were going to stop anywhere for a night, it may as well be here. His shoulders relaxed. "As long as you think it'll be all right, then I'm happy to stay."

A blue light flashed in Mick's peripheral vision. He turned in its direction. Another flash flickered, and Mick blinked from the shock of the sudden brightness. He rubbed his eyes, temporarily blinded.

Light and colours returned in dancing spots in his peripherals until shapes took solid form again. In the middle of the square, a man circled in place with his arms out wide in invitation. He had bits of grey in his dark hair, and a blue light hovering in a sphere over his hand, made the grey strands shimmer like silver. It followed the man's hand wherever he moved it. Vidia followed Mick's gaze, and her eyes lit up. She pulled Mick into the square before it got too crowded. They claimed a place standing near the front, where they could watch the performer.

The man's voice called out loudly so he could be heard over the music and chatter. "If you think magic is myth…" he said in a mystical voice as he addressed the crowd. He peered at all who were present. "You would be wrong." His eyes stopped on Mick. His mouth twitched upward in a sideways smile. Using his hand that was free of the light, he turned his palm down. He held it there until dirt began lifting off the ground.

"Magic," he said as the dirt floated up toward his hand, "is as real as the air you're breathing." His eyes left Mick to search out another captivated viewer.

"It's here." He spoke as the dirt rose higher to reach his hand. "And it's in us all—alive and is a part of you."

As the man spoke, Mick felt a tingling prick up beneath his skin, accompanied by a fluttering in his stomach. The stone was warm against his thigh, through the fabric of his pocket. He closed his eyes as a breeze blew lightly in his face like a gentle caress.

A woman bumped into him as more people crowded in to watch. Jarred out of a trance, Mick opened his eyes and returned his focus to the performer, whose hand had retreated, allowing the dirt to fall. As soon as it hit the ground, Mick felt the thump of it in his chest. He glanced around to see if anyone else had felt it. No one reacted.

The performer did a shooing motion with his lit hand, and his blue light lifted above his head to hover there. It lit up the space all around them, bringing people's faces into clear focus. Every one of them had wide eyes, all enrapt on the performer, who now raised both hands, palms out, facing the crowd. Slowly, he rowed his arms back until his elbows were behind his head. The fire from the nearest lantern followed his motion. The flame left the lantern and bobbed in mid-air toward the man's pulling. It floated over heads as it moved to the centre of the space where he stood. A few gasps came from the crowd. When the flame reached the performer, he clapped his hands together, and the fire went out, leaving his blue light above as the only light source in his space.

The man beside Mick elbowed him. "Do you believe it's real?"

Mick blinked, realizing the question was meant for him. He tore his gaze from the performer to the blond man smiling at him. Mick could tell by the soft lines in his face that he must have smiled a lot. His front teeth were slightly crooked, and his nose looked like it may have been broken once or twice. He had a certain countenance that made Mick want to like him immediately.

"I don't know," Mick said. "It looks real to me."

The way the ground shook when the dirt hit it certainly made it *feel* real.

Or had it just been him who felt it?

"Do you?" Mick asked the stranger. Vidia took notice of them talking and attuned to their hushed conversation. A few other onlookers shuffled toward the front.

The man shrugged. "Where I come from, magic is nothing but tricks and sleight of hand. Look over here while I do this over there. Be amazed!" He added a big gesture with his arms and smacked the woman beside him. She gave him such a dirty look that Mick thought she might smack him back. The man's eyebrows shot up, and his mouth curled down in an exaggerated frown. Behind his eyes was a flicker of amusement.

His frown turned into a smile as he chuckled. "Whoops," he said, then stepped closer to Mick so as not to have to speak any louder. "I've heard stories about Kartha and its magic. I've been studying it and learning all kinds of fascinating things."

The performer was now making a jar of water float over the crowd and spill its contents onto those who stood nearest to him. Those who got wet yelped with delight.

"What kinds of things?" Mick asked the man.

"I heard there's this crystal called Vastgerdite. It used to be mined from the southern parts of Kartha. One day, it just disappeared, and there was no more of it anywhere. They say it had healing power."

"Healing power?" Mick's ears went hot.

The man nodded. "That's what they say, anyway. Most people in Xihngrahv have their opinions of Kartha and its so-called magic. They think the people here are all a bunch of witches and demons. So far, I haven't come across any." He grinned and winked. "I'm Boone," he said.

Mick shook Boone's hand. "Mick." He gestured to Vidia. "And this is Vidia."

"Pleasure to meet you both," Boone said. He glanced at the performer waving his hands about, making water dance in the air in patterns.

Then his attention was drawn back to Boone, who stuck his hand into his pocket and pulled out a handful of something that looked like dried meat. Some fell to the ground as he raised a fistful to his mouth. From the corner of his eye, he caught Mick staring. With a mouthful, he chortled and pulled out another handful to offer Mick and Vidia. "Want some jerky?"

Vidia backed up and grimaced.

Mick wasn't sure whether to laugh or cringe. He shook his head. "No, that's all right, thanks."

Boone shrugged, then ate what was in his hand. "You from around here?" he asked as he chewed.

"Yes," Vidia answered in a crisp tone. "And we're not witches or demons here," she added.

"I didn't say you were," Boone replied. He swallowed his meat. "If you were listening, I said I haven't come across any. That implies that you are not."

Those who stood nearest to them glanced over, frowning.

Boone paid them no mind. "There is one witch in particular I'm interested in meeting, though."

Mick kept his voice quiet so as not to disturb the spectators. "You mean *the* Witch?" Could he mean Laila, whom he and Vidia had just seen?

The performer swept a cloud of dirt around himself and shot it up into the air. He waved his hand in a circle, and the dirt swirled in a circular motion around him.

"As far as I know, there's only one—*the* Witch," Boone said. "I saw her years ago when I was a kid. She saved me and my family, as well as all the passengers and crew of the ship we were on when my family took a holiday to Morrovac." He had a dreamy look in his eyes. "Ah, she was amazing. My brothers laughed when I told them I was coming here to meet her. I hope I really do meet her so I can gloat in their faces when I get home."

The dirt crashed down onto the cobblestone, and the thump in Mick's chest shook him and threw him off balance. He put an arm out to steady himself. Boone's firm grasp steadied him. When Mick had his feet righted, Boone removed his hand. "You all right?"

Mick nodded. "Thanks. That was strange. Did either of you feel that?"

Boone smirked as he shook his head. "Nope. But if I'm a little strange, it's good to know I'm not alone." He laughed out loud, which earned him a scowl from the woman he'd smacked earlier.

A loud bang got all of their attention. All eyes looked to the sky where a burst of light exploded in the air and rained down, disappearing as it fell. A collective *oooh* came from the crowd, followed by applause. Mick clapped his hands.

The performer took a bow. "And now, if you please, give your attention to these next performers, who've been working tirelessly day and night to give you a show to remember. Please enjoy."

The group of people who Mick had seen practicing their light show stepped into the middle of the square. They formed a circle with their backs to one another, while a sixth member sat on a stool with a drum. He banged out a steady rhythm to begin. In unison, the group at the centre began their performance with their arms curled in toward themselves. Slowly, as they stretched their arms out, they each made a light appear, one after another.

With their arms raised and their lights glowing, they waved their arms in a choreographed routine, making their lights dance in perfect coordination with each other. All five of them turned to face each other and combined their lights, making one large sphere at the centre of their circle. They joined their raised arms together, and their combined light floated to the centre.

The rhythm picked up speed, and the performers turned to face the crowd. They danced around the open space in the square, separating the light and each making shapes with it, changing their colours and shooting them up into the sky or out toward the crowd. Their steps were in sync with one another—every step, flick of the wrist, and even their sway as they moved to the beat—were all timed with precision.

At the finale, the five formed their circle, backs to each other, and they created a blast of light that exploded above the crowd and rained down like bright, colourful, glittery snow.

# Chapter 12

Mick had been so engulfed in the display that he continued to gaze up at the sky long after the light had disappeared. He could have stayed lost in a daze forever, staring at the cloudy sky, as the colourful lights burned into his memory.

The crowd didn't disperse right away. People stuck around to speak with the performers. Mick himself wouldn't have minded going over to compliment them on their enchanting displays. Laughter echoed from somewhere. Voices mingled in indecipherable chatter.

"What about you two?" Boone asked, stirring Mick from his trance.

Vidia glanced around. Mick had almost forgotten about her uncle's men. Ighur was tall and would stand out in a crowd. He thought it best to avoid looking and making it obvious they were trying not to be found. He was more concerned about getting caught by the other men, whose faces he struggled to remember.

"What about us?" he replied to Boone.

"You said you're from here." Boone indicated Vidia. "Do you have magic too?"

Vidia shook her head. "Only the Elderace can have magic. It had something to do with a storm a long time ago that changed only those in and around Litlen. The rest of us are just like everyone else."

Although Mick had heard that the magic was limited to only one region, the storm was news to him. How was it that only one city had been affected by the storm? And was it assumed that everyone from Litlen had magic?

Mick hoped not to be put on the spot, but Boone turned to him next. "And you?"

In an attempt to disguise how nervous he felt, Mick looped his thumbs through the loopholes in his trousers and slouched. "I'm not from here either. I grew up near Ectarin."

"Ah, that's what that accent is." Boone winked. "Thought I detected an Ectarin dialect. What brings you to Kartha?"

Mick resisted scanning the crowds. He and Vidia may have lost their pursuers, but would Ighur have thought to follow the throng of people to where the festivities were being held?

"I have family here," Mick said.

"Oh yeah? Whereabouts from?"

Mick bit his bottom lip and forced a smile. Would Boone suspect him of having magic if he told him? Having just established that he was raised away from here, not likely.

"Litlen," Mick said with a shrug.

"Litlen? No way. So are your relatives magical? Or whatever you called it." Boone snapped his fingers. "What was that word? Elderace?"

The term was also new for Mick. He shook his head, genuinely unsure. "Not that I know of. Truth be told, I don't know a whole lot about my family here. My uncle came to see me and invited me to visit him." He raised his hands. "Here I am."

"So you're headed to Litlen then?"

Mick nodded.

Boone scratched his head. "Mind if I join you? I won't be a burden, I swear. I tagged along with a group coming here, but this was their last stop. I'm making my way to Litlen myself and would rather not travel alone. Places around here are prone to thievery—or so I hear." He threw up both hands. "Not that I have anything of much value, but you know…" He shrugged. "A man's gotta eat." This prompted him to reach into his pocket and retrieve another handful of jerky, then stuff it in his mouth.

Boone's having an ulterior motive for wanting to travel with them was unlikely. And Mick had no qualms about travelling in a group, so long as it didn't slow them down. Especially since, as he understood it, the stone was of great worth. The last thing he needed was for it to get stolen.

Vidia sucked her cheek in. "You should know, people in Litlen don't appreciate strangers coming and asking questions."

"All the more reason to ask." Boone's eyes twinkled with mischief.

Mick smirked. Boone would make for some entertaining company, that was for sure. "I think I'd like to hear whatever answers you get to your questions."

Boone winked. "You got it."

Vidia rolled her eyes.

Mick chuckled. "I take it you have a place to spend the night here in Ferenth?"

"Nah, mate." Boone pointed upward. "Was planning a night under the stars. Nights are a lot warmer here than they are in Xihngrahv this time of year." He glanced up at the clouds overhead. "But now I'm thinking I should have had a plan B. Never accounted for rain." A flicker of light from one of the performers drew his attention away from Mick and Vidia. One of the men waved his arms animatedly in conversation, and Boone started walking over toward the group. "Be right back," he said when he was already almost out of earshot.

If they were heading in the same direction, they may as well stick together. Mick nudged Vidia lightly with his elbow. "What do you think? Why not have him join us?"

Vidia fidgeted with her dress skirt. "I don't know, Mick. We hardly know him. Should we really be picking up a complete stranger?"

"We're hardly more than that ourselves." It was hard to believe Mick had only just met Vidia the other day. Yet how quickly he'd felt at ease with her.

They may have only met recently, but Mick felt like he'd known Vidia for years. And the more time he spent with her, the more he noticed how different she and Aira were. While Aira was mostly quiet and reserved, Vidia bubbled with energy. And convincing Aira to do anything required much discussion. In contrast, with every new adventure, Vidia seemed eager to jump in with both feet.

Boone joined right in with the group, speaking excitedly with big hand gestures. Mick liked him already. He glanced over at Vidia. "Should we search him for red?" The odds of him working for either Vidia's uncle or for Riggs were slim.

Vidia playfully smacked his shoulder. "No way he works for my uncle. He's just too…loud. He'll draw too much attention."

As if on cue, Boone's laugh resonated through the square as he waved his arms about.

Vidia hid a smile but not very well. "He could be fun to have around, though. You're so serious all the time."

Mick pointed at himself. "Me? Serious? You take that back." He laughed.

For all his parents' warnings about the dangers here, Mick wondered if they'd only told him those things so he'd stay fearful and not want to come to Kartha. Yet the stone sat heavy in his pocket, projecting that urgency in him, and he couldn't help but feel that the dangers were yet to come. Something was coming, that much he knew. He felt it beneath his feet, through the ground, rising up in him as if sensing the electricity of a storm approaching.

"I guess that settles it then." Mick put his foreboding thoughts aside. "Let's go tell Boone he's bunking with us."

He offered his hand for Vidia to take. She looked at it and paused for only a second before accepting it. After having held her hand while running through the streets of Hywreath, his hand felt empty and cold once she'd let go. He resisted the desire to graze his thumb across her knuckles. Instead, he tugged her along to join Boone and the group of performers. Only one of the men and two women remained behind.

Boone stepped aside to allow Mick and Vidia to join their circle. "Mick, Vidia, these are Corilyn, Eli, and Priy. They were just telling me about Litlen."

"You were the performers?" Mick asked, knowing the answer.

The dark-skinned man, Eli, nodded. His long neck made him appear taller than he was, though he wasn't much taller than Mick.

"You are familiar," Eli said in an accent that was something between an Ectarin accent and one of Kartha. "Do I know you?"

Shrinking back would imply he had something to hide. Instead, Mick raised his chin. "No, I don't believe so."

Without looking over, Mick could feel Vidia's eyes on him. Did she think it odd that two people had said the same thing to him since arriving in Kartha?

Boone bounced on his heels. "Priy was just telling me about the Abberbrat, a tree in Litlen that marks the centre of the city. She says its fruit and most of the plant life glow at night and that the fruit is useful for any ailments. Not only are the people magical, but the plants are too."

"I don't recommend touching the plants, though, unless you know what you're doing," Corilyn said. She had a streak of blue in her platinum hair, which was pulled up in a bun and resting on top of her head. "Not everyone has a knack for handling them properly."

Boone smiled. "I'm on my way to Litlen in the morning. If these two will have me, we'll go together. Is there anywhere else, other than the tree, that I should visit while there?"

Priy wore about half a dozen necklaces of varying lengths around her neck. Her long black hair draped over both of her shoulders. "People often go to Litlen and leave disappointed. The Elderace are not too keen on visitors in their city. You might want to reconsider your holiday destination."

Mick squinted. "Aren't you Elderace too?"

Eli waved his hand. "It's complicated. I'm certain I know you from somewhere."

Boone saved Mick from having to respond. "Reconsidering the destination is out of the question. It's the whole reason I came to Kartha." He clapped a hand on Mick's shoulder. "And besides, Mick here has family there to visit."

Mick clenched his jaw. His lips formed a smile while he raised his brows at Boone. How was he to know Mick wasn't sharing that information openly? In fairness, he did share it with both Boone *and* Vidia. He wasn't being very diligent in his discretion.

Eli's eyes lit up. "What is your name?"

Mick rubbed the back of his neck. "Mick. Mckal, actually, but everyone just calls me Mick. Or Mickey if you like, but I'd rather you didn't."

"You are a Dairner, yes?" Eli asked. "Are you related to Raidan and Dimitri Dairner?"

Priy's eyes widened. "The Guardians?"

Corilyn's jaw dropped.

Mick wished he hadn't dismissed his father's warning so casually. Were his uncle and grandfather really so well known? And did he resemble them so closely that a stranger in the street could pick him out? *Did someone say Guardians?*

Mick supposed there was only one way to know if they thought he was a threat to them and their country. He swallowed and nodded. "I'd rather you didn't announce it to the world but yes, Raidan is my adefa."

"Ah, yes, I remember you now. I have not seen Cassian and Willa in many years." Eli looked Mick up and down. "And you were only a baby. Where are your mom and dad?"

Either Eli had aged very well or, as Mick suspected about Adefa and Uncle Dimi, he was Elderace, and the rumours about their years extending beyond a typical lifespan were true. Eli looked not much older than Mick. Certainly not old enough to have been friends with his parents before they left Kartha.

"My parents couldn't make it."

"Wait." Boone waved his arms to draw attention to himself. "What's an adefa?"

Eli answered. "Eldrace for grandfather."

"Oh. And what are the Guardians?"

Mick would like to have known himself, but having this conversation in a city square at night while people still meandered about was not the ideal time or place. He glanced around, taking in the faces of those around—those he could see in the light of the relit lanterns—and checking if anyone was paying them any attention. The only one who appeared to be looking in their direction was a hooded figure leaning against a wall in the shadows of the nearby buildings. It was hard to tell if the person was actually looking at their group or just in their general direction. Plus, they were probably too far away to hear what was being said. Then again, Boone's voice carried well.

"The Guardians of the Weldafire Stone," Vidia said while looking at Mick with nearly the same awe as Priy had.

*Weldafire Stone?* Mick refrained from putting his hand into his pocket to feel for the stone there.

Eli seemed to become aware of where they were standing as he looked about. "Ah, there is too much to explain. You should visit Elefthan. You will have much better conversations there than in Litlen. But it is late. We must go now." He shook Mick's hand. "It was good to meet you. When you see Raidan and Dimitri, tell them Eli says hello."

Mick nodded. It was all he could do while so many thoughts distracted him.

When the performers departed, Mick glanced back to where the hooded figure had been leaning against the wall. They were no longer there, and the rest of the square had cleared. His nerves were on edge after that meeting.

He ran his clammy hands through his hair, feeling the days-old grease. His face was starting to itch with the prickles of new stubble growth. He scratched his chin.

Well, for a first encounter with someone who'd figured out who he was, he supposed it went well. They didn't call out a mob to drag him to the noose for potentially being the country's cause of destruction. Maybe things weren't going to be so bad after all.

# Chapter 13

Morning sunlight crept in through an open crack in the curtains. Mick lay in bed, bracing to open his eyes to the brightness of its rays shining in. He squinted past his arm and made out Boone's form standing over him.

"'Bout time you woke up. You were like a bear last night. I've never heard someone snore so loud. I could hear you from all the way down the hall."

Mick wiped his elbow across his mouth and sat up. He rested his hand behind him to support himself. "I can't remember ever having had such a restful sleep." Not even in Iptin Province before working for the Governor. "What time is it, anyway?"

"After ten. Vidia cooked breakfast and is waiting downstairs."

Whatever she'd cooked, she'd burned it. "Is that what that smell is?"

Boone grinned and went to the door. "Better hurry up and get ready. She wanted to leave hours ago."

"Why didn't anyone wake me?"

"I only got up not long ago myself. And I don't think Vidia fancies seeing you in your breeches, mate. Or maybe she does." Boone winked, then belted a laugh as he disappeared out of the room and down the stairs.

The cottage they'd spent the night in was the most luxurious place Mick had ever stayed in. It was bigger than his parents' home in Iptin Province. It had a full kitchen, three bedrooms, and water connected from the well through lines leading directly into the house. Mick's room on the second storey had a fireplace on one wall and a window on another. The mattress was more comfortable than the one he had in the Governor's manor.

He packed his few belongings and left them by the door to collect after breakfast, then headed downstairs. The scent of burnt toast was stronger in the kitchen. Three settings were prepared at the table, each with a plate of black toast. A jar of jam that Mick had purchased from one of the vendors yesterday, along with the loaf of bread, sat in the middle of the table next to a pitcher of water. Vidia turned from the countertop after having finished wiping it down. She shook her head. "So much for being out of here by first light. I was up hours ago. Come on and eat, so we can get on the road."

Boone sat and took a bite of his plain toast, then gave a thumbs up. "How'd you know burnt toast is my favourite?"

Vidia's cheeks turned a dark shade of red. "I didn't know how long to leave it for. I can make more—"

"It's fine, Vidia." Boone raised a hand. "I'm messing with you. Really, I like it like this."

Mick sat next to Boone. "You should have woken me. I could have helped." Getting back into a kitchen would have done him some good after the week he'd been having. He helped himself to the jam and slathered it on the toast. Vidia sat down and nibbled on hers. "I didn't want to disturb you."

Mick set his half-eaten toast on his plate and poured himself a cup of water. "It wouldn't have been a bother. But this was thoughtful. Thank you." He took a sip of his drink. "How long do you figure it is to Litlen from here?"

Vidia scrunched her face. "We're about halfway there. We should get going as soon as you're finished."

Boone cleared his throat and set down his cup. His toast was completely gone, save for the crumbs littering his plate and the table. "What were you saying last night about the Guardians of the *What*-fire Stone?"

Vidia looked at Mick first. With a subtle nod, Mick encouraged her to explain. Vidia addressed Boone, likely assuming Mick already knew how important his grandfather and great-uncle were in Kartha.

"The Guardians of the Weldafire Stone are something like the protectors of Kartha," Vidia explained. "They have healing magic that is unique magic that only the stone has. That crystal you spoke of—Vastgerdite—didn't just disappear. All that was here became one and formed the Weldafire Stone. In that stone is Kartha. They say that if it were to be corrupted in any way, all of the country would reap the repercussions."

"Corrupted?" Mick refrained from taking out the stone to gaze at it. "How could a stone become corrupted?"

"I'm not sure," Vidia said. "That's probably a question for you to ask your family."

Mick set down his serviette. "My family doesn't tell me anything. I'd have better luck joining Boone in his quest for answers."

"Hey, I'm not opposed to that." Boone hollered over his shoulder as he took his plate to the sink.

It wasn't a bad idea. Maybe once Mick was with his family and came up with a plan to ensure Riggs wasn't going to come after him, he'd join Boone in his adventure—though he wasn't totally clear on why Boone was going to Litlen in the first place. He tilted his head to the side. "What *is* your plan, Boone? What do you hope to find in Litlen?"

Boone finished washing his dish, and he turned to face them while he began drying it. "Well, originally, I was going to track down the Witch to try to meet her. I heard she's from Litlen. But then, I heard she moves around a lot and is often at sea, which makes sense. But once I'd gotten it in my head to come here, I couldn't get it out. So I figured I'd come anyway and see what I can learn about her and who she is while also exploring the country. The magic fascinates me. My family thinks I'm obsessed. I think they might be right. I can't get this place or the Witch out of my head."

"Somebody's in love," Vidia said in a sing-song voice. She giggled.

Boone's cheeks flushed. "Hey, you're one to talk. I saw you two holding hands last night. And the way you look at each other. Don't go accusing me of being in love when it's clear there's something between the two of you."

Warmth rushed to Mick's face, and he tried not to look at Vidia, who he'd guess was equally embarrassed. Was there something there? They'd only just met. Besides, Mick had too many problems in his life to let himself think of romance at a time like this. Still, there was something about Vidia that made him feel at ease, and he couldn't help but wonder if she felt the same way about him.

Though anyone Mick let himself get close to was just another person Riggs could use against him.

First things first: Get to Litlen, find his family, get word to his parents and Aira to leave Iptin, and avoid Riggs. Above everything, avoid Governor Riggs.

Mick cleared his throat. "It just so happens that you may get an opportunity to meet the Witch after all. She's here. We ran into her in Hywreath. Vidia knows her."

Boone dropped his plate, and it clattered on the floor. Good thing it wasn't glass. His towel hung from his hand, and his eyes bulged as he stared at Vidia. "Really? Do you know her? Can you arrange something so I can meet her? What's her real name? Is she as beautiful as I remember?"

"Whoa, slow down." Vidia narrowed her eyes at Mick, then rolled them while shaking her head. "Her name is Laila, and she was on her way to see my uncle. That was before we left Hywreath. She could be anywhere by now."

Boone picked up his plate and put it away in the cupboard none too carefully. "Well what are we waiting for? Let's go to your uncle and see if she's still there."

"Hold on, Boone." Mick gathered his plate, his cup, and the butter knife, bringing them to the sink. "We're not just going to drop everything to go in search of her. If you want to go, you go, but I have to get to my family as soon as possible. I've wasted too much time as it is."

"And I'm not on great terms with my uncle right now." Vidia picked at crumbs on her plate. "We argued before I left. And…he sort of has people looking for me." She bit her lip. "I don't expect a warm welcome if I go back."

Boone groaned and gripped his hair in his fists. His blond curls needed combing anyway. "Why would you dangle that in my face? Here I tried not to get my hopes up of meeting her, and you go and tell me she's here in Kartha! What am I supposed to do with that?"

Boone's boyish face appeared to age a few years, and Mick almost felt bad for bringing it up. "I didn't realize how much this meant to you." He'd only been trying to get off the topic of him and Vidia. "I'm sorry, Boone. If she is from Litlen, maybe my family will know more and can point you in the right direction."

Boone's shoulders sank as he sighed. "I guess it's something. Your grandfather seems pretty important anyway. I'd wager my chances of meeting the Witch are higher if I stick around with you." He winked. "Guess you're stuck with me now." He perked up and grinned his broad grin that hid the crook in his nose. "We'd better get moving then. But first, the privy calls. Be back in a minute." He headed upstairs, leaving Mick and Vidia to clean up the rest.

Mick washed his dishes from breakfast. Vidia added hers to the pile, then wet a cloth to wipe the table. She didn't move with the same grace and confidence as Aira did in the kitchen, but that didn't slow her down. She wasn't much of a cook, but she had tried. Knowing this added a layer to her that Mick found himself attracted to. He finished drying a cup and put it away, then turned to face Vidia. "Do you think you'll go back at all? To your uncle?"

Vidia stopped wiping the table. She stood completely still, staring at a spot on the table, her gaze unfocused. "I'd rather stay with my brother in Elefthan. He left two years ago, when I was fifteen. But that was then. I can look after myself now." She met his eye. "I just hope I won't have to."

"Any family besides your brother?"

"Another brother. Besides those two, none that I know. My grandmother died years ago, and she and my grandfather had only my dad and Uncle Daegan. My mom wasn't from Kartha. It's why she left in the first place. She had some family dispute she needed to settle. But she'd been gone a long time, so my dad and grandfather went after her to bring her home. That was ten years ago, and I'm still waiting for them all to come home." Her voice quivered, and she quickly wiped her eyes.

Mick placed a hand on her shoulder and released a bit of his healing into her. It wouldn't fix an emotional hurt, but it was all he had to offer. Vidia dried her face using her arm. She sniffed and smiled. "Ack, look at me. Let's talk about something else, okay?"

Mick said nothing, but he nodded. He removed his hand from her shoulder and finished putting the last of the dishes away. Vidia helped. She stood beside him, smelling clean and like lilacs. She must have had time to wash before he'd woken.

She noticed him staring and smiled. "You're not paying attention. Do you always get so easily distracted?" She laughed.

Mick's throat went dry, and his heart sped up. Aira had said the same thing, and here he was, getting distracted when she could be in trouble. For all he knew, Riggs already knew he'd gone off on his own.

Vidia frowned. "Is something wrong? What happened? You've gone pale."

"We should get going. I'll go and grab my things."

"Wait, Mick." Vidia grabbed his hand as he was about to pass her. "The thing you dropped when we first met—was that the…?"

Instinctively, Mick's free hand went to his pocket and grasped the stone. "Maybe." If it was, what did it mean that he had it? What did Uncle Dimi hope would happen after giving it to him? Vidia had said only the stone had healing power. Did that mean it wasn't a common bit of magic practiced among the Elderace? Hadn't his mother told him that too?

Vidia said nothing. After a while, she shrugged, releasing his hand. "I guess that's another thing you'll find out when you get to Litlen."

"Maybe," Mick said again. Unless his family continued to leave him in the dark. He scratched his scruffy chin. Was there time to shave? Probably not. He'd wait. It was already getting late in the morning.

He shifted his weight. "I'll be back in a minute, then we can go."

# Chapter 14

Mick closed the door to his room and leaned against it, enjoying the feel of the sun's warmth shining in and the few minutes he had to gather himself. Vidia would be waiting, and he knew he should hurry, but he wasn't quite ready to go back downstairs yet. It was hard to believe he'd had such a restful sleep when he felt the weight of his worry pulling him down. He tried not to dwell on it, but the more he learned about his family and all that he didn't know, the more difficult it was to put it out of his mind.

A long oval mirror hung in an intricately designed frame next to the door. He caught a glimpse of his rugged reflection. Apart from needing a wash and a shave, he still looked like himself. He thought that coming to Kartha would make him feel better, like he'd know who he was and what he was meant to do with his life.

But he just felt the same as always: confused, unfocused, and without direction.

Sure, the jittery sensation beneath his skin had almost completely disappeared, but if he really concentrated, he could still feel the trembling within. Underneath all his assurance that he was meant to be here, something felt off, and he didn't think it was Riggs trying to breach Kartha's borders. He didn't know what, nor could he place the unease he sensed, but it was as if Kartha rocked on an unsteady balance that could tip either way at any moment. Whatever way it went, Mick couldn't shake this feeling that something was coming. It was difficult not to think about his parents' warning of the sickness. Was that what this feeling was? Some kind of sickness in the land? Did his arrival have something to do with it? He scoffed. *What an absurd notion.*

Things would be so much easier to understand if he had more information. His eyes fell to his hands, reflected in the mirror. No one ever told him about Elderace magic. His whole life, he could heal, but was it possible that he could do what those performers had done last night? Could he make light out of nothing? Or hold fire? He should have asked Eli if Adefa and Uncle Dimi had magic. If so, why keep that from him? Did they not trust him?

Curious, he raised his hands and turned his palms up. Was healing his only power? He snapped his fingers. Nothing happened, but he did feel something stirring in his gut—from where his pool of healing power welled. He tried again, and this time he focused his mind on trying to make a light appear, drawing from that pool he was so familiar with. A spark flashed over his hand. The door opened at the same time and Boone peered in. His eyes fell on Mick's empty hand. His mouth fell open and he entered the room fully. "Did you just—?"

"Shh." Mick placed a finger against his lips.

Boone whispered, "You just did magic. I thought you said you couldn't."

"I didn't know I could." Adrenaline buzzed through Mick's body, and a surging flow trembled in his veins. Not like the usual prickles of his healing at work. His fingers were all jittery and fired up. He wanted to try again.

"Close the door," he told Boone.

Boone obeyed, and Mick opened his hand again, then snapped his fingers. White light flickered and faded in an instant. He tried again, and the light shone in his hand for a full second before it winked out of existence. Boone grinned. Mick stood frozen, staring at his empty hand. Having magic like this could come in handy when he'd inevitably have to face Riggs. Perhaps he could use it to his advantage. Or perhaps Riggs would see it as an opportunity to increase Mick's worth. His stomach knotted.

"Can you do more?" Boone asked.

The sun warmed Mick's back through the window. It would be afternoon soon, and they still had much distance to cover to get to Litlen. He wanted to try again. To master this new power, but Ighur was out there looking for him, and they really needed to get moving.

"When we get there, I'll try again. Maybe I can even get a few pointers from my adefa and get more than a spark."

Boone smiled and shook his head. "Who knows? Maybe one day you'll be performing alongside Priy, Corilyn, and Eli."

Mick rolled his eyes and chuckled. Putting himself on display for entertainment? No, that wasn't for him. He shouldered his pack, and they made their way back downstairs to where Vidia waited with her belongings, ready to go.

"All ready?" Mick looked from Boone to Vidia.

"Like we were never here," Vidia said with a nod.

Boone opened the door. His body went rigid, and Mick almost walked into him. Vidia did bump into him.

Six men stood outside—two at the door, and the others lingered a few paces back, next to a carriage. They all wore an article of red, and they each had weapons—swords mostly from what Mick could see. One had a dagger, and another had an axe.

*An axe?*

Mick blinked. As relieved as he was that these weren't Riggs's men, their presence was still alarming. And they stood in the way of their leaving.

"What's this, then?" the man at the front said with a smile, showing his discoloured teeth. "Three young ones think they can take advantage of Daegan Valca's private cottage while he's not here?" His high-pitched voice sounded hoarse, as though he were trying to make it sound more menacing. His voice might not have had that effect, but the weapons did.

The man scratched a thumb across a scar on his forehead. The way it streaked above his eye in a horizontal line made it look like he had one long eyebrow. His flat cap rested atop his greasy hair, which draped around his face and just touched his shoulders.

Mick shuffled sideways to stand protectively in front of Vidia.

The man pointed to Boone's boots. "Eh, boys, looks like it'll be a good haul. One of 'em's got fancy boots."

Mick's heart raced. His hand inched toward the pocket where he kept the stone. If he could remove it without them seeing, maybe he could hide it or toss it aside so it didn't get stolen. Vidia took his hand, stopping him. She gave him a subtle head-shake—so subtle that Mick wasn't sure what she was doing. But then she stepped out from behind him.

"I don't think Daegan Valca would appreciate it if his *friends* stole from his niece."

"His niece, eh? I'm not so sure." Unibrow squinted past Mick and leaned closer to better see Vidia, though she stood only a few feet away. "You're his niece, are you? Well, I hear he's been looking all over for you, little missy. He'll be positively over the moon to see you well. And I'll humbly accept his reward for your safe return."

Mick set his stance so his feet were planted. "You've got it all wrong, Mr...." He waited for the stranger to fill in the blank.

"Name's Sunny. And it's you who's got—"

"We were attending the festival," Mick continued, "and Mr. Valca wanted to do something nice for his niece, so he offered the cottage for us to spend the night in. You're behind on the times, you see. They've worked things out already. And now, if you'll excuse us." Mick took a step forward, hoping they'd not question him. Sunny crossed his arms and didn't budge from his place. The other men who were a little farther back, slunk closer to the door. Sunny raised a hand in front of Mick, halting him.

"Nice try, boy. You're all coming with us. And if this is all a big misunderstanding…Well, I'm sure Daegan won't mind the intrusion. I'm certain he'll be pleased to see Miss Valca nonetheless. I'm not totally convinced she's really his niece, but we'll find out one way or another. And if not, Daegan will deal with trespassers as he sees fit, but I'll still get paid for keeping a watch on his place. Either way, I win." He stepped closer to Mick until he nearly stood on Mick's toes. "So either walk yourselves over to that carriage or be carried, whichever you prefer. We're all going to take a nice little trip together to Valmain."

Boone stuck a finger in the air. "Um, any chance you might know if the Witch is still hanging around there?"

Sunny grabbed a handful of Boone's shirt and pulled him out of the cottage. He dragged him toward the carriage.

Sunny's men closed in on Mick and Vidia. Mick raised his hands up. "We're coming. We're coming." He took Vidia's hand, and they walked to the carriage and joined Boone inside. Sunny entered last with another man, and they sat in the crammed space with them.

"All set, then?" Sunny grinned, looking at each of them.

The carriage jolted forward and the cottage shrank as they drove away. Vidia stared at the floor. Had she revealed herself to these men just to avoid robbery, knowing they would likely drag her back to her uncle? Mick rubbed her knuckles in gentle motions. She glanced at him and he offered a reassuring smile that was as much for his own sake as it was for hers.

Any day now, Riggs would be informed of Mick's disappearance if he hadn't already been. With warning bells ringing in Mick's thoughts, he tried not to think about what that would mean—to him as much as to Aira and his parents. He'd not been able to warn them, and now he was headed away from Litlen. How was he supposed to get word to Adefa or Uncle Dimi to let him know he was here?

Mick tapped his heel on the floor until Sunny slapped him on the leg.

"Sit still!" Sunny demanded. "Stop shaking the bloody carriage more than it already is."

Vidia rested her hand on Mick's knee, encouraging him with something as simple as her touch. The stone in his pocket seemed to sense his unease, and it gave off a pulse of heat, which moved through him. It helped ease his worry and served as a reminder that he was exactly where he was meant to be. Though lately, he was beginning to second-guess how well he understood the stone's magic. Nothing about this felt right. How could this be where he was meant to be?

Boone shoved his hand into his pocket and retrieved a handful of his jerky. He first offered it to Mick, then Vidia. When neither accepted, he stuffed the handful into his mouth. This earned him a dirty look from Sunny. Not that Boone cared. He went on looking out the window.

Mick gave Vidia's hand a squeeze. Somehow, he believed they'd been destined to meet. Like their lives were meant to entwine. Fate, destiny, luck? Maybe… If he believed in such things. Either way, he was glad she wouldn't be alone when she faced her uncle. And maybe there was a chance that Laila would still be around and might help him. If so, Boone would be thrilled.

As long as Ighur didn't find him, he still had time to fix things. Provided this detour wouldn't delay him long.

# Chapter 15

It didn't matter how little time Laila spent in Kartha these days; it would always be home to her. Since arriving, her bag had become significantly lighter as she made her usual stops on the way to Litlen.

Her last drop-off in the town of Innorsh was the most difficult to make. The bit of medicine she'd concocted and delivered for the little girl with the weak heart was enough to give the girl more time, but it was not a cure for what ailed her. Not even the Guardians' healing power could fix what she suffered from. Raidan's and Dimitri's abilities were limited to internal and external injuries acquired through certain means. They could heal common sicknesses or fatal wounds, for example, but diseases that started from birth were a different matter. Even their power had limits.

Laila's visit to see the mother and daughter left her drained. It wasn't just the visit. The past few months had been exhausting. Worth every drop of sweat and blood, but exhausting nonetheless.

Her shoulders slouched, and she patted the neck of her steed—Vistinn Noreo. Or, as she often called him, Vis. As much as she'd hoped this return home would be a time of resting and catching up with everyone she missed dearly, including her brother Royl, she would probably find something to keep her busy. She always did. Sitting still was never something she was good at. So much so that it earned her the nickname *Tsarioc*—or little bird. Her brother would say she reminded him of a little bird, flitting to and fro, wherever she pleased. He was not wrong.

Vis followed along the road on the way to Ferenth, and Laila didn't have to steer him. The bustling crossroads city was only a short ride away anyway.

She savoured the warm breeze and familiar scents. Unlike the industrial smells in Tsein, where she operated her business, Kartha had a floral fragrance that lingered in every part of the country. Even the coastal cities had a sweet aroma mingled with the fishy sea scent.

In Ferenth, people moved about on the walking paths while horse-drawn coaches drove on the dirt roads. Shop doors were open, and people milled about going from one to another. Laila nudged Vis onto Ruthel Street, toward the seedier end of town. There was a drastic change in the appearance of those who resided in this area. Men and women wore dull colours, and their attire was not as trim and fitted as the fashion of those who lived in the city hub. These people didn't care much about their appearance, and they tended to look a little on the scraggly side.

At the Moceryin Tavern, Laila dismounted from Vis. She tethered him with the other horses, and he took a long drink at the trough. Her hood fell, and she tried her best to smooth the frizz of her long braid. It'd been a long time since she'd felt embarrassed at the attention she would receive whenever she came to places like this.

She entered the tavern and straightened her dark blue blouse, holding her head high. Eyes turned her way. She ignored them all and strode over to the bar counter, where she found Gareth working. Her contact liked to listen almost as much as she did. It paid to have friends like him in her line of work.

When Gareth took notice of her, he smiled, then gave her onlookers reprimanding glares. Laila didn't need to turn and look to know that her admirers had resumed their drinks and conversations. She sat on a stool and rested her arms on the counter. "Gareth, I see you're staying out of trouble. Last time I saw you, you had that nasty black eye and a split lip."

Gareth grabbed a stein from the shelf behind him and set it down. "Now, you know that wasn't my fault." He poured her some ale. His whole left arm was covered in tattoos. Laila couldn't make out one from another. The eyes of a lion were depicted on his shoulder, and she was pretty sure the rest of the lion's head was there too, but spirals and other markings weaved around every inch of skin in knotted designs up and down his arm, making it difficult to tell. He set down the pitcher and passed her the drink.

"That visit was a while ago now anyway. I miss seeing your pretty face 'round here. Have you come bearing gifts?"

Laila withdrew a tub of ointment from her bag. "I have. As requested." She set the muscle relaxant on the counter and slid it to Gareth. He took it, opened it, and sniffed it. He scrunched his nose, and the corners of his lips twitched in approval. He reached into his pocket, took out a small pouch that jingled with coins, and handed it to Laila. He then sealed the container and tucked it away inside his inner coat pocket. "You do know how much Drinke's Apothecaries charges for this same stuff, right?"

She did. Laila winked. "This will cover the cost to make it, but you make up the remainder of the payment with something far more valuable than belds. Speaking of, what have you got for me today?"

There was a glint in Gareth's eye, and the man practically rubbed his hands together with glee. "Oh, it's good. As it happens, I have very interesting news. Something of worth for once."

"No news is worthless. But let's hear what you have."

"Some folks from Ectarin have arrived in Kartha. Rumour has it, they work for the Tax Collector. As if it weren't enough to hear his name pop up here and there, there've also been reports of people going missing all the way from Hywreath to Valmain. I hear they're heading this way. Been telling folks to keep their loved ones close. Anyway, they're looking for someone." Gareth bent over to pull something from the shelf below the counter. He retrieved a piece of parchment and laid it flat on the counter. Laila looked down at it. Staring back up at her was the face of Mckal Dairner. The artist had done a good job of depicting his dark eyes. His name was written in bold along the bottom, above the amount in reward money for his return to someone called Ighur.

Upon first seeing Mick in Hywreath, she'd known exactly who he was. But something about his mannerisms made him come across as guarded. Whatever had him so nervous, she hadn't known then, but now, seeing his face on a wanted poster, she could understand what had him on edge. Wanted by the Tax Collector, no less. She was no stranger to Governor Riggs's endeavours.

Laila rubbed the corners of the parchment with her thumb, and sure enough, at the top right corner was an emblem bearing the ship over the red sea, the crown, and the horned grey bear. Now she wished she'd properly introduced herself to Mick and offered to take him directly to his family. Instead, he could be anywhere, pursued by the Tax Collector's men. Her previous encounter two years ago with the Governor's crew of Collectors had ended badly. And her ribs, though they'd healed, still pained her from time to time. The Collectors had gotten away with a shipload of victims to be sold into slavery, and she herself had nearly drowned.

Gareth smirked. "They've been showing this around to people everywhere, looking for this boy."

What did the Tax Collector want with Mick? Could he have somehow learned of his unique ability?

Straight-faced, Laila peered up from the poster to gaze at Gareth, who grinned and shrugged. "Bad lot to be getting involved with. May want to steer clear of that one. Mind you, that reward is quite fetching. And you're Laila Madx," he said as if that gave her amnesty from the Governor. She may be Laila Madx, but if the Governor caught wind that she and the Witch were one and the same, she'd not be received as a friend.

With her best nonchalant shrug, she said, "Is this supposed to mean something to me?"

*Of course it meant something!* The very man she'd been hunting down for years, unable to touch, was looking for Mick—the grandson of one of her closest friends. And offering a reward! It meant more to her than Gareth could possibly know or understand.

Gareth's eyes bulged, and he shook his head. "Look at the name. Don't you recognize it? Dairner. And his face! Look at him! He looks just like—" He lowered his voice and leaned in close. "Those Guardians. Aren't they called Dairner as well? Don't you know anything? Those twin brothers down in Litlen, who everyone reveres so much."

Laila gazed at the illustration and felt as if she were staring into the eyes of Raidan or Dimitri. Did Raidan know his grandson was in the country? Cassian and Willa had whisked him away in such a hurry when a rumour started going around that he was the Healer. It was true that he had the ability to heal, but Laila didn't read too much into the prophecy. One's future couldn't be predetermined. The family's disappearance put to rest any further speculation, but none of that mattered. Mick was here and in trouble if the Governor of Iptin was looking for him.

She picked up the poster. "Can I keep this?"

"Thought it didn't mean anything to you." Gareth drank Laila's ale, which she hadn't touched.

"Doesn't mean I can't keep an eye out for him. It's like you said. Sixty pounds of xanteén is a hefty reward. And you and I both know how little I charge for my products. Besides, do you really think this boy is likely to come through here? If he's related to those brothers, wouldn't it be more likely he'd head to Litlen?"

Gareth rubbed his rough chin. "Well, I suppose you're right. You're more likely to come across his path than I am, bein' stuck here an' all. And anyway, I don't know if I'd have it in me to condemn a boy to the Tax Collector." He waved his hand. "All right, you take it. But when you get that reward, you remember me, ya?"

Laila folded the parchment and tucked it into her bag. If Raidan didn't already know of Mick's presence in Kartha, he needed to be made aware. It was time she paid her friend a visit.

# Chapter 16

Travelling the dirt roads to Valmain, meant no sleep. Mick tried to close his eyes and get some rest, but with all the jostling about, it proved to be impossible. The many potholes didn't help. He'd have thought that Valmain's streets would be smoother, but the cobblestones were worse than the potholes.

Vidia's leg trembled against his. She bunched up the fabric from her skirt in her fist, fidgeting nervously. If not for the stone in his pocket, Mick might have been just as restless. He cleared his throat and tried to stretch his stiff muscles while seated between Vidia and one of Sunny's men. Sunny sat across from them, beside Boone and another of his men. It was difficult for him not to look at the scar over Sunny's brow.

"You, uh, you have a little something…" Mick rubbed a thumb across his forehead between his eyebrows. "Right there. Did you know that?"

The man beside Mick smacked him upside the head. It might not have hurt so bad if it weren't for the gold ring he was wearing.

Mick laughed softly and addressed Sunny. "He thinks I hurt your feelings."

The man smacked him harder this time.

Vidia scowled at Mick and implored with her eyes that he *stop talking*. Aira had given him that look many times. Even Boone pressed his lips and gave Mick a look of concern.

Mick knew he should stop, but he just couldn't help himself.

"I think he likes you," he said.

Something dug into his side. He glanced down. Sunny's man held a pistol against his ribs, the first firearm Mick had seen in Kartha. Riggs and his Collectors liked to flash theirs often. Mick wondered if the weapon even served a purpose beyond showing off one's status.

He mock-gasped. "Whoa! High rollers. You know how to use that thing?"

Sunny leaned forward and held a dagger to Mick's neck. The tip of the blade touched his flesh. "Keep talking. Give me a reason to slit your throat."

Mick narrowed his gaze on Sunny. Of all the ways for his ability to be discovered, he'd not have thought it'd be because of his inability to shut up. He'd been convinced it'd be because he was in a situation where someone was dying and in need of immediate help, and he'd not be able to walk away. That would be far nobler. He really was being reckless.

Vidia raised her hands in surrender, though she wasn't the one being threatened. "Please, I'll have my uncle increase your pay if you return my friends with me unscathed."

Sunny eyed Mick. He was on the verge of puncturing his skin. He narrowed his eyes for a moment as though he considered it, but then leaned back and released him. He twirled his dagger between his fingers. "I know your face. Why do I know your face?" He squinted at him. "Doesn't he look familiar, Reg?" The man beside Mick shrugged. His nonchalance discouraged any further inquiry. Sunny leaned back. "It'll come to me. Anyway, Daegan has no use for either of you." He glanced Boone's way. "Be grateful your gallant knight is here to speak on your behalf."

The blow to Mick's ego hurt more than the smacks to his head had.

Sunny pointed his dagger at Boone before sheathing it. "But if Daegan doesn't pay up, I expect you to make up for my losses. And those fancy boots alone won't cover them."

The carriage pulled to a stop at the top of a hill, in front of a fortress of a building. Stairs led up to where two pillars welcomed the way to the doors. They were ushered into the entry, which was everything that Governor Riggs's manor was not. The chandelier that glittered above them looked expensive and warm. A large-leafed plant in a pot took up a corner, and the green rug gave the palatial foyer a feel of homeliness.

Surrounded by Sunny and his two men, Mick stayed close to Vidia. Boone shuffled close to them both just as a man with the same vibrant green eyes as Vidia approached. He had fairer skin than hers and looked only a little older than Mick.

"You found her," he said, sounding neither pleased nor disappointed.

Vidia glared at the man who'd greeted them. "Preston…I see you're still Uncle Daegan's favourite pet. I'd like to think my own brother would stand up for his little sister. Waylan would have."

Preston scoffed and shook his head. "And where is Waylan, huh? Oh yes, that's right. He left us. I don't see him standing up for anyone but himself. Who are these two?" He nodded at Mick and Boone.

Sunny straightened. "They were all together, making themselves quite at home in the Valca cottage outside of Ferenth. Thought Daegan might be missing his little princess. She promised a bonus for the extras on his behalf."

"Not likely." Preston waved for them to follow. "But you can bring it up with him. Come, he's in the library. I'll show you to him."

Mick cocked his head at Vidia. "I thought there was no royalty here."

"He doesn't mean actual princess," Vidia said.

Preston led them down the hallway behind the stairs and entered the third room to the left, showing them all inside. Multiple shelves rose to the ceiling in the long room. They were filled with what must have been thousands of books. A dark-haired man with strikingly dark eyelashes sat in an upholstered chair beside a small desk by a large window. Sunlight streamed into the room.

"Visitors, Uncle," Preston said.

The man set down the book he'd been reading and rose, smoothing his clothes. His shirt had embroidered looped designs on the collar and over a breast pocket, and his boots reached nearly to his knees. His outfit made Governor Riggs's clothes seem like a peasant's.

Sunny hovered close behind Mick while his men remained on standby. Preston clasped his hands in front of himself and relaxed. Three men entered the library after them. One wore a bright red headband wrapped behind disproportioned ears, and another had his red sash tied around his plump belly. The third had a long face and wore a red sleeveless shirt. He crossed his arms, flexing his biceps.

Daegan approached Vidia. "You put me in quite a bit of distress, running off like that."

Vidia stood tall. "I wouldn't have run if you weren't trying to force me to marry. I'm not marrying Lord Shorvin, Uncle Daegan. It's not your right to choose for me."

"I am your guardian, and this arrangement will benefit all of our family."

"It benefits you!" Vidia spat. "My father would never agree to this."

"Your father is not—" Daegan stopped himself. He pressed his lips together and threw his hands up. "I'm not arguing with you. It's already been arranged, and you'll do as you're told." He glanced at Boone, then Mick.

Mick lowered his gaze, trying to avoid recognition, if that were possible. Daegan left Vidia to stand before him. He narrowed his eyes and squinted at Mick. Mick met his eye and stared back, but when the staring went on for too long, he yielded.

Daegan smirked. "Ah, there he is. Now you look like Dimitri."

Mick blinked. Daegan knew Dimitri? By the sound of it, not in a good way. Whether or not they were acquainted, Mick was not his great-uncle. There should be no reason for hostility. He extended a hand. "I'm Mckal Dairner."

"I know who you are." Daegan ignored Mick's hand. "All you Dairners look the same."

Vidia moved to stand between them. "Uncle Daegan, please… Leave him alone. I was only taking him to his family. Let him go to—"

Daegan hushed her with a raised finger. "You don't get to speak right now. You took off on me and I'm not ready to deal with you yet." He waved for a guard. "Take my niece to her room and make sure she stays there."

A hand gripped Mick's upper arm. He looked to see whose it was. Sunny shook his head as a warning while the portly guard grasped Vidia's arm and did as he'd been instructed.

"Uncle Daegan, don't be like this." Vidia yanked against the guard restraining her. "Delia would never have stood for this."

Daegan's jaw twitched. He snapped at his guard to take her away. Mick took a step forward when the guard nudged her to go, but Sunny squeezed his arm.

Vidia's voice cracked. "She'd hate you for this! I hate you for this!" She called over her shoulder as she was escorted out of the library. "I don't want to live here! I want to go home!" She continued to shout and her cries rang out through the halls, growing farther away.

Daegan glanced between Mick and Boone. "Who's he?" He nodded at Boone.

"Boone's got nothing to do with any of this," Mick said. "He joined us to avoid travelling alone."

"Hmm… You know, there's some folks from Ectarin—the Governor's men—looking for you. I don't think they realize who your family is or what the name Dairner means around here. Else I think they'd be offering more than sixty pounds of xanteén as a reward for your return to someone called Ighur."

Mick blinked. Had he heard that right? Ighur had put out a reward for his return?

Daegan snapped at Preston. "Bring me that poster over there."

Preston went to the desk against the wall, which was stacked with books on top. He snatched the single piece of parchment atop the pile and walked back to his uncle, handing it over.

Daegan showed Mick the poster. The drawing of Mick's face resembled him exactly. And just like Daegan had said, there was the reward amount. Ighur's name and where he could be reached were written in small text at the very bottom.

Mick swallowed. Boone's gaze turned from the poster to stare at Mick, his eyes wide.

Daegan handed it to Sunny. "Take this. Find this Ighur fellow and tell him I have what he's looking for. You'll receive your payment upon your return."

Sunny let Mick go. "Guess you got lucky." He smirked. "Or maybe not so lucky." He chuckled as he stuffed the poster into his pocket. He waved for his three men to accompany him and they left. With them gone, Mick, Boone, Preston, Daegan, and two other guards remained.

Daegan rubbed his now empty hands together. "That they're looking for you and don't know your worth tells me you must have committed a crime or something deserving of punishment.

"It's not like that. I—"

"apapap… I don't need to hear it." Daegan shook his head. "Save it for your case against Ighur or whomever it is you must answer to."

"Daegan, whatever your problem is with me, I know nothing of it. I just want to get to my family."

"You're a wanted man. It would be irresponsible of me to let you walk out of here without making sure you are brought to justice."

"I didn't do anything wrong."

"We'll see about that. I've got enough to deal with right now and don't need to advocate for any Dairner. Besides, Vidia doesn't need anymore distractions right now. It's enough that I can't get her to stop this nonsense about her parents coming back. She needs to move on. Hanging around with you won't help her do that."

"Have I somehow wronged you?"

"Not you. But if you suffer, Dimitri suffers, and that will do."

What had Dimitri done that made Daegan hate him so much? Mick stared at the open doorway leading out of the library. "Would you at least let Boone go? He isn't part of this."

"I'll let Ighur decide that. If this boy is associated with you, he may be just as guilty. When I'm done negotiating a greater reward for you, who knows? I may be able to strike an even better deal for the extra." Daegan motioned for his guards to take them.

Mick breathed heavily. It was one thing for him to have to face Riggs, but he couldn't get Boone involved. "Please, Daegan, you don't know what kind of man Governor Riggs is. If you hand me over, I'll never see my family again."

Daegan turned his head to look out the window. He breathed in deeply and released it in a long exhale. "It's probably for the better."

The long-faced guard approached Mick. The second guard—the one with the headband and disproportioned ears—grabbed Boone. Any chance of getting out of here was slipping away.

Mick backed away from the guard, raising his hands defensively. "Raidan will pay you more. If my grandfather knew I was here, he'd pay whatever you asked."

Long-Face made no move while awaiting Daegan's instructions.

Daegan scratched above his ear. "A ransom? Hmm… It's not a terrible idea. Except that would mean there would be one more of you in Kartha. No, this is better." He nodded to his men.

"Take them to the dungeon until our guest arrives."

# Chapter 17

MICK'S MIND RACED FOR SOMETHING TO SAY THAT COULD CONVINCE DAEGAN to change his mind. He had run out of time. Long-Face came toward him and Mick hopped back on the balls of his feet. He then ducked low and charged.

Maybe he'd been counting on the guard not expecting him to react, or it could have been that he thought the man weighed less and Mick could shove him enough to get past him, but he'd thought wrong. Long-Face picked Mick up around his torso, upside down, and flipped him onto his back in one motion. The wind left Mick's lungs, and he winced.

While Mick caught his breath, Boone cried out. He grunted, and there was an awful thwacking sound. Mick rolled onto his side, but before he could see what had happened, Long-Face hefted him to his feet and struck his face. Mick's body went slack, and spots danced in his vision. As colours and shapes blurred, he caught sight of Boone lying supine on the floor. The other guard was pounding his fists into Boone's face again and again.

Mick jumped and ran toward him, clawing at the guard to get off. He managed to throw one punch to the man's temple before strong arms yanked him back. The guard over Boone took another swing, and Boone's arms fell limp.

"You're killing him! Stop!" Mick thrashed and shouted, trying to get to his friend. Preston stepped in and assisted Long-Face. The two tugged Mick's wrists, holding them behind his back, restraining him until he stopped his flailing.

Boone's attacker had a mere bloody nose. Boone's, on the other hand, had a mangled and purple face, and blood dripped from his nose and mouth. He moaned and lay still.

Mick's weight sank against Preston and Long-Face. Boone's attacker wiped his bloodied fists on Boone's shirt, and Daegan helped his man to his feet.

"That was completely unnecessary. And you've all made a mess in my library. Get these two out of here and clean this up."

Mick couldn't take his eyes off Boone. He shook all over, and his chin quivered. He wanted to cry, but crying would imply he'd been hurt. Nothing hurt him. Not when he could magically heal. And not when he could heal others…

Boone turned his head and groaned. He was alive and that was enough. The sooner they were taken to the dungeons, the sooner Mick could heal him. If he were discovered because of it, then so be it.

Preston stepped out of the way so Long-Face could guide Mick from the library. Mick didn't resist when the guard led him down a hallway, then through a corridor, down a narrow stone stairway, into a darkly lit room, and then to an even darker room where two cells took up either corner. Long-Face shoved Mick into one. Mick tumbled in and fell, landing on his hands and knees. A few moments later, the other guard and Preston dragged Boone in and tossed him inside with Mick. Preston locked the cell door and they all left.

A torch lit the hall between them and the cell opposite theirs. Boone lay on the cold stone floor and didn't try to get up. Mick didn't think he could. He rushed to his side, turning him onto his back. Without a second guess as to what he was about to do, he put a hand to Boone's chest and accessed the place within himself where his healing magic moved.

Ighur was coming for him. Soon, he would have to face Riggs. He didn't know if Aira or his parents were safe, Vidia was locked up in her room, and Boone was injured badly. Although everything else was beyond his control, healing Boone was the one thing he could fix.

He closed his eyes and poured his magic into Boone. The flow of it filled his heart, and he extended it toward his friend. It flowed through his arms and reached past his fingertips, healing the injuries. Mick kept his hand in place until Boone's raspy breaths levelled into a steady rhythm. Boone's bruised face was cleared of all cuts and swelling. The only evidence that remained of his beating was the blood in his hair and on his skin and clothes.

The healing was complete, but it'd be a few minutes before Boone would be ready to get up. He'd taken a hard beating.

There was only one thin mattress in the cell. Mick dragged Boone over to it and let him rest there while he himself sat on the floor, leaning against the back wall. Apart from the mattress, the only other thing in the cell was a chamber pot in a dark corner. Although, it was likely empty—or so he hoped—the scent of stale urine lingered in the cold air.

Mick rested his hands over his knees. "I'm so sorry, Boone. I shouldn't have let you come with me."

There was no question that when Ighur would arrive, he'd not see any reason to release Boone. Riggs had warned him that he'd take everything from him. And now that meant Boone as well as everyone else. All Mick had accomplished in healing Boone, was prolonging his life for a fate worse than death.

His eyes burned, but tears would not come. This wasn't over.

Boone's hand twitched, then rose to his head. He moaned and sat upright, looking around at their unfortunate situation. He felt around his face with both hands, then his forehead creased as his gaze fell on Mick. He had questions, no doubt.

Rather than offer any explanation, Mick stood and paced, running his hands through his hair. "I gotta fix this somehow." He tried the door, despite knowing it wouldn't open for him. He tapped his thumb against his leg while craning his neck to find any flaw or weakness in the cell. He resumed pacing.

"Fix what?" Boone glanced down at himself, assessing the bloodstains on his shirt. Again, he felt around his head and face. His brows furrowed. "Mick, you have a governor's men after you. What did you do? And how am I not hurt? Did I imagine getting beaten or did that actually happen?"

The pacing made Mick more anxious. He stopped, reached into his pocket, and clutched the stone, allowing the contact to settle him. "You didn't imagine it. And I didn't commit any crime. I denied my employer what he wanted, and he didn't take it well."

"What did you do to your employer that a governor would send his men after you?"

"My employer *is* the governor. I'm his cook."

Boone squinted. "You're a cook? What, did you forget to put salt on his steak?" He waved his hand. "What's going to happen to you when his man gets here?"

"Nothing good."

"And what about me?"

Mick wished he could tell Boone that he'd be allowed to go on his way and pretend this never happened. But that wasn't the case.

He shook his head. "I'm sorry, Boone. I didn't mean to get you caught up in this. I should have just carried on my way and figured this out myself. I should have known better than to think I could outrun the Tax Collector."

"The Tax Collector?" Boone's eyes grew. "You mean your employer is *the* Governor—? *That* Governor?"

So Boone had heard of him too. Mick bowed his head. "Unfortunately."

"Mick, why would you work for that man? Don't you know how dangerous he is?"

Mick scratched his neck. "I didn't when I started working for him." Having seen a man tortured at the hands of Riggs made that pretty clear a short time later.

Boone's eyes darted around their cell. "What about your grandfather? Do you think Daegan will tell him to come?"

The door squeaked on its hinges, and footfalls echoed in the darkness. Mick stiffened. If the guards saw Boone standing, they'd know something was up. He clenched his fist tightly around the stone.

Whatever happened, he wasn't going anywhere without a fight.

A middle-aged man came into the light. He removed his hood, revealing dark hair with bits of silver in every odd strand. His blue eyes landed on Mick. They almost appeared white for how light they were.

"Who are you?" Boone asked.

"My name's Damien, and I have a proposal for you." He pointed at Mick.

Mick released the stone and took his hand out of his pocket so he could cross his arms. He didn't recognize Damien. Whoever he was, he seemed to know who Mick was. But apparently that wasn't unusual around here.

"What kind of proposal?" Mick asked.

"The kind that gets you out of here." Damien tapped the keyhole in the cell door. "I'll free you from this cell if you agree to release an old friend of mine from his prison."

The offer sounded too simple. "Why would you go to the trouble of releasing me when you could just free your friend instead?"

"Because his prison is made from magic, and the only one who can break the enchanted barrier is the one who put him there. Or his heir."

Mick hadn't locked anyone in an enchanted prison, so that must mean... "My father imprisoned him?"

"Your grandfather. So, what do you say?"

"What did your friend do?"

"The reason for his imprisonment is irrelevant and not part of the arrangement. You're wasting time. Will you free him, or wait to see what fate awaits you here when your friend Ighur comes for you?"

Mick walked the length of the small cell and back. Depending on how desperate Damien was to free his friend, if Mick played this right, he could use this as a chance to save Boone at the very least. And maybe, if he was really lucky, himself too.

"I'll do it, but I have three conditions." From the corner of his eye, Mick could see Boone shaking his head slowly. He must know what the alternative would mean. What choice did Mick have?

"Name them," Damien said.

"Boone goes free. We get out of here and far enough away that he'll be safe and can go on his way."

"And the second?"

"Vidia doesn't have to marry against her will."

"I can't speak for Daegan. His choices are his own."

"Then speak to him."

"I can't make his mind up for him either. If I could, I would, but that is one condition I can't adhere to. What's the third?"

It had been worth a shot. Mick would have to find another way to help Vidia out of an unwanted marriage. As for his third request… "As soon as your friend is free, you and I are finished. You don't turn around to collect Ighur's reward for me."

Damien bowed his head and smiled. "Once Beiron is free, our transaction will be complete and I'll have no more use for you. And I promise I won't collect the reward money for you. Let's seal the deal in magic." He extracted a knife from his waistband.

Boone's eyes grew, and Mick took a step back, though Damien could do no harm with the bars between them.

Damien raised his hand, palm up. The flame from the torch bounced out of the sconce and floated in mid-air. Boone's jaw dropped. Mick's breathing quickened.

"It's all right," Damien said. "It's very dark in here, and I can't see you that well." The fire illuminated their faces.

"You're Elderace?" Mick asked.

"And you're half Elderace. Now, you should know that a deal made in magic is no joke. If you fail to follow through with your end of the deal, you'll die. And the same goes for me. Our terms were made verbally, and now all that's left is to bind the contract in blood."

Death was the consequence of failing to follow through? This wasn't what Mick agreed to. There were too many unknowns. "Let's just shake on it. Nice and easy. I have people looking for me... What if they catch up to me and I can't fulfill my part because I'm physically unable to? Or we get separated and I don't know where to go? I don't even know how to free him. What if I can't do it, or it doesn't work?"

"The barrier was made by blood magic. Your blood. You'll figure it out. Your hesitancy solidifies my suspicions that you'll back out of this arrangement the first chance you get." Damien shook his head. "We seal this in blood or I walk out of here and figure out another way to free him. Maybe Ighur and I can work out some sort of agreement. I have a lot to offer. I'm sure I'll have no trouble convincing him to let me take you by force. But wouldn't you prefer to do this on your own terms?"

"My own terms? Is that what this is?"

Damien used his knife to cut deep into his thumb. Blood dripped toward his wrist. He flipped the knife, grabbing the flat part of the blade, and offered the handle to Mick. "Are we doing this or not?"

Boone came up behind Mick, leaning in close. He kept his voice low. "Mick, don't. I've got a bad feeling about this."

As did Mick. But to stay here would be far worse. Before he could talk himself out of it, he gripped the knife and sliced below his thumb on his palm. His healing worked fast, so he thrust his hand toward Damien before the wound could heal completely.

Damien shook his hand. Mick gasped from the powerful surge that shot through his arm. It tingled up to his shoulder and coursed through his body. The stone pulsated in his pocket, and the floor vibrated beneath his feet.

Damien yanked his hand back and rubbed it with his thumb. His eyes flitted around the room, then landed on Mick, who stared at his hand.

Shouldn't his wound have healed? The line where he'd cut remained in his skin, sealed and black. Panic swelled in his chest. He'd never had a mark remain on his body. Not even from some of his worst injuries.

"That'll go away once Beiron is free and our deal is complete," Damien said. He produced a key and unlocked the cell. "The guards in the next room will allow us to go, but we need to move quickly. Daegan could return at any moment."

The mark on Mick's hand was like a ticking clock. He stared, unable to tear his eyes from it. He rubbed it as if that would make it go away. It didn't, and he got a terrible sick feeling in the pit of his stomach. What had he done?

# Chapter 18

RAIDAN'S HOUSE RESTED ON A CLIFF OVERLOOKING THE SEA AT THE southwestern tip of Litlen, away from the busy city. Laila rode Vis around to the front, where she found Dimitri sitting on the bench situated near the cliff's edge, facing the sea. He twisted around and his brown eyes softened the way they always did when first seeing her upon her return to Kartha. They still held a playful gleam, but in them was revealed a lifetime of experience.

Apart from his eyes, he still looked almost the same as when they'd first met. He was, after all, a Guardian of the Weldafire Stone. It didn't make him Elderace, but the magic worked the same in that it extended his and Raidan's years beyond the typical lifespan of a mayanon.

Laila dismounted as Dimitri came around the bench. He wrapped his arms around her.

"Laila. I've missed you. Raidan and Ida aren't here. I've been waiting for them to return. Care to join me?" He gestured to the bench.

Glass chimes tinkled behind her. The glass ornaments were Ida's creation, and many were scattered in strategic places, decorating the garden and around the house. The brick home was painted a deep purple and had lavender shutters and trim. Above the door, an ornament glinted in the low sun. Laila couldn't make out the details from where she stood, but she knew the one. It depicted a pair of cupped hands holding the Weldafire Stone. Ida had even managed to replicate the exact colours and the way it seemed to change from blue to green. She may not have had magic, but she certainly had a gift.

"Actually, I came to show you something." Laila lifted the flap of her bag and stuffed her hand inside, ruffling through her books and belongings. Mostly all she carried were her deliveries, a few extra potions and salves that might come in handy in a pinch, and her notebook. She retrieved the poster of Mick and handed it to Dimitri.

"One of my contacts gave me this."

Dimitri took it and read. His lips parted.

Vis moved away from them to find a better place for grazing, stopping about six feet away.

"This could explain the buzzing I've been hearing." Dimitri glanced around as if trying to determine where a sound was coming from. "I felt a change in the land. There's this subtle vibration in the ground, and I can't help but feel like something is wrong. Like Kartha is anxious."

His and Raidan's role as the Guardians of the Weldafire Stone gave them deep insight into the well-being of Kartha. The life of the country resided within that stone, and the stone was bound to their bloodline.

"That's what I came to speak to Raidan about." Dimitri held up the poster and looked at it again. But this… I was just in Iptin to see Mick. He'd said nothing to indicate he was in any kind of trouble." He uncurled the top corner to look at the emblem there. "This is the emblem of his employer. It was on the banners that were hanging all over the manor when I went to visit."

"Wait, you went to see him recently?"

Dimitri's ears reddened. "I did. Raidan—he doesn't know. He said we should wait until we could get through to Cass, but we both agreed it's time for Mick to come home. We've both been experiencing problems with our magic." He opened his palm. "*Eimis.*" He spoke his trigger word—the Eldrace word for *peace*—and his white light appeared. It flickered and went out.

Laila said nothing. She stared at the empty space above his hand.

"It's time," Dimitri said. "Mick needs to take his place as Guardian."

"Does this mean that when he does, you and Raidan won't have magic anymore?"

Dimitri scratched his chin. "Maybe eventually. I don't think it will work the same as when you lost your magic after the curse. We're relinquishing our place as Guardians, but since we weren't born with magic, I suspect it'll fade away eventually. But with it being so unpredictable lately, I couldn't wait any longer, so… I, uh… I paid Mick a visit and…" He averted his gaze. "Well, I sort of gave him the stone."

A chill went through Laila. "You what?" She said too loud. She thought back to her encounter with Mick in Hywreath. Not only was he being sought by Iptin's governor, but he also had the Weldafire Stone in his possession? Could that be why Governor Riggs was after him? And what of Dimitri sensing a change? Laila might not have put much emphasis into the prophecy before now, but knowing Mick had the stone and was in Kartha… What did it all mean?

These past forty-three years since Litlen's curse was broken had been incredible. She'd been able to put the past behind her and not think about the mines she had grown up in or the two wars she'd lived through. She had even managed to stop worrying that her father would forever have a grip on her life, holding her back from living. Would Mick's being here threaten that peace?

She put it from her mind.

It was silly. He probably didn't have a clue about Beiron and his prison. Besides, it was so out of the way that it wasn't likely he'd wind up there by mistake.

Laila rested a hand on Dimitri's shoulder. "Why did you give Mick the stone? Why not just tell him you had something for him when he got here?"

"I hoped that in giving it to him, the magic would urge him to come." Dimitri covered her hand with his own. "Mick's as honourable as Raidan and as stubborn as him too. As long as he'd made a promise, he'd be insistent on keeping it unless he had a little extra encouragement otherwise." He slid her hand from his shoulder and held it in his. "But I might have also thought that if the stone were in the right hands, it would fill the void in our own magic."

Dimitri wasn't one to be vulnerable around others, but on her last few visits, he'd opened up his heart to her and shown a new side of himself. The lines on his forehead creased. If she didn't know him like she did, she'd mistake his scowl for anger. But she did know him. And this was not anger. Dimitri Dairner was worried.

She squeezed his hand and let go. If she let her guard down, she risked becoming too attached. Over the last years her feelings for Dimitri may have become serious, but he was bound to this country and his role as Guardian of the Weldafire Stone. If she were to let herself explore new territory, evolving their relationship, she may never leave Kartha again.

She rubbed the chill from her arms. "Does Mick know to come here? Does he know you're in Litlen?"

"I told him to find me here, but if someone has put a bounty out for him, he may not make it." Dimitri crumpled the poster. "We'll have to find him. He could be anywhere."

Laila snatched the poster back and stuffed it into her bag before he destroyed it. Raidan would want to see it. That bounty wasn't put out by just *anyone*.

"I can start in Valmain," Laila offered.

"Why Valmain? Why would he go there?"

"Because—" Laila stopped herself. Just because Mick was with Vidia when she'd seen him didn't mean that was where they'd gone. It had been obvious Vidia didn't want to go there, and it was no wonder. Daegan never could figure out how to cope with raising a girl, let alone a young woman. But still, word spread quickly in Kartha and with Mick's face being shown around, the country's capital was where she'd be more likely to hear any news about where he might have been spotted.

"I can ask around," she said. "I have a few contacts there. I'll see what I can find out."

Dimitri nodded. His eyes skimmed over Raidan's place, as he checked all directions around the house. "What's taking Raidan so long? We don't even know if Cassian and Willa are with him."

"I bumped into Mick at Hywreath when I first arrived. They weren't with him."

"You saw him?" Dimitri jumped. "How did he seem to you?"

"He looked fine, Dimitri. If I'd suspected he was in this kind of trouble, I would have asked him to let me take him to you and Raidan. But he was with a girl, and I don't think he would have appreciated a stranger interrogating him in the street." Laila opted to leave out exactly which girl. Dimitri and Daegan weren't on the best of terms.

"You're not a stranger. You shouldn't be." If Dimitri blamed Willa and Cassian for that fact, he'd not given Laila enough credit. She'd been back to Kartha maybe a dozen times since Mick had been born, and never long enough to create a lasting impression anyway.

She flipped her braid from her shoulder. "Not to you, I'm not. But Mick's not going to remember the few times I saw him as a baby."

Dimitri ran his hands through his hair. "Can we try eshuair?"

Laila bit her bottom lip. "Only if your plan is to find Raidan." The pollen from the eshuair flower had been useful in helping Dimitri find Raidan years ago. But it was more likely to reveal the link between the brothers, as their relation as twins was strongest.

"I think he's taken Ida to the market today," Dimitri said. "She mentioned wanting to go."

"Okay, so we go there first and fill him in?" Laila readjusted her bag to sit comfortably against her hip as she sought Vis, who'd wandered in his grazing.

"I'll find Raidan," Dimitri said. "You go to Valmain and learn what you can. As soon as Raidan is back, I'll go to Hywreath to make inquiries and learn if Cassian and Willa are here too or if they know Mick is here. If not, I'm going to have to travel to Iptin Province to let them know. That's not going to be a fun visit."

Laila's heart went out to Dimitri, knowing how Raidan and Dimitri had spent years trying to bring Cassian and Willa back to Kartha. Sure, he was a bit impulsive, but he'd meant well and was only trying to reunite their family again. But giving Mick the stone and failing to share that bit of information with Raidan…

Not his best idea.

Valmain was not nearly as far as Iptin Province. A journey there and back would take around a week's time without stopping for more than a few hours of rest. Iptin would take longer. "Dimitri, if you have to go all the way to Iptin, you should leave right away. I'll catch Raidan and Ida up on what's going on. You go." She placed a hand on his firm arm. Even into his seventies he'd maintained a toned physique. Dimitri placed his hand over hers and gave it a squeeze.

"Did I already tell you how much I've missed you, Laila?"

Laila smiled. It was nice to be missed. She whistled for Vis, who came trotting over from the edge of the tree line where the grass was taller. She mounted and turned to Dimitri. "Try to be civil. Don't pick fights with Cassian."

Dimitri pointed a thumb at himself. "Who me? Never." He smirked.

Laila rolled her eyes. "I'll meet you back here when you return."

She dug her heels into Vis's sides, advancing him into a canter. The sun warmed her back as she rode away from Raidan's house.

Dimitri's premonitions about a changing Kartha stirred a fear in her that she thought she'd overcome a long time ago.

She crouched over Vis's neck and urged him to go faster. For all she knew, Mick could have already caught up with Raidan and Ida, and here she was getting all worked up over nothing.

While she tried to convince herself there was nothing to worry about, her instincts told her otherwise.

# Chapter 19

Getting out of the dungeon hadn't been difficult with Damien paying off the guard. All they'd needed to do from there was make it to the waiting coach. Once they'd made it inside, they didn't have to worry about being seen or recognized. Mick and Boone sat in the coach with the curtains closed while Damien drove.

Compared to the journey to Valmain, their transit proved to be much less cramped. Boone pulled back the curtain for the millionth time and glanced out. The sun was starting to peek over the hilltops in the east.

Mick couldn't stop rubbing the mark on his hand. They'd travelled through the night and finally stopped to rest the horses and stretch. Mick and Boone exited the coach and joined Damien for a breakfast of bread and dried meat. It was a lousy meal, but Mick couldn't complain. He'd been hungry enough not to care that the bread tasted like it was made with a bad batch of yeast or that the meat was too salty.

Boone restocked his pocket with the meat and winked at Mick. It was good he still had his humour and an appetite after taking a beating and waking in a dungeon. "Where will you go from here?" Mick asked him.

Damien handed Mick a second roll and interjected. "Not from here. He'll carry on with us until we make it to the Hayat Forest."

Mick stiffened. "I told you I wouldn't do this unless Boone—"

"Yes, yes, relax. He will go free, just not from here."

"What difference does it make if it's from here or somewhere else?"

"The difference is the time it'll take him to reach your family. If it's your intention to seek out the Guardians and inform them of our arrangement, I want to be sure he'll have no chance of arriving in Litlen before we're done. Once you've done your part, Beiron and I will be gone before anyone comes looking."

Boone stuffed his face with a roll and spoke while chewing. "I'm not going anywhere without Mickey."

"You don't have a choice," Damien said. "It was a condition."

Boone swallowed. "You said you'd let me go on my way. Well, my way happens to be your way."

Mick shook his head. "Boone, I'll be all right." Although they barely knew each other, Boone's loyalty was admirable. Or was he still hopeful that Mick could introduce him to the Witch? There wasn't much chance of that happening now.

The corner of Damien's lip twisted up. "You want to come on your own? Sure, by all means…" He flashed his eyebrows, amused and implicating a threat. "Come." His smile dropped. "Breakfast is over. Let's get moving."

With the horses fed and watered, they got back on the road. Mick picked at his roll. His stomach churned. He didn't know if it was because the bread tasted off or because his muscles were so tense.

Boone opened and closed his eyes as though he were attempting to sleep but was failing at it. He sat back with his head lolled against the back of the seat. Tired as Mick was, he couldn't sleep. Even as minutes turned to hours, his heart raced. He breathed slowly, trying to steady its rhythm to match his breaths.

He didn't know when they'd arrive at Boone's drop off, but they must be getting close.

Ever since he'd made the deal, there'd been a constant vibration under his skin that wouldn't go away, worse than the shakes he'd grown up with. The stone pulsated against his thigh. He withdrew it from his pocket and squeezed it in his fist.

Damien made him uneasy, and he couldn't shake the feeling that things were going to go badly, though he couldn't think how. The terms were set, and the consequence of breaking those terms was straight forward. If Mick's suspicions were correct though, he didn't want to have the stone on him—just in case.

*But what to do with it?*

Mick barely knew Boone, but his new friend had been quick to make a decision to stay with him, even through these horrible circumstances. If his choices were between keeping the stone and risking Damien stealing it versus sending it with Boone to get to his family, he'd take his chances with Boone before Damien any day. Boone may not make it to Litlen in time for anyone to come retake custody of Beiron after Mick freed him, but at least he could let his family know he was here. And as long as his family knew he was in Kartha, Mick would worry less about what awaited him wherever Damien was taking him.

Mick opened his fist.

Boone peeked open an eye. He glanced down at the pouch concealing the stone. "What's that?"

Mick held his breath. It was now or never.

"Boone, I need you to do something for me. It's very important." He didn't give him an opportunity to register his words before continuing. "When we part ways and I go on with Damien, I need you to take this and go to Litlen. Get there, find my family, and tell them what's happened, then wait for me to come. Whatever you do, don't let anything happen to this."

Boone's eyes turned from the pouch to Mick. "I'm going with you. There's something real shady about Damien. You got me out of that dungeon. I'm not going to leave you with him on your own."

The coach started to slow.

Mick dumped the pouch, and the stone fell into his hand. Boone's eyes widened. "Is that the Wel—"

"Shh! Yes." Mick turned it between his fingers. The colour was off. A streak of black cut across a section, marring the beautiful blend of blue-green colours.

"Have you had that the whole time?" Boone squinted at it. "What's that on it there?"

It looked just like the mark on Mick's hand. He transferred the stone to his other hand so it rested on top of the blemished skin. Somehow, they were the same. How could the stone have been affected by his deal?

Boone pointed at Mick's hand and the stone, his jaw hanging open. "Is that from that?"

Mick didn't have an answer. The coach stopped. Quickly, he replaced the stone inside its pouch and stuffed it into Boone's hand.

"I don't have a good feeling either, but I'll feel a lot better knowing you're away from this. I don't know what to expect when I release Beiron. Go to Litlen, look for my family, and be discreet. There's a reason I grew up away from here."

"What reason?"

The door opened, and Damien grinned up at them. He clapped his hands. "All right. Time to send away the friend as per your terms." He addressed Boone. "We're far from Valmain now, so you should have no run-ins with Daegan's men. And if Litlen is your destination, it's quite the hike from here."

Boone stepped out of the coach first. "Where is here?"

They'd stopped on a dirt road filled with potholes, barely wide enough for two wagons to pass each other. The forest at their right extended all the way as far as the eye could see and cut across the road. Damien pointed.

"Southeast will take you to Veryl. Not much there to see unless you're interested in growing barley, potatoes, or corn." He pointed behind them. "Back that way, the nearest town north is Bendreir. If you continue from there, you'll either be heading toward Ferenth, Altrow, or the Gap, depending which way you go."

Boone squinted, looking in the direction Damien indicated. "I've never heard of the Gap. Where is that?"

"It's not so much a place as it is a route. An unofficial road. More like a rough trail between mountains. If you go that way, you'll eventually end up in Litlen, but know that there are a lot of crevices and cracks in the ground, and you'll have to cross the merging rivers. The bridge is in rough shape—has been for a long time. It's not a real road. If Litlen is your destination, I suggest taking the road through the Bludesel Mountains in the west—a nice and long journey."

After Damien had covered every direction, Mick looked around, trying to determine which way they'd be going.

Boone glanced at Mick, then asked Damien, "Which way are you going?" Apparently, he wondered the same thing.

Damien gestured to the woods. "Through there. The Hayat Forest."

Deciduous trees extended toward the sky. Thick branches full of bright green leaves blocked the sun. The rugged ground showed no signs of a path through.

"The forest?" Mick squinted, looking through the dense woods. There was little space for a horse, and no coach would make it past this point.

"My grandfather locked your friend in an enchanted prison in the forest?"

"The mountains beyond the forest," Damien said. "We're only passing through. Hope you enjoy walking because we're going on foot from now on."

Mick raised his brows in mock surprise. "Oh, are we walking? I thought we were going to fly."

Boone sniggered. "I don't know how you've managed to keep your face looking so pretty with that mouth of yours. I say one thing about anything, and I wind up with a broken nose." He indicated his nose to make his point.

Even if Mick had received such treatment for his lack of caution, his healing magic would have erased all evidence of violence. But Boone did make a good point. Mick needed to watch himself if he was going to keep his magic a secret.

Or so he kept telling himself. How he'd managed this long was a wonder.

Damien parked the coach off the road on the opposite side of the forest. He unhitched the horses and released them. They didn't go right away, so he gave one of them a smack to the rear to get it going and the other followed.

He grabbed his coat from the driver's seat and brushed off the grass and hay. "I don't have time to just stand around. Mick, let's go. You"—he jabbed his finger in Boone's face—"go back to wherever you came from. Xihngrahv, I suspect by your accent. You've no business being in Kartha. Go back to your fancy houses and grand dinner parties."

Boone glared at him. He shifted on the balls of his feet. His last attempt at a fight didn't go so well for him, and Mick didn't want to have to heal him in front of Damien. He cleared his throat. "Boone, what we talked about— can you do that for me?"

Boone paused. A moment later, his shoulders sank and he nodded. "I will. Hurry up. And be careful." He turned and only then seemed to realize the horses were gone. He chuckled under his breath and hung his head. "The horses." He turned to Damien. "You couldn't have just left me one?"

"Enjoy your walk." Damien turned on his heel and pushed Mick in the direction they were to go.

Mick staggered, his feet taking exaggerated steps until he found his balance, then he stumbled as he stepped into the forest. He paid attention to where he placed his feet so as not to trip over fallen dead trees, branches, or raised roots. When he glanced back at the road, he caught sight of Boone, walking on his own in the direction that led to Bendreir.

Mick trudged on. He chided himself for not taking a nap in the coach when he'd had the chance. With nothing but trees and mountains ahead, and the fading light above, the journey from here on suddenly seemed much more tiresome.

He slowed his steps. Maybe if he stalled long enough, he could give Boone a head start. Damien's efforts to deter Boone from getting to Litlen in time made Mick want to slow them down all the more.

Sunlight no longer streamed through the dense branches, and the road was no longer visible behind them. The deeper they walked into the woods, the stronger the scent of leaves and decaying logs. Mick found a stump and sat. "I need a few minutes to rest. You don't happen to have proper food, do you? Or do you hunt? I'm a cook, you know. I can make something decent that will actually fill us up, unlike that pitiful breakfast this morning."

Damien popped a piece of dried meat into his mouth and chewed slowly. "Get up. We're not stopping."

"I've not had a real meal for a long while. I'm tired and hungry. Ease up. It'll just be a short rest." Mick showed him the black streak on his hand. "It's not like I'm going anywhere."

Damien grabbed a fistful of Mick's hair and hauled him to his feet. He drew Mick close enough to his face that Mick got a whiff of his beefy breath.

"I am this close to seeing Beiron after nearly a hundred and fifty years. I will drag you the rest of the way if you don't pick up your feet and walk." He propelled Mick forward.

Mick stumbled, then regained his footing and smoothed his hair back. "Dragging me will take longer. You still want to make that threat?"

Damien flicked his fingers in the air as if he were flicking a bug. Blue light sparked out from his fingers—like lightning—and it zapped Mick's foot. The shock stung Mick and sent a jolt of pain from his toes all the way up his legs and throughout his body. Damien flicked again, and his light hit Mick's other foot. Mick's body tingled from the second jolt. He lifted his feet to dodge the next three flicks, laughing all the while. Nothing about this was funny, but it was either that or bark at him to stop.

*Not a chance.*

Damien struck again using both hands, and the electric jolt hit Mick's kneecap. Mick fell to his knees and hands. Another shock struck his shoulder.

Mick raised a hand quickly. "Okay, okay, stop. Stop…" He got to his feet and brushed leaves from his clothes. If Mick really could do that kind of magic, he'd have to learn that little trick and return the gesture.

His nerves still trembled. "No rest. I get it."

Damien straightened his coat and signalled for him to walk. "Glad we could come to an understanding."

# Chapter 20

Mick craned his neck to take in the sight before him. The rock-face at the edge of the forest stood vertically as if confined by an invisible force where the trees ended. A narrow trail opened up through the wall where it split, allowing entry through the pass. The opening was the only way into the mountains without having to climb.

Mick entered the pass first, and the walls rose high on either side. They left behind the forest scents, replaced by the scent of damp rock and freshwater streams. Damien strode over to walk beside him. The rough stone of the corridor-like passage cast shadows in the little daylight that remained.

Damien gave Mick a sideways glance and smirked. *"Truiy."* A blue sphere of light appeared above his hand.

Mick gave him a quizzical look. *"Truiy?"*

*"Loyal."*

"Why'd you say it?"

"It's called a trigger. It helps with control. Every Elderace has their own, and not everyone's is a word." Damien's light glowed like a beacon in the night. He lifted his hand, and the light bobbed above his head, lighting the way. He lowered his hand.

"Do I have one?" Mick asked. There was no sense pretending he wasn't interested. Damien was freely offering information about magic.

"How should I know? I'm not even sure you count as Elderace. Beiron will be able to determine if you have magic."

Mick didn't bother clarifying that he did indeed have magic. He was more curious about Beiron and what he'd done that got him locked up in a magical prison.

"So Beiron… What's he like?"

A smile spread across Damien's face. "He's a visionary. Knows what he wants and doesn't let anything stand in his way. Soon, he'll rule in our country and set things right. You'll see."

"Set things right? How do you mean?"

"The mayanon were not blessed as the Elderace were. Gifted with magic and the heart of Kartha. It's time our people claimed what should have been ours since the beginning. Beiron's always understood this. And I'll be standing by his side when he takes the country and puts the mayanon in their place."

"Their place being…?"

"On their knees."

Mick's feet moved with ease along the smooth stone of the trail. "It seems to me you're grovelling at Beiron's feet. Is that your place?"

Damien chuckled. "You wait. The day will soon be here when you'll look up at me and see that I was right. And maybe as a reward for releasing him, Beiron will bestow upon you the honour of being his personal servant."

*Not likely.* If Mick's grandfather had locked Beiron away once, he could do it again. Evidently, Beiron wasn't as powerful as Damien believed him to be.

After some time, the path ascended out of the low valley and became more jagged. The looming mountains on either side levelled with the path, and the view opened to a vast range of mountains. The light over Damien lit only a small radius around them, but even in the dark, Mick could tell they were in the thick of it. Around them, in the distance, snow-capped peaks reflected natural light so that he could see some distance ahead by the light of the thin crescent moon. Mick drew his shirt closer to himself, wishing he had warmer clothes. Keeping at a brisk pace helped alleviate the chill.

Damien led Mick up a slope that veered away from the path. Mick stepped on a loose rock and tipped forward. He caught his fall with his hands. *No damage done.* While he wiped grit from his hands, Damien reached the peak. Mick hiked the last few feet and caught up to him.

The blue sphere of light remained the same distance above Damien's head. He pointed a finger, directing Mick's attention down the mountain, where still black water filled a small lake. The mountain opposite the lake went straight up with no obvious route in or out. Damien nodded toward the water. "This way." He waited for Mick to go first.

Mick took small steps down the slope. At about thirty paces down, he reached the shore. He crouched to feel the temperature of the water. A shiver ran down his spine—partly because of the cold, but it wasn't just that. It was as if touching the water opened his senses, alerting him to dangers here. The back of his neck prickled. Although he missed the stone's warmth against his leg, he was glad he'd had the foresight to send it with Boone. Something about this place… He wanted to run from here, but he felt drawn to the water at the same time, which in itself made him wary.

He turned to Damien. "There's nothing here."

Damien remained on the incline and didn't come any closer to the water. He crossed his arms. "I'll be waiting for you here."

*Waiting?* Mick glanced back at the lake. The water rippled. He took a step away. "What is—?"

A vine burst out of the water. His eyes grew, and he turned to run.

The thick vine flung toward him from behind. His feet skidded on the slippery rocks, slowing him down. He'd made it a few feet from Damien when the vine caught him around the waist and squeezed, pulling him backward toward the lake. Mick fell onto his backside and gasped in a strained breath. He clawed at the vine. More strands slithered along the lake's surface, moving like snakes toward him while the one clutching him reeled him along the ground, the rough surface scraping through his clothes.

Mick toppled onto his side and tried to pry his fingers between the vine and his body. It did no good. Rocks dug into his arms and stomach as the thing continued to pull him closer to the water, until he was inches from the shore.

The pressure around his torso tightened, and he could hardly breathe. A sharp rock jutted out from the ground nearby. Mick grasped it and held on with everything he had.

Damien hadn't moved from his place on the incline.

Mick groaned. His muscles shook, fighting against the pulling of the vine. "Help! Damien, help me!"

"A word of advice to you, kid: hold your breath." He waved good-bye.

Mick gritted his teeth and cried out when he couldn't bear the pressure. Another vine crept up his back and tangled itself around his shoulders and neck. With all his strength and efforts gone into keeping himself from taking a cold plunge into the lake, he could do nothing to stop them from twisting around his body.

He wanted to scream at Damien, but holding on required all his focus. Whispers of wind blew around him, brushing against his ears. Their indistinguishable words chittered noisily as his hair was blown about. Although the words were unclear, they were there nonetheless. Like magic.

Magic!

Mick would need his hands to attempt to use magic, but if he let go, nothing prevented his going in the water.

A vine at his neck looped around twice. His options were dwindling. He could let go and drown, or hang on and suffocate. Or he could try and use his magic. *Not very good odds.*

The vine around his neck tightened. With little time to decide, he panicked and let go of the jutting rock. Already so close to the shore, water seeped through his clothes at the edge of the lake. He grabbed the vine at his neck and drew from the same power he used for healing, but instead of focusing on healing, he tried to imagine the vine letting go.

His magic flowed from his heart and extended out through his fingertips. The vine loosened. He breathed a little easier as it fell away. *That wasn't so bad.* If he'd gotten one vine, he could get the others. He'd hardly noticed that he was up to his chest in the cold water.

He raised his chin to take a deep breath as his head became submerged. For him to get free of this, he'd need to remain calm. The vine dragged him toward the bottom of the lake.

Mick touched the vine around his chest next, prepared to do the same as he'd done to the other one. The vine, as though it sensed what he was doing, squeezed, and air escaped his lungs.

The light from above didn't reach him at the bottom of the lake. Vibrations shook the water, and a cloud of smoky water plumed up from the base of the mountain, where a cave opening appeared. Mick closed his eyes against his distorted vision. His chest burned.

The vine pulled him through the opening. Complete darkness loomed behind his closed eyes, and an ache throbbed in his ears as the underwater pressure increased.

He opened his eyes, squinting in the water. The vibrations returned and another cloud of smoke prevented him from seeing anything.

Panic swelled in him, impossible to dispel. He reached an arm out to feel his surroundings. All he felt was the rough edge of rock. Walls surrounded him as he was dragged farther into the mountain.

His body glided around a bend.

He needed to try again. He placed his hands on the vine and focused on his magic.

His head collided with the ceiling and all thought disappeared.

# Chapter 21

Mick turned over onto his side and spewed water. He choked and gasped for what felt like an eternity, until he could finally draw a full breath again. And then another. His chest burned. He pressed his hand to his chest to feel his racing heart.

An ache in his head started over his eyes and around his ears. Everything hurt. He lay on his back and stared up into the darkness. The air was dank. Earthy smells filled his nostrils, and the hard surface upon which he rested was uneven and rough.

Exhaustion weighed down on him. He closed his eyes and lay still, listening. There was no difference between his eyes being open or closed. He focused on his fingers, pressing them into the ground to orient himself.

The ground felt rough and hard. Like rock. The last thing he remembered was being dragged into the mountain before passing out. He was likely in some sort of cave chamber within the mountain. If that were so, there might be a way out besides the way he'd come in.

His whole body itched internally, which signalled that his healing ability had kicked in. Already, he felt much better, apart from the fact that he couldn't satiate the itchiness. His head still throbbed, but his muscles had regained some strength.

A blue light flared next to him, temporarily blinding him. He squinted and raised a hand to shade his eyes from the light. A figure crouched over his supine body. Mick gasped. He scurried away on his elbows and feet until a wall stopped him from going any farther.

His eyes soon adjusted to the light, and he was able to see his surroundings. He risked tearing his gaze from the stranger to get a good look at where he was.

The blue light was like Damien's. It had a strange glow, and it rested upon the man's upturned hand. He nudged it upward, and the light rose until it was above his head, where it stopped. It radiated around them, illuminating the chamber, which was circular and had a round ledged pool at the centre. The pool was surrounded by six stone chairs, facing inward, and water dripped into it in a steady flow from the ceiling. A pile of broken vines and twigs sat on the opposite side of the chamber.

The man stood at his full height, towering over Mick. He seemed like a giant in this small space. His light stayed the same distance from his head even with the smallest movement. His black scraggly hair reached past his shoulders, and somewhere beneath all that beard, Mick was sure there was a face. The man pierced Mick with his startling black eyes, his irises as black as the pupils they enclosed.

"Are you Beiron?" Mick's voice was hoarse. He used the wall behind him to help himself stand, and he flattened his body against it. A few paces away, a threshold was impossibly barricaded by a sheet of water, held back by some unseen force.

The man approached Mick and stopped directly in front of him. Of all things, Mick worried about getting a crick in his neck from having to gaze up at the beast. He slackened his shoulders and tried to see around him.

Where was the way out of this place?

depth. Mick figured that if he stretched his arm out over the ledge, he'd be able to just reach the trickling water with the tips of his fingers.

"Give me your hand." Beiron held his hand out for Mick's.

Mick tensed, and he took a step away. "I hardly think it's appropriate. We only just met." He forced a smirk.

"You want to get out of here, don't you?"

"Yes. But what do you want my hand for?"

"I need your blood."

And risk Beiron seeing his healing power firsthand? Mick shook his head. "I'll do it. Give me your knife." He gestured to the knife tucked in Beiron's belt. Its plain wooden handle was chipped on one corner.

In a swift motion, Beiron snatched Mick's hand.

"Hey, let go! Get off me!" Mick yanked his arm, but Beiron's strength proved to be greater than his own.

Beiron linked his arm with Mick's to hold him steady. His broad shoulders blocked Mick's view of his own hand.

Beiron drew the knife from his belt. "It'll give me great satisfaction to cut into the flesh of a Dairner." He paused, then tapped the flat part of the blade against the black mark on Mick's hand. "This have anything to do with me?" His lips turned up in a crooked sneer.

Mick winced as he felt the blade cut into his palm. Beiron stretched Mick's arm over the water. With his thumb, he extended Mick's hand out, palm down.

The cut had already started to heal. Mick strained his neck as he tried to look past Beiron. Seconds passed, and Beiron said nothing. Mick didn't know if the strange man had noticed the now totally healed cut on his hand.

The trickle of flowing water slowed. It grew quieter until it ceased dripping from the ceiling. Mick wrenched his arm free, and Beiron stared with his jaw agape—not at Mick's hand, but at the rippling water as the last drops fell.

The cut on Mick's hand was gone, and with it went the mark from Mick's deal with Damien. It stung for a moment before it faded completely.

Mick took a deep breath and released it. He'd done it. He'd fulfilled his part of the deal.

A tremor shook the cave, and where the water had once trickled down, it now flowed in reverse. A small stream began rising up from the pool's centre. The water flowed up into the ceiling from where it had come from moments ago. Mick was more concerned about the surprise on Beiron's face than he was about the change in gravity. He took a few steps backward, then stopped when the sound of rushing water drew his attention to the threshold, where the wall of water receded.

Amid the sounds of trickling, rushing, and dripping water—leaking from the cave walls, onto the floor—Mick heard the same whispers he'd heard in the wind. The indecipherable voices became clearer. A multitude of soft voices echoed in his mind, speaking all at once and saying different things, but one word repeated several times, standing out among the others: *Theranol.*

*Whatever that was.*

Beiron slowly twisted around to face Mick. His dark eyes bore into him. Could he hear the whispers too? Beiron had the bearings of a man who knew he intimidated others easily. Mick often found himself in the presence of men like this. Riggs for one. How was Beiron any different from him? The man was mistaken if he expected Mick to cower. Instead, he returned the stare.

As far as Mick knew, his secret was still safe. He had only to leave this cave, and he wouldn't have to endure Beiron's company beyond this.

Beiron nodded at the threshold. Mick blinked, not understanding. The water was gone from the threshold, and the way was now clear for them to leave. Beiron walked to Mick, his light trailing wherever he went. He stopped inches from his face. The chair at Mick's back prevented him from backing away any farther. Beiron's lips slowly grew into a grin. "Follow." He turned and disappeared into the tunnel.

As much as Mick wanted to defy the presumptuous command and get far away from the man, he didn't know the way out, nor did he want to stay there in case the water wall should return, trapping him inside on his own.

He treaded slowly after Beiron, maintaining his distance from him. Only a little while longer and he'd be through with him and Damien, and be on his way to Litlen.

# Chapter 22

The blue light followed Beiron's movement, always staying ahead and above him. The bends and turns in the tunnels were too many, and Mick had lost track of which way they'd gone. Beiron confidently led on through the many twists on their way out. None of this was familiar to Mick. But he supposed he'd been unconscious when the Anguivina had dragged him through the dark water.

After yet another turn, they came to a long stretch where the dim natural light of night was visible ahead, coming from outside. They closed the distance and emerged from the cave to the same place where the lake had once been, though now all that remained was wet rock.

Damien greeted Beiron with arms extended and a smile spread across his face.

"Damien," Beiron said, accepting the embrace. "What hole did you crawl out of?"

"The same one as you, my friend. Much has changed since we last saw each other."

Together, their lights lit up the area in bright blue. The spot they stood in looked different without the lake. The ground was shiny from the receded water, and small puddles remained where water had pooled.

"Yes, it has." Beiron glanced around. "Where have you been?"

Damien's face drooped. "I regret my absence when you needed me. After Litlen was cursed and Landon's soldiers tromped through what little remained of our home, when our magic was gone, I feared the war was lost, so I fled. I later returned and searched for you, but when you were nowhere to be found, I'd assumed the worst. By the time I'd heard about the brothers and the reawakening of Litlen, I was too late to come to your aid. But I'm here now. I have brought you the grandson to give you your freedom, and I am at your service from here on out.

Beiron glanced at Mick. "Grandson? How long have I been in that cave?"

"Forty-three years," Damien said.

"Forty-three years?" Mick echoed. That explained Beiron's odd mannerisms. Or was he always like that? "How? How did you survive that long with no food?" He almost added *or water*, but he supposed that particular necessity had been provided in ample volume.

"The Pool of Sovereignty has sustained me," Beiron said. "My captivity in there felt like a long time, but not forty-three years long. Still, I have missed the taste of food."

Damien nodded. "We'll get you some. Now that you have your freedom, which way are we heading?"

Mick raised a hand. "Damien, our deal?"

Damien paused. He squinted as though in thought, then his face lit up. "Ah, right. Yes, you've done well. I release you."

Beiron pointed at Mick's hand. "So that was about me. What did you get out of the deal?"

"My freedom," Mick said. "You have yours; now I have mine. I'll be on my way. Goodbye, gentlemen. I hope we never meet again." He turned to make his way up the mountain. A tug on his shirt pulled him back.

Mick spun around and swung an arm. He half expected this. His hand made contact with Beiron's face.

Beiron scowled. He grabbed Mick's arm, twisting it at an unnatural angle. He leaned closer to him. "Damien may be finished with you, but I'm not."

Sweat beaded on the back of Mick's neck. "This wasn't part of the deal."

"Yours and Damien's deal. Not mine."

Mick squirmed. "Damien, we agreed I would go free."

"No, no," Damien said. "If you remember, I said I'd have no more use for you after Beiron was free. And that's true. I don't need you anymore. You and I are finished. Isn't that what you said?" He showed Mick his hand. It was clear of any blemish. Just like Mick's mark had healed, so had Damien's. "However," he went on, "if Beiron's decided he has some use for you, that's up to him. As you've heard, I'm at his service."

Mick's stomach churned. He tugged against Beiron's grasp, but Beiron held fast. Mick tried again, but failed. He was stuck out here in the middle of the mountains in the dark with only these two. Besides being outnumbered, where could he run to? The mountains stretched a great distance. And he hated to think what kinds of creatures lurked in them, hunting for easy prey. He'd have to play this smart.

He gave up trying to break free of Beiron's grasp.

"What do you want?" Mick asked.

Beiron asked Damien, "Do you have a jar or container?"

Damien produced a canteen. "Just this."

"That'll do. Do you remember the way to the Sacred Room?"

"I think so."

"Good. Go back into the cave and fill it with water from the Pool of Sovereignty. It's disappearing fast, and I'm not leaving this place without water from there. When I was here last, I left a few things up that way, near Deepshadow Valley." Beiron indicated somewhere over the peak. "Meet us there when you're done."

"Will you be all right here?"

Beiron gave Mick's arm a hard twist. Mick bit his cheeks and refrained from crying out.

"I'll be just fine," Beiron said. "Go on."

Damien ran into the cave, taking his magic light with him. Beiron released Mick and shoved him. "Walk."

Mick did so. They hiked to the peak and continued in the opposite direction from the pass. Even with Beiron's light illuminating the ground, Mick stumbled along the uneven mountainside. The farther they went, the more lost he felt.

"Is this going to take long?" Mick asked. "I have somewhere I need to be."

"Forget about your plans. I didn't spend all that time imprisoned in a cave to just let everything go unresolved. Raidan and I have unfinished business. You can go when I have him."

"I think all that time to yourself has gotten to you. Didn't I tell you to see someone about that?"

An electric jolt zapped Mick in the back, and he yelped more from surprise than pain. Beiron grabbed Mick's shoulder and propelled him forward. "You're not going anywhere until I have Raidan's blood. And even after that, we'll see. I could have a lot of fun using you for an experiment."

"I hope it involves food. I'm great at food experimentation."

"Shut your mouth."

"Only when I'm chewing."

Beiron grabbed Mick by his scalp and yanked hard. Mick cried out, but then Beiron squeezed his jaw, pinching his chin painfully. "You're done talking now. Understand?"

Mick's jawbone felt as though it might snap any moment. Unable to nod, he blinked his understanding.

Agreeing to release Beiron might have been the wrong call.

But then he'd still be sitting in a dungeon, awaiting Ighur and the prospect of being sold as a slave.

Beiron released Mick forcefully. He pushed him to keep walking.

Mick massaged his jaw and noted the direction they were going. If he acted soon, he might still be able to find his way back. Beiron had been in a cave for more than forty years. His legs wouldn't be able to keep up with Mick once he'd gotten some ground to make a good run for it. And Mick would wager that Beiron's size would slow him down on this uneven surface.

They descended a steep slope and made it to the bottom of a dark narrow valley. The tall peaks surrounding them would leave little room for sunlight to reach during the day. Mick supposed that was where the name Deepshadow Valley came from.

Beiron shoved Mick again. Then he kicked the back of his knees. Mick fell forward, slamming his kneecap against the mountainside. A burst of pain shot up his leg, and he groaned.

Beiron clutched the nape of Mick's neck and squeezed. "Don't move."

He elbowed Mick in the back, sending a shock up his spine, then he grabbed Mick's feet and pulled his legs out from under him, knocking him flat on his stomach. Mick bit his tongue and tasted blood. He squirmed onto his side and curled into himself.

A boulder beside him rocked in its place. It was bigger than Beiron, and would easily crush Mick if it fell on him. Mick threw his hands up protectively, as if his hands would stop the thing from landing on him. The boulder wobbled but didn't fall.

Beiron raised his arms, and the boulder followed his motion. It raised an inch off the ground, and he moved it by waving his arms, directing it to drop a few feet away from where it had been. The removal of the boulder revealed a hollow space in the mountain. Mick stared at the boulder, awed that Beiron had moved it with such ease.

Beiron bent under the hollowed shelf and reemerged with a bag in hand. "You look like you've never seen magic before."

Mick shut his mouth, annoyed that his face betrayed his surprise. He got to his feet and brushed off his trousers, doing a poor job at feigning pain. Beiron took no notice. He opened the flap of his bag and rummaged around inside, withdrew a neatly wound long rope, and took an end, letting the rest fall loosely to the ground.

Mick raised his eyebrows, understanding Beiron's intention. "Have I given you reason to think you'll need that?"

"Give me your hands."

This would make running a little more difficult. Mick scratched his bristly face. "Can we not?"

Beiron feinted with a flick of his hand.

Mick threw his hands up. "All right, all right. Here." He may as well save himself from another beating. Beiron efficiently bound Mick's wrists together. By the way he knotted the rope, Mick got the impression he'd done this before. Beiron gave the rope a last pull, and it pinched. Mick pressed his lips together and managed not to wince. The end of the rope dangled down to his knees.

When he was finished, Beiron closed his bag and tossed it aside.

Mick raised his bound hands and scratched his nose. "I can't imagine what kind of threat I was before. You must feel so much better now."

Beiron turned his head as if searching for something. His eyes fell on the shelf in the mountain. He gestured to the opening beneath the ledge. "Get in there."

Mick looked at the hole. It looked like a small child might fit but not him.

"I won't fit in there."

"You'd be amazed at how small you could make yourself. Get in."

"You really are insane. I'm not going in there. You've got me. I'm here. I'm bound. I'm yours. What are we even doing?"

"There's someone I need to see. You're going to get in there so I don't have to worry about you taking off."

"You think I know my way out of these mountains? If I run, I'll just get lost. You don't have to worry about me leaving."

Beiron grabbed the loose hanging rope and wrenched Mick's arms so they stood face to face. "I won't say it again."

Mick glared at him. Soon, Beiron would go see whomever he needed to see, and Mick could figure out a way to escape. He wasn't going to let his restrained hands or being stuffed inside a hole in the mountain stop him. Sure, it might slow him down, but he'd make his escape.

He relented and crouched slowly, holding his hands out in front of himself for balance. The hole was wider at the mouth of the opening. The deeper it went, the narrower it became. Mick considered the best way to fit himself inside. He lowered himself onto his knees and shambled in, backside first. He lay on his side, facing out, and wriggled himself into the mountain. Beiron kicked him in the stomach, shoving him in completely. Instinctively, Mick curled his arms and legs into himself. He struggled to move and get his elbows underneath his body. A sharp rock jabbed into his back, and he squirmed as best he could to get off it. It didn't work, so he tried to scoot forward to readjust his position.

Beiron lifted the loose rope and pulled Mick's arms out from under him. He held up the rope, making Mick's hands dangle. The boulder that he'd moved aside moments ago rocked again. Grit crunched against grit as the massive chunk of mountain floated over to cover the opening.

Now Mick understood his cage. The boulder would be impossible to move without at least a dozen men. Or magic. It hovered over Mick's hands. With quick reflexes, he jerked against the taut rope and got his hands out of the way before the boulder came down. They'd have been crushed if he hadn't moved. The boulder did crush the rope, however, and his hands were stuck in place with no give.

Only a sliver of light came in through a tiny crack between the mountain and the boulder. Mick, crammed tight, could barely move at all. He could hear Beiron's voice outside the hole.

"Don't go anywhere. This will only take a moment."

# Chapter 23

A chill crept down Laila's spine. Her hand stopped midway to Vis's reins as she was getting ready to mount. She'd gotten as far as Nivit, a quaint village on the way to Valmain, and stopped to rest and water her horse.

The hair on her arm raised.

*It can't be.* That feeling—it'd been forty-three years since she'd had this sense.

Beiron's voice broke through the quiet, accompanied by his presence, though not in the flesh. "Travelling?"

Laila drew in a sharp breath. How could he be here now? Her mouth went dry and the word to make him go was on the tip of her tongue.

"Well," Beiron said, "aren't you going to say hello to your father? It's been a long time. I've missed our chats. You look different. Older."

More grown up, she hoped, since the last time they'd seen each other. She wasn't the same naïve girl he'd met back then.

"Laila… Look at me." He sounded like he was somewhere close to her left. Her eyes went unfocused, staring at Vis's shining black coat.

With him not being there physically, the only way for her to see him would be if she spoke the words to reveal him. After he'd told her of their relation, it had taken her years to get over the fact that he was her father. She'd spent many of those years trying to prove to herself that she was nothing like him, that she'd never be anything like him. Their shared interest in botany and remedies—her mother had that in common too—it had nothing to do with *him*.

A part of her always feared he'd be back, but as time went on, she'd allowed herself to believe he was truly gone. This could *not* be happening again. If he was able to connect with her after all this time, that must mean he'd been set free. With Mick's recent arrival, it wasn't much of a mystery to solve who'd freed him. The question was: How? Or why? And how could Mick have known about him?

*Okay, so more than one question.*

Try as she might to hide her unease, she was sure her face glistened with fresh perspiration. Beiron's voice stirred the hatred she thought she'd buried long ago.

"Come now." Beiron sounded like he'd moved to stand directly behind her. "It hasn't been so long that you've forgotten the words, has it?"

Not for the first time, she considered hitting him, but if she did, would he feel it?

His voice became terse. "I said look at me."

Vis twisted his head to hers and nudged her, sensing her tension. In past encounters like this, only she could sense Beiron. Unless her horse was somehow attuned to their connection, Laila was sure Vis didn't know he was there. She stroked his neck.

"All those times you came to me," Beiron said. "I answered every question you had. I don't ask for much in return. Only that you look—at—me."

"I never came to you." Her obstinate wall came down. "Not on purpose and you know it."

"But you did ask your questions. And I answered."

She bit her tongue. She shouldn't have engaged in conversation. Why did she say anything at all?

Beiron was quiet, but his presence remained. He exhaled a long breath.

"Tell Raidan I have his grandson and that I want to make a trade. I seem to recall we had a similar arrangement once before? Did we not? Ah, yes, except it was the son for my book. Well, now, maybe I could have spared us all this wasted time if I'd just taken care of the child after all."

A small amount of pressure on her shoulder gave her a start. Even though he wasn't there physically, she felt his hand pressing down lightly.

"I don't regret my decision to make our deal," Beiron said. "I'm curious. What did you do with my book in the end?"

Laila stood quiet for a moment. She wished she could say she'd burned it, and then, for good measure, stamped on the ashes, but that would have been a lie. She still had his book tucked away in her office in Tsein.

She changed the subject. "Better not get too comfortable, Beiron. Your freedom won't last long."

Beiron was quiet.

The night was still and peaceful, save for the sound of rushing blood in her ears.

Had he gone? No, she still sensed him and his hand on her shoulder. If he was waiting for her to reveal him, he'd learn how stubborn she could be when she wanted to be. She steeled herself and held back the renewed emotions that arose with his return. She was not afraid of him.

◊

Under the mountain, contained in the small space, Mick could do nothing more than wriggle his hips. Every time he tried to move, the sharp rock poked into his side. He twisted his wrists and pulled, but the boulder on the rope restricted his mobility.

The small crack was not enough for him to see where Beiron had gone, and he didn't think he'd have a lot of time before Damien returned.

Riggs, Ighur, Daegan, Damien, and now Beiron. How did he manage to attract so much attention from dangerous and powerful adversaries?

He blew air up to move his hair out of his eyes. It was getting warm in this cramped hole. His hair stuck to the sweat on his forehead. What a ridiculous place to be trapped in.

The whispers from earlier gradually returned. Or were they ever gone to begin with? Now, hearing them again, Mick didn't think they'd actually stopped. But with all that had occupied his mind, he hadn't paid much attention.

They grew louder. A breeze drifted across his face, bringing with it a chorus of joined voices whispering loud in his ears. The breeze itself reaching him in here was baffling. There was that word again: Theranol. Apart from that, the words were jumbled and made no sense. The voices spoke in a language he didn't understand.

He closed his eyes, trying to block out the noise of them. He couldn't think clearly. They may as well have screamed for how distracting they were.

A sound like trickling water came from somewhere inside the mountain. Mick tried to twist his head around to find its source. That lake at the cave had vanished. Could it appear anywhere just as quickly? Like the magical barrier that could trap someone in a body of water that only his captor or their bloodline could break?

If that were the case, at least Ighur and Riggs would never find him. But then neither would anyone else. His breaths sounded loud in the small space.

From all he'd seen of magic so far, he thought he had some idea of what could be done with it. He'd seen the performers in Ferenth manipulate light, move fire and water, and create gusts of wind. So knowing that, how could he learn to harness the power and choose which element to use? Was there a way he could use his magic to attack Beiron and escape? Or could he somehow use it to get out of here before Beiron returned?

He closed his eyes and tuned out the voices that weren't helping. Focusing his thoughts on his centre, where he drew his magic from, he set his mind to first freeing his hands. At his core, it was as though he had a pool of power to draw from, like a well. He reached inward and accessed that power. There'd never been a time when he felt his reserve was low, but he'd also never had much opportunity to explore and learn his limitations. Nor did he know what kind of toll it would take if he drew power for anything other than healing. The only time he'd done something other than healing didn't count because he was positive he'd drowned then. That would take a toll on anyone—magical or not.

He twisted his wrists so his fingers could touch the rope. Drawing from his pool of power, he had no clear direction besides breaking the bonds, whatever that looked like. His eyes closed, he directed magic to his fingertips, and soon got a whiff of something burning. Then a cold sting burned on his wrists.

He gasped and pulled his wrists free. The end of the rope glowed red. In its light, he could see the insides of his wrists were black and burned.

He rubbed them, drawing a little extra power to accelerate the healing.

Now he had to find a way to move the boulder. His hands were loose, but his mobility remained limited. He placed his hands flat against the rock and pushed. It didn't budge. He pushed again and grunted with effort. The more he strained, the louder the voices grew.

"Aaargh!" He slammed his fist into the rock.

Mick was sure Beiron would take satisfaction knowing his trap was working if he'd heard the scream, wherever he was.

But everything Mick was trying *wasn't* working. Although he didn't think he could control his magic enough to move the boulder as Beiron had, he still had to try something. He flattened his palms against it once more, and this time he drew from his pool of power. He kept his eyes open in case he burned himself again. Not that he wouldn't heal, but it still wasn't a nice feeling.

His magic flowed from his centre and through his arms toward the rock. It didn't move, but the ground rumbled.

He stopped. If he kept going, he could bring the ledge down on top of himself. If he were anyone else, it might kill him. He took a few breaths and considered which was worse, getting crushed or simply leaving it. Getting crushed could lead Beiron and Damien to assume he was dead. In that case, they might leave him, which would allow Mick to reemerge when they had gone. He'd heal and get on with it, assuming he'd survive being crushed. On the other hand, he could just leave the boulder where it was and wait for an opportunity to escape from Beiron and Damien at a later time.

Better to take a chance now than risk an attempt to run and be chased. He let his magic rush from him into the boulder. The ground rumbled, and the boulder shook. Then, as if a gale swept through, his magic picked up the boulder and threw it into the mountains. Somewhere in the dark, the rock blasted against more rock and crashed.

Mick exhaled a sigh, thankful he'd not have to claw his way out of a rubble heap. He squirmed out of the hole.

Beiron was perched on a rounded boulder, rigid and unblinking. He seemed oblivious to everything around him. His eyes were pure white. The contrast from his usual dark eyes nearly made Mick yelp.

Mick leaned over and waved a hand in front of the man's face. No reaction. Good. He could have laughed out loud at his jumpiness.

He rolled his shoulders and headed up the mountain. He just had to get clear of this area and the cave, then at the pass, he could run back the way he knew to go. That way, he'd avoid getting lost. He could take the road to Bendreir as Boone had done, and make his way to Litlen, meet up with Boone and warn his family about Beiron.

At the top of the mountain, he squinted in the dark, scanning the area for Damien. Having a light of his own would be useful, but that would draw attention. He descended the peak as quietly as he could and slowed his pace while he passed the slope where, just on the other side, lay the cave. If Damien were over there, Mick expected he'd have his blue sphere of light lit. With nothing in sight, Mick crept along the rocky ground, slanting along the slope to make his way back to the pass and the trail that would take him out of these mountains.

He froze at the distinct sound of a pebble tumbling against the rocks. The pebble stopped at his feet. To his left, a few feet away and on the incline, Damien's figure lurked in shadow. He must have been trying to keep quiet and sneak until he was all the way down, but now that he'd been spotted, he bounded from his place.

Mick turned to run. Damien gained on him, then leapt and landed almost on top of him, catching his legs and knocking him to the ground. Mick threw his hands in front of himself to catch his fall and avoid a face plant. He pushed himself up and twisted his hips to shake Damien of, which turned out to be difficult while he gripped Mick's shins, grunting.

Mick managed to pull a leg free and kick Damien, making him let go. Legs free, he sprang to his feet and stumbled away. He got a bit of momentum, then weaved around the jagged rocks, tripping and stumbling as he went. The way to the pass wasn't far. If he could make it there, he could gain more speed on the path and outrun him.

His foot landed in a crevice, and his ankle twisted. He held back a cry. There was no time to stop now. He got back on his feet and hobbled a little farther.

Damien strode across the uneven surface as if he'd done it a million times. Mick's healing worked slow while he put more pressure on his ankle. If he were going to make a proper run for it, he'd need to give it a minute to heal properly. He stopped and turned around, stretching out his hand to ward off his approaching pursuer.

Words usually came a lot quicker to Mick, but he was having difficulty coming up with something to say that might convince Damien to let him go. He took a few breaths and let his heart rate slow.

Damien came closer.

Mick threw his hands up. "Stop, stop… Just… Give me a second!"

Damien flung Mick's arm out of his way. He ducked, dodging Mick's punch, and countered with a quick jab to Mick's stomach. Mick doubled over, coughing. Damien grabbed Mick's hair and yanked him up straight.

He seized his hand and twisted it so that it hurt to try pulling it away. Mick clenched his teeth, trying to hide how much it hurt.

Having control over Mick's movement, Damien steered him back toward where he'd left Beiron.

Mick tripped as he tried to resist but was forced to keep up. His ankle still ached, but only a little. "You knew he wouldn't let me go," he said as Damien guided him. "You twisted my words and agreed to my conditions, letting me believe I could go free. But you knew."

"I know how he thinks. I suspected he might've had use for you, so I kept my options open." Damien twisted Mick's wrist, reinforcing his control. "Beiron doesn't let opportunities go to waste."

He prodded Mick toward Deepshadow Valley, directing him up the mountain, then down into the darkened valley, where Beiron sat on the rounded boulder with his eyes white and unseeing.

They stopped, and Mick slumped his shoulders. After all that effort, he was right back where he started.

# Chapter 24

THE WEIGHT ON LAILA'S SHOULDER LET UP AS BEIRON REMOVED HIS HAND. She trembled all over and hoped it wasn't obvious to him.

"Did you hear me?" Laila forced all the confidence into her voice that she could muster. "I'm coming for you."

Beiron's whisper was right in her ear. "I'm counting on it. Be seeing you soon."

Laila felt his presence depart, and pools of tears welled in her eyes. To be sure he was gone she glanced around. "*Veralnin tushov.*" Her voice quivered.

Nothing happened. Beiron was gone.

That should have given her relief, but her hands still shook.

Beiron was back. She'd spent so much time trying to be free of him, even after she, Raidan, and Dimitri had left him in the cave. She had to warn her brother. Not being of his bloodline, Beiron wouldn't hesitate using Royl against her. He'd done it before.

And now she had to tell Raidan that Beiron had his grandson? Tears slipped down her cheeks. Much time had passed, and in that time, she'd encountered many dangers. Why should facing Beiron be any different?

She sniffed and wiped her face while straightening her drooped shoulders. Vis took a few steps backward, growing restless from having to remain in one place.

The cracked earth in Nivit seemed worse than it had been just yesterday when she rode through here. She steadied Vis and hoisted herself into her saddle.

Raidan had the country and the stone to consider. If he gave himself up to save Mick, Beiron would have all he needed to take the power of the Weldafire Stone, and Kartha would suffer for it.

As much as it pained her to keep this from Raidan, telling him could bring about the ruin of the only place she'd ever considered home.

She'd just have to find and rescue Mick and tell Raidan about it later, after his grandson was out of harm's way. Rescuing people was, after all, what she did best. Then once Mick was safe with her, she'd ensure that not even Governor Riggs could get to him. It'd be a win-win.

She nudged Vis into motion, back the way she'd come. It would do her good to bring Royl this time if she was going to purposely seek out Beiron. His keen senses and mastery in combat would come in handy. And he'd likely bring a company of Warriors to assist in the rescue. They'd arrest Beiron while they were at it.

Laila gripped the reins tighter. She dug her heels into Vis's sides, and he sped up.

◊

Damien pointed at Beiron. "What's wrong with him? Why's he like that?"

"I don't know," Mick said. "Look at him. Forty-three years in a cave, Damien. He's not right in the head. He said he had someone to see. I thought he'd taken off. Aren't you the one who's supposed to know how he thinks?"

"What? So he just left you here and trusted you to stay?"

Mick squirmed in Damien's hold. "No. He—"

Beiron blinked and his black irises returned. They glinted in his blue light hovering over his head. He looked from Mick to Damien. "What are you doing?"

Damien pushed Mick into the space between them. "I caught him trying to escape."

Mick massaged his shoulder. "Yeah, a real mountain lion you are."

Damien nodded at Beiron. "What was that all about? What were you doing?"

"Something I needed to check up on." Beiron cocked his head at Mick. "How did you escape?" He traipsed over to the hole and picked up the burned rope, then turned toward him, holding it up. "You did this?" He scanned around, probably wondering where his boulder of a door had gotten to. When he couldn't find it, he stomped over to Mick and started patting him down.

Mick jumped back. "Whoa! Hey! Get off."

Beiron pushed him into Damien, who held him in place. He continued to pat him down.

"What would I have that you want?" Mick thought he might know. The better question would have been: What made Beiron think he had the stone?

"You have magic." Beiron grabbed the front of Mick's shirt. His voice dropped low and became menacing. "How do you have magic? You're not Elderace."

From somewhere in the darkness, a strong gust of wind blew Mick's hair in front of his face. Beiron let go of his shirt and stumbled backward. His blue light flickered. He stiffened his shoulders. The air stilled, and the tension grew.

Damien created a fire-ball out of thin air. He whipped around and threw it into the darkness behind them like one would toss a ball. A shadow in the shape of a man dove and dodged the fire. Mick couldn't see who it was. The fire went out in a puff of black smoke.

Beiron grabbed Mick from behind and positioned the edge of his knife to his throat.

"That you, Raidan? Not another move, or he dies." He pushed the steel a little harder against Mick's flesh. Mick leaned back into Beiron, to keep the pressure off. He hoped Beiron was wrong about the shadow being Raidan. How could it be? Boone maybe? But that wasn't any better.

His heart sank when Raidan stepped into the blue light that rested over Beiron's head. He'd not seen his grandfather for nearly a year. For a second, he thought he was looking at his father. The two shared the same narrow shoulders. But Adefa had grown his beard out, while Cassian kept a clean shave.

"Adefa? How did you—?"

Beiron pressed the knife harder, and Mick stopped talking.

"I invited him," Beiron said.

Damien lit another fire-ball and held it poised to throw at Raidan. "That's close enough."

Raidan stopped about ten feet away, holding up his hands. "I never received an invite. Kartha's been uneasy, and the only one I could think of who could cause such agitation was you, so I followed my hunch."

Beiron secured his hold on Mick. "Good, then we'll waste no more time. Will the boy's blood do?"

Raidan's jaw twitched. Beiron gripped Mick tighter and angled his arm, readying his aim to slide the knife horizontally.

"It won't." Raidan's eyes locked on Mick's. "Dimitri and I are still bound to the stone. You don't need Mick. Let him go, Beiron. Please."

"I let your son go all those years ago, and it didn't go so well for me. I think I'll hang on to this one until I have the power of the Weldafire Stone. Besides, I'll need a test subject for when we're done."

"Beiron, it won't work for—"

"Enough." Beiron gestured to Damien. "Did you get what I asked for?"

Damien produced the canteen and held it up.

"Good," Beiron said. "Take your knife, draw blood from Raidan, and let some drip into the water."

Mick squirmed. Why was Adefa not fighting? He knew that even if Beiron cut him, he'd heal. "Adefa, it's okay. You don't have to—" He shut his mouth when Beiron shook him.

Raidan clenched and unclenched his fists. "We'll get you home, Mickey." He offered a hand to Damien.

Mick swallowed past the lump in his throat. *Or was that the blade?*

Damien sliced a cut in Raidan's palm. He held the canteen to it and a few drops of blood dripped into the water. The air had a sort of still but tense atmosphere with a silence that Mick had never heard before. The wind had died down, and even all the nightly sounds of critters in the dark were hushed. Damien sealed the canteen and took three steps back.

Beiron waved his free hand at Raidan. "Get on the ground. On your belly, slowly."

Raidan hesitated. He met Mick's eye for a second before lowering his gaze, then he complied, lowering himself down.

Beiron added, "Hands behind your back."

Raidan did as he was told.

Mick grasped Beiron's arm, trying to relieve some of the pressure of the knife held against his neck. Beiron's light flickered again, reminding Mick that he himself had magic too. He loosened his muscles and turned his thoughts to his well of power. If he thought of what he intended to do specifically, could he control it to do what he wanted? He could burn Beiron's arms and make him let him go. He hoped that would be enough for Adefa to get up and fight back.

Beiron moved the knife so the long edge was no longer against Mick's throat—the pointed end now poked upward under his chin.

"Whatever you're planning, stop."

Mick tilted his head back, stretching his neck. How did Beiron know he was planning anything?

Beiron nodded at Damien. "Get your knife and hold it to Raidan's spine at the base of his neck." To Raidan, he said, "If you so much as utter a sound, or if I feel even a slight change in the wind, I'll let him die. And then Damien will kill you after you watch the life bleed out from your grandson."

For all of the healing ability Mick had, the experience did not sound appealing to him.

Raidan raised his head. "Beiron, you don't understand. It won't work for you."

"I don't understand? I understand a lot more than you, *mayanon*. You had no right to the stone."

"If you do this, you won't just curse Litlen. This time, it'll be all of Kartha. Beiron, it didn't work last time, and it won't—"

"It didn't work because Adrik and Norick deceived me. I attempted to take it before having all six trace of elements. With only five, it failed. The curse was their doing, not mine."

"Are you willing to risk your country over your theory?"

"No more talking. We've done enough of that." Beiron nodded to Damien, who crouched over Raidan to do as he'd been told.

"Remember what I said," Beiron told Raidan. "Not even a moan." He leaned forward to whisper in Mick's ear. "Brace yourself."

Before Mick could learn what he was to brace himself for, Beiron removed the knife from his throat and plunged it into his abdomen. Mick opened his mouth but no sound came. Beiron let him go and he fell to his knees.

Mick barely touched the handle of the knife, and pain radiated from his stomach. Finally, his voice remembered what to do, and he cried out.

Raidan's face contorted in silent agony, in keeping to Beiron's demands. Damien pressed his knee on Raidan's back. Raidan writhed, not making a sound.

Beiron left Mick so he could walk over to Damien and retrieve the canteen. He uncapped the topper and swished the contents before raising it to his lips.

Then he drank.

# Chapter 25

The ground shook. It started out subtle, then grew into an earth-splitting quake. The noise of rumbling and breaking rocks cracked the sky. Mick balanced himself on all fours, straining through the pain in his gut. Raidan lay unmoving. Why wouldn't he fight? Mick hadn't noticed if he'd been hurt. He wanted to reach out to where he lay and extend his healing power, even though he knew it wouldn't work without contact.

He moaned. As long as this knife remained in him, his own wound couldn't heal. He needed to get it out, but the pain was unbearable. A crack like an explosion resonated throughout the mountains, and the ground split beneath Beiron's feet. He stepped aside.

The quaking felt like it would rumble on forever.

After what seemed an eternity, it ceased, and an eerie quiet lingered. The light hovering above Beiron flickered, and the blue hue glowed brighter, paler. Beiron closed his eyes and turned his face skyward. He sucked in a long breath through his nose, then settled his gaze on Mick. His lips spread wide in a full smile, and his brows arched downward. The blacks of his eyes shone in the near-white light.

On his hands and knees, Mick could barely hold himself up. It hurt too much to move, so he kept his head down, breathing through the pain of every shallow breath he took. Beiron planted his foot on Mick's shoulder, and he kicked, toppling him onto his side. Mick yowled. He curled his limbs in close to himself.

Beiron crouched beside him. He grabbed the handle of the knife. "No need to fret, kid. I'll take care of this for you."

Mick couldn't hold back his scream as Beiron slowly slipped the blade out. Blood spurted from the hole in his body. His eyelids drooped. He held his hand over the oozing blood pulsing out from him. His strength waned. He had to stay awake. Adefa needed him.

At the rate he was losing blood, he knew he didn't have much time. Weariness pulled him down. He couldn't heal fast enough and was aware that he was going to pass out.

Beiron moved Mick's hands aside and placed his own over the wound. "I'll have you fixed up in no time." He pressed down firmly and closed his eyes.

Whatever he was doing hurt worse than the knife had. Mick screamed until his throat was hoarse.

Beiron stopped what he was doing, and his forehead wrinkled. He lifted Mick's shirt, and his head jerked back. He narrowed his eyes and twisted his body to look back at Raidan, then he stood to his full height and stalked over to him. Raidan didn't stir. Beiron turned him over and patted his face. "Where is the stone?"

Mick replaced his hands over the wound. He focused on healing to gain enough strength so he could help his grandfather, but when he reached inward for his power, it burned. It was like the pool within him boiled. He tried again and stopped immediately when the feeling intensified. Why wasn't it working? He feared to try again, but he couldn't just do nothing.

Beiron hefted Raidan up and over his shoulder.

Darkness filled Mick's periphery. He could hardly see Damien approaching. His vision went in and out of focus.

Damien crouched next to him and looked at him with pity. "I guess Beiron doesn't need you anymore." He then left him there, walking after Beiron, who carried Raidan away.

Mick fought to keep his eyes open. A futile effort. His mind raced with thoughts of all that he hadn't done yet. Of his family—Adefa… What would happen to him? What would happen to any of them? Vidia, Aira, Boone, his parents…

Cold crept over him. He succumbed to uncontrollable shaking. It was too quiet out here on his own. And lonely. He was going to die alone on this mountain, and whatever purpose he'd had here was lost and gone.

He lay still, knowing his end had come. Would Riggs find a contact regardless of Mick's contribution? Would he go after his family?

Even now, while lying there dying, tears would not come. He had to heal. Why was his healing not working?

The ground felt cold beneath him, as though it, too, were draining of life. A growing dread concerning Kartha took root within his soul and drove him further into the abyss.

# Chapter 26

The earthquake had been like nothing Laila had felt before. Immediately after, she'd felt a surge of power that both exhilarated and frightened her. That had been hours ago. Now, she and Royl hiked the pass through the Teiry Mountains with a dozen Litlen Warriors. Speed overruled stealth at this point. Too much time had already been lost since her encounter with Beiron.

Their collectively joined lights made it easy to see in every direction, though Laila refrained from contributing hers to the mix. It no longer shone blue like the others and might incur questions she was not prepared to answer.

Several tremors followed the quake, some more severe than others. Royl led their party. He broke off his light from the others and veered from the pass to ascend at Hayat Point. Laila trailed behind him and stopped when she reached the peak. She'd promised herself she'd never come back here. Of all the treacherous places she'd been to and the dangers she'd regularly faced, this place represented everything she feared most.

As expected, the lake was gone and the mouth of the cave was open. She clutched an arm around her stomach.

Royl approached her, moving with a casual gait. The world could fall apart, and it still wouldn't inhibit his nonchalant mannerisms. He touched her arm. "Are you all right?" He pursed his lips. "You don't have to be here for this."

"Yes, I do. I'm fine." She needed to prove to herself that this place held no power over her. Goosebumps covered her arms beneath her blouse, and now that she was here, she was eager to speed this along. "Let's just find Mick and get out of here."

The Warriors spread out and searched the area. Some of them descended the slope toward the cave entrance. A few joined Royl to look elsewhere. One Warrior remained with Laila atop the mountain, while the rest scattered to where others were not already looking.

This was a waste of time. Beiron wasn't here. Too much time had passed. But he'd told her to send Raidan, so shouldn't he be here? Where was she supposed to send him? Or did Beiron know she wouldn't pass along his message?

She stared at a spot on the ground, hoping they wouldn't find Beiron out here. For as much as she wanted him captured, she didn't know if she was ready to face him again. Forty-three years wasn't enough time.

Royl's voice carried to her and the others, as he called from where he'd gone to search. Only the faint glow of blue light indicated his whereabouts. "Over here! Quick!"

Laila's heart jumped. She rushed down from Hayat Point and scrambled to the next slope, headed toward the light. The remaining Warriors followed after her. She nearly fell several times in her haste to reach Royl. At the bottom of a valley, Stefan—one of the Warriors—caught her arm as she tripped. He steadied her. Even at her full height, she had to look up at him to nod her thanks.

She ran to Royl, and her chest constricted when she saw whose body he was crouching over. Blood pooled under Mick's torso. She gasped and knelt by his side. His face was pale. She checked for a pulse in his neck and found one. A weak one, but that he had one at all was a relief.

*Why aren't you healing?* She peeled his eyelid back. His head jerked, and his eyes fluttered. He tried to move, but when he did, he cried out and grimaced. His head lolled back as he slipped into unconsciousness again.

"Is this who I think it is?" Royl asked.

Mick was the spitting image of his grandfather. Laila nodded slowly.

"Do you have something you can give him?"

Laila spotted the tear in Mick's shirt where it was the most bloodied. A knife lay on the ground nearby, covered in blood. It was the same knife Raidan had given her when they'd trapped Beiron in the cave forty-three years ago. The one Beiron had stolen from her. Her stomach was in knots.

She lifted Mick's shirt to see the wound. Charred skin had crusted around the bloodied spot where the knife had pierced. She lowered his shirt.

"I don't know what this is," she said. "He should be healing, but I can't tell if he is. I'm not sure if anything I have will help this."

Royl grabbed Mick's arm and lifted it over his shoulders. "We need to get him out of here." He then addressed the Warrior standing next to him. "Tilda, run ahead of us and find Adrik. Tell him to meet us at Raidan and Ida's home." To Laila, he said, "Go with her."

He beckoned to Stefan for help. Laila got out of the way as Stefan came around to grab Mick's other arm.

Wherever Beiron was, it wasn't here. Laila couldn't tear her gaze from Mick. What could have happened to prevent him from healing? Her light had changed. And although she felt the surge of power and was pretty sure she knew how she'd attained this new strength of magic in her blood, a part of her refused to believe it was true. Beiron couldn't have. How could he have stolen the power of the Weldafire Stone without Raidan?

The idea occurred to her to take a peek in on Beiron and see where he'd gotten to. She could determine his location and send the Warriors after him. Or ask him what he'd done. But that would require initiating a conversation with him.

"Laila, go!" Royl shouted, jarring her from her thoughts. He waved his arm, using his magic to manipulate the air to help lift Mick's weight.

She'd worry about the magic later. Laila jogged to catch up to Tilda. They ran all the way through the pass. Once they emerged into the fields outside of Litlen, they remounted their tethered horses and maintained a steady pace all the way to Adrik's house in the southern woods. When they knocked on his door, no one answered. They didn't have time to wait around, but if anyone could offer insight into Mick's condition, Adrik would be the one. Laila mentally prepared herself to wait until Adrik returned, while Tilda remounted her horse, looking ready to move on.

Laila opened her mouth to argue that they should wait, but a man came into view on the forest trail ahead. Adrik. Laila recognized his thick hair sticking out at all angles and his coppery skin. He rode his horse, muttering to himself not paying attention to his surroundings. When Tilda approached him atop her horse, he looked up, startled.

"Adrik," Tilda began, "your presence has been requested at the Dairner home immediately. We—"

"Turn around, Adrik," Laila cut in as she remounted Vis. They could fill him in on the way. "Raidan needs us."

His eyes widened. That was all it took for him to tug on his reins and turn his horse around. He picked up his pace while Laila and Tilda caught up and matched his speed.

"Where are you coming from anyway?" Laila asked once they were on the way. She'd never known him to venture far from home unless it was to see Raidan and Dimitri.

Adrik pouted, and his eyebrows curled downward. "The Gap." He'd lived most of his long life in Kartha, but a hint of his Reij accent remained. "It is just as I feared. I don't understand how, but it is as it was when Kartha was cursed, except much worse."

Laila tried to still her trembling fingers while she held on to Vis. That was what she was worried about. "What did you find at the Gap?"

Adrik's expression turned dark. "The ground has split."

Split? When Litlen had been cursed years ago, the ground had become broken up in and around the Gap, but now it was split? To what extent? Before she could ask, Adrik urged his horse to ride faster, putting a stop to any further conversation.

The rest of the journey passed quickly, and the three of them arrived at Raidan and Ida's house ahead of Royl and Stefan.

Laila opened the storm door and knocked on the interior one. She glanced at the glass ornament of the hands holding the stone above the door, then looked away. That wretched stone. She thought she might have some understanding of Raidan's sentiment.

Ida answered the door. Her white hair was pulled back into a loose braid, and her eyes were puffy and red. "Laila, you're back!" When she saw Tilda and Adrik were also there, she drew her eyebrows together. "What is it?"

Adrik barged past her, letting himself in. "Where is Raidan? I must speak to him."

Ida stepped aside to allow Laila and Tilda entry as well. "He's not home. What's happened? Please tell me the earthquake didn't have to do with him."

Adrik never could grasp the concept of compassion. He offered no comfort to Ida as he walked down the hall and popped his head into each room. "Where did he go? And where is Dimitri?"

Laila had an answer for that last question "Dimitri's gone to Iptin Province." She took Ida's hands in hers. "Ida, where did Raidan go?"

Ida's chin quivered. "He went into the mountains. He said something wasn't right, so he went to investigate. He and Dimitri have been so agitated lately. I told him he should wait so they could go together, but he didn't think this could wait, and he's not come home since. I'm worried about him."

Royl was going to be there any minute, and Laila thought it would be a good idea to warn Ida what was coming. "We were just there, and we didn't see him. But there's something you should know. It's about Mick. We found him in the mountains, and he's been hurt badly."

Ida's lips parted. Her eyes searched Laila's. "Mick? But…that's not possible. He's…" She glanced at Tilda, then back to Laila. Mick's healing ability wasn't common knowledge. Laila understood what she wasn't saying.

"I know, Ida. Royl and Stefan are bringing him here now."

Ida shook her head, and tears rolled down her cheeks. "No, he can't though. That's not possible."

"Ida." Laila opened her mouth, then closed it. Should she tell her the rest? She'd find out one way or another. It may as well come from her. She squeezed Ida's hands. "Beiron's back."

Ida's breath caught. Adrik clenched his jaw. Only Tilda was already aware of this bit of news. It wouldn't have been wise to send Warriors out in search of Mick without first informing them of the potential danger they were facing.

The front door creaked on its hinges. Tilda opened it wide for Royl to enter. In he came, carrying Mick in his arms, and Stefan followed in after. The other Warriors had likely been ordered to continue their search for Beiron.

Ida strode over to get a look at Mick, who was unconscious. His clothes were torn and covered in blood. She instructed Adrik to clear the table off so Royl could lay him there.

Laila had been with Ida through every major trial her family ever faced. The woman's strength was admirable. Though she'd been on the verge of tears only a moment ago, she jolted into action and buried her emotions so she could assess her grandson's condition. Laila joined her.

Royl used his knife to cut Mick's shirt off. Most of the damage Mick had sustained was on his stomach, near his side.

Ida snapped at Adrik. "Bring me some water and a cloth." He obeyed.

Laila tried to lift Mick to check his back. She struggled to move him gently on her own. "Help me get him onto his side."

Royl jumped to her aid.

Mick's back didn't look nearly as maimed as his front. The point of injury lined up with the spot on his abdomen, minus the black crusted skin that surrounded the wound. This confirmed Laila's initial thought that he'd been stabbed. But why hadn't he healed? And why did his skin look like that?

Adrik returned with a cloth and a bowl of water. Ida took it and started cleaning around the wound. Her gaze met Laila's. "Can you help him?"

Laila knew what she meant for her to do. She was no stranger to blood magic. Ida, like few others, believed it had its place and proved useful at times. Using blood magic now wouldn't heal Mick, but it would give them better insight into what they were dealing with.

She turned to Adrik. "Would you like to check?"

Adrik raised his hands. "You are better practiced than I am."

Unlike the elements, which could be manipulated from the exterior, blood had to be grasped from within. It needed to be controlled with care as it weaved through the heart, lungs, and veins to its intended place of use. Misuse could do serious harm both to her and Mick. It took skill to be able to manipulate your own blood flow and mingle it with someone else's.

She caught Royl watching her from the corner of her eye. Elder or not, he'd not disclose her use of the forbidden magic to the senior elders. Leaving Kartha had been Laila's way of spreading her wings and proving she could handle herself. But it was also her chance to get out from under the elders' constraints in their rules of the uses of magic and of her concoctions. Royl knew this. Informing them of her continued use of both would incur punishment, and neither she nor he wished to go down that road. Still, he'd never gotten over the fact that she'd freely use blood magic if a situation arose where it might serve their purpose. At the moment, he gave no objection.

"If something goes wrong," Laila said to Ida, "it could make things worse. Are you sure?" She said it even though she knew Ida was not unfamiliar with the dangers.

Ida didn't blink. "Do it."

*Okay.* Laila took a deep breath. She placed a hand flat on Mick's chest; closed her eyes, unifying mind, body, and spirit; and drew from the magic that resided deeper than her typical power.

Tilda gasped behind her. "But you can't—"

Adrik shushed her. "Do not distract her focus."

Laila's fingers tingled as they served as the connector from her to Mick and vice versa. She pressed her power into him to stir up his blood's movement and find the reason why he wasn't healing. While her magic worked its way closer to the wound, something deadly lingered within his body. She imagined inky black tendrils reaching up toward her as her magic inched closer to the injury. The substance made contact with her touch and stung her. She jerked her hand back, yelped, and clenched her hand into a fist.

"What was that?" Royl asked, reaching for her hand. She kept it close to herself and shook her head.

*What was that?* That was the same thing that had touched Kartha long ago. The curse that had left her home in a lifeless state for a century. That was death.

She met Ida's gaze. "He's dying."

# Chapter 27

Laila stepped outside, leaving Ida and Adrik to wrap up Mick's wound and clean him up. Tilda and Stefan exited a moment later. Tilda gave her a side-eye and attended to her horse. Royl would speak with her and Stefan later about Laila's meddling with forbidden magic, though Stefan was no stranger to her disregard for certain rules among their people. He approached Laila at the bench overlooking the cliff. "How are you holding up?"

The truth: not good. Beiron was free and now had the power of the Weldafire Stone. The last time he'd attempted to take it, he cursed all of Litlen. Now he had it, and Mick showed the same symptoms as the once cursed Litlen had. She shuddered to think what would happen if Beiron tried to use the power of the stone. Or had he tried already? Could that have been what happened to Mick?

Although Laila had known Stefan a long time, she'd never shared her relation to Beiron with him or anyone else aside from Royl, Dimitri, Raidan, Ida, and Adrik.

Her worry for Raidan grew.

She assumed Stefan's question referred to her use of blood magic and not the fact that Beiron was at large. "I'll be all right," she said. "I just wish I knew how to help Mick."

Stefan nodded. "Me too. But if I know you, Laila, you'll figure something out. You always do."

The wind off the sea gusted, carrying with it a fresh salty fragrance. Laila rubbed her arms where goosebumps still prickled under her long sleeves. "It would help if we knew where Raidan was."

Stefan nodded. He touched her back, between her shoulder blades. "We'll do what we can to find him." He made his way to his horse, where Tilda waited for him, ready to go. He mounted. "Someone will come as soon as we have news."

He and Tilda rode off.

Laila shivered, chilled by the breeze, but she wasn't ready to go back inside yet. She rubbed her shoulders and sat on the bench.

She'd not heard Adrik come outside. He came around and took the seat beside her. "I take it Beiron has come to you," he said.

Laila let out a soft laugh despite her tension. Always right to the point. She'd sought Adrik's help years ago to help sever the connection she shared with Beiron, but Adrik admitted it was beyond his understanding. Needless to say, he couldn't help her. Thankfully, Beiron's prison kept him from bothering her anymore. Until now.

"He did." Laila swallowed. "It was before the earthquake. He had Mick and asked me to deliver Raidan in exchange for him."

She didn't need to clarify her course of action. Adrik knew her well enough to know she'd do everything in her power to protect Raidan and Dimitri. He tapped his foot. "You've mentioned the connection goes both ways?"

Laila cocked her head. She thought she knew where this was going and was ready to shut down what he might suggest. Seeing Beiron wouldn't help Mick's condition.

Her teeth chattered. She really should go back inside.

Adrik removed his golden coat and wrapped it around her shoulders. Its warmth did little to settle her shaky nerves. He sat back down and drew a breath. "You say you wish to break the connection, but maybe you can use it to your advantage."

Laila pulled his coat tighter around her shoulders. She could… But to what purpose? "Mick had the Weldafire Stone, Adrik. Now it's in Beiron's hands. What good will it do to speak to him?"

"To know if he has Raidan. You can glimpse him and confirm whether or not he is alive. It isn't much, but it's something."

"You don't know what you're asking." Not only did she think she couldn't handle speaking to Beiron again, but he'd also used their connection before to get to her and learn things she didn't want him to know. "I don't know if I can." Admitting so felt like a disservice to all the years she'd spent breaking the hold he'd had on her.

Adrik twisted to look at the house, then turned back to Laila. "I won't pretend to understand how it works, but if Raidan is in danger, wouldn't you rather know what we're up against so we can help him? If this connection you share is a way to do that, isn't it worth a try?"

Adrik's role as a delegate meant it was his job to protect the Guardians. And while Laila wasn't a delegate, the well-being of Raidan and Dimitri affected everyone, since it was they who protected the Weldafire Stone, which in itself was the heart of Kartha. Not only that, but they were also her closest friends. All the evidence pointed to Beiron having Raidan with him. It was the most plausible explanation for his disappearance. How else could she explain the strength in her magic, except to assume Beiron had used Raidan's blood to steal the power of the Weldafire Stone? What did that mean for Raidan?

And what would happen now that Beiron had obtained guardianship over the Weldafire Stone? Guardian didn't seem the right word. Warden was more like it.

"I think it might be too late to stop Beiron." Laila made a fist and opened it. A burst of white light shone bright over her hand. Her light should have been blue, but it was more than just the colour. "I can't explain it, but I feel different. Stronger, and yet—there's something else; something…sickly." The best way she could describe the feeling was that it was like the black tendrils that had touched her when she assessed Mick. It was like the thing that was killing him was also killing Kartha. But that didn't make any sense.

She closed her hand, and her light went out.

Adrik scratched his short, scraggly beard. "Do you remember when Litlen was cursed?"

Laila hadn't even reached her first hundred years then. She'd been young but not young enough to forget that night. She nodded. "I remember."

"I went to the Gap because the earthquake reminded me of that time, when we lost our magic. Whatever has happened, we haven't seen the worst of it yet. We warned Beiron this could happen and he refused to see reason. If you speak to him, you can tell him what I saw. We may not agree on many things, but we all share a love for our country."

If Beiron hadn't listened when Adrik and Raidan tried to warn him, why would he listen now? Just because he cared about Kartha didn't mean he'd make the right choice and give Raidan and the Weldafire Stone back— assuming he even had Raidan.

"Even if we get Raidan and the stone back, is there a way to fix this?" Laila asked. Without the delegates, what could be done?

Adrik said nothing for a minute. He stared at his hands. "As of right now, everything is speculation, and until we know something for certain, we can do nothing. But if there's a way to get through to Beiron, there may be hope."

He gave Beiron more credit than she would have.

But he was right. As long as Mick wasn't waking up, they couldn't learn from him what had happened in the mountains. If she could get over her fears and tap into her connection to learn from Beiron, they may be able to fit the pieces together. Beiron had done the same to her when he sought Raidan and Dimitri. It was tempting to return the gesture, but this was Beiron.

She dropped her head into her hands. Why did he still affect her like this?

Her thoughts turned to Mick and his curse. Beiron had done that to him. She didn't hold much hope of Beiron having a change of heart. Even now, after all those years in isolation and captivity, he would have the stone and its power one way or another. He was determined, she'd give him that.

But Adrik was right. Beiron didn't hide the fact that he cared about Kartha and the Elderace. If she could get through to him—make him see what he'd done—maybe he would fix this, though she couldn't understand how.

She raised her head. "What about Mick? What can we do for him?"

Adrik breathed deeply. "When Mick awakes, I will take him to Kameron."

During Litlen's cursed years, Kameron had led a camp that functioned as a rebellion against the Valca Order. When the war ended and the Valca Order no longer ruled in Kartha, Kameron continued to lead his camp and welcomed visitors seeking refuge and rest.

"What's Kameron going to do?" Laila asked.

"I believe his magic will help us to know what the boy's trace of element is."

Laila perked up. "Mick has a trace of element? How do you know?" A trace of element was only present in the delegates' blood. If Mick had that, could there be others too? Maybe they wouldn't have to rely on Beiron making the right choice after all.

Adrik folded his hands in his lap. "When Mckal was born, Raidan, Dimitri, and I could sense the trace in his blood. We don't know which element he has, but we know it's strong. We discussed testing him when he got older, but Cassian and Willa left, and we never got the chance."

Laila gazed at the sea beyond the cliff. Questions arose in her mind. Could they do a search for others with delegates' blood? If they found others, was it possible to take back the power of the Weldafire Stone? Would Mick and Adrik be enough? The only reason Beiron had all six elements was because he'd stolen them. When he'd finished drinking the delegates' blood to acquire their traces, he killed all but two of them, who happened to be his father and uncle.

Laila slumped in her seat. She needed answers, and Beiron was always quick to give them. He was always the one who had them. If she went to him, might he oblige and give Raidan up? This was hopeful thinking, she knew, but it offered more hope than sitting here guessing. It wasn't like she'd be going to him for real. It would be only in their minds. She shivered when she thought of his phantom touch on her shoulder. The thought didn't inspire her.

"Adrik, what if he's already killed him?" She could barely voice the question.

Adrik rested a hand over hers. "It's possible Beiron might have killed Raidan, but we must believe he is alive. We have no way of knowing for certain. If you can check, we'll have a better idea. I will be here with you if that helps."

His presence was a comfort. And knowing she wasn't alone here did help.

Laila made up her mind and resolved that she'd do it. She'd speak to Beiron.

She sat up straight and nodded. "All right, I'll do it."

"What do you need?"

It'd been a while since she'd done this, but there wasn't much to it. "Just…hold my hand?" It would help to keep her grounded here and let her know he was there when she couldn't see him.

Adrik took her hand with both of his. She closed her eyes and blocked out the gulls and crashing waves, then focused on Beiron and where he might be.

# Chapter 28

The atmosphere changed. Pine and damp soil scents filled the air. Laila opened her eyes to find herself standing in a wooden shed with cracks where the sun's rays crept in. The single room was bare, with a few empty shelves on one wall. Rotting logs were left piled in a heap underneath them.

"*Veralnin tushov.*"

Laila turned to the sound of Beiron's voice. He leaned against the wall with his hands in his trouser pockets. She'd forgotten how frightening his black eyes were to look at. Besides looking a little older—with more white in his black hair and an extra wrinkle or two around his eyes—he looked the same as the day she'd left him in the cave.

"*Now* she'll see me." Beiron laughed softly and shook his head.

Laila squeezed her hand and felt Adrik's squeeze back. She could do this.

"Where's Raidan?"

Beiron's face softened in a smile. It didn't make him any less frightening. "And as usual, you have questions. I should have guessed. But I'll tell you something, Laila, I'm not answering your questions anymore until you come to me."

All the heat left Laila and her knees almost gave out on her—though she wasn't truly standing. The last time she'd been with Beiron in the flesh, things hadn't gone so well. She had never learned how to leave these meetings at will, but she was ready to give up and go back to Adrik. Determination kept her there. She'd come for Raidan. She wasn't leaving until she knew if Beiron had him.

She licked her lips. The plain room held no clues to lead her to where this was. It looked like it might have been a storage shed at one time but had long since been abandoned. Through a hole in the door, she could see trees outside. Bright deciduous, with blue-green leaves. This was the Forest of Litlen.

"Is Raidan alive?" She held her breath, worried she'd not like the answer.

"Come see me and we'll talk."

"I'm not coming. You don't have him. Why would I come if he's not here? I have nothing more to say to you." She closed her eyes, about to make her first attempt at leaving.

Beiron's next words gave her pause. "He's alive. For now." He walked toward her. She took a step back and reminded herself that she wasn't physically there. As far as she knew, he couldn't hurt her, but he'd used this connection a previous time to see into her surroundings. Beiron reached for her face, and she stumbled backward to avoid his touch.

The corner of his lip quirked up. "I'll make you a deal."

"No deals. Not again."

"Well, fortunately for you, blood magic is off the table since we're not having this discussion in person. We'll do this the mayanon way." He wrinkled his nose at this.

"I'm not making any deals with you. Just tell me where to find Raidan, and I'll be on my way."

Beiron chuckled. "That's not how we're going to do this. I'll tell you where he is; in fact, I'll even have him delivered directly to his doorstep. But first, you'll have to come."

A sinking feeling came over Laila. She bit back her building emotions. "Why? You want to take your revenge on me? Hurt Royl because I prevented you from having your way?"

"No." Beiron shook his head. "No, I'll leave your brother out of this if you come. You have my word. On the other hand, Royl, Dimitri, Raidan and his little family—none of them will escape my rage if I have to hunt you down."

Tears rose, but Laila kept them at bay, though it wasn't easy. She feared to say anything and betray her emotions. "Why?" she croaked.

"When you come, you can ask all the questions you want. Save it for when we're together. But you better hurry. I don't think Raidan has much time if he doesn't get the proper care."

"What did you do to him?"

Beiron placed a hand on his chin and studied her. "All right, you get this one. I'm sure you already know I possess the power of the Weldafire Stone. I imagine you felt it." He tapped his temple. "Didn't I tell you you'd benefit from my gain?" His smirk disappeared. "I missed a lot in that cave and needed an update. Raidan was more than helpful there. I was surprised by his wealth of knowledge, courtesy of the knowledge of the stone. I've learned what I needed, and now I have no use for him."

"Then let him go."

"I will. When you come. I assure you he'll be returned home. If you hurry, he may still have a chance at surviving."

"What you've done will be the end of Kartha. Adrik warned you this would happen."

"I have some thoughts on that, which I'll be happy to share with you when you come."

Laila stared at the floor, and her vision blurred. She needed to think. His thoughts meant nothing to her. If she could just get Raidan back, he might have an idea of what to do. But how could she get Beiron to hand him over without giving herself up? She could tell Royl, and the Warriors could comb through the Forest of Litlen in search of Beiron, then arrest him and demand he tell them where he left Raidan. But if Raidan was hurt badly, he may not be alive when they got to him.

She couldn't breathe. The last thing she wanted was to willingly go to Beiron, but if it meant she'd be saving Raidan's life, how could she deny him? Again, she squeezed Adrik's hand and he returned the gesture.

Beiron went back to leaning against the wall. "You're wasting time." He crossed his arms. "Go to Hayat Point in the Teiry Mountains. Be there by nightfall. If you bring anyone—and I mean *anyone*—I'll come for Royl. Of that, you can be sure."

Laila took a shaky breath. It wasn't fair. He knew she'd do anything to protect those she loved. "And then what? What happens at the Point?"

"Then you'll see." Beiron winked. "*Farino.*"

The shed disappeared in a flash. Laila blinked rapidly. The sun blinded her and she squinted. There were no trees or shed to block its light as it arced toward the western horizon over the sea. Adrik's eyes searched her face. The corners of his lips turned down. "Was he there? Did you see Raidan?"

Laila was near bursting with tears. She shook her head. "He wasn't there. But I know how to get him back."

"He is alive then? That is good news." His brows drew together. "What is it? What did he say?"

Laila bit her bottom lip and shook her head again. "That getting him back comes at a price."

Beiron was many things, but a liar was not one of them. She didn't need her gift to deduce whether he spoke the truth. If Beiron said Raidan was alive, then it was true. And if they had any hope of keeping him that way, there was only one thing to do.

# Chapter 29

At the entrance to the pass in the Teiry Mountains, Laila dismounted Vis. He'd not go far without her. The passage was too narrow in places, and low ceilings required ducking, so this was as far as he went. She hoped this wouldn't take long and that she could be back before morning. To make Beiron's deadline, she'd had to leave Raidan's home right away.

Signs of Kartha's sickness were already becoming evident as she'd journeyed toward the mountains. Her heart sank upon seeing the dying plants. Trees and leaves were losing their vibrancy and colour as everything suffered from Beiron's corruption. It was as it had been during Litlen's cursed years, except back then, everything had died at once, and only Litlen had been cursed. Now, who was to say this wouldn't affect all of Kartha? At what rate did it worsen?

Before leaving Raidan's home, she'd had to come up with an excuse to appease Royl so he wouldn't become suspicious of her absence. She'd told him she needed supplies for healing potions, then left a message with Adrik, asking Royl to come and get her in the Teiry Mountains as soon as Raidan was returned home. She assumed he'd find her at the Delegates Cave, which was located in the valley of Hayat Point.

Her heart raced faster the closer she got to the meeting place. Unlike the last time she'd met Beiron in person, this time she came prepared. Her little ankle dagger wasn't much, but it gave her a sense of security. It'd come in handy in certain binding situations, which she'd experienced her fair share of. But as an extra precaution, she carried an extra dagger at her waist. Remembering Beiron's massive size, her knees wobbled. She hoped her experiences against her previous adversaries would be of some help.

She touched the scar on her chest where a thrown knife had found her instead of Beiron, who'd been the intended target. He'd saved her life then. Part of her still believed she could make him see reason. Having read his journals and understanding his desire to learn and educate their people, she hoped she could appeal to this side of him. Now that he'd gotten what he'd always wanted, maybe he would finally see how wrong he was. Maybe now he'd listen. The little voice in the back of her mind reminded her that this was wishful thinking, but it kept her going along that path toward him. If it weren't for Raidan, she'd just as soon never speak to Beiron again, regardless of whether there was hope for him.

Remnants of the sun's light cast an amber glow to the west, behind her, while straight ahead, the darkness loomed.

Laila put one foot in front of the other as she contemplated a plan of action if he tried anything on her.

Magic was her first line of defence, but it didn't matter how much practice she'd had with that. Against her own father, she'd only wind up hurting herself if she tried using her magic to hurt him. Now she wished she'd had more practice in the art of martial combat. Or perhaps with a firearm. She'd tried using one once and swore she never would again. She'd break that promise to herself if she thought it could protect her now. Though acquiring such a weapon was not easy in Kartha, even for her. Her dagger would have to suffice, but she hoped it wouldn't come to that.

In thinking of firearms, she considered Governor Riggs and his men prowling about Kartha. When all was said and done here, she still had to find a way to put a stop to their plans, whatever they entailed. Any plans of the Tax Collector's wouldn't be good. Of all the times for him to make his way here, it had to be now. As if she didn't have enough going on.

She veered from the path and gazed up the slope to Hayat Point. Beiron must be by the cave. All she had to do was stall until Raidan was returned, then wait for Royl to come. He'd get the whole division of Warriors spread out in the mountains. There'd be no place for Beiron to run. She took a breath and reminded herself that this was why she was here. She could do this.

She hiked onward. When she crested the peak, Beiron was nowhere in sight. At the bottom of the basin was the cave's entrance. A shiver ran down her spine. Was she meant to go inside the cave?

She slowly descended, remembering the Anguivina and her encounter with the creature. She'd controlled it then. More than likely, Beiron had claimed control since then. Usually it dwelt in the lake, but now that the lake was gone, she didn't know if it left the cave and the Pool of Sovereignty.

A line of darkened stone marked where the shoreline used to be. Laila went no farther.

This couldn't be right. Beiron had said Hayat Point. If he wanted her to go into the cave, he would have said so.

"I'm here!" she shouted. So where was he?

Beiron appeared at the top of the Point. He meandered down toward her. Laila stepped sideways, getting herself positioned where she had room to run up the slope. How had she managed to put herself in this situation *again*? The impassable vertical wall of mountain behind her forced her to have to go past Beiron to get back up to the Point.

"I'm impressed." Beiron smiled, then shrugged. "But then I shouldn't be surprised you came. You're predictable."

Laila extended her dagger as he came closer to her. "Stop there. Where's Raidan?"

Beiron didn't stop.

She walked sideways on the slant. "I said stop!" Her voice came out stronger than she felt.

Beiron didn't slow, and she wouldn't be able to keep her dagger trained on him if she turned and outright ran, which she'd tried the last time she'd been in this absurd position. How could she have been so foolish?

She sliced the dagger through the air. "Stay away from me!"

He reached for her arm, and she jumped back, moving out of the way, while taking another swing with the dagger. The blade made contact with his forearm. He grunted and lunged for her.

She stumbled and nearly fell back. Beiron caught her by the wrist, stopping her fall, then with his other hand, he pricked something into the side of her neck. She gasped and touched the stinging in her neck.

Beiron let her go and took a step back. Laila's eyes focused on the alcunic flower in his hand. She blinked, trying to remember the properties of the alcunic.

Her neck seared with pain that spread throughout her body. It occurred to her what was happening and she gaped at Beiron. That couldn't be right. She'd seen it wrong. She looked again at the plant. Maybe it just looked like the alcunic but was something else.

As if reading her mind, Beiron held it up. There was no mistaking the red flower, open and exposing the sharp needle-like spathe of the venomous plant. From what she knew of it, the venom didn't take long to set in. She'd be dead in minutes.

"That'll kill me."

Beiron held up a small bud of the same plant. The red was a lighter shade than the fully blossomed alcunic. "Not if you eat this. The chemicals in the bud will counter the venom and work as an antidote."

Laila bowed her head to ease the spinning. She knew this. The same as she knew that eating the bud would render her unconscious for as long as it took to clear her system of the venom.

He held the bud up for her to take. There wasn't time to weigh the options.

*Like she had any.*

"You're not dying today, Laila. Take it."

Her dagger slipped from her fingers and clattered against the rocky ground. Her head lolled, and she felt herself fall forward. Beiron caught her. She had no strength to fight him off as he stuffed the bud into her mouth and clamped his hand there.

"Chew it and swallow," he told her. "It'll work fast."

She obeyed, only half aware of herself. She swallowed, and within seconds her throat was on fire. As it made its way down, it burned her insides.

Beiron pulled his hand from her mouth, and he took her weight into his arms. He lowered her to the ground and onto her back, then cradled her head, smoothing her hair. "You'll be all right. Once we're away from this damned place, I'll tell my man to take Raidan home, just like I said I would."

Laila clutched her stomach and curled her body in on itself. She had the fleeting thought that the bud might not work—that she was going to die and she'd fail everyone she loved: Raidan, Royl, her mother. Dimitri. Tears streaked her cheeks, and she closed her eyes. Sleep dragged her down, and all her cares became distant thoughts.

# Chapter 30

An ache in her gut woke her. Laila groaned. She was going to be sick. She swallowed and remained motionless in her seated position until the nausea subsided. Wherever she was, it was dark. She couldn't make anything out.

Her hands were tied behind her back. She wriggled them and rope dug into her wrists. They were secured around some kind of beam. The walls felt close, giving the impression that this room was small. The place held Beiron's scent of pine mingled with a floral fragrance and was mixed with a lingering burning smell.

"*Bludevint.*" Beiron's face lit up behind the glow of his white light—like hers, it'd changed. It blinded her, and she turned her face away, blinking until her eyes adjusted.

Beiron crouched to her eye level. A bandage was wrapped around his forearm where she'd cut him. He pushed his light upward, then offered her the drink he held in his other hand. "For your stomach."

Laila raised a leg and planted her foot against his chest. She kicked him. The drink sloshed from the cup, and Beiron toppled, laughing. *Laughing?* Laila fumed.

"You keep pushing me away," Beiron said. "Don't you want to learn more about our connection?"

More than he knew. But not this way. She kept her leg up as her defence and braced herself to kick him again. She could feel her ankle dagger hadn't been taken and it remained hidden beneath her pant leg. That would come in handy.

Beiron stood and set the cup on the counter against the wall. He stepped toward her, keeping his arms outstretched over her legs. As he bent down, approaching closer, she drew her knee to her chest, ready to thrust out at him again. He moved toward her, and when she kicked out, he grabbed her ankle, stretched it, and wrapped his arm around both of her legs. She wrenched them, but his grasp tightened.

The nausea came back, and she had to stop moving to keep from throwing up. She took a few breaths until the feeling passed. Her nerves wouldn't stop trembling. It took much restraint to keep from lashing out.

Beiron lowered her legs but kept his arm extended over them as though he might grab them again at any moment. He crouched down next to her, and when he reached for her face, Laila leaned away. He paused with his hand hovering in the space between their faces. "I'm not going to hurt you."

"You just poisoned me and could have killed me."

"I wouldn't have let you die. But I had to get you here." Beiron lowered his hand. "I wouldn't have to resort to such extreme measures if you would just cooperate.

"I don't blame you for the way you are. You're my daughter. I'd be disappointed if you didn't have such a strong spirit." He shifted his weight and rested his elbow on his knee. "Unfortunately, I'm going to have to break that spirit and make you understand."

"Make me understand what?"

"Why you need me."

Laila scoffed. "I don't want anything to do with you. You're not well, Beiron."

"I will be. When everything is as it should be. But first, you have much to learn." He reached for her head again, and she jerked away.

"What have you done with Raidan? You promised to return him home."

Beiron sighed and lowered his hand again. "And I have. I had an old friend return him this morning. I always follow through with my word, Laila. You know this."

*He had friends?*

Laila squirmed in discomfort. He told the truth. He'd done what he'd said, and Raidan would get the care he needed. Now she just needed to get herself out of here. *Wherever here was.*

There wasn't much chance Royl would find her in this place. With their being half siblings, even eshuair pollen would lead him to the stronger connection with their mother before it would lead him to her.

"You're wasting time here," she said. "Kartha is dying, and you have the power to do something about it. You don't need me for that. Just let me go and leave me alone."

Beiron lowered his eyes and frowned. "Pleading is unbecoming of you. I'm a patient man, Laila. I'm going to teach you many things."

Laila squirmed. It did nothing to loosen the bonds. Heat rose to her cheeks. "Nothing you teach me will ever change how I feel about you. You're a monster. You were a monster when we met, and you're one now."

Beiron grinned a crooked grin, and his eyes gleamed. "That's the spirit." He raised his hand yet again. "Now, are we doing this?"

He was mistaken if he thought she'd not find a way out of here. She stopped struggling against the rope and asked, "Doing what?"

"I'm going to show you something. Something about our connection."

Learning about their connection could help Laila come up with a way to break it. She had no idea what he intended to do, but he had his hand poised to touch her face. "No. Tell me."

"I'm going to show you."

"Get away from me."

Beiron dropped his hand but stayed down and in her face. "I'll wait until you're ready."

That would be never. She let a few minutes pass, hoping he'd get tired of waiting. But this was the same man who'd spent half her life imprisoned and yet somehow didn't lose sight of his goals or give up. Granted, he may have lost his sanity somewhere along the way, but she didn't doubt the extent of his patience. Though she wondered how sane he'd been to begin with.

Either way, he'd not leave her alone until he had his way, and as long as he hung around, she'd never get a chance to work on her escape. But to relent would feel like she was giving him a win.

He watched her, probably knowing the exact thoughts going through her head. She couldn't stay here like this all day. She bit her lip, hating that she was giving up so easily. Just this once.

"Fine. Show me."

The smile Beiron gave her was full of satisfaction. "See, you're getting it already."

He reached for her face, and she didn't stop him. He could enjoy his small victory. She'd take hers when this was done.

# Chapter 31

Beiron placed his hands on either side of Laila's head. Her stomach turned when she breathed in his scent, as he knelt so near. She closed her eyes so she didn't have to look at him.

A tugging sensation pulled on her mind, and the cool glow in the cellar-like room faded away. A flurry of colours and shapes whirled around until the shapes took the form of a spacious hall with a raised long table at the front. Eight men and women were seated at the table, looking down on Laila—Beiron. She was Beiron. This was his memory. But fragments of her own memory flashed in her mind. The eight people seated, shifted to only five, including Royl.

A wall of mirrors behind the elders faced Beiron, reflecting his black hair and icy blue eyes—not the black emptiness Laila was familiar with. The scar over his eye was non-existent. She recalled in her own memory how the mirrors had shown her reflection when she went before the elders, how small they'd made her feel. The sun shone through the high windows, letting in the morning light in her own memory. It flashed again, and the eight elders were back.

In Beiron's memory, clouds drifted across the sky out the window. He—she—stood before the table with a solid black leatherbound book in hand. The very same book Laila had taken from Beiron's home years ago when she was collecting books to preserve Elderace knowledge and history.

"If you would just look at my discoveries." Beiron's voice was up an octave from his typical smooth, confident tone. He raised the book and jabbed a finger at it. "There is so much more to discover. If you would allow me a chance to prove to you that what I'm doing is for the good of our people. Allow me to demonstrate the benefits of my ointments and potions and you'll see—"his voice united with Laila's in the memory as Laila recalled quoting a similar pitch—"how useful they are as medicine. If you knew—"the voice altered back to Beiron's—"how many of our own Karthan plants contained active ingredients that have yet to be discovered—"

Noli, the senior elder situated at the middle of the table, between Sisco and Darrin, raised her hand, silencing Beiron. Her straight white hair framed her heart-shaped face, accentuating her blue eyes.

"It is not your discoveries we disapprove of, Mr. Cailt. It is your methods of discovery. They are unethical and, to be frank, cruel."

Beiron huffed. "What do you know of my methods?" He let his arms fall to his sides. In his memory, Laila experienced his emotions in the moment. His anger at their stupidity. Not willing to even look at his work. They'd never appreciate what he was doing for them. He'd just have to show them. Laila's own feelings were not so unlike his when, one by one, each elder denied her request to put to use the things Beiron had learned. She'd made it clear that she did not approve of how he'd come to learn them, but there was no denying the usefulness of the medicines. But unlike Beiron, she had taken her knowledge out into the world to make use of it without their approval. It wasn't for them to say whether or not they should be used.

Her thoughts were torn from the scene, and she was back in the cellar-like room with Beiron and the man he'd become since that time. He withdrew his hands from her head and sat back on his heels. Silence lingered between them.

Laila hadn't understood it then, when the elders denied her, but Vix, Darrin, Maire, and Zulu had been present when Beiron approached them with his request. Her own audience with the elders had looked very much like his. How had she been so blind? She'd not realized how like him she'd been. That alone could have been their reason for refusing her. She didn't blame them. How similar their memories were frightened even her. So much for trying to not follow in his footsteps.

She met his eye. "That doesn't explain our connection."

"No, but it confirms what I suspected." Beiron reached for her head again.

She pulled away. "Stay out of my memories." His rummaging through her thoughts unsettled her.

The corner of his lip twitched up. He said nothing as he placed his palms against her temples. This time she was expecting the tug on her mind and she leaned into it.

She—as Beiron—stood on a doorstep just as the door opened. Freya, Laila's mother, answered. Laila's heart leapt. Her mother was younger here. Her dark curls were tugged back into a sloppy bun and her casual sky-blue dress draped to her toes. Her sad eyes wrinkled at the corners when she smiled. She waved Beiron inside and clasped her hands in front of herself.

"Thank you for coming." She sounded meek, speaking in a formal tone. This was not the Freya Laila knew. This version of her mother was sad and hesitant, uncertain.

Experiencing the memory from Beiron's point of view, Laila felt his chest swell as he approached Freya, taking her hand in his own. "You know I look forward to our visits. How are you today?"

Freya peered into his gaze. Even then, Beiron exhibited confidence in his appearance and person. He was handsome, and he knew it. Laila didn't need to see him to know he carried himself with pride. She supposed she could understand how her mother might have been attracted to him. She shuddered. This was not what she wanted to be thinking of while he was in her head.

Freya's lips quirked up in a smile. "Better, now that you're here. Come in. Royl's asleep. I want to show you something."

Beiron entered the sitting room with Freya. He sank into the sofa and Freya sat next to him at the edge of the couch. She opened her clasped hand to reveal the thing she'd been holding. Beiron dropped his gaze to look at the lacrut. His pulse quickened as he reached for the plant. He paused. "I don't know, Freya." In his mind, it wasn't fear of getting caught using the illegal plant that made him hesitate. It was fear of what Freya might find in his own mind. Lacrut was a two-way connection allowing thoughts to be shared. Theirs was a fragile new relationship. Was he ready to let her in?

Freya placed a dainty hand gently on the rough skin of his own.

"Please, I want to share with you."

She seemed ready to let him in. So why shouldn't he do the same?

Beiron took the root. "Why don't I make us some tea?"

A moment later, he was in the kitchen brewing tea and breaking up the root into each mug. He walked back into the sitting room and handed Freya one of the mugs. He sat beside her. They drank while Freya smiled and talked about her day in the market with Royl. A tot who couldn't keep his hands to himself. She chuckled, recalling the way he'd stretched his arm up to touch every vendor's product as they passed by.

Beiron let the warmth of the tea and Freya's voice soothe him. Was this what it felt like to love someone? Could this life be his someday? Sharing stories about his children and laughing at how embarrassed he was when the child repeated back words that weren't meant for their ears.

He'd loved once before, but not like this. Gilia, his sister, was the only one who'd stood by him on those nights when their mother had taken her fury out on them. Their father had spent many nights away. Busy nights, meeting with the delegates. *Important matters, you understand*, he would say. It hadn't taken Beiron long to figure out they were excuses. For all his father's bravery and honour when it came to his duties as a delegate, he was a coward when it came to facing the woman he married when she'd had too much to drink and was in a bad mood. Beiron had vowed that if ever he had children of his own, he'd be there for them and a part of their lives.

Again, he envisioned the possibilities of what the future might hold.

Freya's smile relaxed, and she gazed into Beiron's eyes. She leaned her face just a touch forward, then hesitated. Beiron's senses took in everything. The scent of the ginger in the tea mixed with the lacrut that would soon allow them to share a connection in their minds. The way Freya's hair wasn't holding very well in its bun. A loose curl fell in her face and he tucked it behind her ear. The dim candlelight flickered, casting shadows on the wall.

She took his hand and pressed it to her cheek. "What now? How do I share?"

"Through physical touch." Beiron gently caressed her jawline. "Just think whatever you wish to show me."

Freya's eyes searched Beiron's. Her mind became an open book, revealing her thoughts—her confusion. She had intended to show him a memory—to share with him something from her past, a time she missed with a man she missed. But in his arms, here now, she no longer wished to share that part of her with him. She wanted to make new memories—with Beiron. To cherish this friendship and possibly even find love again. She leaned away, her wide eyes darting between Beiron's eyes, to his lips and his face, to his gentle hands cupping her cheek.

Before he could think himself out of the moment, Beiron drew her in for a kiss. Freya moved her hands to his face. She ran her fingers over his bristly chin and leaned in to him.

Laila pulled her mind back, which took effort. She squeezed her eyes shut, wishing she could erase the image from her mind.

The warmth of her home disappeared, and the flickering candlelight was gone, replaced by Beiron's glowing white light hovering above their heads in this dark room. She opened her eyes and had to turn her face away from Beiron's. Seeing his gentleness with her mother and his hope for a future with her, and then seeing the man he'd become… She couldn't look at him.

His desire to have children of his own had been strong. When they'd spoken of Royl, Beiron had even considered the idea of raising him alongside Freya. Laila could only imagine how much it must have hurt him to find out he had a daughter and had missed her whole life. But she couldn't feel guilty for him. He'd made his choices. Her mother hadn't been wrong to keep her from him.

Beiron shifted his weight. "You understand?"

That her parents had consumed lacrut the night she was presumably conceived? "I got it," she said. The question of how had been answered but it raised another question. Could she and her mother connect in the same way she and Beiron could? If so, why hadn't she been able to in all this time? She shook her thoughts and questions aside for now. It didn't matter. Now that she knew, she could start figuring out a way to break the connection with Beiron. If it was a simple matter of lacrut, there had to be a way to shut off the thought-sharing. Or block him at least.

But first, before she could look into it, she had to get out of this place.

"So now what?" she said. "You've got your power, you've had your way with Raidan, and now you have me. What now?"

"Did the boy live?

Laila tugged at the bonds, wishing she could move her hands.

"You stabbed him and left him for dead."

"Did he live?"

In her time abroad and working with the kinds of people Laila often worked with, she'd learned that sometimes you had to tell a convincing lie. A few lives had been spared thanks to her many years of practice. Whatever Beiron's interest in Mick, he had no business interfering with him or his family any longer. Unblinking, she made direct eye contact. "No."

Beiron inhaled a deep breath. He shook his head. "Don't lie to me, Laila. Asking is a courtesy. I can take whatever I want from your head if I wish to."

Laila's blood boiled. Only Royl had ever been able to call her out on her lies. Did Beiron possess the same gift as she? Was he able to tell lies from truth? Was that hereditary?

Beiron reached for her head again. She pulled away. He was in there enough as it was. She didn't need him poking around anymore and perceiving her plan to escape.

His fingers grazed her temple, and she spoke quickly. "He lives."

His hand froze. She went on. "You did something to him. He's dying. As is Kartha." She used her head to bump his hand away, then glared at him. "You said you had thoughts on how to fix that. How?"

"I've since learned of the boy's unique ability. The Dairner kid is going to fix things and make Kartha whole. Somehow, he and Kartha are connected. I don't understand it, but I will. Where is he?"

That Beiron cared about what became of Kartha was a step in the right direction. Regarding Mick, was there much point in trying to lie? Laila rolled her eyes. "Where do you think he is?"

Beiron took a second to consider where. He pursed his lips. "I've been in the dark for a long time. Tell me." His voice betrayed a hint of weariness.

Laila searched his face, looking for signs of vulnerability. "What happened to you? When you were with my mother, you seemed so…different."

Undeterred by her attempt at distraction, Beiron sighed. "Where is the boy?"

So much for that idea. "What will you do to him?"

"I'm going to make sure he gets to where he needs to be."

"Which is…?"

Beiron stared at her, unblinking. The room fell completely silent, which felt unsettling. After a few minutes, he moved and extended his hand for her head. "I gave you a chance."

Laila leaned back against the beam. "You don't need him to fix this if you'd just return what you've stolen."

Beiron ignored her. He placed his hands on her temple and tugged at her thoughts. She closed her eyes, trying to keep from him the thing he wanted, knowing she was losing the battle. How could one lock away fresh memories? Within seconds, he had what he was looking for. He backed up and scrunched his nose. "Are they really that obvious?"

Laila's head throbbed from her failed efforts at having her memories appropriated. "Considering any normal person would have died from such a wound, why would he be anywhere else?"

When Beiron stood, Laila jumped despite herself. She tensed her legs, getting ready to kick him again. He glanced from them to her face, then laughed softly. "I'll be back soon. We have much to discuss, but first I've got things to see to." He stopped before a door, then with a wave of his hand, he extinguished his light and left, closing the door behind him.

*Took him long enough.*

In the dark, Laila listened. It sounded like he was going upstairs. Something heavy scraped along the floor—twice. His shuffling footsteps above faded away until there was nothing.

Evidently, Beiron did not know her as well as he thought if he believed she'd be here when he returned. To ensure he was truly gone, she'd wait a little while before making her getaway. These ropes and doors wouldn't keep her from her freedom. Beiron could not take that from her. No one could.

# Chapter 32

A nutty, citrusy scent filled Mick's senses and slowly drew him from his sleep. He recognized it as the spice that his Adema gifted him whenever she visited, claiming it was popular in Reij. She favoured cooking with it, and the smell reminded him of Adefa and her visiting him at his family's home in Iptin.

Vidia whispered from somewhere close by. *Vidia?* Mick blinked open his eyes, searching the room for her. She sat cross-legged on the floor across from someone past the bed who Mick couldn't see. He glanced around, taking in the small bedroom. Under a window, a three-drawer dresser rested against the wall, leaving enough walking space between it and his bed. In the corner on his other side, an immaculate blue chair sat next to a bedside table with a cup on it.

The room spun, and Mick had to close his eyes until the dizziness subsided.

"You're cheating," Vidia said softly to her opponent. "You have to place a card down."

"That doesn't make any sense." Boone's deep voice spoke quieter than Vidia's had. "I know a game just like this one where you don't have to discard. Are you sure you're playing it right?"

"Yes, I played it all the time with my older brother. Discard."

"I did."

"You didn't."

"You weren't looking. You did that thing again. You're supposed to take your mind off it, that was the idea of the game."

"I know, I know. But it isn't working."

Mick's own voice was groggy and rough. "Vidia?" He tried opening his eyes again. Vidia gasped and leapt up from the floor.

"Mick!" She bounded over to him and wrapped her arms around him. He groaned, squeezing his eyes shut. She jumped back. "Oh, Mick, I'm sorry. Are you okay? I didn't mean to…"

Mick pressed a hand against his stomach where the pain radiated from. "I'm all right," he said through clenched teeth.

"It's about time you woke up," Boone said, smiling. "You were out for days."

While the pain dissipated, Mick relaxed. He tried to return Boone's smile but couldn't make sense of his surroundings and how Boone and Vidia were here. He gazed at Vidia. Her stunning green eyes and loose, unruly curls framed her petite chin. She really was beautiful. "How are you here?" The last time he'd seen her, she was being escorted to her room in her uncle's home.

Vidia's face drooped. "That man who was looking for you…" She paused. "When he showed up after my uncle sent for him, and you weren't there, he didn't take it well." Her chin quivered as she contained her emotions, but her voice faltered. "He took Uncle Daegan." Tears fell down her cheeks. "I didn't want to live with him, but that doesn't mean I wanted him gone." A sob escaped her throat, and she wiped her face in a futile effort to dry her eyes.

Ighur took Daegan all because Mick wasn't where he was supposed to be? And now Daegan would face the same fate that Mick was trying to escape. "Oh, Vidia, I'm sorry."

She sniffed. "I came here because you were coming to your family for help, so I thought… maybe they could help him too."

Mick kept still to prevent his stomach from throbbing. The pain nagged at him, but he ignored it. He couldn't get hurt. Not really. This was something new, that was all. He'd heal, just like he always had. He sought the comfort of the stone he'd become accustomed to having on him, then remembered he didn't have it. Looking at Boone, he had the question on his lips, but Boone spoke first.

"I tried to get here as quick as I could, but by the time I made it, you were already here. I told your family what happened in Valmain and with Damien, and I told them I wasn't going anywhere until you woke up." He flashed a crooked grin. "Well, I asked if I could stay, and they said it was all right. Your parents are nice."

Mick drew his brows together. His parents?

As if on cue, his mother entered the room, her eyes wide and teary, yet somehow more vibrant than he'd ever seen. She let out a sob, ran to his side, and mimicked Vidia's action from only a moment ago, flinging her arms around his shoulders and jostling him. This time, he braced for the pain in his stomach, but it didn't help. He moaned, curling himself in. Pleased as he was to see his mother, Mick couldn't reciprocate her affection.

"You're still hurt?" She let him go and reached for the hem of his shirt to check. He stopped her before she could lift it. "I'll be all right." He didn't need everyone gawking at him with his shirt off.

A man Mick had never met before entered the room, waving his arms about. "Out. Now. Everyone, out." He shooed Vidia and Boone away. Mick's father burst in after him, breathing hard like he'd tried to beat the man to the room and had been too slow.

Willa stood and went to Cassian's side. Cassian straightened and pointed at Mick. "Adrik, Mick. Mick, this is Adrik."

"Very good," Adrik said. "Now we're all friends." He waved his arms in an upward motion. "Up, up. Let's go. Enough time has been wasted. We must go now." Mick couldn't place his subtle accent, but wherever he was from, he must have left there a long time ago.

Vidia squeezed Mick's hand. "We'll just be out here."

Boone patted his pocket and winked. The stone was safe. The relief eased Mick's pain, if only for a moment.

With Vidia and Boone gone from the room, Cassian gave Adrik a hard stare.

"Adrik, he's only just woken up. Give him time and let him rest."

"He's rested for days. We don't have time."

On top of the stinging in his abdomen, Mick's mind buzzed. He put pressure on his forehead, and it helped to lessen the developing ache. He couldn't wrap his head around everyone being here now. Or how he'd come to be here, wherever here was. Apart from the nutty scent permeating throughout the house, a subtle woodsy vanilla fragrance reminded him of Adema and Adefa. Was this their home?

If his parents had come, then where was…?

"Aira!" Mick sat up too fast and bent over himself until the pain lessened. His mother sat next to him and put a hand on his shoulder. "She's all right, Mick. When you'd gone to Kartha without saying anything to her, she knew something was wrong. She left to stay with her cousin, and we departed Iptin to make our way here. We ran into Dimitri on the way, as he had just arrived in Iptin on the ship we were preparing to board."

Relief flooded Mick. If Aira would be safe with anyone, it'd be with her cousin Krie. The man was a guard of the Lord's Sentinel. She'd be well protected with him. At least one thing had gone right. Luckily his parents had crossed paths with Uncle Dimi in the small harbour of Iptin Province rather than the busy port at Ectarin.

"What about Adefa? Beiron took him! We have to find him!"

Cassian raised a hand. "He's here. He and Uncle Dimitri are tired, but they'll both be fine."

So many questions filled Mick's head. What had Beiron done that affected Raidan the way it had in the mountains? How did they get him here? Where was Beiron now?

Adrik tapped his foot. "Save your reunion for later. Kartha does not have much time."

Cassian opened his mouth to protest but Mick cut in. "What do you mean by that?"

"Kartha has been cursed. As have you." Adrik pointed toward Mick's stomach. "Every day the sickness grows, worsening. It won't be long before it will be too late to do anything about it. I must get you to Kameron as soon as possible."

The sickness? Mick had done it—the very thing that had been foretold. Kartha was sick somehow, and it was because of him. "The prophecy."

"Mick." Cassian shook his head. "This isn't your fault. You didn't do this. Beiron did."

"But I released him. This is my fault. I did this!"

"You didn't know," Willa interjected.

"That doesn't matter. I let it happen."

Adrik crossed his arms. "If you would get up already, there is still time to fix this."

Mick's eyes shot to Adrik. "How? How can I fix it?"

"You're not ready to go anywhere," Cassian said. "You were hurt—cursed. Rest awhile." He turned to Adrik. "I told you Kameron can come here."

Adrik gestured out the window. "Kameron has everything he needs in Elefthan. I will bring the boy there to—"

"Mick! My name is Mick. If we're going to get along, then let's be clear: Don't call me boy. I have a name, use it."

The room fell to silence as all three of them stared, Cassian with an amused spark in his eye.

"Apologies," Adrik said. "Mick. Get whatever you need for a journey. We leave immediately."

Cassian stood. He pointed a finger in Adrik's face. "I told you—"

"Dad!" Mick's shout got their attention. "If there's a way to fix this, then I'll do whatever I can. This is on me."

Cassian's lips drew into a thin line. He shook his head and tears welled in his eyes. "No. It's not on you. And you're not ready, Mckal. You're not all right. You were…" He bit his bottom lip. "We thought you were dead." He choked the last word out.

Dead? Mick felt the bandage under his shirt. It was wrapped around his torso. Willa squeezed his hand. "We can't lose you again."

Adrik sighed. "If we do not hurry—"

"I need a minute with my parents." Mick sat back against the bed-frame, suppressing a wince as he did so.

Adrik raised his voice. "Have you not been listening? We need to—"

"I said—I need a minute. Get out." Mick had never sounded more like his father just then. Adrik closed his gaping mouth and pressed his lips into a pout. "One minute. No longer." He swivelled on his heel and exited the room. Mick quirked a brow at his father. "What's his problem?"

Cassian wiped tears away and chuckled. "He takes some getting used to. I'd say the trick is to be direct with him, but it looks like you've already figured that much out."

Willa took her hand from Mick's and rubbed his arm lovingly. Mick couldn't ever remember seeing his mother look so fresh and rested. At home, she always looked so frail. And with everything going on, he'd have expected her appearance to worsen. Had being away from Kartha affected her as it had affected him? Yet, even though her face glowed, her eyes were sad. "I'm sorry we didn't tell you more, Mick. If you'd have known about Beiron… If we'd have told you everything…" She dabbed her eyes.

If Mick had known what releasing Beiron would have caused, would he still have done it? The alternative wasn't great, but if he'd been aware his actions would have caused so much damage, he might have tried to come up with another way to avoid facing Riggs. Regardless, he'd made his choice.

"What's done is done" he said. "If Adrik knows a way to fix this, then I'll go with him and learn what I must do."

Cassian grabbed the chair from the corner and brought it closer to the bed. He sat, facing Mick, and leaned forward. "Adrik believes you have something called a trace of element. He wants you to go with him to a camp in the Bludesel Mountains. A family friend who lives there has magic that can help draw forth which element resides in your blood."

Mick got goosebumps thinking about magic. "Do you have magic?"

Willa adjusted her position on the bed, and the metal springs creaked. "I do. Your father doesn't. But having a trace of element is not common. For centuries, there were only six who gained one element each at the time of the Chronicle Storm. Adrik's father passed his trace of light on to him. He is the last remaining delegate from the time before.

"Beiron stole the trace of elements from The Six, and that's why he was able to take the stone's power and bind it to himself. Without all six, it wouldn't have been possible. As far as we know, you're the first besides the original delegates to possess a trace of element and the first to have been born with it. If we can determine what your element is, we can figure out what that means and how you can use your delegates' blood to..." She hesitated, frowning.

Willa glanced at Cassian, who finished for her. "To stop Beiron," he said. "As it stands, Kartha needs a healer. As long as Beiron wields the power of the Weldafire Stone, things will not get better. You and Kartha share a connection. Your adefa and Uncle Dimi have always said so, and recent events have proven it to be true. Kameron's magic can help you to better understand what can be done."

Adrik reemerged. He stood by the door and crossed his arms. "Now you've had your minute. Do you feel better? Kartha is dying and so are you. We need to go."

Throwing in that he was dying too didn't exactly spark motivation. Mick got a sinking feeling and touched his stomach. A twinge persisted where Beiron had stabbed him, but it didn't feel so bad as to feel like he was dying.

Uncomfortable, maybe, but not dying. He couldn't die. Could he? He was the Healer; healing was what he did.

And if a healer was what Kartha needed, then he was ready to do what needed to be done.

He swung his legs over the side of the bed and gritted his teeth, hiding his discomfort. Willa stood and offered him her hand, which he accepted as he got to his feet.

"Let me grab some things and I'll be ready in a few minutes," he said.

Adrik, assured that Mick was going with him to Elefthan, left him to get what he needed. Willa hugged Mick, wary of his injury. "Be careful, Son."

"You're not going to come?"

"No. Adema is not well enough to travel. She's grown weary these past months, and the last few days have taken a toll on her. Your father will join you, but…" She spared a glance at Cassian. "Someone needs to stay here and look after her and Adefa. He's slept almost as much as you since we got him back."

Got him back how? If every movement didn't cause Mick so much pain, he would have sprinted from the room to lay eyes on his grandfather and see that he was there and well. A burst of emotions rose in him, and he held them back. He needed to stay strong. If it was true he was dying, he needed to make the remainder of whatever time he had left impactful, not sit here crying on his mother's shoulder.

He stifled the emotions and asked, "What about Vidia and Boone? It's my fault Vidia's uncle was taken."

A dizzy spell threw his balance off. Cassian reached a hand out to steady and support him. "You focus on Kartha and getting better. I'll see what we can do for Daegan."

Mick set his jaw and bore his own weight. "Be careful, Dad. There's no limit to what Governor Riggs will do to those closest to me."

"I'll be careful. And you do the same, Mick. No more of—"he pointed to Mick's stomach."—that. Understand?"

Mick refrained from pressing his hand there. He wasn't about to go queuing up for another round of knife in the gut anytime soon. "I'll do my best." He gave a soft laugh.

Once his parents had vacated the room, Mick turned to gather things for the journey, only to realize he had nothing. Anything he'd brought from Iptin had been left behind at Daegan's Keep after Sunny and company had taken Vidia, Boone and him from Ferenth to Valmain. How long ago had that been? He'd lost track of the days and deduced that Riggs probably knew he'd been unaccounted for in Ighur's party. At least if he did die, he'd not have to worry about them catching up with him.

Mick lifted his shirt—which, he presumed was, his grandfather's—and stared at his bandaged torso, contemplating whether he should unwind it. He wanted to see what damage had been done, but at the same time, he didn't.

Deciding against it, he lowered his shirt. For now, he didn't need to know what lay beneath the layers of gauze. Instead, he placed his hand flat against his abdomen, over the bandage. If he could make the pain go away, he might feel a little less reluctant to look. He reached inward for his pool of power and flinched when his stomach experienced a sharp pain. His body shook all over, and he dropped his hands. Dread filled his heart at the idea that he may never heal from this.

But he couldn't think like that. Too much needed to be done. He put his doubt aside. His healing magic would kick in again. The injury had been traumatic. It just required more time for healing, but it would work. It had to.

# Chapter 33

Mick took a last look around the quaint bedroom. Had he been allowed to come to Kartha growing up, would this have been where he'd have slept? The wall by the window displayed markings starting from near the bottom and ascending toward the top of the doorframe, each line labelled with Cassian's name, representing his height and age at various stages. Mick stood taller than the latest addition. The hurt in his heart was of a sort he didn't know how to heal from. He swallowed past the lump in his throat and turned his gaze from the wall.

Boone poked his head in. "Hey, the, uh, thing you wanted…" He whipped his head over his shoulder, glancing back, then faced Mick as he entered the room and closed the door. He reached into his pocket and retrieved the leather pouch. "This."

Warmth filled Mick before he'd even laid hands on it. His sadness forgotten, he reached for the stone, and Boone dropped the pouch into his hand. Whatever it was about this stone, when he held it, it was as if he suddenly had a pulse again, where he didn't think he'd been missing one to begin with. He could have chalked up his previous anxiety to all that had happened in the time he'd given it up, but now holding it, the way it alleviated his unease, he'd not realized how much he'd missed it and needed it. Especially knowing that Beiron wanted it and had failed to get it.

Having the stone back gave him some peace of mind, but it didn't relieve the pain in his abdomen. He avoided opening the pouch for now. If the marring of his flesh from his deal with Damien had been revealed on the stone, he hated to think what it must look like now. He paused, staring at his closed hand. A fraction of curiosity tempted him to look.

But not enough to win him over.

Mick stowed the stone safely away in his pocket and clapped a hand on Boone's shoulder. "I owe you, brother."

"Good." Boone grinned and winked. "I'm counting on you to introduce me to the Witch someday."

In theory, his request didn't seem like too much of a challenge. Provided Mick survived the journey to Elefthan and this wound would heal. And after all that, if he managed to avoid Riggs, though he didn't know how he was going to do that if he was going to try to get Vidia's uncle back. A sharp stirring in his stomach broke his train of thought. He winced.

Boone's forehead creased. "They told us you were stabbed. How are you standing right now?"

"Sheer force of will." Mick straightened his back slowly and breathed deeply. The discomfort subsided, and he offered a shaky smile. "I'll manage. Come on, let's go join the others."

Outside, Vidia had packed some things in a saddlebag. "You're coming too?" Mick asked.

"My brother." Vidia raised her brows as though Mick should already know this.

Adema exited the quaint home that Mick now took a good look at. A garden expanded along the side of the house, and creeping vines slithered up its purple walls, looking like they might swallow it whole and make the house one with the earth. The location was beautiful, perched at the top of a cliff overlooking the sea. To one side, a row of trees bordered an open green, and the cliff's edge bordered another, and to the left, the lush grassy ground sloped gently downward.

Adema headed straight for Mick and embraced him in as tight a squeeze as her thin arms could muster. Tears rolled down her cheeks. It'd been less than a year ago that Mick had restored some health into her bones. How quickly she'd declined. As soon as he got his healing back, he'd take care of her.

She patted his rough beard that had reached the point of no longer itching. "You only just got here, and now you're leaving. I've missed you." She offered him a pack with some food and water and a change of clothes. Her white curls fell loosely around her shoulders. Somehow, she seemed fragile on her own, but Mick remembered how she always looked more youthful next to Adefa. Their contrasted appearances in age never seemed odd. It was just the way they were to him and he never thought much of it until now.

"I'll be back soon, Adema. How's Adefa holding up?"

"He's feeling his years catching up to him, but he'll live. He didn't sleep well, and I don't want to wake him now. See him when you return."

Mick liked the sound of that. He would return. These goodbyes were not final.

At the door, Mick's parents hugged. Vidia and Boone were nearly packed and ready to mount. Adrik came from the field beyond the tree line, leading two horses on either side of him. There must have been a stable somewhere that way. Mick's heart did a little leap when he spotted Uncle Dimi, standing by a bench near the cliff with his thumbs in his trouser pockets. He watched them all, but didn't look like he was going to come say goodbye. His standoffish behaviour was unlike him.

Mick laid down his pack and walked away from the others to join him. Dimitri's brown hair had more silver in it than when Mick had last seen him, and the skin around his eyes appeared sullener. He still didn't look his age, but he looked older than he had just weeks earlier.

"While we still have daylight!" Adrik called over as Mick walked away.

Part of Mick wanted to laugh at the man's insistence, but more than that, he wanted to slap him.

Dimitri waved off Adrik's remark. "Relax, Adrik. This'll only take a second."

Mick didn't rush to meet his uncle. Every slow step was a reminder of his injury. Dimitri's eyes softened, missing their usual spark. Instead of swallowing Mick in a giant hug as usual, Dimitri looked him over. His lips turned down and his eyes filled with tears. Mick didn't know if he could take any more crying if he was going to hold back the dam behind his own eyes.

"Don't tell me you're going to get all sappy on me now too." Mick forced a smile.

Dimitri's tension let up as he laughed. "Don't you take anything seriously, Mick?"

Mick drew in a long breath. "Life's too short to be serious." How short it was indeed.

"Do you still have the stone?"

He nodded. "It's safe."

"That's good. How did you keep it from Beiron?"

"I didn't have it on me. But I don't understand. If Beiron got the thing he was after, why does he still want the stone? He searched Adefa for it after he'd …" *Drank his blood.* Mick shuddered at the memory. Then Riggs popped into his head, blood dripping from his fists and the evil gleam in his eye when he'd spotted Mick in the hall outside the study. Would that tortured man be him next? A strange tingling extended from his wound and an escalating fear rose in him that he had to stifle before it consumed him.

"That stone is the heart of Kartha," Dimitri said. "As long as Beiron doesn't have it, there's still hope to reclaim the power."

"Why did you bring it to me in the first place? Anything could have happened to it, and I didn't have a clue how important it was." That wasn't entirely true, but what Mick knew of its importance was more instinct than actual knowing.

Dimitri pinched the bridge of his nose. "I'm sorry." He took Mick into an embrace. "I should have waited. I didn't think giving it to you would lead to all this." He released him and his eyes flitted to Mick's stomach, then back to his face. "Adrik says you're not healing. Is it true?"

Mick shrugged and pretended like it didn't bother him. No one else could heal in seconds, and he never heard them complain. "I'm sure I'll be fine." But he doubted it. He glanced over his shoulder. Cassian, Boone, and Vidia were mounted and waiting alongside Adrik. He faced Dimitri again. "Are you not coming?"

Dimitri ran his fingers through his hair. "I told a friend I'd help him find someone. But I'll catch up with you as soon as I can."

Adrik walked toward them, bringing Mick's horse. "Longest second ever."

"Okay, Adrik, hold your horses." Dimitri nudged Mick's arm and winked, a spark of his humour returning. "You better get going before he drags you behind them."

"He wouldn't do that." Mick smirked. "It would take too long." He grinned and Dimitri laughed. "Cheeky kid. Go."

# Chapter 34

The whispers were back. Mick thought they'd have left him alone by now, but they still echoed on, growing louder in the silent moments of the journey. *Theranol*, the voices whispered. The same word as before, along with the jumble of other words he couldn't understand.

Cassian rode with Adrik, leading Mick, Vidia, and Boone through a luminous forest. As the sky grew darker, the leaves and grass gave off a subtle glow. Mick didn't recognize most of the plants that grew here. Even the shrubs had a yellow hue, and their jagged leaves were like nothing he'd ever seen. Adrik paused in places along the way and examined some of them. Many of the blue-green leaves of the trees were duller than others. Flowers that Mick didn't know the names of grew in clusters along the trees' roots. While some were vibrant and full of life, others looked like ash. Mick trailed behind the others. He reached out and picked a greying leaf as he passed under a tree. The leaf crumbled between his fingers.

Sickness was a good word for this. He imagined his own body slowly turning to ash, the wind carrying what remained of him throughout a dying

Kartha. As if the thought spurred it on, his wound flared in a burst of pain. He hunched over, squeezing his abdomen and slowing his horse. After a few seconds, he felt a little better. No one appeared to have noticed. He straightened and tried not to fall too far behind.

Heavy clouds threated an afternoon rain. After some time, the forest trail tapered from soft soil to a packed gravel road that took them into the mountains. The Bludesel Mountains, as Mick had learned, named for the red sandstone.

Cassian held his horse back and waited for Mick to catch up so he could ride beside him. "How bad is the pain?"

"It's not bad," Mick lied. "How soon until we get there?"

Adrik pointed to a path that diverted from the main road. "We'll bring the horses this way and will follow that road. We'll be there shortly."

"Should we stop for food?" Boone asked, looking a little too hopeful.

"We keep going." Adrik nudged his horse to move. "It's not far now."

Probably best they didn't stop anyway. If they did, Mick didn't think he'd want to get back on his horse again. He dismissed his father's frown. "I'll be all right, Dad. Let's just get there."

Adrik led them off the road and onto the new path. Whether or not Cassian believed Mick, he left it alone and trekked after Adrik. Boone nudged his horse to follow.

Vidia rode up on Mick's other side, catching his eye.

"Really, Vid, I'll be fine."

She said nothing as she trailed after Boone. The path they turned onto was narrower than the road had been, and they only had room to ride single file.

From the front of their line, Adrik spoke about the mountains with a cheeriness that didn't suit Mick's mood. "The Bludesel and Teiry Mountains were the same at one point," he told them all. "They spanned across the width of Kartha as one long range. The Chronicle Storm not only affected the people within the vicinity but the land as well." He didn't wait for any response as he went on explaining how the gap between the ranges came to be, and how the Vastgerdite had been torn from these mountains.

As fascinated as Mick was to soak up every bit of Kartha as possible, the grandness of what he might have to do started to weigh on him. So much history and life here and he knew next to nothing of any of it. *Or how to save it.* And now, just as he was finally learning everything, he was going to die.

Adrik started getting into talk of curses when Mick stopped listening. He didn't need fuel to feed his fear.

The trail widened, and Mick had room to guide his horse up next to Vidia. Boone sped up ahead to ride next to Adrik and probably ask him a million questions about magic.

Mick shifted his backside in his saddle, trying to relieve his tailbone from the pressure. He squirmed, and Vidia eyed him, her brows raised.

He stilled his fidgeting. "Vidia, I wanted to apologize for leaving without you. We were—"

"Don't." Vidia raised a hand. "My uncle had no right to lock you up like that. Boone told me everything. You don't have to apologize. Don't beat yourself up about it."

Mick smirked. "The curse is doing enough of that." He chuckled, but Vidia didn't reciprocate. Her frown deepened. "Is it true you can heal?"

"I can. They have a name for me. Healer. Some healer, right? I think I'm broken."

Cassian peered over his shoulder at them but said nothing.

"Don't joke," Vidia said. "You're lucky to be alive."

"All the more reason to have a little fun, don't you think?" Mick gave her a crooked smile.

Vidia's lips pressed together, and she furrowed her brows.

Mick winked. Did all women lack a sense of humour, or just the ones he knew?

The path narrowed again, and Mick allowed Vidia to ride ahead of him as they returned to single file. Shale crunched underfoot, and the humidity increased as they descended on a slow decline. Clouds drifted across the sky, still looking on the verge of letting loose. The peaks of the mountains blocked what remained of the daylight, leaving them in hazy dusk. Adrik raised his hand, opening his palm toward the sky.

"*Luzen.*" A light appeared over his hand, much like Beiron's or Damien's except Adrik's was white. It lit the area in a bright glow.

Mick opened his hand to try making his own light with magic. "*Luzen.*" He repeated the word Adrik had used. Light sparked over his fingers, but at the same time, pain exploded from his wound. He cried out and wrapped his arms around his torso. Cassian dismounted his horse and ran to Mick, looking ready to catch him should he fall. "What's happened? What did you do?"

Mick took a minute to catch his breath. "That." He pointed to Adrik's light. "I made a spark, but it was excruciating. That's not supposed to happen, is it?"

"No," Cassian said. "It's not. Your light—it wasn't blue."

Mick shook his head. The little bit that flared had been white.

Adrik shared a meaningful look with Cassian. He waved a hand at him. "Get back on your horse. We will talk more when we get there." He glanced up and around, then carried on without waiting for them.

Cassian didn't go right away. He looked up at Mick. "Are you still able to ride?"

"Yes." Mick held back from adding, *I'm not dead yet.*

Cassian didn't press for more, although he looked like he wanted to. He remounted, and they continued riding.

They trekked farther into a valley until they reached a plateau, where huts made of clay and straw were scattered. Two large timber-framed buildings stood out near the centre of the valley. One was rectangular, and the other was shaped like an octagon. Off to the side, a square took up a large space where chairs were lined in haphazard rows.

People milled about. Walking the grounds, standing and talking, playing cards or dice at the tables outside the octagonal building. A few people took notice of them coming in, but mostly everyone carried on with what they were doing.

Adrik dismounted. Cassian, Vidia, and Boone followed his lead and did the same, but Mick struggled to bring his leg over the horse's neck to dismount. Two boys who looked around twelve years old came to relieve them of their horses, and Mick felt a flush of heat rise to his cheeks at his predicament. What kind of grown man couldn't get off a horse? He braced himself for pain as he stretched a leg across until they were both draped over one side. Boone took the reins and steadied the horse for him.

"Give me a second." Mick lifted a finger. He took a big breath and held it as he hopped down. His feet landed hard on the ground, which jostled him and sent shooting pains all over his midsection. He wrapped his arms around himself and hunched over, seething through his teeth. Cassian took him by the elbow until he was ready to stand again.

The stares didn't help.

Mick glared back at them. "Would you all stop looking at me like I'm about to drop dead any second?"

A husky blond man approached to greet them. Mick straightened, and his legs managed to take his weight. Blondie looked at all of them, but his gaze came to rest on Vidia. Adrik scanned the camp, then said to the man, "Waylan, where is Kameron? I must speak with him immediately."

"He's in a meeting at the Hall with Keshlyn." Waylan jabbed a thumb over his shoulder but didn't take his eyes off Vidia.

Adrik started on his way. He paused and looked back at Mick. "Don't go far. I'll be right back." He ran past the huts in the direction Waylan had indicated.

Waylan took notice of Boone, Mick, and Cassian. He kept his attention on Vidia. "Hey," he said.

"Hi." Vidia rubbed her arm.

"Who are your friends?" Waylan eyed Mick.

Vidia bit her lip. "Cassian Dairner." She gestured to him. "And these are Boone and Mick." For their benefit, she added, "This is my brother Waylan."

Mick gathered that his father had already known this, but not because of any resemblance. The only similarity Mick could see between Waylan and Vidia was their bright green eyes. Otherwise, it was hard to believe they were related at all.

"Can we talk?" Waylan asked Vidia.

She nodded, then turned to Mick and peered up at him with her doelike eyes. "You'll be okay?"

Her concern gave Mick the strength to want to prove to her that he would be. "I'll be fine. You go."

Vidia didn't go right away. She continued to hold Mick's gaze. "Kameron will be able to help you. Come find me when you can." She hesitated, looking like she wanted to say more. When Waylan started walking away, she slowly turned and went with him.

Cassian waved for Mick and Boone to follow him. "Come this way. We'll wait over here." He led them toward the square with the lined-up chairs. Mick moved slowly, and the others matched his speed.

"You know Vidia's family?" Mick asked his father, but it wasn't really a question.

"What makes you think that?"

"When we met Daegan, he brought up Uncle Dimi once or twice." Mick shared a look with Boone, who would have already given the details of that visit, but might have omitted this particular subject. "I take it they don't get along."

"No, they didn't." Cassian rubbed his neck, which sometimes gave him problems. Mick always thought it was because he never loosened up about anything.

They passed the small huts. A handful of residents exited the rectangular building and meandered in the same direction as them.

"Their conflict started before you were born," Cassian said. "They used to get along fine, but that was before the incident." He paused long enough that Mick thought he wasn't going to elaborate, but then he continued to share the story.

"The woman Daegan was to be married to got sick. Uncle Dimitri and your adefa tried to help by using the healing magic of the Weldafire Stone. It worked initially, but the sickness came back and she didn't make it.

"Daegan thought they didn't try hard enough, that they should have done more. Dimitri cared for Delia like she was his own, and knowing that, Daegan believed he should have been more invested. They all took it hard, but Daegan took it the hardest.

"Then, not long after, his father and brother went missing. When they were declared lost at sea, Daegan was given the responsibility of their three children. He barely knew how to take care of himself, never mind three kids barely in their adolescence. He got himself mixed up with some bad people and hasn't been the same since."

Boone scratched his ear. "You mean someone actually wanted to marry that man?"

Mick had to agree with Boone. But the part about the woman's sickness returning nagged at him. Was Adefa's and Uncle Dimi's healing power only temporary? Could the same thing happen to him with his own magic, and would he make enemies if he couldn't get it right?

Not that he didn't do a fine job of making enemies already.

Couches made up the last row of the square. A few instruments were left on the grass at the front where the chairs faced, including a marimba, two djembes, and a conga. A shekere rested on a chair.

"Are there many here from Ectarin?" Mick recognized the instruments from his studies on the nearest neighbouring land to Iptin.

"Kameron and Keshlyn came from there years ago." Cassian found them an empty couch in the back row and directed them toward it. "They travelled with others and settled in Litlen. After the Chronicle Storm, they came here and started this camp as a place of refuge. They call it Elefthan—freedom. You should be all right here. Kameron and his people will make sure you're looked after."

A handful of men and women trickled over from the buildings to find a seat.

Mick took a seat on the couch, immediately regretting it. How was he going to get up now?

Cassian shuffled into the row after them but remained standing. "They must be getting ready to start soon. Most nights, after sundown, they have music sessions."

A woman strolled around the perimeter of the square, lighting standing torches with a magic flame. Boone stared, then circled in place. "Can we stay for it?" he asked.

More people made their way over, taking seats with the others.

"We will," Cassian said, "but Mick is going with Kameron and Adrik. You and I will have to wait here."

Mick hadn't thought much about what he was here for. It was overwhelming to keep up with everything he was learning about himself and Kartha. The whispers were a constant distraction. As was his fear of dying—again. Had he died? There was the stabbing, but before that, he'd nearly drowned in that cave. Had he died then too?

He dismissed those memories. They were still too fresh to think about. He was here now and among friends and family. His father seemed confident that he'd be safe in this place. Safe from Beiron and Damien perhaps, but what about Ighur? Would he make his way to this secluded corner of the country?

"Where's Mick going?" Boone asked Cassian, drawing Mick from his thoughts.

Cassian pointed to the octagonal building. "The Acteg."

Mick swallowed. He rubbed his hands on his trousers. "What will they do?"

"I don't know. But you can trust Adrik and Kameron. Mick, you have to understand. There's never been anyone like you before. Karthan magic doesn't include healing power—that comes only from the Weldafire Stone. And your blood—no one knows what any of this means. Adrik and Kameron have been around since the time of the Chronicle Storm and have the most insight into what we're dealing with. Adrik has dedicated his life to protecting and studying the stone and its power. If anyone can tell you what's going on, it's him."

"What's the Chronicle Storm?" Mick hated that he didn't know.

Cassian dropped his head. "I'm sorry I haven't told you anything, Mick. That stone has brought nothing but pain to our family. I thought that by keeping all this from you, it would stop these kinds of things from ever happening. I thought I was protecting you.

"The Chronicle Storm is the storm that changed the people of Litlen. Vastgerdite, the healing crystal that used to be part of the hills and mountains in the southern regions of Kartha, had been summoned from the earth to join and create one stone—the Weldafire Stone. That was the storm that gave magic to those who were present in Litlen at the time."

Half the chairs were filled now as more people had come to claim a spot. Vidia hadn't returned from wherever she and Waylan went. Mick's tailbone ached, but more than that, his wound throbbed beneath the bandage. He'd been avoiding unwinding it to see the damage and didn't dare look now. For having never had so much as a scratch last more than a few seconds, he didn't think he could handle what he'd find underneath. The black scar on his hand from making a deal with Damien had been bad enough.

Boone sat beside Mick, leaving a space between them. Cassian sat on the arm of the couch, not making himself too comfortable. Mick scanned the grounds for Adrik, who was nowhere to be seen. He couldn't tell if his nerves were on edge because of his anxiety over what he would have to do or because of the curse that was killing him. Whatever Adrik and Kameron had planned, he hoped it would help calm the storm in him and shed some light on how he was meant to heal Kartha. If he didn't have this strange connection to the land, he might have laughed at the prospect of healing a country. A country that was dying because of him.

# Chapter 35

IT'D BEEN A WHILE SINCE LAILA HEARD ANY SOUNDS COMING FROM UPSTAIRS. Now was as good a time as any to make her move. Beiron's bindings were well mastered, but Laila had plenty of practice at escaping. In the time she'd waited—hopefully for Beiron to get far away from there—she'd used her foot to rub against her opposite ankle and draw her dagger from its sheath. It was a small thing—nothing glitzy or fancy about it. Just something with a sharp edge that came in handy in tough situations.

Like this one.

Unfortunately, experience had taught her to always keep one tucked away. While she was grateful to have learned a few things from her misadventures, she was even more grateful to have survived them.

She used her leg to slide the dagger toward her hands, which proved to be difficult while tied to a post. After all her efforts, she was sweating. She managed to get her dagger to her hands, then used it to carefully cut through the rope. It snapped apart, and her hands were free. She rubbed her wrists and felt the blood return.

She said, "*Bludevint*," and a white light appeared over her hand. That would take some getting used to. She didn't mind the dark, but the light helped her find the door quickly. It would help to know where she was so she could determine how she might get away undetected. All she needed was to find somewhere safe to lay low until she could safely return to Raidan's place. Then she'd send Royl and the Warriors to wherever this place was.

She tried opening the door. Locked.

*Not a problem.* She touched a palm to the door and, as much as she preferred not to rely on using blood magic—sometimes it couldn't be avoided—she drew from the power in her and combined it with her essence. The door groaned. It shook violently, then exploded into tiny fragments of wood splinters. Depending on where this place was, the noise might have attracted attention.

Laila replaced her dagger, unstrapped the sheath from her ankle and secured it at her waist, making it more readily available should she need it again. She stepped over the mess of the shattered door and bounded up the stairs, where another barricade blocked the way. This one didn't have a doorknob—not that it mattered. She snuffed her light, put her hands to the solid object in her way, and felt around. It moved. She pushed it and discovered that she could slide it sideways. It was heavy, and it took great strength, but she strained against it until it slid open enough for her to slip through.

She emerged in what appeared to be a study or a bedroom in a home. A desk and chair sat against the far wall. Curtains were drawn across the window, but they were thin enough that she could see it was nighttime. The wall she'd just moved aside was actually a bookcase. It was slightly raised from the ground and on a rail to make it easier to slide. The books on it explained why it was so heavy.

Beyond the scent of mildew and dampness, the smell here had a certain familiarity to it. She knew this place. In fact, she'd been in this very room before. She hadn't known about the secret room downstairs, but it explained a lot. She'd always thought Beiron would have had some sort of laboratory for all of his work in experimentation.

She ignited her light, knowing that this window faced the back garden and that no one could see the light from the street. She directed it so she could read some of the titles. The books confirmed her suspicion that this was indeed Beiron's home. She recognized some, but many of them hadn't been here during the time she'd scavenged this place more than a century ago, including titles such as *Zareff Continent: The Countries of Ecstein; Natural Remedies for the Everyday; A History of Kartha: Government, Resources, and Geography; and Kartha's Power Over the Nations—Dive Deep into Kartha's Rich History—Learn About the Chronicle Storm and the Chosen Race.*

Laila rolled her eyes at that last one and noted the author. Whoever Regal Norm was, she didn't think she'd get along with him.

No doubt Beiron had written his own works in the many books that bore no title on the bindings. She was struck with a sudden urge to set fire to the place. Nothing would give her greater pleasure than to destroy all that Beiron had invested his life's work into. She paused, staring at her hand. How easy it would be to spark her flame and touch everything in this house so that it burned. The idea tempted her, but then she considered the knowledge in these books. They contained information obtained through awful, horrible means. Everyone who'd been used for the sake of amassing it would have been sacrificed for nothing. The least she could do was preserve the learned information and ensure it had not all been in vain. Besides, there was no time for vengeance. Now that she knew where she was, she ran.

She hadn't even made it out of the room when a figure jumped out in front of her. She gasped, and the assailant put his hand to her chest, cutting her breath short. Her knees buckled, and she clawed at him with waning strength as he used blood magic to draw from her well of power, building his own power while weakening hers.

Laila knew his face. He'd been a visitor at Daegan's Keep. Damien. Wasn't that his name? He pushed her into the room she'd been trying to escape from, and she stumbled backward while he guided her with firm pressure on her chest. Her head slammed against the wall, and her legs gave out. She slid down the wall, but he maintained his touch.

Her breaths came short and quick. When she slumped on the floor, he removed his hand. It felt like she'd been suffocating and, at last, could suck in a harsh breath.

Damien crouched. He sniffed the air around her and licked his lips.

"Would you look at this? Laila Madx…lurking about in places she shouldn't be. I thought that was my job." He chuckled. "What would Beiron think if he knew you were sneaking around in his house? You do know this is his house, don't you? Of course you do. You're the Witch. You know a lot more than you let people believe. Cunning, crafty Laila." He leaned away so she could see more than just his lips and nose. "Apologies. I know who you are, but you've never had the pleasure of meeting me. I'm Damien. Beiron and I go way back."

Laila drew in a raspy breath. Her power was drained, and she didn't have the strength to stand.

Damien smiled, showing off his straight, discoloured teeth. "He'll be very interested in why you're here."

Laila closed her eyes and opened them slowly. A bit of strength seeped back into her body, but not fast enough. She needed more. She barely made a sound on her breath.

"What's that?" Damien turned his ear toward her.

When he leaned in, Laila placed a hand on his chest, mimicking his move from a moment ago. She imagined setting fire to his blood from the inside and letting it simmer hot. His lips twisted in agony, and he went rigid.

"Didn't you hear?" Laila whispered into his ear. "I was invited. You can't be that good of a friend if he didn't tell you about me."

A flood of strength came over her as she drew from his power. Once she'd depleted his strength, she pushed him over, and his body fell lopsided to the floor. A glass vial stuck out of his pocket, nearly falling out. Without thinking, Laila grabbed it. The liquid inside had an unusual dark pink colour, distinctive to the sap from the tandernion—which she knew had only one prominent use. What was Damien up to?

She stuffed the vial into her pocket and hopped to her feet. There was still time to get out of here. She left Damien where he lay and ran into the hallway toward the front door as quickly as she could manage while still recovering from his assault. Her heart leapt when she turned the knob and found it was unlocked. She swung it wide and didn't look as she bolted out and ran straight into Beiron.

Panic flooded her. She flung her arms in front of herself while trying to scoot around him at the same time. He grabbed her wrists and twisted her around. Her arms crossed over themselves. He pinned her against his torso as he guided her back inside. Laila dug her heels into the stony ground. She shook her head and threw every ounce of power into her fight, then screamed when it accomplished nothing. His hand released one of her wrists to cover her mouth as he pushed her into the house.

Once inside, he removed his hand from her mouth so he could close the door and lock it. His grip on her wrist tightened.

Laila kicked him, but he held on, unaffected. He shook her arm violently and she let it go limp. A sinking feeling came over her that nearly brought her to her knees. She had been so close. If Damien hadn't slowed her down, she might have gotten away.

Her dagger hadn't gone unnoticed. Beiron ripped it from her waist and tossed it aside. But thanks to Damien, she had one last resort. If she were right about the vial's contents, it might come in handy to get past Beiron. Depending on this particular concoction, maybe it had some sort of sedative mixed in with it.

He thrust her into the sitting room, and she nearly tripped over the table in the middle. The boarded-up windows blocked her view of outside. And anyone's view in. Not that this neighbourhood was teeming with people.

Beiron rubbed the back of his neck. "I should have known you'd be clever enough to get yourself out of there. I'll have to take better care where I leave you next time."

There wasn't going to be a next time.

Damien came out into the hallway and faced them in the sitting room. He supported his weight against the wall and clutched his chest. He looked from Beiron to Laila and then back to Beiron.

Beiron took one look at him and his eyebrows flashed. He grinned. "I see my daughter got the better of you, my friend."

Damien's jaw dropped. "Your—? She's—? Laila's your *daughter?*"

"You sound surprised."

"I…" Damien closed his gaping mouth and shook his head. "I didn't realize you and Freya were close, that's all."

"They weren't," Laila said, hoping her words cut deeper than any knife could. "My mother wanted nothing to do with him. She didn't even tell him she had me."

Beiron crossed his arms. "That's all right. We'll make up for lost time, won't we, *Deihara?*"

Laila flared her nostrils.

Not if she could help it. "I think you spent too much time alone and you've gone insane. Or have you always been this disillusioned?"

"It's true. I had a lot of time to think. But all that time gave me clarity. See how quickly I got the power of the Weldafire Stone after I'd been released. Now, once Kartha is restored, we can work on purging the powers that be and starting fresh. The elders had their chance. Now it's time they stepped down so we can try something new. And I'll have you by my side one way or another. I've seen into your mind. Your sentiments are not so different from my own. Kartha will be ours to make it as we like."

"You really are delusional." Laila reached slowly for her pocket containing the vial. The tandernion sap had a component in it that could inhibit magical abilities. The tree was a dying species and wasn't one Laila had come across often, but she'd also made a special point not to. Based on the little she did know of it, she was unwilling to risk contact with it for fear that the effects would be permanent. Now she didn't think she'd mind so much if they were.

Beiron's chuckle lacked emotion. He turned to Damien. "What did you find out?"

Damien bit his lip. He gestured to Laila. "You really want her here for that conversation? She's close with the twins."

"She won't be seeing them for a while. She can hear what you have to say." Beiron indicated the couches in the sitting room. "Come in. Take a seat." He nodded at Laila. "You too. Sit."

Laila jutted her chin out. She had no intention of making herself comfortable here.

When Beiron started toward her, she whipped the vial from her pocket. She wound her arm back, ready to throw it hard enough to smash it at his feet. This being a potion she was unfamiliar with, she didn't want to risk removing the stopper and having the fumes affect her before she had the chance to use it.

Beiron froze and assessed the vial. "Where did you get that?"

Laila nodded in Damien's direction. "Ask him. I'm not sure what's in here, but I have a pretty good idea of one ingredient. I'm sure you've come to that same conclusion."

If he did, it didn't stop him. Beiron took another step toward her, and she panicked. She threw the vial downward toward his legs, but his reflexes were sharp. Beiron swung his arm and caught the vial before it hit the floor.

While he reached for it, Laila bolted to the door, though she still had to get past him. In one motion, Beiron caught the vial and swooped for her, catching her shoulder. He clamped his grip there and shoved her back into the sitting room. The force of the movement gave her whiplash. She stumbled, and the backs of her knees bumped against the couch behind her. Damien rushed to the door and stood in front of it, creating an extra obstacle in her way. Laila growled and projected a ball of white light at Beiron, hitting him square in the chest. It stung her, which meant it stung him too, but it didn't deter him as he barrelled toward her.

She placed a hand flat against her chest. "Stop! Don't make me do this."

Beiron paused. He was within arm's reach, but he didn't try to stop her. He leaned back and put his hands on his hips. "All right, Laila. Do it. Remember how well it worked for you last time? I seem to recall you losing consciousness while I stayed on my feet."

Laila's mind raced to come up with something she could use against him. Her dagger lay on the floor on the other side of the room. Even if she had it, it wouldn't do her much good against the two of them. She didn't have the physical strength or the skill to fight both of them, which left her with only her magic. But Beiron was right. She wouldn't get very far if she exhausted her power.

She lowered her hand, conceding.

Beiron placed his hands on her shoulders and forced her to sit. She sank onto the couch, averting her gaze from them both.

Just because she had failed to escape this time, didn't mean Beiron had won. This wasn't over.

# Chapter 36

Damien took a seat on the couch opposite the one Laila was on, and Beiron plonked himself down next to her. She pressed herself into the corner on the couch, getting as far away from him as possible. It wasn't far enough, as their knees still touched.

Beiron linked his fingers together and leaned forward over his knees. "The boy? Did you learn anything new?" he asked Damien.

"He's awake. Adrik escorted him to Elefthan earlier this evening."

"How did he seem?"

"I didn't have eyes on him myself, but they rode on horseback, so he was well enough to make the journey."

"Did you find out why he was going there?"

Damien shook his head. "My spies could learn only that Adrik was taking him to see Kameron."

Beiron rubbed his stubbled chin. "His being there does pose a problem. He'll be well protected. I won't be able to get within a hundred feet of the camp without being seen."

Damien crossed his ankle over his leg. "I might be able to help with that. I have men at my disposal. I can have them create a diversion that will force the Healer from the camp. Once he's out, I'll ensure his path crosses with yours."

Laila's ears burned. Why couldn't she have shared a connection with Royl instead of Beiron? She could have used it to warn him.

Her frustration mounted, and she couldn't stay silent. "You don't need him to fix anything if you would just give back what you took. What can Mick do? You're the one with all six trace of elements. You can't expect someone else to fix what you broke."

Beiron sat back and put his arm around the back of the couch, behind her head. "Welcome to the conversation. Tell me more about this prophecy."

Laila stuck her nose out, determined not to further encourage this course of action. She'd have given Beiron her best look of contempt, except she already didn't like how close their faces were. Turning hers toward his— they'd practically touch noses.

"Now, Laila, have you already forgotten our conversation from this morning?"

Their conversation? Laila had to think for a minute. He'd shown her why they shared a connection. The lacrut. She lowered her gaze to the floor.

He didn't have to ask when he could just take.

"It doesn't make any sense," she said. "Our people have taken this prophecy and made it out to be more than what it is: the drunken ramblings of an old woman."

"What exactly does it say?" Beiron asked.

Damien uncrossed his leg and sat back. "That the Healer would bring a sickness to Kartha. One that would bring about the end of the land. In other words, Kartha's doom."

"That's not how it goes," Laila cut in, unable to restrain herself. Beiron and Damien both turned their focus toward her. She squirmed in her seat and shifted her gaze to stare at the floor instead of at either of them. So much for not encouraging this topic.

She felt both pairs of eyes staring, but refused to look up.

"Go on," Beiron said after a long moment. "You've already started. You may as well finish now. Do tell. How exactly does this prophecy go?"

"It's nothing. I don't remember it all anyway."

"Are you always such a bad liar? Tell me."

Laila rubbed her clammy hands together. Was there a convincing half-truth she could give instead? Something to appease Beiron's wondering? How much of the prophecy did Damien actually know? Could someone just remove that plank from the window to let in the fresh air? Perspiration tickled her neck.

Beiron took a noisy breath in, and Laila's heart thumped hard against her breast. Beiron's patience would only last so long. How far could she push it before he decided to steal the answer from her thoughts? She supposed that if he was adamant about learning these details of the prophecy, he may as well hear what had actually been spoken and not Damien's misinterpreted version of it.

She cleared her throat and relented. It was confusing and made no sense anyway. "Separated are the heart, the spirit. The land—torn in two. Sickness will bring the end when the Healer comes. Blood must be spilled to right the wrong, to restore. Return. Blood of the cursed. Blood of the offender. Blood of the land. Return. Heart. Spirit. Return. Return."

No one said anything. Laila rolled her eyes. "Like I said, the ramblings of a drunken woman."

"It means the Healer must die," Damien offered. "Blood must be spilled. That's what it said, right?"

"It means nothing." Laila locked eyes with Damien. "Mick didn't bring the sickness." She shifted so she could turn her face to Beiron without being so close to him. "You did. Besides, you've already spilled enough of his blood, don't you think?"

"Apparently not," Beiron said. "Damien makes a good point."

Laila wanted to smack the sneer from Damien's face.

Beiron shifted around on the cushion, retrieving Damien's vial from his pocket. He fiddled with it between his fingers. "Is this what I think it is?"

Damien's eyes twinkled. "What do you think? I used your own recipe."

"I take it you have a good reason for having this on you."

"If I'm going to instigate a fight with the valients of Elefthan, I like the odds better when I have the upper hand."

Beiron hefted himself from the soft cushions and stood. He stretched his back. "Right, well, gather your forces to smoke the boy out." He handed Damien the vial. "And keep an ear out for where the Weldafire Stone is."

Laila looked at her hands in her lap to hide her surprise. She'd not realized Beiron didn't have the stone. Had he not checked Mick before leaving him for dead?

Damien got to his feet. "The land at the Gap has been split apart. Torn in two." He raised his eyes at Laila. She ignored his patronizing. Just because it was as the prophecy claimed, didn't change the fact that Beiron was to blame. Not Mick.

Damien walked to the door. "I'll lead an attack on the camp and will coax the kid out. Once he's away from Kameron's protection, I'll take him along the forest trail. If you don't have anywhere else to be, I can have him converge paths with you at the old Cotyr mill."

"Excellent." Beiron clapped his hands together. "Ah, I've missed having you around, Damien."

"You've been missed as well. When all this is said and done, I'd like you to meet some folks who sympathize with your cause. I've established new contacts through the Valcas' connections and have grown a bit of a following. Many of whom would like to see new leadership rise up in Kartha."

"I should like that."

Damien had his order. He left and closed the door on his way out.

Beiron stood over Laila. He chewed on his cheek and tapped his bottom lip. "Now, what to do with you?"

Laila eyed the door behind him. Damien hadn't locked it on his way out. Should she try and make a run for it? Would it do her any good? If she weren't quick enough, Beiron would have no trouble subduing her. She licked her lips. If she were going to run, she couldn't afford to hesitate.

Beiron shifted his weight. "I've got an idea." He motioned for her to stand.

Laila's heart sank. She'd missed her chance. Her only comfort was that there would be another. Beiron's last trap hadn't successfully contained her. Why would this next one be any different?

But that didn't mean she would make things easy. An idea came to mind. "You like making deals, don't you? Let's make a deal."

"The time for deals is over. Now's the time for obedience."

Laila trembled. "What if I promise to visit you regularly? You can teach me anything—everything—and I'll listen willingly."

"I don't need you to listen. You and I are already in agreement. But you're soft and unwilling to do what needs to be done. Luckily for you, you've no need to. I will. But you're staying out of my way until it's done. Enough stalling. Let's go."

Laila stood on shaky legs, and Beiron led her back down the stairs and into the secret room in the cellar. He ignited his light and stood at the threshold where there should have been a door. The shattered splinters lay on the floor in a heap.

Beiron glanced sideways at her with a twinkle in his eye, not hiding his amusement.

"I like your style. Now, get in."

Laila stood, frozen. "What are you going to do?"

He placed a hand on her back and guided her in. She moved at his prodding, and when she was in the room, she quickly turned on her heel to face him. He backed away through the threshold. Instead of answering her question, he produced his knife, sliced a thin line into his palm, and rubbed his hands together so both had blood on them. He raised his arms and smeared his blood along the top of the frame where the door used to be, then along its sides, outlining the shape of the threshold.

*"Vee aim bludevint, in triguznin. No an"*—he cocked his head at her—*"vychlemoland aim ernind—dororon craxn."*

He swept his fingers across the opening, as if feeling along a smooth surface. When he finished, he rested his hands at his sides.

"Do you remember at the lake? All those years ago, outside the cave? How I told you I put a spell over my book that should have prohibited anyone from being able to take it, except for me?" He paused.

Laila remembered. And hearing his incantation just now, she already knew she'd not be exempt from his spell because of their relation. Not this time. *Including my heir…*

She balled her hands into fists.

"No one but me will be able to come or go through here," Beiron continued. "Not even you. The only way you're leaving this room is if I allow it." He rubbed his hands together. "As you heard, I have somewhere to be. When I return, we'll have a conversation about what comes next. Your mother robbed me of the chance to know you, and now it's going to take some time to establish how to move forward from here. But first, the boy." His chest heaved, and his eyes, though already black and full of hate, darkened further like he had murder in his heart."

"Beiron, don't do this. Leave Mick alone. Give up the power and stop this pursuit."

Beiron raised his chin. He sniffed and wiped his wrist across his nose. "Get comfortable, Laila. We'll speak again soon."

He turned and went back upstairs.

She heard him slide the bookshelf back into place. "I won't be here when you return!" she called up to him, but her voice lacked conviction.

At the threshold where he'd created his invisible barrier, nothing indicated she'd be stopped from getting through. She stepped over to the door fragments. Was it possible his spell hadn't worked? Or maybe he thought he'd only deterred her and that she wouldn't try to escape. But—as much as it pained her to admit—he'd proved time and again how capable he was. He wouldn't have left her there if he wasn't certain she couldn't go anywhere.

She ignited her light and prodded it to float above her head. As best she could, she braced herself for whatever might happen as she attempted to reach through the opening.

A zap stung her fingers and shot up her arm, all the way through her body. She retracted her hand, and her light flickered. Her nerves tingled, and she cradled her hand close to her chest, feeling her racing heart. The realization sank in, and she wanted to cry.

She circled in place, scouring the walls of the small room for anything that could serve as an alternative exit. Unlikely. Beiron was a thorough man. But he didn't know just how resourceful she could be.

The room was a misshapen rectangle—one wall jutted in a little more than the others. Beiron hadn't bothered to cover the stone walls with anything to make it a more inviting atmosphere. Like a hidden room beneath his house was a place anyone would wish to visit.

A long, narrow table was positioned along the back wall with a single shelf beneath the counter. On the table were a lamp and weighing scales, and the cup he'd brought down for her earlier. Jars and vials were strewn messily over it and on the shelf below it. Most were empty, but a few had remnants of whatever they'd previously contained. She examined one jar that had yellow powder stuck to the bottom. She sniffed it. Motus. Useless. She smelled the next one that had hard bits of empty shells at the bottom. Harbury. Even if there were any left, it wouldn't have helped. Another jar had only a few drops of clear goop in it. Salve. If she had to guess, it was made from pink raimai.

These were useless. She'd be better off trying to break the barrier. Beiron had cast the spell using blood magic. Could she use the same to tear it down?

She broke a vial and took a sharp shard of glass. Blood to cast the spell, blood to undo it. *Maybe.* She faced the barrier.

Only one way to find out.

PEOPLE CROWDED INTO THE SQUARE, FILLING THE CHAIRS AND COUCHES. Mick had such a habit of keeping a lookout for Ighur that he couldn't help but scan the faces for his. He'd see better from a standing position, but he didn't have it in him to rise just now. From his seated viewpoint, Ighur was nowhere to be seen.

Adrik weaved through the empty spaces in the square and parted through where crowds blocked his path. He was easily distinguishable in the night with his white light bobbing over his head. With him was another man, who, like most of the residents here, had dark skin. Much darker than Adrik's copper tones. Mick watched as Adrik searched the faces of those around him until they landed on him, seated on a couch with his father and Boone. Adrik led his companion toward them. The man carried himself like a leader; his posture boasted authority as he walked. His mostly silver beard matched his head of silver hair. Those who caught his eye as he passed smiled and gave a little bow of the head or at the shoulders, showing respect. Mick deduced this to be Kameron.

Kameron's eyes fell on Cassian first. "Cassian, it is good to see you again. I am sorry it is under such circumstances." He had a faint Ectarin accent.

Cassian rose from his half-seated position on the arm of the couch. "Yes, I wish it weren't so, but it seems a visit was long overdue."

The man grasped his shoulders. "It is good to see you." He turned to Mick and scratched his silver beard. "You must be Mckal. I am Kameron." He offered his hand. Mick joined them standing and shook Kameron's hand. His friendly manner relieved some of Mick's tension.

"And who is this?" Kameron indicated Boone.

"Boone. He's a friend," Mick said.

Boone stood, and then smiled awkwardly. He stuffed a hand into his pocket and offered the other to shake.

The brief introduction seemed enough for Kameron, who shook Boone's hand and rested it on his shoulder. "Make yourself at home, friend."

A handful of men and women began setting up at the front and picked up their instruments.

Kameron stretched his arm toward the Acteg. "Come, Mckal. The music is about to begin. Let us go and see what your power holds."

When Mick looked for his father's reassurance, Cassian wrapped him in a hug. "This is where you're meant to be, Son." His words filled Mick's spirit.

Yes, of that, Mick was certain. Having his father's blessing gave him peace about whatever he had to face next.

He followed Kameron and Adrik to the Acteg, where, inside was an open space. "Welcome." Kameron's voice resonated. Wood floors and a high ceiling gave the room echoey acoustics. He extended his arms out wide and hummed a note. His blue light popped into existence and joined Adrik's white light. They danced to the ceiling and lit the spacious room.

"This is the Acteg," Kameron continued, "It is used on our music nights like these when we cannot gather under the stars. Grab a chair and take a seat over there." He pointed to the middle of the room.

A stack of chairs leaned against the wall. Mick took one and brought it to where Kameron had indicated. He sat and leaned over his knees. He'd thought Kameron and Adrik would grab a chair as well, but neither did.

Mick scratched his neck. It felt like he was about to get interrogated. "Should I have a witness present to hear my plea?" He flashed a crooked grin, but neither man cracked a smile. Kameron walked behind Mick and placed his hands on his shoulders.

Mick tensed. "Is it something I said?"

Kameron hummed another low note. His voice carried the tune around the room, maintaining its melodic sound even after he'd stopped humming.

"This requires you to focus, Mckal. Outside, the music will begin in a moment. All that you must do right now is listen. Close your eyes."

Mick caught Adrik staring at him with narrow eyes. The man was bossy even without saying anything.

Mick closed his eyes.

Kameron removed his hands from Mick's shoulders. "Let everything go from your mind. I want you to think of your magic. Your healing ability is directly correlated with Kartha, but I also want you to search deeper for the elements."

Apparently, Mick's healing power was more widely known than he realized. Or maybe it had become obvious after he'd survived being stabbed.

Outside, someone started banging out a rhythm on a drum. Another drummer joined, and soon the other instruments added to the sound in an upbeat tune—loud, even inside the building.

Kameron hummed again, mixing his bass vocals into a song with no words.

"Do you hear?" he asked after a moment.

Mick didn't realize the man had stopped humming. If Kameron was referring to the music, the volume of it coming from outside was loud enough that Mick felt the pulsing rhythm of the bass instrument in his throat. He couldn't tell the pace of his own heartbeat apart from the beat of the drums.

"I'm pretty sure everyone can hear it."

Kameron made a mirthful sound. "You are correct. But what each person hears and sees is different and unique to each individual. When you clear all things from your mind and listen intently to the sounds of the music—to the voices of the elements—the spirit of the song will entwine with yours and reveal to you the things meant only for you. As someone with delegates' blood, it will draw out your trace of element, and allow us to observe your power as you are entranced in the music."

Mick twisted back and looked up at Kameron. Out of everything he'd seen and heard in all his time in Kartha, he'd have thought talk like this would seem normal by now. But the spirit of the song entwining with his? Voices of the elements?

He'd once seen a woman claiming to be a seer. She'd take people's money and coax them into her caravan to show them *mystical things*. Kameron hadn't asked for anything yet, but Mick waited for the catch.

Kameron bowed his head and motioned for Mick to turn around. Mick did so while trying not to be skeptical. He closed his eyes again and listened. The mood of the music transitioned from an upbeat rhythm to a low, compelling chant. It had a tribal sound that carried an intriguing invitation to dive deeper into the low, gravelly tones. Mick slumped lower in his seat, letting the sound move through him.

Slowly, he became aware of little things, such as the sound of his breath, and his foot tapping along to the music. His chest rose as he inhaled, and he swayed in sync with a woman humming a melody. She sang no words, but her voice was haunting on its own.

Shadows flitted in his mind's eye. Shapes and colours without form. Fragments became clear in flashes: a river—two rivers—and the place where they met. A trench, split lengthwise across the land, stretching from south to north. More shadows crossed over the clear images and left a remnant haze over what Mick thought was meant to be Beiron's soulless eyes staring down at him with pure hatred in them.

Flashes of light burst behind Mick's closed eyes, and he squeezed them tighter. His wound tingled like it was on the verge of erupting in pain but wasn't quite there yet. He placed his hands over his abdomen, and he touched something warm and sticky. Although he was aware that he was still seated in the Acteg with Kameron and Adrik, somehow all that he was seeing and feeling seemed so real. He looked down at himself and took his hands away, horrified at the amount of blood on him. Something glinted in one of his hands beneath the blood. The Weldafire Stone. *How'd that get there?*

The music had changed. It grew louder. A group of what sounded like all male singers sang a song with perfect harmonies.

Mick's head throbbed.

The voices in his thoughts returned in full force, their chanting overpowering the male vocalists. *Blood of the cursed. Blood of the offender. Blood of the land.* Over and over, they continued to chant, growing louder. *Return. Return.*

In one instant, Mick was staring at his blood-soaked hands, and in the next, he was standing at the bottom of the trench, where water poured down the rocky walls. He stared at a stream that trickled in a rut along the ground. The haze remained, making it difficult to see clearly. The water on the ground appeared to be flowing in the wrong direction. Rather than running down the slanted earth, it flowed uphill. Mick squinted at it. He no longer held the stone, nor were his hands covered in blood.

His injury flared up and burned from within. It started subtly, then grew until he couldn't ignore it any longer. He screamed and doubled over, clutching both arms around his torso.

His head spun and felt like it might explode as the images tore from his mind. When the ringing in his ears subsided, he realized the music had stopped playing outside.

He opened his eyes.

At some point, he must have fallen from the chair, because he was on his knees on the floor in front of it. He touched his upper lip, where something tickled down from his nose. Blood. In rushed motions, he wiped it away using his forearm. The visions he saw lingered in his thoughts, and the chanting still resounded in the back of his skull. *Blood of the cursed, blood of the offender, blood of the land. Return. Return.*

The door slammed open and a woman entered. Her eyes darted from Kameron to Adrik to Mick. "What has happened? Is everything all right?"

Kameron's face had lost a shade of colour, and his forehead creased as he gazed at Mick. His eyes were all white—as Beiron's had been—like he was in some sort of trance. Adrik's mouth hung open, and his pupils were rolled back into his head. He too, was not fully present.

Mick shook his head. "I… I don't know what happened. He told me to listen. I—"

Kameron gasped, and his eyes returned to normal. They focused on Mick, "You were hurt. Let me see." He moved toward him, but Mick jumped to his feet and extended his arm out in front of himself. "No. I'm fine. It doesn't hurt anymore."

Adrik blinked twice, and his eyes returned to normal, but they glazed over right away. "I don't understand."

Kameron turned to the woman at the door. "Keshlyn? Is there something wrong?"

Keshlyn's shoulders dropped. "We heard screaming. I thought someone was dying."

Kameron and Adrik fixed their gazes on Mick.

"What?" Mick said. "I'm still here, aren't I?" Although, at the time, he'd certainly felt like he was dying.

His cheeks went hot. Had everyone heard him scream?

Kameron dipped his head at Keshlyn. "Thank you for your concern, Kesh. Everything is all right."

Keshlyn nodded and left, closing the door on her way out.

Kameron approached Mick. "Come now, let me see how it looks."

There was no point in arguing. Truthfully, Mick wanted to see how it looked too. After seeing it in his visions, covered in blood and feeling like he'd been stabbed all over again, he needed to lay eyes on it and see for himself what he was dealing with.

He removed his shirt and unwound the bandage.

Where Beiron had impaled him with the knife was all black. The wound itself had sealed and there was not even a hint of blood, but a mark the size of Mick's hand marred his flesh. He wobbled on shaky legs. Kameron offered his arm to help steady him.

The wound was not painful when Mick touched it. All the pain he felt came from within, and only in bursts. His breaths came in quick, short huffs. Kameron rested a hand on his shoulder. "Relax, Mckal. Breathe."

Mick held back tears.

He was okay.

He'd heal.

He always did. *Right?* But from this? He didn't know what would happen to him.

Kameron put pressure on Mick's shoulder, grounding him. "Your blood—"

"But how can it be?" Adrik finally spoke, cutting Kameron off. "I don't understand. If I still have mine, how could he possibly have it also? When Beiron stole it, I felt a change in its strength. But I feel no different."

Mick slipped out from under Kameron's grasp. He picked his shirt up off the floor and put it back on, covering the awful mark. "What are you talking about?"

Kameron rested his hands on his hips. "It seems your blood contains not just one trace of element but all of them."

If Mick knew what that meant, he might have understood Kameron's and Adrik's bafflement. "What does that mean?" he asked.

The music outside began playing again, quieter this time.

"It means…" Adrik began, but he squinted and looked away, thinking it through.

"You have the means to take back the power of the Weldafire Stone," Kameron finished for him. "What did you see during the music?"

Mick thought back to the images in his mind. "It was like seeing through a thick fog. Everything was hazy and unclear." Whatever energy he'd had prior to the visions, it was quickly depleting. He shook his head, trying to keep himself alert. "Nothing made sense. It was all backward." He remembered the water flowing in the wrong direction. "I didn't understand any of it. And there were these voices chanting, 'Blood of the cursed, blood of the offender, blood of the land. Return. Return.' Over and over again." His eyelids drooped. Why was he so tired all of a sudden?

The look Kameron shared with Adrik was one of understanding.

"What?" Mick asked. "What's it mean?"

Kameron frowned. "You need rest."

Mick didn't argue. He could have closed his eyes right then and fallen asleep while standing. He willed his eyes to stay open.

"This has taken much out of you," Kameron said. "Go. Sleep. We will further discuss this in the morning."

Part of Mick wanted to protest and hear everything now, but in this state, he wouldn't retain anything. He nodded.

"Adrik will show you to a hut where you may spend the night. I will point your friend in the right direction of where to find you."

Adrik's lips pressed together. He didn't seem to like this plan. "There isn't much time, Kameron."

"Maybe not, but a Healer without rest cannot heal. And what will we do? Send him out in the night? Besides, you and I have some things to discuss anyway. We do not know for certain if the Gap is the correct destination."

Adrik crossed his arms but relented under Kameron's stern gaze. His posture relaxed. "Very well. Come, Mick, I will show you to where you will sleep tonight." He started for the door, and Mick dragged his feet, following. Before exiting, Adrik stood in his way. "Mckal, it is best if you keep what we've learned here tonight to yourself for now. Until we have a plan going forward. Understand?"

Mick lacked the energy to say more than two words. He'd have no trouble keeping it to himself. He nodded, and with that, Adrik led him out.

# Chapter 38

Mick lay awake on his bed. The dawn's light crept in under the door of the small hut. Boone moved about on the bed opposite him. Mick didn't remember him coming in, but that could have been because he'd passed out the second his head had hit the pillow.

The hut consisted of only the two beds and a small table along the wall. Mick had woken with a start to a tingling sensation where his wound was. He couldn't help but think that each time it flared up could be the end. Would this be the one to kill him?

"You up?" Boone broke the silence.

"I am. How'd you sleep?"

"All right. I'd venture to say you didn't though."

Though he'd been exhausted, Mick's sleep had been fitful. He sat up and tousled his hair. "Your venture would be correct. Did I scream?" He chuckled and wished the joke was only a joke.

"No. You just moved a lot."

Relieved, Mick got to his feet. "Do you think we could get something to eat at this hour?" There weren't any fragrances to indicate food was being made just yet, but Mick's stomach grumbled. Maybe they'd accept assistance in the kitchens if he offered his services. He contemplated heading to what the locals called the locameen—the kitchen and eating hall. When nothing else eased his anxiety, cooking always did the trick. And being away from work for as long as he'd been, his fingers itched to chop a few vegetables, stir a stew, fry a fish, stuff a potato—*something* that would keep his mind from wandering into the unknown.

"It's a bit early for breakfast," Boone said. "Hey, what happened last night? I tried to go to you, but a very intimidating-looking woman wouldn't let me into the building."

Mick smiled. Keshlyn did have a kind of look that said, *Don't mess with me.* He'd not want to get on her bad side. He vaguely remembered Adrik telling him to keep quiet about the evening's events. "I don't exactly know what happened," he said truthfully. The vision of seeing the stone in his bloodied hands flashed in his mind. What he'd seen was confusing, and he couldn't make sense of any of it. "I expect Adrik and Kameron will find me later and let me know what I'm supposed to do. I was barely able to keep myself awake last night."

"You were out of it when I came in."

A bang on the door startled Mick. Boone jolted. Adrik opened the door without waiting for either of them to answer. He hardly acknowledged Boone. "Come," he told Mick. "Kameron and I would like a word."

*This early?*

Boone raised his eyebrows at Mick, who shrugged. Adrik didn't seem to notice or care about the hour. Or that he'd just barged in without first checking if they were even awake.

"I'll find Vidia, and we'll catch you later," Boone said. "Your dad's around somewhere. He stayed in his own hut last night."

Mick nodded. He donned a coat and went with Adrik. The air was cold without the sun's heat. Mick could see his breath. He drew his borrowed coat closer to himself. In the sky, pink-tinged clouds touched the peaks of the mountains in the east as he followed Adrik in the direction of the Acteg.

Despite the early hour, a handful of people made their way to the locameen. Mick walked slow, unable to keep Adrik's pace, so Adrik was forced to slow down for him.

Although mornings were not Mick's favourite time for talking, he didn't think he had too many left, and he had too many questions rolling around in his mind. It was about time he started getting some answers.

"What's going to happen now? Did you and Kameron learn anything useful last night? Like why what Beiron did to me affected Kartha too?"

Adrik took many short, quick steps beside Mick, clearly wanting to move faster. He looked at Mick walking beside him. It was the first time he properly looked at him. "Kameron will meet us in the Acteg. We will discuss what we know, and then what will happen next. We have spent years trying to make sense of the prophecy. Your visions last night may help us understand it better. Everything points to the Gap, but we're not certain if you are to go there. That's what we will determine."

The Gap? Mick recalled Adrik ranting about the place on the journey here. He didn't think he could handle another long walk beyond the distance from his hut to the Acteg. His body ached.

At the octagonal building, Adrik held the door open for Mick. They entered and Mick came to an abrupt stop at the entrance. The room was unrecognizable from what he'd been in just last night. The couches and chairs that had been lined up in the square outside the night before had been brought inside. The chairs had been stacked in uneven numbers, looking like they'd been dragged in and left as they were. The couches were situated at the far-right corner, left in no particular arrangement.

Adrik's head swivelled, scouring the big open space. He threw his hands up. "Where is he? He said he'd be here."

"Maybe he's on his way," Mick offered as excuse for Kameron. He didn't know the man well enough to know if his lateness was unusual.

Adrik scanned the space again as if he'd somehow missed seeing him. It would have been hard to miss him. He made a clicking sound with his tongue and sighed. "Wait here," he told Mick, then pointed at him. "Don't go anywhere." He left the building and closed the door behind him.

Mick walked to the corner with the couches. He lowered himself to sit on one, then stood back up, not letting himself get too relaxed. When he was young, he'd train in swordsmanship with his father, and after a day of training, his muscles would be sore the next day. He remembered how he'd keep active and moving so his muscles wouldn't hurt so bad. He'd feel it the worst only after sitting still for long periods. This ache he felt was nothing like that, but he thought he'd try the same method of keeping active in hopes that he'd minimize the pain. He was afraid to sit down and possibly not be able to get back up.

He paced back and forth slowly, dodging the stacks of chairs, walking from one end of the room to the other. Noises outside grew. Swords clanked somewhere in the distance. Perhaps the residents trained in the mornings.

After making his way back toward the couches a second time, he stopped pacing. His stomach grumbled. He didn't have much of an appetite, but he craved the comfort of food and could use the sustenance. A couple of times, he nearly convinced himself to go hunt down Adrik or Kameron so they could get this over with. Then he considered whether Adrik would know to look for him at the locameen if he went there for some breakfast.

Shouts came from outside. Mick stilled. He tilted his ear to listen. More swords clanging. Shouting and grunting. Screaming. *Screaming?* Those did not sound like everyday kinds of sounds. He glanced about the room.

What was taking Adrik so long? Should he go look for him? He'd told him to stay there, but what if something had happened to him and he wasn't coming back?

Mick reached for the door, then froze as his muscles tensed and his wound began to tingle. "No, no, no. Not now." He stopped moving and placed a hand gently over his abdomen, squeezed his eyes shut, and focused all of his thought and energy on keeping the pain at bay. There was enough going on as it was without the added dilemma of these excruciating episodes. He inhaled deeply, then held his breath, allowing himself to relax as he exhaled. The tingling went away.

The door burst open, and Mick tripped backward when it swung into him. He flung his hands out to catch his fall and landed on his backside. Three armour-clad men entered and looked down at him on the floor.

"Well, look what we have here. A rat hiding out in his hole." The man in the middle wore no helmet, but he probably should have. His face was ugly, and his smile only made it worse to look at him. His moustache made him look like he had the whiskers of an animal.

"Speaking of rats," Mick said, "have you looked in a mirror lately?" He scuttled backward until he was safely out of their reach, then hopped up onto his feet.

The man on the left removed his helmet. It was a wonder he had even fit it over his thick hair. "You're the one on the poster." His voice was deep and gravelly.

Mick had forgotten how famous his face was thanks to Ighur's posters. He took a step back, setting his feet apart in a better stance to defend himself. Unarmed combat wasn't his strength. He'd do better with a sword.

Whiskers smirked. "I think you're right, Kurstier." He gripped his sword. "I can't remember. Did it say if he had to be brought in dead or alive?"

Kurstier's grin revealed crooked teeth. "Alive. But it didn't specify that he couldn't be maimed. That sixty xanteén is ours. Such a high reward for an easy catch."

"I think you underestimate me," Mick said.

Whiskers straightened and tightened his grip on his sword. "This whole camp is surrounded by our men. Where are you going to go?"

"What's that?" Mick shouted. "I'm sorry. That caterpillar on your lip muddles your words."

*A weapon would be good right about now.*

The third man didn't remove his helmet. He bent his knees and hunched his shoulders, lifting his arms up from his torso, blocking Mick's escape.

Whiskers dove forward first. Mick pivoted to the right and dodged his sword, nearly crashing into a stack of chairs. He righted his feet and quickly angled himself so he faced them all.

"You think you're so scary with your swords." Mick provoked them. "Why don't you lose them so we can call this a fair fight?"

Kurstier threw his helmet to the floor. He sheathed his sword and took a step forward, accepting the challenge. Whiskers eyed Mick, his eyes scanning him from top to bottom. He smirked. The third man maintained his wide stance, guarding the door like a goalkeeper in a game of ternex.

Sweat tickled the back of Mick's neck. He rolled up his long sleeves to his elbows.

Whiskers smiled, and his big teeth added to his ratlike appearance. He tossed his sword to the floor, out of Mick's reach. "All right, you cocky bastard, show us what you've got."

# Chapter 39

MICK KNEW HIS MOUTH WOULD GET HIM INTO A SITUATION LIKE THIS someday. He rolled his shoulders and bounced on the balls of his feet. If he didn't think using his magic would be the thing to kill him, he'd have given it a shot. However, with the searing pain he'd experience every time he attempted to draw from his power lately, he opted to settle for a good old-fashioned brawl. One he honestly didn't believe he'd win.

Unless he could get his hands on one of their swords.

He kept his eyes on Whiskers, not letting them shift to the abandoned sword on the floor and betray his thoughts.

Whiskers leapt at him, his fist hurtling toward Mick, who ducked and threw a punch upward, making contact with the man's jaw.

Mick hopped back and shuffled his feet.

Kurstier took slow steps outward and sideways, slinking around to get to Mick's other side and put him in the middle. Not a position Mick wanted to be in. He countered his steps so the two facing him stayed in front, but the movement brought him around, so the man by the door would end up behind him. Mick stopped circling. He didn't like that position either.

He bounded after Whiskers, who was closest to him, and psyched him by twitching to one side, then fully twisting in the opposite direction and snapping his elbow into his temple. Whiskers stumbled. Kurstier lunged toward Mick. Mick pivoted but was too slow this time. Kurstier moved in step with him and flung his fist, striking Mick's arm. It stung and Mick swept his feet back to get clear of another blow. He slid backward, away from the door and the three men. The stack of chairs he'd nearly tripped on earlier was at his back, limiting his places to go.

The sounds of battle outside intensified. Mick needed to end this before the camp was completely overrun and he'd lost his chance of getting out of here. He crouched low and pounced, using all the power in his legs to launch himself at the sword Whiskers had thrown on the floor. Bracing for the hard impact, Mick stretched out his arm, reaching his hand for the hilt. At the last second, Whiskers stamped his foot on the blade and slid it out of reach.

Mick followed through with his fall, pressed himself up to his feet just as quickly as he'd gone down, and wasted no time considering his next move. In a flash, he dove at Kurstier, who was closing in on his left. The man's hair bounced as he flailed his arm. Kurstier shuffled backward but was too slow. Mick grabbed the hilt of his sword and drew it from its sheath, then pointed it at the three soldiers. He puffed his chest out and raised the sword. He'd done it!

The big one at the door stepped forward and took up a guard with his own sword. Mick widened his stance. If it was to be a duel, that he could win.

The tingling returned and settled over his abdomen.

*No, no, not again!* Mick gripped the sword tighter and tried to focus his breathing like he'd done earlier. The tingling grew. His opponent must have sensed something was off because he strutted over to Mick, not looking the least bit concerned about his weapon.

Mick thrust his arm out with the point of the sword directed at the man. He tried not to think about how much his wound hurt.

"Don't come any closer!" The pain grew. He clutched his free arm around his torso. His grip on the handle loosened. His stomach felt like it was on fire. He doubled over and let the sword clatter to the floor as he fell to his knees. He cried out, and still the pain grew.

It seemed to last forever until Mick's muscles finally relaxed and he heaved heavy breaths.

Whiskers took advantage of Mick's vulnerability. He kicked Mick in the back, dropping him flat onto his stomach, then, taking Mick's hands, he thrust them behind his back, clamping them in cuffs. Mick didn't have the strength to resist.

Kurstier aided Whiskers, and they hauled Mick to his feet. He wobbled, unsteady. He'd done his best. He'd tried, but it meant nothing in the end. They were going to drag him before Ighur, who would then return him to Governor Riggs, and that would be the end of it. Mick might not even make it back to Iptin before the curse took him. The image stamped in his memory of Riggs's bloodied fists flashed in his mind. Dying before he could face Riggs would be a blessing. But then what would become of Kartha?

His eyes burned. He squeezed them shut, refusing to let the tears come. That'd be just perfect in front of these three.

He opened his eyes and swallowed his emotions, while straightening as best he could with the ache in his abdomen still lingering. "You have no idea what you're doing. If I don't get to where I need to be, Kartha will die."

Kurstier wiped sweat from his brow. "That's a new one."

"You've seen the sickness, haven't you?"

The door burst open, and Adrik appeared, wide-eyed, with two people Mick didn't recognize. A strong scent of fire filled the room with their entry. Whiskers, Kurstier, and the big one were slow in reacting to the new arrivals. Before any of them registered anything, Adrik called, "*Luzen!*" and the light that filled the room was blinding.

Mick shut his eyes tight and turned away. He felt a gust of wind blast across his cheek, whipping his hair every which way. Adrik shouted, adding to the chaos of the voices coming from outside. Additionally, the howling wind in Mick's ears was like being caught in the middle of a tornado. He opened his eyes to slits, allowing them to adjust and see what had happened.

Kurstier and the big one had been subdued by Adrik's companions. Whiskers was on the floor; Adrik stood over his prone form, patting down his pockets. Mick blinked. *What just happened?*

Adrik stepped over Whiskers and walked to Mick. He fidgeted with the cuffs until the pressure released around Mick's wrists. Mick rubbed them, expecting the itch that typically came with his healing, but all he felt was a dull ache in his abdomen.

Adrik grabbed Mick's arm and pulled him toward the door, barely giving him a moment to process what was happening. The two others remained behind to deal with the trio of soldiers.

"We must get you to the Gap. There's no time to waste," Adrik said.

Mick ripped his arm free. "Now? I thought you didn't know if I had to go there."

"We've no time to speculate. We're under attack." Adrik flailed his arms out the door to prove his point. The camp was overrun with soldiers. Men and women charged in battle all throughout the grounds. Swords clanked against each other. Orange sparks and blue light flashed in various places. A few huts were aflame, which explained the smell. Bodies lay scattered, and blood stained the earth where they'd fallen. Near the edge of the mountains surrounding the valley, more people fought. Plumes of black smoke billowed in places all around the camp. Mick searched the faces for his father. No doubt he'd have offered to help. Not seeing him, he kept an eye out for Vidia and Boone, pushing aside the fear that gripped his heart.

Adrik tugged Mick's shirt. "Move quickly. We must get into the mountains."

Now wasn't the time to argue or resist. Mick's feet moved instinctively. He kept watch for his friends, but there were too many people and too much chaos around him.

As they hurried around burning huts and strewn bodies, attackers came at them, but from nowhere the wind changed, blowing stronger. Help came to them from residents of the camp, who were equipped for battle, wearing thick leather armour and carrying swords. They either engaged in duelling or used magic to fend off the soldiers. Red rocks flew past Mick and hit their enemies square in the head. Roots popped up through the hard ground and tripped whoever its intended victims were. All around, magic and light dazzled Mick's eyes. The only thing keeping his pain at bay was adrenaline and fear. Adrik swept his hands about, and the wind moved wherever he commanded it.

They wove around bodies, charging past, and Mick couldn't bear it. He could help these people. It wasn't too late. For those who had fallen, as long as their flesh was warm, there was hope. He stopped in his tracks and bent over a fallen woman, nearly tripping Adrik.

Adrik yanked Mick's shirt, pulling him up. "Don't stop. We—" He screamed and fell. Mick's heart jolted. He caught Adrik in time to ease his landing.

An arrow had lodged into Adrik's calf. He stretched his leg out and leaned back, clenching his teeth. It had gone straight through to the other side. Thinking fast, Mick snapped the fletching off the end and grabbed the front, ready to pull it straight out.

Adrik gripped Mick's wrist. "No, stop! Not yet."

"I can help."

"Can you?"

Mick knew what Adrik was implying. Could he heal him? "Maybe. I don't know." Probably not. But healing was all he'd ever known. He had to at least try. He couldn't give up.

Another arrow swooped overhead.

Mick stole a glance at their surroundings. Straight ahead, the space between them and the path out of the valley was littered with bodies and a swarm of chaos. He looked over his shoulder, back toward the hut where he'd slept last night. In the crowd of unfamiliar faces, he searched for Boone and Vidia. He fought the impulse to go look for them.

He returned his attention to Adrik and his wounded leg. Maybe he couldn't use magic to heal him, but the arrow had to come out either way. He reached for it, but Adrik stopped him again by pinching his wrist. He squeezed it. "I will tend to this. You have to get to the Gap! Go and do not stop until you get there."

"Adrik, I can't leave you like this."

Adrik waved a hand for Mick to help him stand. Beside them, a man wearing leather armour magically created a spear by weaving roots into the shape of a shaft with a pointed tip. He flung it at an oncoming attacker, then glanced over his shoulder. "If you're not fighting, you need to get to the Hall. Now! Adrik, get that leg taken care of."

Adrik ignored him and gripped Mick's shirt, partly to hold himself up and partly to implore Mick to obey. "Go to the Gap. Get there and mend the tear."

Go to the Gap, mend the tear, break the curse. *But how?* "I don't know where that is." Mick struggled with Adrik's added weight on top of his own. His stomach burned.

Adrik called to the man with the spear. "Corbin!" The man spared a look back at them. Adrik hobbled toward him on his good leg, using Mick's support. "Take Mick to the Gap. It's imperative that he get there."

Corbin squinted at Adrik but only for a second. He swooped his arms through the air and blasted fireballs and electric shocks of light at their attackers. Light flashed, illuminating his nearly white blond hair in a blue glow. "I'm a little busy, Adrik. Now's not a good time. Word's been sent to Litlen for Warriors, but until they get here, we need all able valients and anyone who can fight."

Adrik stretched his fingers out, exasperated. "If Mick doesn't get to where he needs to be, all of this is for nothing!"

Mick looked about again, searching for Boone and Vidia. In all the chaos, he didn't see them.

Adrik withdrew his sheathed knife from his belt and handed it to Mick. "Go with Corbin. Take this."

Mick accepted the knife. "I'm better with a sword."

Adrik frowned. "It's not for battle. These things usually require blood."

The knife suddenly felt heavier. Mick nodded, understanding. He let Adrik go so he could bend down and strap it around his ankle, where it was hidden by his boot.

Corbin whipped up another spear and threw it at two soldiers heading their way. It struck one. Adrik conjured light and blasted it at the other. He toppled after doing so and Mick caught him, nearly falling over himself.

"I can't, Adrik. I won't make it." Nor did Mick want to leave Adrik like this in the midst of enemies.

"You must. Look, Waylan comes now. He can help me get to the Hall in the mountain."

Among the many bodies, both fallen and standing, Waylan approached them. He carried a sword and fought his way toward them. He fought well.

An arrow flying overhead plummeted toward them. Corbin thrust his arms up and the wind swept the arrow off course from its trajectory.

Waylan finally caught up to them. "You picked a bad spot for a meeting." His gaze swept over Adrik's leg with the arrow sticking out of it. He swapped his sword to his opposite hand and used his free one to take Adrik from Mick. "You're not looking great, Mick. Follow me and I'll get you to the Hall with the others."

Mick spoke before Adrik could insist yet again for him to go. "Did Vidia and Boone make it there?"

The corners of Waylan's lips pulled to either side. "Not yet. We've got valients gathering people and bringing them in groups. I'm sure they're okay." His voice was tight with concern. "Come on."

"Mckal." Adrik's voice became fierce and demanding. "You have your instructions." His urgency put all disputes aside. Corbin heeded his order. He stretched his arm out, putting Mick in front of him to lead him away from Adrik and Waylan.

# Chapter 40

No matter what way they went, they'd face danger. Corbin chose the most direct path out of the camp. He continued to counter oncoming attacks all the way to the trail that would take them out of the valley and into the mountains. Fewer contended them here.

Mick wanted to help the people in Elefthan, and this seemed like the wrong way to do it. This felt like running away.

A soft whisper tickled his ear. *Return. Return.*

He reminded himself of his task. This wasn't running away. Adrik had been right. He had to do what he could to save Kartha, and if the Gap was where he needed to do that, then that was where he had to get to.

They trekked along the narrow path through the mountains. Mick proceeded with caution, twisting his head to see in all directions at once. Even up. The ledges of the mountains that towered over them were wide enough for someone to walk along. It wasn't impossible for an attack to come from above. Mick noted the lack of attackers here. It seemed all of the battle stayed contained within the Elefthan grounds. Why had no one followed them?

"Wait!" a woman called out. Mick turned toward her call. "Mick, wait!" Vidia ran up the path, followed by Boone, who tried to keep up with her while carrying a sword and watching their backs. As they neared, Mick could hear Vidia's heavy breathing. Despite the danger and his fear, Mick felt some of his tension let up. Vidia and Boone were all right.

"What are you doing?" Corbin's shoulders were visibly tense. He looked up and around them all, behind Vidia and Boone. "Were you followed? You should be in the Hall with the others."

The burning feeling in Mick's stomach spread and he stilled. He closed his eyes and tilted his head back, breathing through the pain. He couldn't fail now. He had a mission. Standing there, he attuned his senses to the wind on his cheeks, sweeping through the space between the mountain walls. He let the whispers calm him.

Boone took Mick's arm, jarring him back to the moment. Mick didn't realize he'd leaned so far that he'd just about toppled right over. Boone righted him. "You expect Mick to get anywhere like this? He can barely stand." He let him go, and Mick swayed, proving the point to Corbin. Adrik's mission did feel like an impossible feat to accomplish without help.

"I told Mick I wasn't leaving his side, and I meant it." Boone stuck his nose up and pressed his lips together. Vidia linked her arm in Mick's. "I'm not going anywhere either. Where he goes, we all go." Mick's heart swelled with gratitude for these two. They were here. They'd made it to him, and he wasn't going to have to do this alone. Whether or not going with him were any safer than going to the Hall, Mick didn't know, but he was glad to have his friends at his side.

Corbin looked at the three of them and shook his head. He sighed. "Keep up then. And if he falls, I'm not carrying him." He led on.

They reached the road and had gone far enough away from the camp to feel safe from attack. Mick felt that tingling sensation rise to his abdomen again. He inhaled deeply, held his breath for a second, then slowly released the air through pursed lips. The tingling subsided, and he rested his hands on his knees, taking a few more deep breaths. If he was calm, the pain wasn't as bad, nor did it become as debilitating. Maybe he could survive this journey after all.

A flash of movement caught his eye. In the time it took for him to register the motion, an arrow struck Corbin in the chest, piercing through his armour. Corbin went rigid and fell to his knees.

Mick's heart jolted, and he twisted to see where the arrow had come from. Another one whipped past his face, and Corbin cried out when it caught him in the leg. Mick crouched to his level to tend to him. The next arrow hit Corbin in the eye, the impact throwing his body backward. He lay unmoving, and blood pooled around him. Mick stared dumbstruck, while Boone placed himself in front of them, holding his sword at the ready. Vidia crouched next to Mick, wrapping her arms around him. Was she afraid, or was this her way of protecting him?

Mick hesitated to touch the arrow sticking out of Corbin's eye. He didn't know if he could remove it and still save him. He reached within and drew from his healing power. Already, he could sense the pain from his wound growing, so he quickly pulled back. It wouldn't work. He couldn't heal him. Just like he couldn't heal himself.

He stood and faced the direction where the arrows had come from. He used an arm to shield the sun to look about for the assailants. About half a mile up the road, a band of armed men and women walked toward them. Too many to count, but at a glance, Mick guessed about two dozen approached. Vidia rose and took his hand in hers, taking a stand beside him. Boone gripped his sword tighter, raising it in a guard.

The archer had an arrow nocked and aimed, but he didn't loose it. As the band came closer, Mick recognized the gait of the leader.

Damien. The limp was subtle, but he favoured his left side when he walked. Mick had noticed it when Damien had chased him down in the mountains and brought him back to Beiron.

A chill crept down Mick's spine. He forgot to breathe.

Damien carried no weapon. He extended his arms in greeting. "Well, look who's still alive and kicking. You know, I didn't think that would work, to be honest. But here you are." He smiled. Mick drew in a shaky breath. His eyes darted around, checking for others. Or one person in particular.

Wherever Damien went, Beiron was bound to be close.

# Chapter 41

MICK REGISTERED DAMIEN'S WORDS. THE BATTLE... THE ATTACK AT THE camp... "That was you?"

Damien signalled his people, and they split up, half going left and the other half going right until they surrounded Mick and his companions. Corbin lay unmoving, and Damien toed his limp body. Mick wanted to scream, though he knew it wouldn't bring the man back. Was that how others felt when someone died? Completely helpless?

The archer kept his weapon raised and directed at Mick. Another of Damien's men relieved Boone of his sword.

"What can I say?" Damien curled his lips up in a sneer. "I had to get you out of that camp somehow." He gestured to Boone. "I see you found your friend." Boone's clenched knuckles cracked.

"And Miss Valca has found her way to you. What a nice little reunion this is." Damien winked at Vidia.

Mick wrapped his arm around Vidia's waist and pulled her close, but she stepped out from him and toward Damien. "You'll pay for what you've done."

Her threat didn't seem to faze Damien. He sucked his cheek and shrugged. "I heard your uncle fell into a bit of trouble. From the sound of it, it's all on account of Mickey here."

Mick took Vidia's hand and squeezed, drawing her back to his side. Damien sought to instigate something. It would do no good to rise to the occasion.

Damien's face lit up. "You know, it's crazy! The twins look so alike and are often difficult to tell apart at a glance, and I've never met your father. But then you—I look at you and I think: Dimitri. How is it you can look more like him than Raidan when they're literally identical? I think I understand Beiron's fascination with these things." He scratched his head.

Mick didn't know how to respond. An ache settled in his gut and grew. He winced. "Kartha is going to die if I don't get to the Gap." *Wherever that was.*

"Oh good. That's where we're heading. We can walk together. I'll lead the way." Damien indicated the trail Mick and his companions had already started on.

"That's what he was doing." Mick pointed to Corbin.

"And now you don't need him. You have me. Come, let's go."

If Mick's discomfort were any gauge of how much time they had, it wasn't much time at all. Damien had allowed Boone to go free once as per Mick's condition. Mick wondered if he'd be so lenient this time. "If you're to be my escort, allow Vidia and Boone to return to Litlen. They don't need to be here."

Vidia opened her mouth, but Mick gave her hand another squeeze, cutting off her objection.

"They'll come," Damien said. "Consider them my surety. Or if it makes you feel better, think of them as moral support."

Mick held Vidia's hand tighter. He'd have to be careful not to jeopardize her and Boone's safety. Damien's minions pushed Boone to move. A dark-skinned woman with a shaved head, ripped Vidia from Mick, and the archer pulled his bowstring back, keeping his aim locked on Mick. The others were dragged up ahead. Damien signalled for Mick to walk. He did. His chest tightened as he left Corbin's body behind.

Damien strode up beside him. "There aren't too many things that get by me. I'm beating myself up for not realizing who you were sooner. The funny thing is, as soon as I learned you were the Healer, I remembered the rumours going around about Cassian Dairner's son. I'd just figured there was confusion because of the Guardians' healing ability with the power of the Weldafire Stone. Speaking of which, you wouldn't happen to know where I might find that, would you?"

Mick leaned away from him. "Even if I did, I wouldn't tell you."

"That's all right. Beiron has the means to get answers, whether you want to tell or not. He's always been good at taking what he wants. But between you and me, I think he's gone a *lit*-tle mad during his long captivity."

Mick couldn't deny the man's insanity. Nor could he imagine what implements of torture Beiron had for extracting information. Really, though, how much more damage could be done at this point? He felt the curse grow a little more with each debilitating episode.

Beiron wouldn't have to look far for the stone anyway. It rested against Mick's leg, lacking in extending its usual warmth.

They headed east along a trail, between the edge of the mountains and a forest—the same brightly illuminated forest that Mick had travelled through just the other day with his father and friends on their way to Elefthan. In the afternoon light, it looked like any old forest, except the colour of the leaves and grass were tinged with blue hues rather than green. However, more greys now stood out among the colours.

After some time, they came to a fast-flowing stream and followed it at a slow incline until they reached a log cabin. Attached to the cabin was a water wheel. It hung crookedly on its axle and had two broken spokes. No smoke came up from the chimney of the cabin, and the windows had no glass pane or shutters. The tattered couch and fireplace in the darkened living area were visible from outside. It looked to have been a long time since anyone had lived here.

Mick was about to ask what this place was when he heard Beiron's deep voice.

"Ah, good. You're here," Beiron said.

Mick's shoulders stiffened. Beiron rounded the cabin and came to meet them. He'd cleaned up since Mick had found him in the cave. His beard and hair were washed and trimmed, and his face was clean. He was nearly unrecognizable, if not for his beastly size and those unnatural black eyes of his.

"I was beginning to wonder," Beiron said.

Damien tipped an invisible hat. "The Dairner boy: delivered. And on a mission apparently."

Beiron rubbed his finger and thumb on his chin and looked Mick up and down. "A mission indeed. You're not looking too good."

Mick raised his arms and shrugged. "I have you to thank for that. I can't say I'm loving this new me."

Beiron flashed a crooked grin, unaffected by Mick's lip. "Let me look at you." He reached for Mick's face, but Mick swatted his hand away.

Beiron's reaction was like lightning. He wrenched Mick's wrist, and with his other hand, he took Mick's chin between his fingers, squeezing his jaw. His sudden burst of violence frightened Mick more than he'd actually been hurt. He flinched, and Beiron squeezed harder.

Mick's abdomen twinged. Pain spread to his sides and around his back. He relaxed in Beiron's grasp and breathed a hard breath in through his nose.

Nothing mattered except this pain and keeping absolutely still until it passed.

Beiron's brows drew together. Mick closed his eyes. The throbbing lasted a minute before it eased and dissipated. He waited a minute more, then let his muscles go limp.

"Are you finished?" Beiron said.

Mick didn't dare fight now in case the pain returned. He barely moved his head in a nod.

"Good."

Beiron turned Mick's face to look at him. Mick met his hollow eyes. They were like black tunnels, fading into nothingness. The longer he looked, the more frightening they were.

Beiron broke eye contact and turned Mick's head to examine his neck. He released him, then tugged the collar of Mick's shirt and stared too long at his chest underneath the fabric. Mick tilted his head down, curiosity getting the better of him. A sob caught in his throat. The black tendrils had extended up his body and were nearly to his neck. It spread in narrow web-like streaks all across his front and, he suspected, toward his lower body and back as well. Sweat beaded on his brow, his heart raced, and his legs shook. The flutters in his stomach became unbearable, manifesting in another searing burst from his wound. A burning sensation spasmed up his spine and wrapped around his heart.

He tried to breathe in slowly, but if he didn't get air, he was going to pass out. His breaths came in short bursts. He crunched his shoulders in toward himself, trying to grasp a handle on the pain. But it was too late. He was past the point of recovering from this one.

Was this it? Was this the one that would kill him? He clutched his stomach and collapsed to the ground, landing on his knees. The taste of blood was on his lips. One thought carried him through the pain. *Get to the Gap and finish this. This is why you're here*. He groaned and planted a fist on the ground.

*Get—up.*

It took him every ounce of strength to push himself up, gritting his teeth all the while. By sheer willpower, he straightened to his full height. Slowly, the pain let up until all that lingered was a dull ache.

From the corner of his eye, Mick saw Vidia with her hands to her mouth and tears streaking down her cheeks. The archer had his bow slung around his body and a firm grasp on Boone, who looked disgruntled and like he had put up a fight.

The wind rustled the leaves, carrying the voices through the air. Apart from these whispers, only the water's flow in the stream disturbed the silence.

Beiron pinched Mick's chin and nudged his cheek with his knuckles. "You're worse off than I thought. Where's the Weldafire Stone?"

Although Mick was unable to ward off Beiron, he wasn't going to just hand it over. He hung his head and stared at his feet, not answering. Beiron patted Mick's pockets. He slipped his hands into the pocket containing the stone and withdrew it in its leather pouch.

Mick's heart lurched. When he'd given Boone the stone to hold onto, nothing had changed, but now… Somehow it was different. It was like Beiron had stolen a part of him. Now a hollow hole took up space in his heart.

Beiron emptied the leather pouch into his palm and gazed at the stone. Its black mark was bigger and had extended all around the stone, just like Mick's marring had grown.

The corner of Beiron's lip twitched. He looked Mick up and down. "What are you?"

What he was, was a dead man.

Beiron pocketed the stone. He smacked Mick's arm. "Let's move. Would hate to have to carry your corpse to the Gap."

Mick squinted. *The Gap?* "Wait, why do *you* want to go there?"

"I'm going to make sure you do your job, Healer. Move."

Damien prompted everyone to go.

Vidia dragged her feet. She wouldn't take her eyes off Mick. The archer shoved Boone in the back, making him walk. Beiron went along with them, leaving Mick standing there. No one prodded him or pushed him to go. They didn't need to because Beiron was right. He had a job to do.

# Chapter 42

Mick caught up to the others and strode past Beiron to walk next to Vidia. He took her hand in his. She walked tense and fidgeted with her skirt. Mick was aware that anything they'd say to each other would not be private.

They left the cabin behind and walked for some time until Vidia finally looked at him. "Are you all right?"

The answer to that seemed obvious. Mick didn't speak right away. He should have been the one asking her that.

"I'm as well as I can be," he said.

"Your eyes, Mick—they're…"

"I know." He flashed her a grin. "So serene. Dreamy. Easy to lose oneself in." He chuckled, stopped short, and clutched his stomach.

Vidia wrinkled her brow. "They're like that." She pointed to Mick's chest.

Although it was covered, Mick knew what she meant. He imagined his eyes with veiny black lines extending into the whites and was glad he couldn't see for himself what they looked like.

The forest thinned out as they strode alongside the stream. After walking awhile, they eventually reached the edge of the tree line, where the land opened up before them. The Bludesel Mountains and the Teiry Mountains flanked the land on either side, and from the Teiry Mountains, a river flowed and converged with the stream. The water continued, cascading down into a long trench that stretched north as far as the eye could see. The noise of it carried, barely overpowering the steady stream of water next to them.

Cracks everywhere broke up the ground, and ruts that dipped in various places looked deep enough to lodge a foot in if they weren't careful.

Beiron strode up next to Mick and wedged himself between him and Vidia, forcing their hands apart. He put his arms around them both.

"Here we are. The Gap. See that big tear ripping the land apart? That's not supposed to be there." He grasped the base of Mick's neck in a tight squeeze and pulled him close to speak directly into his ear. "Fix it."

He let them go, pushing Mick in front of him. Boone was already up ahead with Damien and the others. Mick didn't know how Vidia and Boone would get past the henchmen while Mick did whatever he was meant to do here. *Mend the tear.* That's what Adrik had said. And Beiron had just called the trench a tear. Somehow, Mick had to find a way to move the earth and bring these pieces of land back together. Simple. No problem.

He *could* just take one out of Beiron's books and move it with his mind.

Except for the fact that he was broken, and he didn't even know if that would work. Nothing about this was simple.

Mick stepped carefully across the ruts, watching his every step and avoiding breaking an ankle. He didn't think he'd recover from something so minor. As they reached the edge of the trench, the noise of the waterfall boomed. Beiron led them away from where the water fell. Mick gazed down the forty-foot drop. The stretch of space across to the other side was about half the distance as the trench's depth. He thought the ravine would have been filled with water and rising, but the only spot that contained water was directly beneath the waterfall.

Mist drifted from the spray. The voices it carried were faint, but the words were clearer than they'd ever been. *Return. Return.* For the first time since Mick had heard them in his visions at Elefthan, the jumbled nonsense was not so incomprehensible anymore. As if aware of what was at hand, the whispers grew in intensity.

Beiron clapped. "All right, here's what's going to happen. The girl is going to go down first, followed by me. Dairner, you're last, and your friend—"

"Go down?" Mick asked. "What do you mean?"

Beiron pinched his lips together. "Don't interrupt. Your friend is going to stay up here with the rest." He gestured to the two dozen men and women who stood tense, weapons drawn, then he pointed to Mick. "You're going to find a way to fix what's wrong with Kartha. When it's done and we're all back up here and everything is as it should be, these two can go on their merry way. But if you try something clever, I'll kill the girl first. Then, depending on whether you cooperate after that, Boone over there might take a shortcut to the bottom of the trench. You understand?"

Mick caught Boone's eye. Beiron's lack of bringing up Mick's release hadn't gone unnoticed. He supposed he was dying, and this could very well be his final resting place. How fitting—the place he'd dreamt of his whole life—the country that had called to him—had brought him here for this purpose, only to have him end up decomposing in its soil. As long as he could finish what he'd come here to do and Vidia and Boone were allowed to go free, he'd not make any demands for his release just yet.

He nodded his understanding.

"Good. Let's go." Beiron searched along the inside of the trench for a good place to climb down. There were a few spots where there'd be nowhere to get a good foothold or have a place to hold onto anything, but a little farther down, about midway, one section had a narrow ledge that stretched almost all the way to the bottom.

"You're up first," Beiron snapped at Vidia.

Vidia's lip quivered. She peered over the edge where Beiron pointed. One misplaced step could kill her. Was there any point in begging Beiron to let her stay up here? Mick had to try.

"Beiron, it's too far down. Let Vidia stay here with Damien. We're here with a common goal. What am I going to do?" *Steal back the Weldafire Stone, for one.* Somehow…without getting his friends killed. Mick gave Boone a sideways look. His new friend had been bold in each unfortunate situation they'd found themselves in. Mick had confidence that he could improvise if he had to.

Boone added his own plea to Mick's. "Allow her to trade places with me. I'll go down, and she can stay. The climb is too dangerous."

"She goes." Beiron nodded for Vidia to carry on.

Vidia hesitated, fear evident in her eyes. It was either climb down or… well, the other way down wasn't good.

She sat and dangled her feet over the edge, then turned herself around so she could climb down backward. Her movements were slow and calculated as she descended the steep wall. Mick couldn't look. He bit his lip and counted the seconds until Beiron found his footing on the wall and climbed down after her.

Damien folded his arms over his chest, looking very proud of himself.

Between him and Beiron, Damien was the lesser of two evils. But getting out of this would be so much easier if they weren't in league with each other.

Mick might not make it out of here alive, but if he did, he liked his chances better if they weren't unified against him.

He met Damien's eye. "Do you know who else is loyal, Damien? Dogs. Dogs are loyal. I've met a lot of men like you. Eventually, your master will grow tired of you. Or he'll do something you don't agree with, and just like that, your loyalty wavers. Then what? What happens when Beiron isn't the master you hoped he'd be? Are you just going to live your life going from one person to the next, hoping someone will take you in and love you?

"Who says you have to be the dog? You have the men—clearly." Mick gestured to Damien's well-armed band. And this wasn't even including however many people he'd sent into Elefthan. "What do you need Beiron for? Look what he's done to Kartha? Do you really want to follow the man who cursed your homeland?"

Damien stood closest to Boone. He clutched the front of Boone's shirt and pushed him toward the trench. Boone stumbled and grabbed Damien's hand. His heels rocked on the edge.

"Divide and conquer. Is that your plan, Mckal? Speaking of dogs, I met a friend of yours yesterday. He's been looking for you everywhere."

Mick's heart beat faster, if that were possible. Had Ighur finally made his way south and was on his way here now?

"Are you planning on handing me over to him after this? What about our deal?"

"I'm not interested in any reward money. That was the deal, Mckal. That I'd not take any reward for you. I'll gladly gift you to him as an offering of what's to come. I have big plans, and I can't have you getting in my way, trying to stop me."

"What will Beiron think?"

"Beiron likes to experiment with oddities such as you. But I think he'd be willing to consider what Kartha has to gain by handing you over."

Mick ignored the tickling sensation of sweat dripping down his neck. "You know I'm dying, don't you? I don't think Governor Riggs will appreciate you tricking him by gifting him a dead man. I take it you're familiar with his work?"

"Oh, I'm aware of his endeavours." Damien grinned. "I'm scheduled to meet him. Turns out he's looking for a contact here who he can do business with. I think he and I will get along well."

Damien and Riggs meeting to do business. It was exactly what Riggs had sent Mick here to do and exactly what Mick had intended not to do.

Mick put a hand to his heart where the black tendrils stretched up his chest. "Until he realizes you've given him a bad product."

At this point, who knew what Riggs would do to Mick for his insubordination?

"We'll see about that," Damien said. "You and Kartha are connected. Succeed here, and you may just survive this yet. Better get going."

# Chapter 43

Heights had never been an issue for Mick, but since any moment he could experience another bout of those painful episodes, the idea of scaling a forty-foot wall didn't seem like such a good idea. Vidia was more than halfway to the bottom. Even if she fell from there, she'd be seriously hurt. Beiron climbed faster than she did and was halfway down.

Mick sat at the ledge as Vidia had done. He turned around to climb down backward and found a hole for his foot to step into. He began his descent.

The key to preventing his wound from flaring up right now was to keep calm. He scaled sideways along the wall, moving wherever he could find ledges and footholds.

His foot slipped, and he dug his nails into the rock. His legs flailed and he swung them around, feeling for purchase. A subtle ache started—the first warning.

His arms shook as he struggled to hold his body weight. He pointed his toes and found a crevice, then got his foot in it and anchored his position.

*Deep breaths.*

He breathed in. He breathed out.

The ache settled, but it felt like it wouldn't take much to return.

He glanced down. Vidia was near the bottom. Beiron wasn't far behind.

He himself hadn't gotten very far. Spray from the waterfall dampened his face. His chest lightened, and he exhaled. He could do this.

Slower this time, he descended. A little over halfway down, a narrow ledge creased along the wall, and Mick could climb down it like how one might climb down a ladder. He continued like this the rest of the way until he could jump the distance to the bottom and land safely.

His feet touched the ground and the whispers ceased. The air thickened, and his skin prickled. Never had he experienced such stillness. Ahead, the waterfall roared, filling what must have been a very deep hole in the ground, though Mick couldn't understand it. It poured into the trench and yet maintained its boundaries. He'd seen something like it before, in the cave, where the trickling water had filled the pool that never overflowed. Vidia rubbed her arm and looked down the length of the trench. It went on for miles.

Beiron's dark eyes bore through Mick, who felt no compulsion to do any specific thing to fix the trench or *mend the tear*.

"I don't know what I'm meant to do," Mick told him.

"Blood must be spilled."

A dizzying sensation came over Mick, and his breath caught. *These things usually require blood.* That was what Adrik had said. He'd tried to put the words from his mind but had sensed there was truth to them. Wasn't it enough that he'd nearly bled out in the mountains?

Beiron drew a knife. Apparently, he'd replaced his last one. Mick took a step back. Adrik's knife chafed against his ankle bone, but he'd refrain from using it unless he had a plan—which he was working on.

Something cold seeped over his foot. He chanced taking his eyes off Beiron to look down. Water. It flowed around and over his foot—through his boot—and travelled up the slant. Just like he'd seen in his vision.

"What is that?" he asked, more for the sake of drawing Beiron's attention away from making him bleed.

Rather than wait for Beiron to speculate, Mick followed its trail to where the water congregated beneath the falls. The noise was too loud to be heard over. He twisted his torso around to look back at the others. He was startled to see that a woman had appeared beside Beiron and Vidia, and he nearly stumbled into the pool. He'd seen her before—in Hywreath, when he'd first arrived. It was Laila. Vidia knew her, yet she acted as if she weren't there at all. Beiron made no indication he'd seen her either. Mick squinted at the woman and curled his lip up. Where had she come from?

Laila faced Beiron, and her lips moved like she was talking, but Mick couldn't hear. She looked his way. When she realized he was staring at her, her eyes grew.

Mick wanted to hear what she was saying. He walked back over and pointed a finger at Laila. "You. What are you doing here?"

Vidia cocked her head and looked around. Beiron's jaw dropped, as did Laila's. The way they looked at him… Had he done something wrong?

"You can see her," Beiron said.

"Mick," Laila cut in. "Raidan—is he all right?" Her words were rushed.

Mick blinked at her. "He'll be fine. How did you get here?"

Beiron tucked his thumbs into his waistband. "*Veralnin tushov.* She's not. You're still where I left you, *Deihara?*"

Laila ignored the question and turned to Mick. "Mick, if you see Dimitri, tell him I'm at—"

"*Farino,*" Beiron interjected before she could finish. She vanished, and only Mick, Vidia, and Beiron remained.

"What just happened?" Mick stared at the place Laila had just been standing. "Where did she go?"

"I sent her away. You have other things to worry about right now." Beiron had that murderous gleam in his eye again. Mick took two steps backward. Beiron matched them, then stopped. His face contorted into a grimace. He then doubled over, moaning while clutching his chest.

Mick took another two steps back. He caught Vidia's eye and gave her a subtle nod. If they needed to make a quick getaway, he wanted her to be ready to run. She blinked once. She understood.

Beiron growled and stood to his full height. He slicked his hair back and spoke through clenched teeth. "Enough of this. Time to bleed, Dairner."

◊

Laila fell to her knees, panting. She caught her fall with her hands. She would have kept using her magic against Beiron if it weren't for how much it hurt her too. She needed to stay strong. Unfortunately, she didn't think she'd ever be able to use magic against him without bringing harm to herself. Perks of a blood relation. She would probably never be able to sever that connection, but the one brought on by the lacrut... That she'd see about breaking. She'd have to look further into experimenting with the tandernion as a means to cut him out.

Just as soon as she was out of here.

She couldn't be sure if Mick had heard where she was. That he could see her at all was amazing. What made Mick so different from the rest of them?

Whatever the reason, it didn't matter right this moment. He was in danger. And if Damien had more of that concoction, then she had more than just Iptin's governor to worry about as soon as she was out of here. But how to get out? She'd tried the barrier countless times, thinking maybe the next time would be different. Her hopes of freedom were fading. Beiron was too clever and strong.

A door slammed upstairs, which made her jump. It couldn't have been Beiron. He couldn't have gotten here so quickly. From what she could tell, and based on Damien's information, Beiron and Mick were at the Gap, though the split across the land was new. Damien had said the land was split in two. He'd not been exaggerating.

Laila wondered whether Damien was at the Gap as well or if this visitor upstairs might be him.

No, if Beiron had Mick with him, Damien would not have left his side.

Royl perhaps? Her stomach fluttered. Had he come looking for her here, thinking to check Beiron's home? If so, he'd not know about the room downstairs, hidden by the bookcase.

Footsteps creaked on the floorboards. More than one set.

She rose to her feet and listened for more sounds. She had Royl's name on the tip of her tongue, ready to call out, but something held her back.

Even if she did call him, what could he do to help her? He'd only end up sticking around until he could free her and risk putting himself in danger in his attempt to protect her. Her brother was almost as stubborn as she was.

Not that Beiron would have any difficulty getting to Royl if he really wanted to. Once Beiron set his mind to do something, he usually got his way. And the time he'd spent in captivity seemed only to sharpen his will and drive. If he caught Royl in his home trying to rescue her, what might he do to him if he viewed him as a threat?

No, Royl staying away would be for the best.

If Mick had heard her message, she hoped he'd tell Dimitri. At least her blood couldn't be used against *him*. He'd come and would bring with him the entire Karthan regiment.

She listened to the footsteps walking through the house on the main floor. Whoever it was, they were scouring the whole house by the sound of it. Should she call out? She bit her bottom lip. What if it was Dimitri?

Her heart raced. If she were going to do it, she'd have to soon, or she'd miss them.

The footsteps came to a stop somewhere near the hallway. More floor creaking. Laila strained to hear voices. Someone was speaking, but their voice was too muffled.

She went for it. "Hello? I'm down here!"

Nothing.

"Please! Someone!"

With only a bookcase between them, they should have been able to hear her. Did Beiron's barrier have some sort of sound-blocking magic?

She tried again. "Help!"

The sounds started again. They were heading toward the front door. The door slammed, shaking the house, and then there was silence.

Laila's shoulders drooped. They hadn't heard her. She was right there!

Tears flowed down her cheeks. She hugged her arms close.

What could they have done anyway? The barrier was created using blood magic after all. Thanks to Litlen's elders, no one would dare meddle with it. If Adrik knew where to find her, he might have some thought as to how to counter Beiron's spell.

It made no difference now. Whoever it was, they were gone and probably not coming back. She glanced around, but nothing had changed since she'd been put here. Everything was the same. There had to be another way to get out. She just hadn't thought of it yet.

But she would.

# Chapter 44

MICK SCRAMBLED TO COME UP WITH AN IDEA OF HOW TO FIX THIS WITHOUT getting himself stabbed again. Bile rose in his throat at the thought. If at all possible, he'd avoid that.

Beiron took a step toward him, flashing the knife in his hand. Mick raised his hands and rushed his words. "The water is the same as from the cave." Beiron paused and focused his eyes beyond Mick, to the waterfall. He gestured for Mick to walk toward it.

Above them, the towering walls on either side blocked the sun. The trench grew darker with evening upon them. Mick glanced at Vidia. She scrunched her skirt in her hands at her sides.

Turning his back on Beiron when he was so determined to draw blood was not something Mick cared to do. But he needed time to think before Beiron's patience came to an end. He turned and walked toward the pool, expecting to get stabbed in the back at any moment.

The surface of the water shimmered with blue-green hues, just like the Weldafire Stone. Except not anymore. Now the stone nearly resembled a chunk of coal. Mick shook off the image of it bloodied in his hand.

Beiron hovered close behind him. He jabbed Mick's back with the knife, an action meant only to get his attention. Still, Mick straightened his posture.

"How can you tell it's the same?" Beiron asked loud enough to be heard over the thunderous pounding of the falls.

Mick crouched by the shore—if that was what it could be called. Did it qualify as a shore if it wasn't technically an official body of water? The closest thing he could compare it to was a giant bowl.

He couldn't say how he knew it was the same water as from the cave. Something about the way it reflected the sky. Or maybe the magnetic pull it had, drawing the water into it despite the natural inclinations of the land. His fingers touched the surface. The water climbed up his hand and swirled around his wrist. He jumped back and lost his balance, his backside landing on Beiron's feet. Beiron kicked him off.

The whispering voices returned. Their words were clear and sharp, speaking in unison. Chanting was more like it. *Blood of the cursed, blood of the offender, blood of the land. Return. Return.* Over again. Mick righted himself and stayed in a crouched position.

Beiron leaned closer to Mick's ear. "How do you know it's the same?"

Knowing what to expect this time, Mick touched the water and let it trail up his hand. It covered his arm, up to his shoulder and chest, then his back and stomach. Its soothing embrace gave him clarity.

"It speaks," he said, though probably not loud enough.

This was it. Whatever he had to do, it had to do with this water. His blood offered to the pool in the cave had broken the barrier there. Beiron had drunk from this water and cursed the land, cursed Mick. Blood of the cursed. Blood of the offender. It wasn't just Mick's blood that needed to be spilled. It was Beiron's too.

Mick once again felt Adrik's dagger digging into his ankle.

His heart sped up as he inched his hand toward his boot to retrieve it without Beiron noticing. *Return.* Return what? Blood? The stone? Both? And what blood of the land? Was it reference to this water? Maybe it wasn't water at all.

Whatever it was—whatever Mick was meant to do here—the Weldafire Stone was a part of it.

There was no preparing himself for what he was about to do. He pointed in the middle of the pool for Beiron to look. "There… Do you see?" There was nothing there.

Beiron stood over him, peering into the pool where Mick was pointing. He leaned closer. Mick had his other hand on the hilt. He remembered to breathe.

Now.

He pivoted on his toes and jammed the knife into Beiron's thigh. Beiron howled and arched his back.

Mick wobbled on his toes, lost his balance again, and fell backward into the water, which was surprisingly shallow. Like a puddle in a pothole. He scrambled to his feet and planted them shoulder-width apart, ready for anything. If he hadn't fallen, he might have been able to snatch the stone from Beiron's pocket and slip past him as he'd intended to do.

He'd missed his chance.

Beiron grasped the hilt and tore the knife from his leg. In the dying light, his eyes were endless pits. He gritted his teeth and groaned before tossing Adrik's knife into the pool. *Blood of the offender.*

Mick set his jaw. Now it was his turn.

Vidia ran toward them, frantic, drawing Mick's attention to her. Beiron too, tore his gaze from Mick to look her way. He peered back at Mick and grinned.

*Not good.*

Vidia halted as Beiron gripped his knife and started toward her. Despite the evident fear in her eyes, she clenched her hands like she had it in mind to charge at him with nothing but gumption and her fists, the little good they'd do against Beiron.

Had she not been paying attention?

"Vidia, go!" Mick bounded after Beiron and jumped in front of him with his hands out. He'd not avoid getting cut, but he was beyond being cautious.

Vidia hesitated. Her face betrayed her warring emotions, her eyes darting back and forth between them.

Mick tried to keep Beiron's attention away from her. "Get out of here, Vid!" He said it with enough force to stress his urgency. It worked. Vidia turned from them and ran for the wall, then began the climb. But she had the entire length of the trench. Why would she go back up?

Mick blocked Beiron's path to her. When Beiron tried the other way, Mick matched his step. Vidia needed more time.

Beiron flared his nostrils. He grabbed the front of Mick's shirt and reeled him in, piercing the knife through his abdomen—in the exact same place as he'd done before.

Mick cried out. He bent forward and clutched Beiron's hands on the knife. Vidia's scream was like a distant sound over the waterfall.

Although he'd been asking for it, it didn't make the pain any less. He stuttered in a breath. Beiron leaned close enough so that Mick could feel his hot breath on his ear; close enough that Mick could reach his hand into Beiron's pocket.

Mick sagged, and he tasted blood in his mouth.

Beiron spoke just loud enough to be heard. "You must be really stupid, boy."

Mick's eyes fluttered. He squeezed them tight, trying to stay focused. His fingers poked around inside Beiron's pocket. They touched the soft leather pouch, and he wrapped his hand around it. Beiron favoured his injured leg, but he didn't appear to struggle with holding Mick's weight. Whether it was because of the pain of his own injury or the noise, or that he was distracted,

Beiron hadn't noticed Mick's hand in his pocket or that he'd removed it, clutching the stone.

Beiron put pressure on the knife. Mick clenched his teeth and seethed, and every excruciating breath set his body afire. Beiron eased the knife out, drawing a scream. He took a step away and looked Mick up and down, snarling. Mick pressed his hands to the wound on his stomach, failing to stop the flow of blood. *Blood of the cursed.*

Mick fell to his knees. His hands were hot and sticky. The stone pressed into his palm.

*Return.*

He sat back on his heels. Vidia was a quarter of the way up the wall. Thankfully, *thankfully*, she'd not turned back. Whatever she'd face up top, Mick prayed Boone would get them both to safety.

He sucked in a breath. As much as speaking would hurt, this moment was too good not to share it. "I fixed it." His words slurred.

Beiron eyed Vidia, watching her go. With Damien and his men up there, he probably wasn't worried about her getting very far, despite Mick's hopes.

Mick's breaths became shallower. "I just…needed…this." He emptied the stone from the pouch onto his bloody palm, then held it up to make sure Beiron could see it clearly. Beiron's face turned bright red, and the veins in his neck pulsed. He saw it. Mick tossed it over his shoulder and relished the satisfying *plop* as it hit the water.

It was done.

# Chapter 45

The ground vibrated, and the falls ceased to flow into the pool. Beiron's face contorted. His eyes darted from the walls, to the ground, to the pool, to the waterfall that no longer poured down.

To Mick.

He bared his teeth and grabbed Mick by the throat while letting out a guttural roar. Mick had little fight in him. He tried to pry Beiron's hands off his neck, but his fingers weren't working. He couldn't get air into his lungs. His eyes bulged.

"What have you done?" Beiron spat. His grip tightened around Mick's neck. He then lifted him and threw him. Mick landed in the pool, and dark water splashed around him.

Shadows deepened within the trench.

By the time Mick had taken a few raspy breaths, Beiron had waded into the water, up to his thighs. His eyes scanned the opaque surface.

What had started out as subtle vibrations beneath their feet grew into trembling. Mick got onto his hands and knees. Where he knelt, the pool's depth was only enough to reach midway up his forearms, but the water defied gravity and crept up his arms, over his shoulders, and around his chest and back. It offered soothing relief from his agony. His muscles shook, and the familiar itching sensation of his healing magic prickled under his skin. He never thought he'd be so happy to experience that unpleasant itch.

While the trembling grew to quaking, Mick wondered vaguely if he'd be crushed by the walls of the trench closing in if he stayed there, assuming that was what they would do now.

Vidia still made her way up the wall. She was nearly to the top. It was a good sign that Boone had not come hurtling to the ground, but Mick had no way of knowing how his friend was faring.

Mick closed his eyes and let the water's healing magic rejuvenate his own. He would survive this. Already, he felt strong enough to stand.

Beiron crouched low in the water, feeling around for the stone. He froze, and his body tensed. His face scrunched up in pain. The noise of rumbling and quaking earth drowned out his scream.

Mick rose on shaky legs. Surviving his wounds was one thing. Surviving Beiron's rage was another. He had to get out of here, and as long as Beiron was distracted, he had an opening. He took it.

He trudged out of the water, not yet able to straighten his back fully. As he reached the wall, a scream came from above. The cry became louder as a man plummeted past him, splatting on the bottom of the trench. Mick's heart stopped. His hand trembled as he clutched his chest and looked over the jumbled form. The man who'd fallen had dark hair. Relief flooded him, followed immediately by guilt, then shame. Although it wasn't Boone, a man had died. Mick gazed at the blood pooling around the man's head. Should he try to heal him? As long as he'd not gone cold, there was time. Yet, he himself could barely stand.

Beiron bellowed another roar.

Mick bounced on the balls of his feet. He had yet to catch his breath. He needed to heal and wanted to save the fallen man.

But he had to move. He found a foothold in the wall and started the climb. He'd have to live with the guilt of knowing he didn't try to help. *Some healer.* His words from the other day echoed in his mind.

He'd gotten a hurried start and was making good progress. Vidia was at the top. He could see her lifting her legs over the edge. Mick climbed faster. He glanced down to see Beiron at the base of the wall, starting the climb with his injured leg.

The quaking continued at a steady rumble. If these walls were closing in, it was subtle and the only thing to go by were these vibrations.

Mick grabbed a jutting rock, pulled himself up, found a foothold, found another place to hold onto, and went on this way until he'd worked up a good sweat. Not once did he look down to see how far below Beiron was. Getting to the top was his sole focus.

Mick sped up as he got closer to the top. With each step, he felt stronger. Any pain he'd experienced since Beiron had first cursed him was gone.

Dusk was upon them now. The navy hues in the sky were slowly darkening. After climbing out of the darkness of the trench, the additional light, no matter how faint, was a welcome change. Mick made it to the top and paused before climbing out. Swords clanged above, accompanied by the sound of a host of people engaged in battle. As long as Mick kept his head low, he'd not be seen just yet. A quick glance down confirmed that Beiron hadn't caught up. Or, at least, he'd not yet reached where the light touched. It was difficult to see, but Mick caught sight of his shadow moving in the darkness. He'd be a while still. Mick didn't want to be around when he eventually made it to the top.

Nothing good would come of his lingering here any longer. He peered over the ledge, and rough hands grabbed him under the arms, pulling him up. He flailed and kicked before he could see who'd lifted him, though he panicked at the thought that it might be Ighur.

An electric jolt shocked Mick's nerves, and his body went limp. He crumpled to the ground. Apart from a ringing in his ears, he was aware of fighting happening around him. Bodies danced in motion, and every once in a while, the glint of a sword reflected the light of someone's blue magic light, hovering above. Blue and orange lights flashed in all directions, except over the black opening of the trench.

The trembling ground was almost beginning to feel normal. From a brief glance at the battle in what light was available, Mick couldn't see Vidia or Boone anywhere.

Damien straddled Mick and flipped him onto his back. He planted a knee on each wrist. "It appears Adrik has sent reinforcements for you." He smelled of sweat and earth. "Too bad. Now they're going to die." He touched a hand to Mick's chest and grinned. The light from above created shadows on his downturned brows.

Mick braced himself. Whatever Damien was doing, it looked like he intended to inflict pain. But nothing happened. Damien's brow creased.

Mick took advantage of his flop. He raised his knee and kicked him in the pelvis—not quite where he was aiming. Still, Damien hollered. The assault was enough for Mick to be able to rip one of his wrists out from under Damien's knees. At the same time, a lunging force ploughed into Damien, toppling him off Mick. The two rolled in a tangled heap. They stopped near the edge of the trench. The attacker was on his feet in less than a second. Fireballs formed in his hands and he threw one at Damien, engaging him in a fight.

With Damien distracted, Mick hopped to his feet. Multiple blue spherical lights hovered over the span, from where he stood to the edge of the forest, where men and women fought in a protracted battle. Much like the battle at Elefthan, magic was a favoured choice of attack. Having not mastered any magical skills besides healing, Mick needed to see about how he might obtain a sword. He made his way past duelling opponents and nearly tripped over a few bodies in his haste to flee. He again felt guilty for leaving someone in such a state when his healing power had been restored.

Mick glanced back at the open space of the trench. For all the peril they were in now, he would not dismiss the danger that Beiron would present once he emerged from that darkness.

Where were Vidia and Boone? He dismissed the thought of them lying dead somewhere in the dark. Never again did he want to experience that helplessness of not being able to save a life. And here he thought that nothing could hurt him. Even though he could heal again, he feared the pain that would come if anything happened to his friends.

A pale, dark-haired woman approached Mick. She raised her free hand and lowered her sword so the blade tip pointed away from him. "You're Mick?" she asked, but she didn't wait for a response. Her voice carried over the noise. "I'm Pepri. We got your friends. They're returning to Elefthan with some of our Warriors. The curse—is it broken?"

A flare of light whipped past Mick's arm, grazing him. He grabbed his arm, but he already felt the stinging fade. "It's done!"

"We've been sent to get you home. Get back!" Pepri set her stance and took up a guard as one of Damien's followers ran toward them. She thrust a flame at Pepri.

Mick glided out of the flame's trajectory and tripped backward over something sticking up out of the ground. He landed on his back, and the thing that tripped him extended further out, twisting around his ankle. His skin crawled.

While Pepri fended off her attacker, Mick sat up and floundered while searching for anything with a blade. Enough bodies were strewn about, so he was sure to find something to use to cut the root from his foot. A second root sprang up and twisted around his other ankle and he was reminded of the vine that dragged him into the lake. *Not this again.*

He pulled his legs, which did nothing to loosen the bonds. His eyes caught a glint of something on the ground, and he saw that someone had dropped a dagger. Mick shimmied himself toward it, his feet fixed in their place. He'd nearly reached it when a third root popped up and wrapped around his extended wrist.

Afraid to lose the use of his remaining free limb, he kept his other hand up and away from the ground.

But he needed that dagger.

He reached with his restrained hand, but it was still too far. He flinched when the root tightened against his stretching. He abandoned the dagger for now and tried to pry his fingers between his ankle and the roots.

"Ah-ah, Mickey." Damien rushed Mick and shoved him, knocking him so he lay on his back. He waved his fingers, and the roots grabbed hold of Mick's free wrist. They tightened and twisted further up his legs and arms. The trembling earth vibrated underneath him.

"This should be over in a minute," Damien said. "You've got an appointment, in case you forgot." He twisted around and fought one of the Warriors, who'd come charging at him.

How could Damien tell it would be over soon? Were there more of his fighters than there were Warriors? Or was it just a confidence boast?

Mick strained his limbs. He'd not accomplished his goal here only to be brought back to Riggs. Assuming Beiron didn't decide to unleash vengeance first. Mick glanced toward the ledge. Beiron hadn't climbed all the way up yet, but he would soon, and once he did, he'd be a force to be reckoned with—even with his injury. The man had a freakishly strong will.

Mick took comfort knowing Boone and Vidia had escaped. Now if only he could do the same. He was so close to finding his family. No way was he going back to Iptin to be made into a slave. Kartha was where he belonged. Wasn't he supposed to be connected to this place? If that were the case, why was it attacking him?

Bodies lay on either side of him. Contenders, preoccupied in battle, skirted around them and him—tripping hazards. No one came to his aid. He tugged his arms and legs, and the roots tightened, constricting his blood flow. He let them go limp. Frustration led to anger.

This was ridiculous.

"Let go!" he shouted as he pulled his limbs. The roots loosened, no longer binding him. But his elation lasted only a second. Heat seared his face as a flash of fire cast light into the darkness, then disappeared, leaving him temporarily blind. He raised his arm to cover his eyes.

Squinting, he spotted Damien striding back toward him. Mick, his reaction too slow, hadn't even had the chance to rise. Damien grabbed his left wrist and wrenched it to the ground. He raised a sword and brought it down, piercing it through Mick's hand and into the ground on the other side.

A cry came forth from Mick's throat before he even realized he was screaming. Every time his hand flinched, it was like feeling the initial pain all over again.

"Stay!" Damien left the sword stuck there and faced another opponent.

*Stay, says the dog.* Like he had much choice. Mick gritted his teeth and stretched out his right hand to try to grab the hilt of the sword. It was too high, and he couldn't reach it without pulling on the hand that was pinned. Now that his healing power had returned, his magic worked to mend his flesh back together, but with the blade pierced right through the middle of his hand and with his skin prickling, trying to regenerate around it, it only made it hurt worse.

Blue light flickered, and a few of the spheres went out completely. The battle-ground grew darker. It was hard to tell how many were left fighting and which way things would go. The clattering of swords and the grunting of exertion had diminished.

A figure appeared beside Mick. The man stepped on his arm, grabbing the sword hilt. Mick breathed through his teeth, bracing himself for the next part.

The stranger added pressure to Mick's arm. "This is going to hurt."

"It already hurts. Just do it!"

In one swift pull, the man removed the sword. Mick turned over, howling. He used his good hand to lift himself onto his knees.

Another blast of fire barely missed the side of his face.

The stranger's dark skin glistened with sweat. He hoisted Mick to his feet and waved a hand. "Get out of here. Go!" He turned to face Damien, who charged at him.

Mick ran. His hand itched as he raced past the bodies of the fallen and past those who remained fighting. What began as maybe fifty men and women had dwindled down to little more than a dozen. How many of those were Damien's, and how many were Adrik's reinforcements?

He wasn't going to wait around to find out. He kept to the shadows, places where the light was no longer touching, and headed for the trees.

"Don't let him go!" Damien shouted. His voice sounded distant. "I'm coming for you, kid. You hear me? I know how to find you!"

Mick sped up and sprinted the rest of the way to the shelter of the trees. When he reached the tree-line, he didn't stop. He ran until sweat dripped from his head into his ears and eyes; he ran until he couldn't breathe and still kept going. He stopped only when he couldn't hold back his stomach's contents any longer. He leaned his shoulder against a tree, bent over, and vomited. When he finished, the only sound to disturb the quiet was his own raspy breathing.

# Chapter 46

Mick required no light to find his way through this forest. The leaves on the trees, as well as the grass and insects, let off a bright glow. The colours and the way the leaves and branches swayed reminded him of the aurora lights that danced in the sky back at home in Iptin. The similar shades of turquoise and blue swooped up and down in gentle motions. A breeze kissed his cheek.

His heart still pulsed in his throat. All he wanted to do now was collapse and sleep right where he stood. His fear and pain had accumulated over the past few weeks, and he just wanted it all to be over. But he couldn't stop now.

Boone and Vidia were headed for Elefthan. If Damien valued his life, he'd not show up empty handed to meet Riggs. No doubt he'd be coming for Mick. But where could Mick go where Damien wouldn't look for him? Damien's forces had already attacked at Elefthan just to lure him out. If Mick returned there to catch up with his friends, could the camp handle another attack?

He slumped against a tree.

A twinge of fear for his father rooted itself in his thoughts. Had he survived the fight? Clearly, if Adrik had sent reinforcements for Mick, that must mean they'd gotten control of the situation there. Otherwise, why send for them to be returned there? If Mick was to be Damien's focus, he should stay away from the camp while they were vulnerable and recovering. But he had to go somewhere.

He gauged his direction based on the path. If he continued heading south, away from Elefthan, he could make his way toward Litlen and perhaps throw Damien off his scent for long enough to find a safe haven. Provided Ighur wasn't already waiting for him in Litlen.

The quakes continued to rumble beneath his feet and he wondered if they would ever stop. Or if Beiron had made his way out of the trench. Probably, knowing how persistent he was. The hate in the man's eyes would haunt Mick's dreams for a long time to come.

Dwelling on these thoughts made him weary. He put them from his mind while he walked in silence.

By the time Mick had reached a road and oriented himself, it was well into the night. He'd been curious to check his stomach but feared what he might find. Although he knew he'd healed, part of his mind still held onto the idea that a mark remained. He'd not want to arrive at his grandparents' house and discover something there while in front of them.

He lifted his shirt and checked all around his navel and sides. In the dim glow of the bioluminescent forest, he could see no black charlike webs marring his skin. Every inch of him was clear and unmarked. His clothes, on the other hand… His shirt was torn and bloody, hanging loosely; his hands and arms were covered in dried blood; and he could only guess what his beard and hair must look like, or how much blood was in them.

He lowered his shirt. He'd have to borrow more of his grandfather's clothes until he could get himself sorted with his own wardrobe. Or maybe his parents had thought to bring him several changes of clothes.

As he carried on his way through the pre-dawn morning, dragging his feet all the while, the road widened and the trees thinned out. This was familiar. He'd taken this route on the way to Elefthan. From here, he retraced his path back to where they'd started out—at his grandparents's home, near the cliffs.

In Litlen, few people were out at this hour. A glow on the eastern horizon hinted at the sun's imminent rising. As he walked through the cobbled streets, he'd garnered one or two turned heads from the few people he passed. Thankfully, no one stopped him or inquired about his appearance.

Further into the city, more people went about their morning, getting their shops ready for the day, flipping closed signs to open, brushing the front steps, or setting a mat outside their front entrance. Mick caught bits of a conversation from a couple while they walked past him, going in the opposite direction. Words such as *earthquake* and *curse* stood out. They ceased speaking as soon as they saw him and blatantly stared as they went past. He supposed the only thing he had going for him with the way he looked was that he'd not be easily recognized from Ighur's posters.

By the time the sun had risen, he'd made it to his grandparents's house and knocked on the door. His adema opened it, and her bright green eyes sparkled. She yelled and flung her arms around Mick, squeezing him.

"Mick!"

When she pulled away, she crinkled her nose. "You smell awful." Her eyes scanned him, moving up and down his torso and face. "And you look worse than you smell. What happened?"

*What didn't happen?* Mick shrugged and gave a half-hearted chuckle. "I didn't die."

Raidan sat on the sitting room couch, watching them. His lips were tight and he stared for a minute, unblinking. He stood slowly, putting a hand to his heart as he did so. Mick crossed the room and touched a hand to his shoulder. "You're hurt." Without waiting for confirmation, he drew from his power and expelled healing into Raidan. Using his magic felt different than it had his whole life. Somehow it seemed…fuller. More complete.

Raidan brushed Mick's hand aside gently. "I'm all right, Mickey. Just tired. I've been bound to the Weldafire Stone for so long. It's taking me a bit to adjust to these changes."

"It hurt you to lose it, didn't it?" Mick hadn't seen what exactly had happened after he'd been stabbed.

"It felt like someone reached inside me and ripped out part of my heart."

"And Uncle Dimi?"

"Yes, him too. He was on his way back here from Iptin with your mom and dad when it happened."

"Is Dad all right?" Mick's concern grew. "And Mom—where is she?"

Ida answered. "Your father is well. But as soon as we heard about the attack at the camp, there was no stopping your mother. She went as soon as she could."

"Is that where Uncle Dimi is too? At the camp?"

"No," Ida said. "He— Well, he went to look for Laila. She's a friend of—"

"Laila?" Mick only now remembered her sudden appearance and disappearance. "I saw her. She was there, at the Gap. She just appeared and then she was gone."

"You saw her?" Raidan asked. Beiron had had a similar confused expression when he'd asked the same. Had Mick seen an apparition? He tried to recall if Vidia had seen her too. She'd given no indication that she had.

Raidan pinched his chin. "Was Beiron with you at the time?"

Mick nodded.

Ida pursed her lips. "He and Laila share a connection that allows one to be where the other is—though not physically." She glanced at Raidan and he continued for her.

"We learned about it right before he was trapped in the cave. Since then, they've been cut off from each other. It's an unusual thing. When you saw her, did she say where she was?"

Mick shook his head. "She tried to tell me, but Beiron sent her away before I could hear. Why do they have a connection?"

No one answered. Ida and Raidan shared a look. Finally, Raidan spoke. "We don't know why. Not truly anyway. But right now, she's in trouble. She gave herself over to Beiron to save me. Not for the first time has she done something like this. She's family as much as you are, and Dimitri has gone to find her and bring her home."

"I'd better be on my way." Ida shuffled toward the door.

"Where are you going?" Mick had just gotten there. She was leaving so soon?

"We received word that you had fled the camp during the attack to go to the Gap," Raidan said. "We told the elders we'd report to them if you came here. Adema offered to bring the report."

Ida pointed to her handbag on the couch, and Mick picked it up and gave it to her. "Why don't we all go?" he suggested. It would be a good excuse to get somewhere no one would expect him to be. How familiar was Damien with his grandparents' address?

Raidan rubbed the back of his head. "You and I need to have a chat, Mick."

Warmth rushed to Mick's cheeks. Was he in trouble? Even now, after everything, was Adefa going to give out to him for leaving Iptin against his parents' wishes? He was a grown man, fit to make his own decisions. Sure, the consequences had cost him, but this was his purpose. He sensed that. Something in his heart let him know he'd fulfilled the objective that had drawn him to Kartha. How could they still be upset with him?

Raidan kissed Ida. "I love you."

Ida returned his affection and his kiss, then she hugged Mick and kissed his cheek. "Don't look so worried, *Eduso*." She cupped a hand to his cheek. "You've done well."

*So she says.* The look on Raidan's face made Mick think otherwise. The door closed behind Ida when she left, and Mick had no one around to soften the blow of what might be coming. Left alone with his grandfather, he suspected this wasn't going to be the happy reunion he'd always imagined.

# Chapter 47

A muted sound stirred Laila to her feet. It sounded like the front door.

Something had happened with Mick. She'd felt the power leave her, just as she'd felt it come. The ground had trembled for a long while before there was stillness. Her body still ached from the way it felt like a piece of her had been ripped away.

Mick had done it. He had to have. How else could she explain this feeling?

She'd had the power in her bloodline for only a short time, and it had been painful to lose it. She couldn't imagine what Raidan and Dimitri must have endured when Beiron had stolen it from them.

Footsteps descended the stairs, and Laila shook herself, making herself more alert. Damien appeared at the threshold. He stopped at the opening and ignited his blue light, then prodded it upward to rest over his head. His dishevelled appearance gave Laila fuel to aggravate him. "Failure suits you," she said.

Damien smoothed his hair down and brushed off his shoulders. He examined the opening between them and the edges around the threshold. Laila let him take his time checking it out, not interrupting his thoughts. Would the barrier keep him from stepping through? She held her breath as he stretched a finger out. The zap made a sharp *zzt* sound, and he drew his finger back. He sucked his finger like he'd been burned.

The results were to be expected, but Laila didn't know if she was relieved or more afraid now that he'd put to rest any doubt she'd had of the barrier working only for her.

"Did you really think it'd be that easy?" She leaned her weight to one side and crossed her arms. "You didn't think I'd tried that at least a hundred times?"

Damien said nothing as he continued to examine the edges of the doorframe.

He was here, which meant Beiron couldn't be far behind. Unless something had happened to him. A cold chill swept over her. "Was Beiron killed?" She tried to hide her panic. If he'd died and she was stuck here… She swallowed and got a hold of herself. Surely if he'd died, his enchantments would cease to exist. Wouldn't they?

Damien's lips slanted in a sneer. "You'd like that, wouldn't you? Or are you afraid you'll be stuck here forever?" That would make my life easier. But only if it actually worked like that."

Was that an answer to her question? It sounded like Beiron was still alive, but Laila wasn't sure. If he were still alive, then what was Damien doing here without him?

"What do you want?" she asked.

"I want a lot of things, Laila. Right now, I want you, but it looks like Daddy's managed to successfully cage his little bird." He winked.

If Damien's life would be easier if she were stuck there for all time, why would he want her? Laila disregarded his little bird remark. "You can't handle me. That little sample of my power earlier was only scratching the surface of what I can do." Maybe she was exaggerating, but wasn't that what reputations were made of? Exaggerations and half-truths?

Damien's eyes softened, and he smiled, amused. Laila expected a snide come-back, but he made no comment. He drew his knife from his waistband and made a small cut on his fingertip.

Laila rolled her eyes. Did he think she hadn't tried that either?

While Damien pressed his thumbs to the doorframe and whispered an incantation, Laila tried to understand his reason for coming back for her without Beiron. She couldn't come up with any. "Okay, you've got me," she said. "I can't think of what you'd want with me, so why don't you enlighten me?"

Damien gave up trying to break the barrier. He leaned back and stuffed his hands into his pockets. "Wouldn't you like to know?" He chuckled, and his blue eyes sparkled. Even though their lightness contrasted Beiron's dark eyes so greatly, they glistened with the same cruel intent. "I really wanted you to see for yourself what I have planned. But all right, I'll tell you, only because you won't be able to do anything about it, and that is the point."

He extracted from his pocket a vial filled with the same pink liquid as the one Laila had stolen from him and had confiscated. The tandernion concoction. She kept her face composed.

Damien studied the vial. "Unless…" He opened the stopper and splashed the contents at the barrier. It sizzled and smoked, and the transparency of the barrier became a visible window for a moment. The window disappeared, and it was impossible to tell if the potion had destroyed the invisible wall. He gave Laila a single nod.

She raised a brow. Why should she be the one to try it? She doubted it would be such a simple solution as that. When she set her weight back, Damien relented. He touched a finger to the barrier and received a shock.

He grimaced. "It was worth a try." He eyed the empty vial. "I have plenty more of this and other variations of the potion. You're not the only one who's benefited from Beiron's experimentation. I've been saving these for something big."

"Thought you would have used those up at Elefthan."

"Only a few. And only when it was absolutely necessary, but the thing about using something like this is there's a risk for me and my people when handling it. More than half my followers are Elderace. There's not much room for mistakes when it comes to this."

"So, what's the point in making and storing so much of it?"

Damien grinned. "That's the best part. I'm to meet a new acquaintance soon. I plan to gift him a generous amount. You might have come across him in your adventures. Maybe you know him. Governor Tormin Riggs. He has his henchmen roaming about Kartha looking for the Healer. I'm going to deliver the boy myself.

"That's not all, though. Beiron was on the right track to setting things right in Litlen, but he's failed too many times now. I've lost faith in his abilities to accomplish this goal. Governor Riggs, on the other hand… Now there's a man who can get something done right. He's in the market for some new stock-—something unique that only he'll have to offer to his buyers. I can help him get what he wants." Damien patted his pocket. "I've got a list. Would you like to see it? Your brother's on it. And you. And a few others who might make taking Litlen more of a problem for me. Once I've eliminated anyone who could oppose me, I'll step in and begin implementing some changes around here with the Governor to back me. I see a productive future in the making."

Laila couldn't believe what she was hearing. "You would turn against your own people?"

"I'm a businessman, Miss Cailt." Damien tapped his forehead. She clenched her fists at his use of her father's surname. He sought to get a rise out of her and she would not oblige.

"You risk using the potions because it will affect you too. You don't think that Governor Riggs would turn on you and use it against you the first chance he gets?" Did Damien truly fail to see the flaw in his plan?

Damien shrugged. "It's a risk, but if the Governor is serious about business in Kartha, he'll be careful not to burn bridges before he makes them. But look at me. I'm rambling now. I have plenty to do before I meet him. Beiron should be back any moment. Thanks to Mick, he's not at his best. We'll give him time to lick his wounds. Hang tight, Witch. I'll come back for you when all is said and done."

He blew a kiss as he backed away, and his light followed.

He was leaving, and Laila would be alone again. Trapped here. Unable to go after him and stop him from setting the Tax Collector upon Litlen and the people on the undoubtedly long list he carried.

She waited until he turned and skipped up the stairs before she bent over and clutched a hand around her stomach. These walls, that shelf, the discarded vials and jars…this stupid room! Whenever Beiron returned, he would soon find that she was done playing his games.

# Chapter 48



"Have a seat, Mick." Raidan offered the couch across from him.

Mick's infrequent time spent with his adefa made a moment like this feel awkward. He walked over to the couch and flopped onto the cushion. As soon as he let his legs rest, he sank back, letting the softness of the couch swallow him. He could have gone to sleep for how tired he was. But the tension in the air kept him alert and awake.

This wasn't over. Damien was still out there looking for him. He'd said he knew how to find him, but did he mean to look here? Or in Elefthan? And Ighur…was he already here? Mick was banking on his family helping him out of that predicament, but with Damien and a legion at his side, what chance did he have? A personal guard would certainly put his mind at ease, but while the smoke still smouldered from the battle in Elefthan, he'd not request their help only for the sake of peace of mind.

Raidan studied Mick's face with the same brown eyes that matched his. And his father's. And Uncle Dimitri's. Mick wished Uncle Dimi were here right now to make this less uncomfortable. He was never quite so serious as Raidan.

"I would have been here sooner, but the, uh…the roads were pretty rough." Mick's lips twitched. His chuckle was forced.

Although Raidan had just recently taken a hard hit, he still looked young for a man in his seventies. He could have easily passed for a man in his fifties. His face remained stern—not in an angry way, more like he had too much on his mind to be amused.

Mick dropped his smile. Now was not a time for jokes. "Adefa, I'm sorry I messed things up in coming here—"

Raidan raised a hand. He shook his head and lowered it into his hands. Still, he said nothing.

Mick tapped his thumb on his leg. Why did it still feel like he was in trouble? Was it because he'd gotten himself caught by Beiron, which forced his grandfather's hand and set in motion the curse that nearly destroyed Kartha?

"Adefa… When you came for me in the mountains…why did you let Beiron take your blood? You knew what I could do—that I'd heal. He didn't know it, but you did."

Raidan raised his head from his hands, revealing the tears streaking down his cheeks. He shook his head again. "I would never abandon you, Mick. Never. You have incredible power, but you are not invincible. Your heart does not heal as you would like to believe it does. You've been through much since you've set foot on Karthan soil. So many trials to test the strength of your heart and spirit. I will not add to that hurt and have you believe that I'd let anything happen to you just because you can heal.

"Beiron had been after the same thing since long before our time. But sooner or later he was bound to succeed at taking what he's always wanted. I wasn't going to stop him by refusing him then. He had all but the one thing he needed to complete the ceremony.

"That's all resolved now, though, isn't it?" Raidan asked. "I felt the change, as I'm sure, everyone in all of Kartha did as well. The curse is broken, and you're here and whole."

*Until Ighur came for him.* Mick tried not to squirm.

He opened his mouth, but Raidan interjected, not letting him speak.

"There's something I need to say, Mick. Before anything else. I owe you an apology for not visiting you as often as I should have." He raised his hand to stop Mick from interrupting. "It wasn't that I didn't want to see you, or couldn't handle the journey. In the same way you felt a discomfort under your skin when away from Kartha, Dimitri and I experienced the same. It was worse when we came to visit together, so we started staggering our visits. Over the past seven years, while we sensed the stone's power reaching— searching for you—it became more difficult for me to visit without feeling ill. Dimitri's always been a better pretender than I ever was." He smiled. Mick always knew his truest smile when his eyes softened the way they did.

Raidan looked his grandson over, taking all of him in. "I've missed you, Mick. And I can't tell you how pleased I am that you're here. Now that you are, there are certain things you must learn about Kartha and the Weldafire Stone.

"Your connection is unique, as I'm sure you know. When Adema and I had your father, it was before I ever became bound to the Weldafire Stone. The time came when we were ready to settle in Litlen and expand our family, so we..." Tears pooled in his eyes. "We were unable to bear any more children. Even to this day, I don't understand why, but we think it has something to do with the magic in my blood. So when your father married your mother—he, my heir and she, an Elderace woman—we wondered if they would face the same challenges.

"When you were born, our fears were put to rest. But then..." He hung his shoulders and dropped his gaze to the floor.

Mick knew what then. His sister had been born without breath. Mick bowed his head, honouring the sister he never knew.

Raidan took in an uneven breath and let his unspoken words speak for themselves.

"Of our bloodline," he continued after a while, "you're the first to have been born at a time when the Weldafire Stone was bound to our bloodline in a time of peace. I believe that has some significance in your unique power and your connection to Kartha, but there is still much to learn. We'll have plenty of time to figure it all out, but for now, it'll have to wait until Dimitri's present. Until then, fill me in on what's happened since you fled Elefthan. What of the Weldafire Stone? What of Beiron?"

What of Beiron? Mick's jitters may have faded since arriving in Kartha, then completely disappeared after throwing the stone into the pool, but now a new sort of anxiety simmered beneath his skin.

"The stone is where it belongs."

Raidan didn't blink. "Which is…?

"It's no longer bound to Beiron. Or you. Or anyone. It's where it belongs."

"Good." Raidan clasped his hands in front of himself and took a long breath, then released it—like he'd been waiting a long time to let this go. "The Weldafire Stone was never meant to be bound to anyone. War drove the delegates to summon the storm centuries ago—the Chronicle Storm that condensed the healing crystal of our land into the stone. Then war again drove them to bind it to our ancestor Marc. The delegates called him Sermarc, the Entrusted. When he died, the stone wasn't passed down to the next generations as it was meant to be, until it came to me and Dimitri. When Cassian came of age, we never felt it was time to release the role of Guardian to him. And then, when you were born, something changed.

"The heart of Kartha was the Weldafire Stone, Mick—but you, I believe you are its spirit. Now that you're here and the curse is lifted, Kartha is truly whole again."

Mick let that sink in. There were still so many questions about what it all meant. One thing he understood, though Raidan hadn't said it outright, was that Kartha wasn't just a place; it was a living thing—alive with a life of its own, a life not meant to be captured and claimed, much like any life.

He snorted. *Tell that to Riggs.*

He gazed out the window and looked at the cliff and the vast sea. What would happen now? Was he to forever go on the run? He swallowed and tried to settle his mind. He couldn't think of that just now.

Raidan sat back. "Now we've established the outcome of the stone, but what about Beiron? Is he alive?"

"Yes." That stirring again. Mick looked down and stared with unfocused eyes at the floor. "He's hurt, but he's alive. And angry. As is Damien. And…" He bit his lip. "My employer."

"You mean the one flashing that handsome portrait of you all over Kartha? Why is the Governor offering a reward—a generous one at that—for the return of his cook?"

Mick detected the concern edging his words.

"Governor Riggs runs a side business. I learned about it, and now he thinks I mean to sabotage him."

"What side business?"

"Have you ever heard of the Tax Collector?"

"The name rings a bell but only from news abroad. The slaver, if I recall? Has his toes in all the countries of Ecstein. All but Kartha."

"Yes, well, he's got his heart set on Kartha now. I was pushed into a corner and made a deal to find him a contact here in exchange for my freedom. I've no intentions of following through, but Riggs is not the kind of man you double-cross."

Raidan's lips made a thin line. "So you've made a few enemies, have you? Unfortunately, it seems we have that in common." He stood and brushed the crinkles from his trousers. "So, this man who seeks you out now—will he know to come looking for you here?"

Mick nodded. "By now, yes." He was surprised Ighur hadn't already crashed the door in and hauled him away. It was only a matter of time before he learned of Mick's ability if he didn't already know.

Raidan offered his hand and helped Mick to his feet. "Adema's right. You stink. And I don't think I've ever seen so much hair on your face. You're catching up to me." He ran two fingers along his cheek, patting his beard. "There's a place around the side of the house where you can wash. The pipes pump water up from the stream. It's not as cold as you may think."

A foul smell wafted up from Mick's body and hit his nostrils. He wrinkled his nose and looked down, reminded of his bloodied and ragged appearance.

"Go wash up," Raidan said. "Afterward, you can cook us up something quick, and then we'll head out by nightfall and make our way to Elefthan. Probably best to get on the road before your pursuers think to come here." His jaw twitched, and Mick knew he was thinking the same thing he was. Neither of them wanted a repeat of the night they'd encountered Beiron. Raidan alone wouldn't be enough to protect Mick from what was coming.

Even though Mick's fear lingered, he was slow to move. All those years of being in the dark and not knowing what he'd been missing here with his family. In his homeland. The curtain had been pulled back, and he now longed to draw out this moment, standing there with his grandfather, finally understanding this bond they shared after all the distance and time between them.

And knowing that his fight was not over and that danger still loomed over him, threatening to rip all this away, he couldn't bring himself to walk away. Nor could he express how afraid he was to lose it all. His chin quivered, and he held back a wave of emotions.

"Mick." Raidan placed his hands on Mick's shoulders and rested his forehead against his. "You're not alone. You don't have to harden yourself to your pain. Just because your body heals doesn't mean you don't feel the hurt. But you don't have to bear it alone. I'm here. Adema is too—and Uncle Dimi, your mom and dad, your friends… You'd be amazed at how much sharing a burden helps you heal."

Mick wiped his cheek and brushed away wet streaks. In eight years, he'd not cried. Now, he was on the brink of breaking open the dam. He feared he'd not be able to stop the flow. He felt more release from his eyes, relieving some of the weight he carried. He brushed them away. This was no time to break down. He sniffed, then he stifled the emotions before he could become overwhelmed by them. The time would come for this kind of healing. Just not yet.

Raidan patted Mick's shoulders and gave him a playful nudge. "Go on. Get ready.

Mick nodded. He swiped his wrist under his nose, wiping the snot and composing himself. His clothes clung to his body, sticky with blood. He peeled his tattered shirt away from his skin and gave his grandfather a guilty smile. The clothes had been his.

"I may need to borrow another shirt." He glanced at the rest of himself. "And probably trousers too."

# Chapter 49

The door slammed and vibrated the house. Specks of dust fell from the ceiling. Laila stood from her seated position, her muscles tight. Beiron's scream resonated past the floorboards and into the room beneath the house, reaching her ears. Footsteps tromped, coming closer. It had been too long since Damien left. Every minute she remained trapped down here, was another minute he had to do what he said he would do.

Laila's heartbeat quickened. Now, at last, Beiron was coming—angry, by the sound of it—and it should have been a good thing, except that meant she'd face the brunt of his fury.

The bookcase moved on its rail. Laila wiped the sweat from her brow. She tried to slow her breathing so she could come across as calmer than she felt. After Damien had gone, she lit her own light, and it now hovered above her head. The original colour had returned, blue and bright, filling the room.

Footsteps descended the stairs. Beiron came into view on the other side of his barrier in the threshold, where the door used to be. His eyes were the first thing she noticed. The black endless pits had been replaced by icy-blue irises. She gaped at him. Around his leg, he had a bandage wrapped over a wound where blood had seeped through. She was grateful their shared pain only came through means of magic and that she'd not had to experience whatever beating he'd brought upon himself physically.

He paused briefly, glaring at her with a wild and crazed look about him, though he no longer accomplished the same frightful effect with such bright eyes. She returned his stare.

Whatever Mick had done that left Beiron in this state, she had to give him kudos. But then she had to wonder what state Mick had been left in. Still alive, apparently, if Damien was planning to bring him to Governor Riggs. But in what condition?

As if there were no magic wall before him, Beiron stepped across the threshold and into the room without consequence. No shocks or jolts like she'd experienced every time she'd attempted to go through. Would it shock her if she went through with him? She'd have to get closer if she were going to try. But before she could go for it, Beiron took long strides, closing the space between them. Although he limped, he moved quickly. Laila's feet scurried backward without her telling them to. Her backside hit the table, trapping her between it and Beiron. The weighing scale was to her right on the countertop. That could make a nice weapon. It would be heavy enough.

She fixed her gaze on Beiron, who stood so close that he nearly stepped on her toes. The pine and floral scent was one Laila had come to associate with him. It made her stomach turn. He loomed over her, studying her. She could only hold his gaze for so long before breaking eye contact. His eyes disconcerted her more now than they had before. She glanced at the open threshold across the room. How was she going to get him there?

A messy plan formed in her head. It was going to be tricky, but if she were fast enough, it could work. But first, the scale. She'd have to reach it somehow without him discovering what she was up to. To do that she needed to distract him.

"I take it things didn't go so well for you out there." If her darting glances weren't already obvious, the quiver in her voice was sure to give away her thoughts of escape. She held her breath and peered up at him. She could do this. *Keep it together.* Her right hand gripped the ledge of the counter.

"Looks like you could use something for that leg."

Beiron reached a hand toward her face, which she smacked away. He grabbed her wrist and squeezed, while placing his other hand on her temple. His fingers were cold as he laced them through her hair and around the back of her neck.

Little pinpricks poked like needles in her fingers of the hand he squeezed. She tugged her arm, but Beiron tightened his grasp. His large frame blocked her escape from every angle.

Laila closed her eyes. She'd spent decades training in all different ways to use her magic, but never had she considered how to protect her thoughts from invasion. Beiron dug his nails into her scalp, enough for her to feel a pinch. Her thoughts swirled to times when she'd spoken with Raidan or Dimitri about Mick, then to her meeting Mick in Hywreath. While these memories were forced to the forefront of her mind, she sensed Beiron's thoughts. He was looking for something. Something about Mick.

She strained her mind to put every memory she had of Mick from her thoughts. She winced when Beiron latched onto those thoughts and fought to bring them back. Back to the day of Mick's birth, when she visited Ida and gazed upon her grandbaby for the first time.

An ache grew at the base of her neck.

Still, with eyes closed, Laila yelled, fighting for control of her mind. "What do you want?" As if shouting could keep him out of her head.

In contrast to her volume, Beiron brought his mouth close to her ear and spoke in barely more than a whisper. "How did he do it?" His bristly stubble brushed against her cheek. "I didn't open access to the trace of elements in my blood. So how did he do it, Laila?" Again, he tugged at her mind.

The scale forgotten, Laila doubled her efforts to keep him out. But doing so drained her strength. She'd need a reservoir of energy if she were going to get out of here.

Her head pounded. "I don't know!"

*Did she?*

She faltered against his pull. Adrik appeared in her thoughts, telling her of Mick's delegates blood.

How could he have stolen the power with one trace of element?

Already, she'd given Beiron too much. She blocked her thoughts again. This connection existed because of the lacrut plant, meaning it went both ways. She countered Beiron's assault on her mind and forced herself into his, probing about for anything she could use against him. Images of faces and memories that were not her own flew by in her mind's eye. A woman came into focus, and the image froze on her pretty face. She had dark hair like Beiron's and the same green eyes as Laila's. The woman's features were lined with kindness—nothing like Beiron's. In the memory, the woman, whom Laila understood to be Gilia, smiled.

Laila was ripped out of the memory, back to the cellar with Beiron, who'd taken his hands off her. He faltered back, his face redder than it had been a minute ago. Laila's head spun. She blinked, grounding herself. Her blue light flickered. It reflected off the scattered jars on the floor. The threshold lay open across the room, and the scale was just within reach.

She looked at it, and in that same moment, Beiron caught her eye. He leapt for her, but she got hold of the scale and bashed it into the side of his head before he could stop her. He screamed and clutched his head.

She dropped the scale and dove forward. He snatched her around the waist, blood trickling down his temple.

She couldn't quit now. Keeping the momentum, Laila flopped herself sideways, throwing all her weight into the motion. Beiron's grasp slipped, and she fell to the floor. On all fours, she crawled out from under him. She then grabbed one of the jars and twisted, throwing everything into her swing as she smashed the glass against his head. His legs bent, and he stumbled. It slowed him but wasn't enough.

They were halfway to the threshold. Adrenaline held Laila's exhaustion at bay. Beiron gritted his teeth and glared at her. Determined and desperate, she hopped to her feet and braced herself for his full rage. He'd cornered her for the last time. She was done being afraid.

She charged at him, yelling as she kneed him in the groin. Beiron cried out and stumbled back another two feet toward the threshold. She extended her arms and shoved him closer to it. He grabbed her shoulders, thrust her off him, and backhanded her across the face. Her cheek stung, but the pain was nothing compared to her desperation to get out of there and the hatred that now drove her.

The barrier was five paces away. Beiron set his feet, blocking her way—not that she could leave without him. Laila screamed and rammed her shoulder into him, failing to accomplish her goal.

Beiron threw her aside, and she hit the floor, scraping her hands on shattered glass. Undeterred, she snatched up a shard and jammed it into his already injured leg, not concerning herself with the fragments piercing her palm, though she knew she'd feel it later.

Beiron howled. He collapsed down to one knee, taking his weight off the injured leg. He rested a fist on the floor, and Laila jumped to her feet. This wasn't working. Broken as he was, Beiron still had the advantage of his size and strength. It was time to use his own tricks against him.

Laila flung her hands toward him and grasped both sides of his head. She plunged into his mind, searching for whatever she could use against him. Flashes of colour flew through her mind. The memories belonged to someone else but felt as if they were her own. A grey-haired man with a proud posture much like Beiron's stood before her—as Beiron. Sorrow filled his blue eyes. He wore his sadness like a badge—like he'd earned the right to forever mope about everything.

A woman's voice shouted into a blend of indistinguishable shadows, yelling at a girl. A light glowed, creating a silhouette around the girl—a young Gilia. She stood over a smashed vase, tears in her eyes. Beiron, only a teenager at the time, had his arm around her protectively. The ferocity in his gaze was not unlike the one Laila knew, but his expression back then had a certain noble quality to it.

The colours swirled, and Laila could sense Beiron trying to boot her out. She gripped harder and plunged deeper. Freya—her mother—lay with her face so close to his. Laila steered away from that memory. What was she looking for?

Gilia's face became clear and focused. She had the perfect mouth for smiling. Symmetrical and dainty. Her loose dark hair splayed around her shoulders and swished back and forth in her playful movements. She was dancing. With Beiron. He held her close and protectively just as he'd done all those years ago when he'd taken the blame for the smashed vase. Tonight, it was matters of the heart. Gilia had been rejected by a man she believed had loved her, and rather than simply leave the fair with her that evening, Beiron had stepped up and asked her to dance. He swept her along in a graceful waltz, cheering her up so the night wouldn't be completely ruined.

All the light and colour were ripped from Laila's mind. A force drove her out of Beiron's head with such violence that the hard smack produced an explosion of pain in her forehead. Darkness cascaded over every thought and memory.

# Chapter 50



"Laila?" Beiron spoke from somewhere close.

A light flashed from behind Laila's closed eyes.

The concern in Beiron's voice didn't match her impression of him. She hated him, wanted to kill him. How dare he sound so frightened?

"Laila, wake up." Beiron shook her shoulders.

Pain in her head began in a dull ache and grew as Laila blinked her eyes open. She squinted and raised an arm to shield her eyes from the too-bright light over Beiron's head. He was on his knees. The shard of glass was gone from his bandaged leg, but blood continued to seep from it. She'd forgotten how eerie his bright eyes were.

His shoulders relaxed, and he let out a breath. "I thought…"

Laila scooted herself out from under him, but the movement brought on a wave of nausea. She clutched her arms around her torso and supported herself with her elbow. "That I was dead?" She might have laughed if it didn't hurt so much. "Why would that matter to a murderer?" Even speaking hurt.

She cupped her cut-up hand to her forehead. The room was spinning. She closed her eyes.

Beiron sat back on his heels. He dropped his head. He was centuries old and, for the first time, truly appeared so. Both eyes were swollen and starting to bruise. Blood stuck in his dark hair where she'd hit him with the scale and jar, and under his blue eyes were dark shadows. He looked less like the monster she knew and more like a wounded creature.

And her state was no better than his. To reengage in another fight would probably very well lead to one of them getting killed—which of them was anyone's guess.

Shattered glass littered the floor, and blood dappled it in spots.

Was this what her life was to be now? Fights to the death over who had the stronger will and the most control over the other? She wanted to cry, but no tears would come.

Ever since learning that Beiron was her father, all she'd wanted was to prove to herself and others that she was nothing like him. Her love for using plants in healing and potions—that had come from her mother. Her knowledge of them may have come from Beiron, but she'd never use them in the way he'd intended. Blood magic—she'd come to appreciate its uses when used in the right context. And she'd certainly never go so far as to murder anyone. But had she been strong enough, she'd have killed Beiron without a second thought. It frightened her that not only was she capable of murder but that she'd also entertained the idea of it. Maybe she wasn't so unlike him after all. That scared her most.

She gazed at the open threshold. Her way out. Only a few feet away. Beiron's guard was down. He was weak and vulnerable, and yet she couldn't muster up any strength to get up and try to get past him again. Everything in her ached. She missed her friends. Royl. Her mother…

She sat up slowly and drew her knees up to her chest. "You want to know something? I'm like you in a lot more ways than I care to admit. And you're right. Our elders can be insufferable. But they're doing their best, just like the rest of us are. It's not your job to make them think like you."

Beiron stared blankly at his hands. After a minute, he stood and limped out of the room without a word.

*Figures.*

Laila rose on shaky legs. It was another few minutes before she felt she could stand up straight without retching. She tensed when Beiron descended the stairs again and returned with a fresh bandage wound around his thigh. He set down a bowl and cloth that he'd brought, placing them on the floor before Laila, and then he handed her a cup of water. She accepted it and took a small sip. The taste of blood was in her mouth.

Beiron pointed to her forehead. "You're bleeding." He directed his finger to the bowl of water on the floor. "Clean the wound or it will get infected."

Laila didn't move. Beiron had a bad habit of giving orders and expecting compliance. But she knew he had a point. She would get to it, just not yet.

The misshapen windowless room never felt so small as it did now. Beiron crossed the space and was still not far enough away from her. He picked up the scale and replaced it back on the counter, then he stared, facing the wall. Something in him had changed. This strange behaviour wasn't like him. His madness was gone, replaced by something else. This new aura he emanated was difficult to pinpoint. Was it remorse? Resignation?

"What do you want, Beiron?"

He said nothing, and the silence grew uncomfortable, so Laila continued. "You sought the same thing for centuries. You found it and lost it, so what now? The Weldafire Stone rejected you, and you nearly destroyed our country. Are you going to try to get it back?" Her head throbbed at the prospect.

She knelt and set the cup down, then wrung out the cloth as best she could with her hands stinging from the bits of glass in them. She would need tweezers to properly remove the shards. For now, she tended to her head. The cut there stung when the cold cloth touched it, but its coolness eased the throbbing. Had he struck her? Was that what had knocked her out? Or had she smacked the floor, hitting her head in her fall?

Only a few days here and already she didn't know how she was going to survive any more of this. She dropped the cloth back into the bowl and stood.

"One threat against Kartha has been seen to," she said, "but right now, another threat against our people is growing."

Still facing the wall, Beiron asked, "What is the boy's trace of element?"

Laila exhaled, and it came out as a laugh. Was he even listening? "I never found out. You saw that for yourself. That conversation with Adrik happened just before I came to meet you."

"He deprived me of mine. All of it."

Laila examined his eyes. Was that what had happened? *But how?*

When she said nothing, Beiron asked, "How did he see you?"

Laila wondered about this as well. She sighed. "I don't know. I doubt Mick even knows. Maybe it's because of his connection to the Weldafire Stone. I could make up a bunch of theories, but they'd change nothing. What's been done is done."

Beiron turned and faced her, leaning his backside against the counter. He crossed his arms and stared at her for a long time. Eventually, his eyes glazed over.

She shifted her weight, growing accustomed to these drawn-out silences.

When all she'd seen in his eyes was the darkness, it was easy to hate him. Now she saw a remnant of his old self. The same broken man who'd laughed with her mother and envisioned for himself a future that held the promise of love and family. The same man who'd danced with a heartbroken Gilia to cheer her up.

In the same way that she studied his features, he gazed intently at her, then broke eye contact at last. The silence lingered between them. In the time they'd settled, a bit of strength had returned to Laila, and she was getting anxious about the time they were wasting while Damien was plotting against their people. She had to stop him before he could give the Governor the tandernion. That in the hands of the Tax Collector would greatly hinder her efforts to put an end to his business.

Laila refrained from picking at the glass bits embedded in her hands. "Damien is about to hand the tandernion potion over to a very dangerous slave trader. My crew has been hunting this man down for years and hasn't been able to get close enough to stop him. His business is growing and with access to Kartha and our people, his influence will expand. If I can stop Damien now, before he meets him, I can put an end to their plans."

Beiron locked his gaze on her. A fresh patch of red showed through his clean bandage. "You're crew?"

Laila blinked. Of course, how would Beiron know of her work? He knew nothing about her life, nor did he ever think to ask her. "Yes, my crew. I have a crew and a home. I have work and a business partner. I've made a life for myself." Funny… How much of that life had been derived from her studies in Beiron's books? He'd taught her things that played a major part in who she was today. The biggest differences in where their lives had wound up were the choices they'd made along the way. In the end, that was what it all came down to. Even his mistakes had taught her what not to do. He'd inadvertently taught her much, despite her best efforts to have nothing to do with him. Evidently, he didn't realize how much of a role he'd played in her life without even trying.

Laila crossed her arms over her chest, taking care not to disturb her hands. "You can't change the world, Beiron. No one can. The most you can do is make a footprint. Then another. And another. And you keep making them until you've made a thousand footprints. Then, when you look back, you can see the impact you've had on those around you.

"Your discoveries, for example. I by no means condone your methods of how you came to discover them, but I've made a business from using the knowledge I've learned from your books. You've taught me, but you can't choose for me. It's up to me to take what I've learned and make my own decisions and discern for myself what's right and wrong. Let me make my own footprints."

Beiron's blue light reflected in his eyes as he stared at the floor. He took too long to respond. Laila glanced at the threshold and wondered, if she caught him off guard, could she push him through and make a leap for the stairs? But that wouldn't do. The time for fighting was over. She had to cut to the core of Beiron. What drove him? What went through his head that had him dead set on this path of making others think like him? Gilia's face came to mind—and Beiron's memory of her. While they danced at the fair, his heart had been light and free—sad for his sister but pleased to be the one to make her smile.

Laila relaxed her tense shoulders and smiled. "That memory—" she didn't need to clarify which one she meant—"it was beautiful. *She* was beautiful." She watched Beiron's expression for any softening. He kept his eyes to the floor and pinched the bridge of his nose.

"How did she die?" A question Laila had wanted to ask for forty-three years. She might have even asked once before but had received no response. But now, Beiron looked up at her, and she knew today would be different.

He walked across the room, passing her, and stopped at the threshold, still within the room. He faced the opening and spoke with his back to her. "She had a gift, as many Elderace do. But the people feared her gift and what she could do with it. They had no reason to. If you'd known her, you'd know she had the gentlest spirit. She understood blood magic like no one else. And more than anything, she wanted to help our people understand it as she did."

Beiron's fists clenched, and his knuckles turned white. "My grandfather unleashed a mob on her, letting them tear her apart, all because she saw good in something he feared.

"When Gilia died, I tried to continue what she'd started, but the magic didn't work the same for me. Blood magic is a tool that can offer life. I saw Gilia demonstrate that. I've never been able to use it the way she did, and I've accepted that." He faced Laila, and their eyes met. "It's possible you can, but the elders—our people—they'll kill you because of it. I won't let that happen."

Laila looked away. What did it matter to him? "You've nearly killed me several times now. Why should you care what happens to me?"

"You're all I've got left."

Weariness left Laila unable to arouse her anger. She couldn't help but feel sadness in its place. Whether it was for herself or for him, she wasn't sure. Throughout her life, she'd always been surrounded by those she called family, those she loved. Beiron was not among them. Was that truly something he valued? Did he even know what it meant to be family?

She closed her eyes. Too much to unpack. Damien was out there. The Governor's Collectors were too. And whether or not Damien would travel to Iptin Province or send for Riggs to come to Kartha didn't matter. She wasn't going to let it come to that. She drew her shoulders back and stepped toward Beiron at the threshold. Here she was, within reach of freedom, yet unable to go any farther beyond the invisible wall. Not for much longer.

"I've been telling myself all these years that I'm not like you," she said. "Well, maybe I am, but I've made better choices than you. I've let you hold me back all this time, even while you weren't there."

Standing toe to toe, she tilted her head back to meet his gaze. No longer did his size intimidate her nor did his power and strength. She had strength of her own. And it was about time he recognized that. "No more. You're done holding me back. I have work to do."

# Chapter 51



Every inch of Laila yearned for rest, but her body shook with the need to make things right, to protect her friends. Mick needed to be warned if Damien didn't already have him, She'd not set eyes on Raidan since knowing Beiron had used him to fill in the gaps of time he'd missed. Dimitri… The last time she'd seen him, he had set out to bring Cassian and Willa to Kartha. And Royl… He'd be so worried about her.

Enough of this. Laila pointed at the barrier and received a shock when she accidentally touched it. She ignored the sting. "Break it down, Beiron. I'm leaving."

The heavy shadows under Beiron's eyes made him look tired and old. He looked as tired as she felt. Worse, in fact. It was over. This centuries old quest of his—he'd lost. He posed no threat to Kartha anymore.

But Damien did. Laila stuck her chin out and narrowed her eyes, making her thoughts clear.

Beiron breathed out and his shoulders fell. "You can eliminate this threat?"

"I know I can."

Seconds passed, every one of them giving her less time to act.

While never taking his eyes from Laila, Beiron raised his left hand—bloodied from holding his wound—and placed it against the threshold frame. "*Craxnin thei embiyer.*" He dropped his hand.

He'd broken the barrier? *Just like that?*

Laila blinked past a surge of light-headedness. Her head still pounded, but that wasn't going to stop her. What more was there to do now except go? Questions popped into her head. Would he continue to use their connection when she was gone? Was he planning on taking vengeance on Raidan and his family? Where would he go after she left? But these weren't pressing enough to ask now. She'd been here long enough as it was.

She took a step away from Beiron, and he grabbed her wrist. She froze, more angry than startled. *What now?* She pinched her lips together.

Beiron opened his mouth, but no words came out. She waited, glancing down at his hand, then peering back up at him.

Beiron's usual confidence withered. He averted his gaze. "Be careful." He released her arm.

Whoever this man was, he was not the Beiron that Laila knew. Something had happened to him after he'd lost the power of the Weldafire Stone. She took another step back, and he did nothing to stop her this time.

She turned quickly and bounded up the stairs. No footsteps in pursuit. She ran past the hole in the wall where the bookshelf had been pushed aside, then out of the room and out of the house. When she'd run as far as the end of the yard, she glanced back, taking one last look at Beiron's house. Would he stay here? Or would he find some place else to collect himself in?

The idea of Beiron roaming free didn't evoke the same kind of anxiety as it had before. Beneath her skin, within her well of power, something new bubbled. This feeling—it was the most freeing sensation she'd ever experienced. Beiron truly had no hold on her anymore.

The sun was shining. The late afternoon was brighter than any she remembered in a long time.

She hopped into motion, starting at a jog, moving between houses in her old neighbourhood. Her sedentary days were evident in her weary body. It would take her a while to get to Raidan's house, but she needed to pace herself if she would be travelling to Hywreath, assuming that was where Damien was going. As long as the Collectors were still looking for Mick, she imagined they'd still be at the port.

The houses she passed looked almost exactly the same as they had when she was growing up, except now the vines reaching up the walls of the homes had been trimmed and the gardens were contained. Bright flowers created colourful murals from house to house, reminding her that life thrived here after so many years in darkness.

For the first time in as long as Laila could remember, no curse touched Kartha. If Governor Riggs got his foot in the door here, he would bring with him a curse of another kind.

"I'm coming," Laila spoke aloud, while picking up the pace. Governor Riggs. Damien. They were going to regret the day they ever made an enemy of the Witch.

# Chapter 52

A section on one side of Raidan's house had a protruding cubicle built beside it. Wooden walls nearly as tall as Mick made up its sides, and a curtain hung across the opening, creating a boxed-in area for washing up. Mick washed himself in the cubicle, using the pump to pour water over his head. The water, no longer a stranger to him, swirled up his legs and around his arms. After a shave, he could feel his face again, and he no longer smelled like he'd washed up out of the Setter Sloughs in Iptin, where sewage often made its way into the stagnant lagoon.

In the still air, he took note of the quiet. No whispers echoed in his head. No jitters or ringing in his ears. The ground no longer shook. The sun shone warm on his bare skin. This was right.

But as refreshing as it was to wash up, it didn't alleviate his exhaustion. He couldn't remember the last time he'd slept properly. It'd be late soon. Much as he revelled in this moment, his stomach grumbled, and he and Adefa needed to be on their way.

The last of the water streamed out of the pipe. Mick grabbed a towel and dried himself. He donned the fresh clothes Adefa had given him and stepped out into the cool air. A breeze whipped through his wet hair, and he shook, suddenly chilled. He'd have to see about borrowing a coat from his grandfather too.

Mick tousled his hair while walking back to the front door. He rounded the corner and caught a flash of something flying toward his face right before feeling it strike him.

◊

Litlen was unusually quiet. So few people were out compared to the usual bustle of the city. She guessed many of them were out only because they had their shops to run. It was almost as quiet as it'd been during the curse. Maybe not that bad, but she hadn't felt this kind of tension since that time. Between a battle at Elefthan and the lifted curse, she'd wager everyone was staying in until they knew what was going on. Or maybe they did know and it wasn't looking good.

But knowing how proactive the elders were in keeping up with the happenings around here, she'd say they were probably still trying to piece together how the country had been cursed in the first place.

They really needed to work on their priorities.

Laila headed south toward the edge of the city at a brisk walk to conserve her energy. Once she had reached beyond the developed areas, she started at a run on her way to Raidan and Ida's but had to walk again when the exertion put too much pressure on her head.

The dips in the land dropped deeper and the inclines climbed higher as the terrain became hilly. Evergreens and deciduous trees grew denser the farther south she travelled. Sunlight streamed through the canopy, making it difficult to see, and low-hanging branches made the light that did breach through dapple the rough ground. In all of Laila's travels, she'd never seen trees that came anywhere close to the roundness of these. It would take at least ten of her, arms chained together, to hug one a full circle around the trunk.

She stopped at an incline close to Raidan's house. Ahead, two carriages were parked on the road behind the house. Men surrounded the coaches, looking like they were not in any kind of hurry. Even from this distance, Laila could make out the branded mark of the Tax Collector on each of them. They all wore the black sigil of a whip in the shape of an *R* on either their arm or neck. For all the Governor's discretion, he certainly wasn't subtle about the brand. Then again, what did it matter to him that anyone knew who he was? No one could touch him.

That was about to change. The Governor of Iptin Province had made a mistake in thinking he could do business in Kartha.

*And he dares to come to the home of the Dairners?*

Governor Tormin Riggs would regret the day he interfered with her family. When she dealt with his Collectors this time, she would succeed. She had to. For the sake of Kartha. When the Governor learned his efforts here failed, he would not be so quick to do business in Kartha.

Laila tucked behind a tree and watched as three men hauled a body toward one of the carriages. Another two of the Collectors pried open a crate, and they put the body into it. Laila squinted to see who it was. Her first thought was Raidan, but he was too young. That was Mick.

Usually, Jude and her crew were around to back her up whenever they raided ships and released slaves. Today, it was just her, and that wouldn't do. If she were going to instigate a fight, it would be unwise to attempt to go it alone. It was likely that these men were taking Mick back to the docks at Hywreath to set sail for Ectarin. Their numbers and their cargo would slow them down and give her enough time to put together a last-minute crew in Jude's stead.

She watched Raidan's house for more movement. A few men left there and made their way back to the carriages. Among them was Damien, speaking with a broad man who, instead of bearing Riggs's brand, had matching tattoos around both biceps. Laila's whole body slumped. She'd been too late.

Damien had caught up to them and now her adversaries would have an advantage against her. Damien and the other man joined the Collectors at the carriages. They loaded the sealed crate onto the back of the coach and then drove off.

As soon as they were gone, Laila ran to the house. She let herself in. "Ida? Raidan?" She hurried from room to room and found the place empty. Had Damien gotten them too?

Laila's heart wrenched. Ida was in no condition to be handled with such disregard for her well-being. And Raidan… She had no idea what state he was in. She hadn't seen him since before Beiron had taken him. And although Laila wouldn't be surprised if the healing power of the Weldafire Stone still coursed through his veins—having had it as a part of him for so long—if her experience of losing the power had been as excruciating after having had it for only a few days, she could guess he was in no condition to defend himself or his family.

She did another check through the house. No one was here. Her sense of urgency increased. Where was everyone? If she knew her brother, he would be with his Warriors at Elefthan, cleaning up the after-math of whatever mess had been made there. Dimitri should be here. And Willa and Cassian. Unless Dimitri had failed to bring them here.

Outside the house, Laila clutched her scalp and circled in place. Whose names did Damien have on that list of his? Had he already gotten to everyone she loved?

Someone called her name from the field beyond the tree-line, where the stable was just down the hill. She could have melted right there. Dimitri called to her as he ran up the hill toward her. Tears of joy slid down her cheeks as she ran and met him the rest of the way. He wrapped his arms around her and squeezed her so tight that she couldn't breathe.

He let her out of his embrace, but kept his hands on her shoulders.

"I've been looking everywhere for you." He, too, had tears streaking down his grimy cheeks. His hair was a mess of tangles, and his clothes looked like they'd been through all kinds of weather and terrain. "Where were you?

Are you all right?" he asked her, but she felt like she should be the one asking him that given how distraught he looked.

"I'm all right," Laila said. And she meant it. "Where are Ida and Raidan?"

Dimitri shook his head. "I thought they were here. I came to check in before going out again to look for you."

Laila's head still ached from earlier. She rubbed her forehead. "I just got here, but…" Now for the bad news. "Dimitri, Mick was taken."

Dimitri had been looking at the house, squinting to see in through the windows. He whipped his head toward her. "Taken?"

"The Governor's Collectors were here. I saw them take Mick. I didn't see Raidan or Ida, but there's a good chance they're in danger too." If Damien was crossing names off his list, Laila was certain Raidan's name was on there.

"Daegan's gone missing too. Vidia said the Governor's men took him. This has to end."

"It will. I'm going after them."

"*We* are going after them. I'm coming with you."

Laila wouldn't have expected anything different from Dimitri. She took his hand in hers and squeezed. "I was hoping you'd say that. But we're going to need more help than just us. Has Vis returned?" They were going to need to hurry if they were going to make it to the port before the Collectors could leave Kartha with their extra passengers.

Dimitri nodded. "Vis is here. I found him wandering in the southern woods, near the mountains. Come on, Royl's at the stable too." He started walking backward, facing her. "He'll want to see you. Until recently, I don't think I've ever seen him look like he didn't have it all together."

Laila didn't go just yet. "Dimitri, wait." For what, she didn't know. Dimitri stayed put and watched her expectantly. What was she stopping him for? She should go with him to see Royl and put her brother's mind at rest, knowing she was safe. And why wasn't she rushing to make a plan to stop Damien? Mick had been taken. Daegan too. Who knew where Raidan and Ida were? Why was she stopping when there was still so much to do?

Dimitri tilted his head and quirked an eyebrow. "Laila?"

Laila's heart raced. Her chest rose and fell as if she'd still been running. She closed the short distance between them and reached her hand behind his neck, holding him. She stretched onto her tiptoes to look directly into his eyes. Dimitri followed her lead and wrapped his arm around her waist. Their noses nearly touched. She could feel his breath mixing with her own. It hadn't been just Beiron holding her back. She'd been letting her own fear hold her back, and now she couldn't think of why she'd been so afraid to let Dimitri know her feelings. She lowered her gaze, lingering in this place of desire. "I'm done holding back," she whispered. Then she kissed him, letting him feel how much she yearned for him. He leaned in and returned her affection. He drew her closer and wrapped his arms fully around her.

He pulled his lips away and grinned. "It's about time." His gaze fell to her lips and stayed there.

Laila wished she could stay right here like this and not break away from him, but too many things nagged at her mind to let her get lost in this moment. She had more to tell him, and they'd need a plan of action. And they still had to stop and recruit some Warriors.

She slid her hand to his shoulder, down his arm, and reluctantly let him go. "Let's go show the Governor what he gets when thinks he can bring his business into Kartha"

# Chapter 53

A hard jostle startled Mick awake. He banged his head on the wood beneath his head, then again on the wood above when he tried to sit up. His wrists were tied and curled in close to his body, and his knees were drawn up to his chest. This was nearly as cramped as the hole in the rocks that Beiron had stuffed him into. Rain pounded hard on the top, and water dripped in through tiny cracks in the wood. The scent of stale urine wafted toward his nose. How long had he been in there for? His trousers were wet but so was the whole bottom of the box because of the rainwater.

Where he'd bumped his head didn't hurt, but he felt groggy. His healing should have kicked in and removed any of that. He could have sworn he'd dreamt of faces crowding around him, holding him down, touching his face. Damien was there, and Ighur.

A taste of lavender and dill was on his lips, along with something sour he didn't recognize. He squirmed, unable to move much in the tight space. He had no way to gauge the time of day. Then panic gripped his heart when he remembered the hit to the head. Damien and Ighur taking him had been no dream. His breath caught. *Adefa!* Had they taken him too?

Mick listened for voices. From behind came the sound of horses' hooves clopping and the wheels of a carriage grinding against wet dirt. If they were passing through villages, he could yell and maybe someone would hear him and help. But then again, they might not. The rain would drown out his voice. Besides, what would it matter? Few would stand against these men.

Mick's hands were stuck uncomfortably close to his body, and the rope dug into his flesh. He had no doubt as to where they were headed. And now with the prospect being so real, he trembled. His breathing was loud in the confined space. He couldn't go back there. Not when he was only just beginning to see all the possibilities for his future. A future that was about to be stolen from him.

Word would have reached Riggs about Mick's magic, and he'd make certain not to lose his prize. Never mind marking up his price to sell him. Why would Riggs ever let Mick out of his sight when he'd make better use of him as his own personal healer, guaranteeing him a long and healthy life?

Mick clenched his hands into fists. If he was to be brought before Riggs to have his freedom taken, he wasn't going without a fight.

Beyond the rumble of the wheels, and the jostling of the carriage, jarring him, he perceived a deep pulse, growing stronger, as if the pulsing were Kartha's lifeblood trying to connect with its spirit—with him. With every beating *thump* of his heart, Mick relished the charge he felt. It reminded him of his roots here and that this was where he belonged. Not in Iptin. Not as someone's slave.

Those old jitters that had disappeared when he first arrived at Kartha had returned, though now he understood that it was his magic building up, needing to be released.

With his hands so close to his body, he struggled to gain leverage and pull them apart. The last time he'd used fire to burn through the ropes, he wound up burning himself. He could bear a little sting for the sake of his freedom. Besides, he would heal.

He twisted his wrists and arched his fingers so they touched a bit of rope. He then released a smidgen of his magic. The last thing he needed was for a spark to catch and ignite the whole crate, burning him alive. The crate might be soaked, but this was magic fire. Control was key. His fingers emitted heat that singed through the thick rope. The smell of burning overpowered the foul odour that exuded from him. His hands shook with an insistence to release more power. He held back, allowing the amount he released to be enough. The ropes snapped, and the burning smell lingered in the box. It beat the other smell.

With his hands now free, he directed them toward the lid of his little box and let his magic pool into them. No ball of light or electricity appeared, but the growing energy was palpable. It wouldn't take much to blast the top off. If he got a few splinters in the process, so be it. Of course, there were other possible ramifications, but he'd deal with them. He first needed to get out of this box.

The steady motion of the carriage slowed. If he didn't hurry, he'd run out of time to act. The energy building in his hands was near its bursting point.

He turned his face to the side and closed his eyes while he thrust his hands up to release the power. The top of the crate blasted apart into tiny shards, leaving the top open for the rain to pour in freely.

He shimmied himself so he could sit upright. Heads turned his way. People in the vicinity stopped and stared. Mick's crate sat strapped to a carriage that had now come to a stop. Ahead, a pier extended out into the sea where a familiar flag blew on a ship, bobbing in the water, while Collectors—each with their branded marks—hauled crates on board. Any one of those could have contained Adefa, but Mick couldn't save him if he himself were not free.

Behind Mick, on the road, Damien stood with Ighur, and both were staring at him. Nearly a dozen Collectors flanked them. Mick's stomach dropped. He flopped out of the crate and fell onto the road flat on his belly. At the same time, both Ighur and Damien ran toward him. Mick scrambled to his feet. His hands trembled, with magic still at his fingertips. Damien, having magic of his own, was the more dangerous threat. Mick directed his palms out toward him and thrust them, launching a burst of wind or light or something—he didn't care what it was exactly, so long as it gave him time. Ighur was big and slow—strong, no doubt, but that would only matter if Mick got caught.

Mick's aim had been off. The magic spark that emitted from his fingertips missed Damien, only grazing his shoulder.

Ighur moved sideways to Mick's left, while Damien went right. Collectors spread out on the road in the middle, closing in on him. Behind them, on the pier, more Collectors inched forward. Options were few. Mick could dive into the sea and swim, but he'd be slow. If he could weave through the Collectors and put them behind him, he could make a run for it through the city and lose them.

Every passerby scurried out of the way, darting frightened glances back as they went. Were there no guards anywhere? Or did everyone work for Damien?

Damien was getting too close. Mick feigned running at him, spurring him to flinch, then he twisted on the balls of his feet and sprinted down the middle of the road. Damien tripped, and Mick ran in a zigzag past the Collectors.

He dodged the first two, who were too slow to read his direction, and another whose feet skidded in a puddle. One nearly got a swipe at him, but Mick teetered on his feet and pivoted at the last second. A Collector who wore his brand on the back of his bald head ducked and rammed his shoulders into Mick. They toppled onto the road, rolling around each other, getting drenched in the muck. Mick landed an elbow on the man's temple, then hopped to his feet. He threw his hands out toward another Collector coming his way, and white light shot out from them, striking the man—not what he'd meant to do, but it gave him an idea. This was the last stretch. He only had to get past two more Collectors, and he'd be clear.

Breathless, he drew from his power and focused on what he wanted. Over each hand appeared a small flame that grew to the size of an apple. He raised his arms, ready to strike.

A sharp blast cut through the air, followed by a force that whacked Mick in the back. It flung him forward, and his fires sizzled in a puddle as he caught his fall. The force that hit him was like fire, but it burned cold and radiated throughout his right arm and chest, taking his breath away. White-hot pain seared through the back of his shoulder where the bullet had hit him. He gritted his teeth against the pain and leaned his weight onto his left side. He'd had worse pain than this, but not by much.

Ighur lowered his gun and stalked over to Mick.

One of the onlookers who had stopped to see what was happening finally spoke up from where he witnessed the scene.

"Hey, you can't just—!"

Ighur pointed the gun at the man, who shut his mouth, tucked his chin, and raised his hands.

"Walk away. Mind your business." He aimed his weapon at him until the man took slow steps away backward. At least he'd tried.

Ighur grabbed Mick by his upper arm and lifted him to his feet. Blood stained the ground where Mick had fallen, but his front had no wound. Which meant the bullet was still lodged in his shoulder. Ighur pulled him along, dragging him toward the ship, his grip unrelenting. Witnesses watched curiously. Some went back to work as if there were nothing to see. Nothing at all. Just someone being shot and abducted in the middle of the day.

Did Riggs truly have the power to get away with this? When had he achieved such immunity?

Damien caught up with them and joined in step beside Ighur.

Mick grimaced and bit back his pain. "Beiron know you're here?" he asked Damien.

"Guess I took to heart what you said about not needing him." Damien flashed a grin. "The man's losing his touch. And Ighur assures me the Governor is good to his friends."

"Still a dog, then. *Truiy*, right? *Loyal* to your master." Mick chuckled despite his agony. "Sure you are. You just can't keep straight who your master is. But if you've any love for Kartha, you'd reconsider opening the door for Riggs."

"Kartha's not your concern anymore. As I understand it, you won't be returning. Hope you enjoyed your visit."

Mick had no time to assess the weight of his words. Ighur picked up his pace, directing him toward the gangplank, where Collectors resumed going about their work, loading crates and unloading barrels. Goods, stolen from Kartha, most likely.

Rain turned into a mist that blew through the sails of the *Dominance*. And while the tall masts overhead were daunting and the grey skies created a foggy gloom, it was the figure awaiting them aboard the ship that raised the hairs on Mick's arms.

The Tax Collector himself had come to collect.

# Chapter 54

After Mick had discovered Riggs in the study, torturing a man, he'd developed a fear of the Governor that only grew after nothing had come of that night. The pleasure in Riggs's eyes at inflicting such horrors on another human being frightened Mick the most, and the thought that it could be him next.

But the way Riggs presented himself like a perfect gentleman—well-practiced in all his pleasantries and wearing a smile—one would never believe him to be a sadist. Even now, he grinned at Mick with his perfect eyebrows and charming smile, his arms extended as though Mick were his long-lost relative returned. Beside him, Rugio, his wild hair wet and frizzled even more than usual, had lost colour in his face. Evidently, sea life didn't suit the poor butler. Had the man, in all his eagerness to please Riggs, volunteered to come on this trip? Or, as Mick now suspected half the staff at the manor were doing, was he just trying to survive in the Governor's employ?

Ighur prodded Mick to board the *Dominance*. Once they were aboard, Riggs grasped Mick by the shoulder, sending shooting pain through his upper body. Gently, he kissed his cheeks, one side, then the other.

Theérl crossed his arms. His large biceps twitched. The dark man's pierced brows curled down at Mick, daring him to try something.

Mick flinched at Riggs's touch. This pretending was worse than if he'd outright struck him.

"Riggs. You didn't come all this way just for me, I hope."

"*Governor* Riggs, boy. It seems I have a potential contact here and thought I should come meet him myself." He tipped his head to Damien, then his eyes turned cold and focused again on Mick.

"Enjoying your little holiday?"

"I was. Until someone hit me on the head and stuffed me in a box."

Riggs rested his hands on his hips and quirked an eyebrow. "Is that all?"

"Well…" Mick glowered at Ighur. "There was the shot in the back, but I'd hate to bore you with the details."

"I never thought I'd miss your cheeky remarks." Riggs laughed and clapped Mick on his shoulder.

Mick's knees nearly gave out, and bile rose in his throat. Itching pinpricks tingled where muscle and other tissues tried to heal around the bullet in his shoulder.

The rain picked up and wet his hair so that it clung to his face and neck. Gusts of wind sprayed water that pelted his face, feeling like tiny bites on his cheeks.

"Theérl," Riggs said, "see that the crew is ready to set out as soon as possible. Mckal's caused a bit of a scene, and I'm afraid we may have overstayed our welcome."

Theérl began barking out commands to the crew, using colourful language he'd never used at the manor.

Mick stole a glance at the streets. Most of the onlookers had gone back to whatever they'd been doing before he'd burst out of the box. In the lashing rain, people scurried indoors or under nearby shelters.

Mick wouldn't get very far if he tried to run now. Apart from Damien and Ighur hovering close behind him and Riggs in front, his shoulder hurt with every little movement. But his options were shrinking. Escape would become impossible as soon as they arrived back in Iptin. He'd not be returned to the manor. No, he'd be brought to one of the warehouses, where Riggs was sure to have an excessive amount of security in place to keep his "products" from escaping. Mick hadn't seen these places, but he'd heard rumours.

He needed a plan. More than that, he needed time.

"I think you overstayed your welcome the moment you arrived," he said. "In fact, was there ever a welcome to begin with?"

Riggs nose wrinkled. "Careful, Mckal. My patience extends only so far." The Governor then turned to Damien. "Now, I understand you wish to do business, Mr…"

"Brendte. Damien Brendte." Damien extended his hand toward Riggs, who reciprocated.

The simple gesture of a handshake made Mick's heart sink. He'd done this. Kartha would suffer at the hands of Governor Riggs, thanks to him.

Damien fixed a loosened button on the cuff of his coat sleeve. "I think it's about time Kartha is given a chance for trade and business beyond our borders. I'm pleased you've not been deterred by our reputation."

"Not in the least. I see your country's…" Riggs searched for the right word "…uniqueness, as an opportunity. Mckal, you look like you're in pain. I was told you heal, so why the face?"

Ighur pressed Mick's shoulder where the bullet was stuck. Mick yelled and jumped away from his touch, but Ighur looped his arm around Mick's throat, holding him still. "The bullet is still in him. But the wound has healed over it."

Riggs rubbed his smooth chin with a thumb and forefinger. "Fascinating. I want to see. I'd hate for it to get infected." His forehead creased. "Is that even possible? Can you even get sick? Ah, no matter. We'll have plenty of time to learn all there is to know. In any case, we'll remove the bullet and see how the magic works.

"Damien, please accept my invitation to come aboard and travel with us. As you know, I cannot stay. But once we arrive in Iptin, we'll discuss a contract, and my men should be able to take care of routine visits from here on out."

Damien surveyed the ship, then he met Mick's eye. "I'm honoured you would have me. And if I may, I have something that should be of interest to you that will help to manage this one." He gestured to Mick.

"Help how?"

"Suppresses his power." Damien retrieved a small jar from his pocket. It was nearly full to the top with a pink viscous gel. "Use it on his gums and under the tongue, and he'll give you no trouble. Consider this batch a gift to go with the boy."

"How long does it last?" Riggs put his hand out, and Damien handed it over. Mick was overcome with a sense of dizzying dread. That must have been how he'd missed the entire journey to the port.

"A few hours," Damien said. "But you can top it up and extend it so it lasts longer. And use more or less of it depending on how cognitive you want him."

Mick closed his eyes and tried to feel his connection to Kartha, tried to call upon the land to offer some solace. But his feet were no longer touching the land. Below these wooden planks were the lower levels of the ship, then nothing but the sea. He'd not even left the harbour yet, and already, a part of him was missing.

"Excellent!" Riggs tucked the jar into his pocket. "I'll see a demonstration of his healing, then we'll give him this. Bring him below. I'll be down shortly. And then, once we're on our way,"—he leaned forward, toward Mick—"I have a surprise for you. But let's get settled first, shall we? Come, Damien, allow me to show you to your accommodations." He headed toward the bow. Rugio followed with quick steps.

Damien's lip quirked up in a crooked smile. "Enjoy the voyage, Mickey. Our business has only just begun." He swaggered after Riggs.

Ighur then pressed his forearm against Mick's neck, constricting his airflow before guiding him to a nearby ladder leading below decks.

Was it too much to hope that the ship would capsize? He could heal from drowning, right?

# Chapter 55

Giant raindrops splattered onto the ship. Mick's shirt stuck to his skin, soaked and bloodied. Another shirt gone.

His feet were like lead as Ighur dragged him toward the ladder leading below. The upper deck bustled with more than two dozen men working their stations: loosening ropes, unfurling sails, and battening down hatches.

Ighur released Mick and shoved him down the ladder hole, not giving him the chance to climb down. Mick threw his hands out to catch his fall. Dark circles swirled in his vision from the pain in his shoulder. At the landing below, he sat back on his heels. The fumes of burning oil and the smell of livestock on this level overpowered the fragrance of sea and rain.

Ighur's feet stamped to the bottom of the ladder. He hauled Mick up by the collar of his soaked shirt and dragged him forward. Mick's feet faltered. They fumbled behind him until he was able to match Ighur's steps.

In the middle of the deck, cannons were strapped together and secured to the floor. Ighur scooted Mick past them toward the next ladder, which they descended in similar fashion as the first.

A shift in the motion told Mick they'd shoved off from the pier. This deck was busier than the last. Barrels were stacked on their sides, chained together; crates lined one wall and crewmen moved about, checking the contents of their cargo and taking inventory. Two Collectors lifted the lid to a crate similar to the one Mick had been stowed here in. It shouldn't have come as a surprise to see them lift a young man out. Mick's hands trembled. The man looked only a year or two younger than him.

Mick turned on Ighur, flailing his hands out wide. "You can't just take people! They have families and lives."

The young man looked his way. The two Collectors clamped a metal collar around his neck and led him toward the back of the ship. Ighur slammed his fist into Mick's cheek, the impact throwing him against a support beam. Mick blinked and hardly had time to stand up straight before Ighur grabbed his wrist and twisted his arm behind his back.

"What'd you think? I'd sit around doing nothing while you were off sightseeing? Ighur gripped Mick's shoulder, purposely pinching his wound. "Move!"

Mick shook, but not with fear or pain. Frustration and anger fuelled his power.

The ship rocked side to side as they altered course. There had to be something he could do. How many more people had Ighur taken? Would Mick find Daegan here? And was Adefa among those stolen? Was that the mysterious surprise Riggs had told him about? Mick's blood ran cold. How many more lives was Riggs about to ruin?

Ighur stopped Mick at a small corner of the ship designated for storage, except instead of containing what one might expect in a ship's locker room— sails, repair kits, blankets, pillows, hammocks, and the like—the room was filled with chains, shackles, metal collars, whips, and things Mick didn't recognize nor care to know about, all hanging from the walls. He took a step back, bumping into Ighur, who pushed him inside. Ighur entered after him, leaving barely room for a third man in the small space. A lantern was mounted on a square table, which looked more like a tall stool, situated against the bulkhead.

Ighur reached for manacles hanging on the wall. He attached them to a chain that hung down from the rafters. "Boss thinks you deserve special treatment. He's even given you your own room. Lucky you." He clamped the manacles around each of Mick's wrists, then pulled on the chain, which raised Mick's arms above his head and lifted his feet off the floor until his toes could just barely touch the surface. Ighur linked the chain through a reel in the bulkhead, letting Mick dangle there in the centre of the room.

Mick's shoulder was on fire. He was sure that, even if they managed to remove the bullet, he'd forever be tormented by the memory of this pain. Although if he didn't somehow get out of this predicament, he had no doubt he'd endure much worse.

The ship rocked and swayed, adapting to the rhythm of the waves. Chains clinked together, setting Mick's nerves on edge even further.

Ighur brandished his knife. His eyes gleamed, and the corner of his lip twitched. "If I cut out your tongue, will it grow back? I don't think the Governor will mind at all if it doesn't."

"I don't know, Ig. You heard the man. He missed my voice." Every bit of common sense told Mick to shut up, but he had no more moves—if he'd even had any to begin with. All he had left was a chance to stall. For what, he didn't know. He was making this up as he went.

His comment earned him a whack on the side of the head. Ighur steadied him and straightened him so he faced him. "It's like you're asking me to do it. You're a fool who doesn't know when to shut his mouth."

The truth hurt. Mick didn't disagree. He opened his mouth to say more but stopped when Riggs showed up at the door.

"Ah, good, we're all set, I see."

Theérl lingered closely behind him. Riggs crossed his arms and leaned against the door frame. "Let's see this, then."

Ighur spun Mick until his back was to him. Mick balled his hands into fists, bracing himself as best he could. How did one brace for a knife in the back? He'd been stabbed enough times, he should know. Still, he wasn't ready when Ighur touched the knife to his skin and pierced it.

Mick breathed through his teeth, while Ighur cut deep through the mended tissue. He flinched, unable to pull away. Ighur dug the knife around in the back of his shoulder like he had a personal vendetta against him—which he probably did. As hard as Mick tried to keep from screaming, he let out a yelp when Ighur twisted the knife in the wound.

At last, the bullet came out, and relief flooded Mick when the familiar itching started to work its magic. He let out a breath and hung his head, enduring the dissatisfaction of not being able to scratch where the wound had been. It would heal in a minute, probably a little longer thanks to Ighur's hacking around in there. But with the bullet gone, it no longer hindered his movement. Riggs came fully into the room, and he, Theérl, and Ighur stared at Mick's back as it healed.

Mick caught his breath and felt he was capable of anything now. It wasn't too late to have another go at getting off the ship. At this point, his limited knowledge of his magic was going to have to do. He drew from his power.

Riggs spun him so they were face to face. He must have sensed Mick's thoughts because he retrieved the jar that Damien had given him, opened it, and sniffed it. His nose crinkled. He then dipped two fingers in and signalled Ighur to hold Mick still.

"Let me know if it tastes better than it smells," he said to Mick.

Mick's toes touched the floor, and he tried to spin away, but Ighur turned him to face Riggs. Theérl left his place just outside and entered the room with them all, cramming the space entirely with his presence. He did nothing yet, but his change of position let Mick know he'd step in if he had to.

Riggs brought his fingers closer to Mick's face. The stuff smelled like lavender and dill—the same as the taste that Mick had wondered about when he awoke earlier. Any lingering doubts as to whether it would work left his mind. Seeing as he remembered nothing from the journey to the port, he'd say it worked as it was supposed to.

He pinched his lips tightly together, and his breathing quickened. Any hope of getting out of this was dwindling.

Riggs squeezed Mick's jaw with one hand and with his other, he pressed his fingers against Mick's lips and into his mouth, touching his top teeth.

A sudden jolt shook the ship, throwing all of them off balance. Riggs rocked on his heels and waved his arms about. Ighur released his grip on Mick as he stumbled backward and bumped his head on a hook protruding from the wall. And Theérl, hardly affected by the jostle, uncrossed his arms and set his feet shoulder-width apart. Mick didn't wait until they had their wits about them again. He lifted his knees to his chest and flung both feet at Riggs, who'd not yet righted his footing. His kick knocked Riggs against the wall, and he sent himself swinging in the process.

Theérl hunched, his eyes set on Mick. He looked ready to charge. Ighur found his balance, using the wall to stand straight.

Mick's chest tightened. He stretched his toes, barely skimming the floor, and gained enough traction to steady his swinging.

A loud crack thundered throughout the ship, followed by the wood groaning. Shouts erupted.

# Chapter 56

The flag of the *Dominance* cracked wildly in the wind. That the Governor's ship was here could only mean that the man himself had come. And while it saved Laila from having to hunt him down later, she felt ill-prepared to face the one who'd evaded her for so long. Yet this might be her only opportunity to get this close to him.

Laila's feet touched down on the deck of the ship. She was followed by Dimitri, Royl, and a dozen Warriors. Another handful rowed over in a second longboat. In the aftermath of the attack on Elefthan, it was all they could spare. It had to be enough.

Thanks to the foul weather, the crewmen paid and hired by the Tax Collector—Governor Tormin Riggs—had been caught off guard by the arrival of Laila and her party. If not for the use of her and her comrades' magic, it would have been foolish to attempt to row in these waves.

Laila's hair whipped about in the gale, threatening to come loose from its band. She wiped the rain from her face and assessed her quarry. The brigantine consisted of a typical crew of two dozen. The extras on board, who sported the Governor's brand, were Collectors—mere men, no different from those on her usual raids.

How fitting that the Tax Collector's ship should be her fiftieth, marking it as a memorable occasion.

The closest of the Governor's men faced Laila, choosing her as his rival. He had to have heard of her. Everyone who sailed the Bantevv Waters knew who the Witch was. But no matter how many times she'd done this, these situations never got easier or less frightening. Part of her greatest power was not letting her fear show. And now, she had this new strength bubbling up in her—that powerful feeling of nothing holding her back anymore.

She spoke over her shoulder to Dimitri. He had one job. "Find Mick and anyone who's been taken. Get them out of here."

Dimitri didn't need any more convincing. Without a word, he took off to go in search of others.

Laila drew her attention back to her chosen opponent. She fanned her fingers, swirling them in circular motions, already feeling her power swirl like never before. Her challenger narrowed his eyes. He wouldn't realize what she was doing until it'd be too late. The weapon she conjured in the sea behind her took shape. Although she couldn't see or hear its formation, she trusted her magic. She raised her chin, confident, and ready to accept this confrontation.

Royl stood next to her, grasping his short sword in one hand. His kept his other free for the use of his magic. His Warriors took similar stances, with their feet set apart and their swords poised. They each raised their free hand in front of themselves, as magic would be their first action in combat. Laila had no use for a sword here. Not as long as she had her magic. However, if Damien were brought on board, she would be at risk of losing it. She dismissed the thought, using her focus to fabricate her weapon.

She raised her arms, and the waves responded to her summoning, rising from the sea in a lofty wall, stretching above the taffrail. It hovered and funnelled, dipping lower toward her outstretched hands, which were now bandaged and glass-free. All eyes gazed upon the churning waters above.

Laila resisted turning to look back at it herself. The power in her belly swelled and continued to grow. Now the governor would know the true power of the Witch.

She grasped the handle of her newly created weapon even though its construction was incomplete. The current of water flowed in her grasp. She flicked her wrist, and any loose water fell away, leaving only the whip she'd envisioned. Its length curled on the drenched deck.

Now she was ready.

This fight could end only one way. Governor Riggs had made a mistake in coming to Kartha. Not only had he stolen the lives of thousands and evaded her for years, but he'd made her animosity toward him personal by coming after the Dairners. Today was the day that she would put the Tax Collector out of business once and for all.

◊

In the lower decks below Mick, wood creaked under immense pressure. The *Dominance* rocked to starboard. Mick's body swayed and angled with the motion. He spat the bit of gel Riggs had rubbed on his teeth, but the flavour stuck.

Theérl glanced backward, out of the room, toward the growing noise on the upper deck. He whipped his head back to Ighur and pointed at Mick. "Watch him."

With that, he disappeared, leaving Mick alone with the others. Riggs was dusting off his knees and trying to stand straight on the slanted floor.

Screams now accompanied the shouts. Ighur and Riggs shared a look. The Governor picked up the dropped jar of gel—still intact—and handed it to Ighur. He jabbed a finger at Mick's chest. "We're not finished." Then to Ighur, he said, "Keep him quiet. I'll be back."

Another swaying of the ship threw him off balance as he left the room to investigate the happenings on his ship.

*Down to one.* Mick's hopes soared. He still had no plan on how to get off the ship, but one enemy was better than three. Better still, there was no bullet to slow him down. Ighur didn't seem bothered that he'd been left alone with him. He smiled as if it were exactly what he'd wanted.

They were past words. Having had success with his earlier kick, Mick tried to repeat the same move on Ighur. He lifted his legs, aimed, and thrust them out. Ighur didn't recoil. He pounded Mick's legs down, and in the same movement, wound his elbow back and slammed his fist forward, striking Mick square in the jaw. Mick sagged, drooling. *Should have tried something new.* He lifted his head in time for another blow. Everything went black.

◊

Mick blinked. He opened his eyes to the empty room. Had he been unconscious? He couldn't tell if the blood on his shirt was recent or from an earlier wound. He had that taste of lavender, dill, and something sour in his mouth, stronger than ever.

Realization sank in.

*No.*

Ighur was gone. The door to the room was closed, and the now half-empty jar of gel had been left on the square table, next to the hook where the chain was latched onto. Mick might be able to knock it over with his toes if he could raise his leg high enough.

All of his weight hung on his arms, and he felt heavier than he had earlier. He couldn't shake the grogginess. If he were going to attempt anything, getting out of here took precedence.

Shouts came from everywhere on the ship. The wood groaned again, sounding on the verge of snapping. Mick might survive drowning, but in order to do that, he'd have to get to the surface to breathe again. If the ship went down while he was chained to it, his chances of survival would be slim.

He thought of the young man Ighur had abducted, of Daegan and Adefa. How many more victims were on board? This wasn't just about getting himself out of there. The others—however many there were—needed help. Drawing upon his magic proved fruitless. What he really needed was more energy. This drowsiness made his muscles feel like stone. *Must be a side-effect of the gel.* He wasn't going to let it stop him.

Mick grabbed the chains that were attached to the manacles above him. He stretched one leg and kicked it behind, then forward, until he had a fluid rhythm of motion. Whenever he swung forward, he reached his leg, aiming for the reel and chain. His foot hit the wall and he kicked off it, getting a more powerful swing. Another kick, and this time, his toes tapped the reel.

Not enough.

He kicked off again, harder, and this time, he hurtled toward the wall. His heel whacked the chain and loosened it. The chain dropped him by a few inches, then caught again. But now his feet fully touched the floor, and he could loosen the rest. He kicked the reel hard, and the chain released, letting him lower his arms at last. Blood flowed back into his hands.

The cuffs on his wrists rubbed against his bones. This room was all chains and restraints but no keys. There wasn't time to turn the place upside down in search of one. He'd have to find one on the way. On the other hand, this room had no shortage of weapons—and those he could use. Any one of the metal rods would do. He picked one up off the floor.

When he tried the doorknob, it turned. A stroke of luck. Mick hoped it was the start of a streak.

He stepped out of the room. Across from him were the extra sails and rope he'd expected to find in the storage room of horrors. A couple of casks lay beside the rope piles, sacks were stacked in groups of three and netted off against the bulkhead, and a mop and bucket looked like they'd been tossed and left exactly where they'd fallen. Dividing the room and the chaotic mess was a thick support beam in the middle, and to his right, a curtain blocked off access to the bow of the ship. Mick had no interest in going that way. As far as he could tell, what he wanted was astern. He started in that direction.

# Chapter 57

Mick's wrists itched under the restraints, but it could have been worse. At least he had some mobility thanks to the length of the chain between the cuffs, which extended about as long as his forearm.

The light coming in through a porthole went dark, blocked by something large and moving. Whatever was out there was green and shimmering in the rain and sea-spray. The thing clung to the hull of the ship on the outside. It looked like seaweed. With the taste of the gel on Mick's lips, it crossed his mind that he could be hallucinating.

In his periphery, he saw a form storming toward him. Mick moved before he looked, chains jangling. He jumped aside, and Ighur just missed him. Ighur turned, surprisingly quick for a man his size, and Mick issued a two-handed swing of the metal rod. Ighur caught it, mid-swing and ripped it from his grasp, baring his teeth. His palms had taken the brunt of the blow, but rather than thwart him, it further provoked his fury. He roared as he adjusted his grip so *he* could wield the rod as a weapon.

With supplies on either side of the bulkheads, another support beam in the middle, and the only thing behind him being the room he'd escaped from and the ship's bow, Mick had nowhere to go but through Ighur.

Ighur swung the rod, and Mick skidded backward, barely dodging the assault. He slid his feet left, then right in a quick motion, thinking to dive past on the side Ighur least expected. But he'd done this before, and Ighur had expected it.

While Mick dove, arms first, Ighur caught him in the stomach with the rod. Mick hit the floor. Hard. He coughed. He rose to his hands and knees, then quickly got back on his feet. If he lingered too long on the floor, he might never rouse the energy to keep fighting.

Without any thought, Mick charged at Ighur, taking out his legs. A difficult feat while trying not to get the chain snagged around the rod. He landed on top of him and fumbled to get off. He may not win in a clash against him, but he could definitely outrun him. Where he'd run to was an entirely different matter, but he'd figure something out.

Mick's feet slipped. He righted his balance, but not quick enough. Ighur grabbed his ankle at the last second and yanked. The rest of Mick's body followed through with the motion. He twisted while he fell, and dropped his fists down on Ighur's head. It barely did anything. Mick struck again. He reared both arms back to do so a third time, but someone grabbed him from under his armpits and thrust him off Ighur. Mick was about to go berserk on the newcomer, but it was Dimitri who faced him and held up a hand to stop him. Mick blinked, not understanding. Dimitri pounded a fist into Ighur's face. Ighur's body toppled and went limp.

Mick could hardly comprehend his great-uncle's presence. He opened and closed his mouth, his thoughts struggling to keep up with what he was seeing. Was this another effect of the gel?

Dimitri urged Mick to move. "He might not stay down. Let's go."

Mick forced his mind to focus. Ighur may not be an immediate threat anymore, but they were by no means clear of danger.

Before going, he bent over the unconscious man. In a pocket, he found the key to free his hands. He then secured the manacles around Ighur's wrists and left him.

Dimitri led Mick to the first ladder, which would take them back up to the gunner deck. He nodded for him to go first.

Mick backed away from the ladder. "There are others. Daegan and Adefa might be on board the ship."

Gunfire cracked and swords clanked, adding to the chorus of screams and shouts.

Dimitri glanced up at the deck above. "I know. I'm going to look for them. But my first priority is to get you off this ship. Laila and a crew of Warriors are here. We came over on longboats. Get to those and wait. If things start to look like they might take a turn for the worse, leave and don't look back."

Run away? Leave all these people here while he saved his own skin? "No." Mick stood a little straighter. "I'm coming with you." This wasn't up for debate. He bypassed the ladder and ran farther down the ship toward the stern, where the two men had led the boy after taking him from the crate. If more prisoners were anywhere, he guessed they'd be held in the lowest part of the ship.

Dimitri raised no argument. Mick would see this through with him, whether he liked it or not. He would have done the same for his nephew. He kept pace with him as they ran the length of the ship, toward the steps that would take them down.

The thing outside, creeping up the ship, covered the portholes on both sides. Pieces of it stretched upward, blocking the view. Mick could have sworn it was some sort of strange seaweed octopus with many tentacles. He stared, trying to understand what he was seeing while trying not to trip on anything or run into a beam.

From the sound of it, most of Riggs's men were on the upper decks, too preoccupied to come for him. For now.

They reached the ladder. Mick descended the steep four steps first and went to the very back of the ship. There, he got a quick glimpse at the men and women sitting on the floor, shackled and chained to one another by the collars around their necks.

The lone Collector who stood guard faced Mick, and his eyes bulged. He reached for the knife in his waistband.

"I got this," Mick said as he charged him, ramming him into the bulkhead, where the man smacked his head and crumpled to the ground. Mick kicked his heel into the man's face. He then searched him for the keys to the collars and shackles.

Not long ago, he might have felt bad for how hard he'd hit the Collector. His instinct was to heal, not hurt. But when nearly forty Karthans stirred in chains, which jangled in this shallow hold, he felt no remorse for the downed man. These people were probably thinking the same thing he had: that they were never going to see their families again.

He'd make sure they would.

The young man who Mick had seen removed from his crate caught his eye. Next to him, a teenage girl looked up at him with tears in her eyes. Upon seeing them, Raidan sat up straight. Dimitri went directly to him and crouched to embrace his brother. Relief came over Mick, but they weren't through this yet. He surveyed the small compartment and gauged the condition of each prisoner. How were they going to get everyone out of here safely?

Near the back of the rows of chained people, Daegan glanced up at them. His eyes grew with hope, and he shuffled to his knees from his seated position.

Dimitri took the keys from Mick and got to work freeing the prisoners, starting with Raidan. Once released, Raidan placed a hand on Mick's shoulder. He squinted while he examined his face, then raised a hand to Mick's head and grazed his thumb over his eyebrow. "You have a cut here. That should be healing."

Mick gently brushed his hand away. "They have something that blocks my abilities." Just thinking of the gel made his head ache. His knees wobbled. How was he still standing?

Dimitri freed Daegan, and an awkward moment passed between them. Daegan nodded his thanks. "I—If I'd realized…"

Dimitri hit him on the shoulder in a lighthearted kind of way. "Save it for now. We'll have a talk when we're home and everyone's safe."

He wasted no more time as he moved to the next prisoner to release their restraints.

Daegan met Mick's eye, then averted his gaze. Mick couldn't hold a grudge. Who knew what he'd been through in his brief time with Riggs? And seeing the look on Vidia's face once she saw that her uncle was okay would make up for Daegan's behaviour toward him.

In the next row over, a woman sat with her knees drawn up to her chin. Her long matted black hair covered her face.

Mick swayed in a wave of dizziness. *Aira?*

He took one long stride over to the woman and gently swept her hair from her eyes. She jerked back, then looked up. Aira's lips parted, when she saw him. Tears streamed down Mick's cheeks. He crouched in front of her. This must have been the surprise Riggs had in mind for him. Her dress— filthy and not something Mick imagined she'd picked out herself—left her shoulders exposed. On one side of her neck, near a vein, at least a dozen small ticks had been made in her flesh—little red lines, each at various stages of healing.

"Uncle Dimi, give me the keys."

Dimitri finished helping the young woman he'd been freeing, then handed the keys over. Mick released Aira, removing first the collar around her neck, then the irons clamped around her bruised wrists. He handed the keys to Adefa, who was closest to him, then helped Aira to her feet. She wobbled at first, and he helped steady her. Her face had thinned, and her pale skin looked like porcelain. Mick feared she'd break if he touched her.

He turned his focus inward and sought out his pool of healing power, but was met only with fatigue. He swallowed a lump of emotion and set his jaw.

Chaos ensued above, and somehow, they had to get all these people past Riggs and his men, and off this ship. As tired as Mick was, rest would have to wait. No way was Riggs getting away with this. Mick may not have access to his magic, but that wouldn't hold him back. As long as he was still standing, he'd fight. Or die trying. Or at least…get seriously hurt trying. But preferably not.

# Chapter 58

Seawater danced through the air as Warriors manipulated the wind and waves to do their bidding. Laila spun in fluid motion, swishing her whip, lashing from one Collector to another. She flicked her wrist, and the water whip struck a mountain of a man, maiming him just the same as any old whip would.

A burst of pink smoke exploded to Laila's right. The pungent decaying scent of the sap reached her nostrils. Tandernion. Damien had to be close. Governor Riggs had yet to show his face too.

The second boatload of warriors came aboard and aided in the fight. The moment they boarded, another blast of pink smoke billowed at their feet. The Warriors who got the brunt of the blast bent over, coughing. Laila searched for Damien or the Governor or whomever was throwing the tandernion potions. Her last raid on the Governor's ships had ended badly without the added obstacle of a magic-hindering potion. She relied too much on her magic for her to have no access to it here and now. Her fingers shook, and she gripped the handle of her whip tighter.

The ship had stopped moving, but Laila hadn't had a chance to see why. A pair of Collectors came at her, and she whisked them off their feet by swooping the long length of her weapon across the deck of the *Dominance*. Water trailed in its path.

At last, the Governor appeared at the top of a ladder. He froze, turning his head about and taking in the scene. Laila set her sights on him. She strode across the deck, which was drenched from her whip and the rain that had briefly let up.

Governor Riggs's eyes fell on her and hardened. Laila's lips curled up. She waved her arm and cracked the whip at him. As the Governor brought his hands up to cover his face, Damien leapt to his side and grabbed the airborne tail of her whip. The water broke free from its form and showered the deck in a puddle.

Laila took a step back, reeling from her lost momentum. It wasn't often that she contended against other Elderace. She quickly recovered and raised both hands, slamming them down through the air fast and hard, bringing with them an onslaught of water.

Damien dove out of the way, but the Governor stumbled backward and sputtered in the torrential downpour that blasted him. The goal was to arrest the man. The state in which he was brought to the authorities didn't matter much, so long as he was breathing. That went for Damien as well.

While she had the Governor where she wanted him, she marched toward him, relieving a fallen Collector of his dagger along the way. Riggs continued to cough air back into his lungs. She was so focused on him that she almost didn't see the flash of pink hurtling toward her. At the last second, she dove in the opposite direction, and the vial smashed where her feet had been, polluting the air with its smoke. If all it took were the fumes to diminish her abilities, it mightn't be long before the effects kicked in. A pink haze hovered over the deck of the ship.

Before Laila could stand, Damien rushed her and knocked her onto her back. He leapt on top of her, pinned her forearms with his knees, and grinned down at her. She tried not to lose sight of Riggs. She turned her head toward where she'd last seen him and caught the swish of his coat as he fled back down the ladder from which he'd come. She groaned.

Damien bared his teeth, a crazed ferocity in his eyes. "Busy, busy, Laila. Beiron couldn't even keep you contained." He reached for her chest.

*Oh no you don't.* Laila thrust her hips upward, and Damien fell forward over her shoulders. One of his knees ground deeper into her arm, but the other slipped. She twisted her body on the loosened side, freed her hand, and touched his chest, executing the same assault he was about to unleash upon her. Damien's muscles sagged, his weight bearing down on her. Still, she held her hand in place until he passed out, his body slumping on top of her.

Laila squirmed, trapped under him. Glass vials tinkled against one another in his pockets. With effort, she rolled him over and wriggled free, then rummaged through his pockets and took whatever vials he had left. Six of them consisted of the thin liquid like the one she'd almost taken from him in Beiron's home. The other two contained a thick gel of the same colour. Damien had told her he had the potion in various forms.

She picked wet, stray hairs from her face and scanned the faces of those around her. Two Collectors challenged one Warrior on his own. Their footwork and technique proved they knew what they were doing. Another Warrior, however, jumped to the aid of his comrade. Laila had to trust they could handle themselves. She had her mission.

Damien moaned and twitched. Laila retrieved one of the potions. She yanked the cork from the opening and dumped the stuff over his face. He sputtered and spit, while still clutching his chest.

He'd done this.

All across the deck, her people fought. Of the couple dozen they'd brought along, too many lay unconscious from the effects of the tandernion. And of the Warriors left standing, the remaining Collectors who faced them almost matched their numbers. Laila's chest tightened. She hoped these few Warriors would be enough to be victorious. If things went south for her and her party, at the very least she needed to get Mick and the others off the ship.

Royl still had his magic. He moved as in a dance, his every footstep like a work of art like he'd choreographed prior to setting sail. Dimitri had disappeared below decks to go in search of the others and still hadn't returned. He had his job, and Laila trusted his capabilities. Damien was down, but Riggs was still around somewhere.

Laila started for the ladder. Royl appeared at her side and grasped her hand gently. They'd come a long way since leaving the mines all those years ago. If he still worried for her safety, he hid it well. His eyes searched hers.

She answered his unasked question. "The Governor will not evade me this time."

Wood snapped as the taffrail broke apart. A long length of seaweed crawled aboard, joined by dozens of other pieces, all of various sizes at every edge of the ship. It slithered, not unlike the Anguivina had at the delegates' cave. Everyone engaged in the fighting began shuffling inward toward the centre of the ship as the seaweed glided onto the deck all around them.

Royl set his jaw and squeezed Laila's hand, encouraging her before releasing her. "We've got this. I'll keep an eye out for Dimitri. You go do what you do best."

# Chapter 59

While Uncle Dimi released the rest of the prisoners, Mick helped each man, woman, boy, and girl to stand. Some had been taken from their homes days ago and had to shake out their sluggish muscles. Mick deduced that Aira had been here the longest, having been taken from Iptin and brought here—all for his sake. He glanced back at her for the dozenth time. The oldest of the prisoners, a man who must have been a few decades older than Mick, had his arms around her shoulders, keeping her steady on her feet. Aira stood stiff and closed off, but she allowed him to help her stand.

Mick fought against the effects of the gel, trying to keep himself alert and clear-headed until they were free and clear.

As long as they remained on this ship, their chances of getting home dwindled. Someone would have to take them to the longboats, wherever those were. Just about half of the prisoners had been freed. If they went in groups, Mick and Adefa could finish freeing the rest while the others could start making their way. He went over to Aira and reached for her elbow in a supporting gesture, but she backed away from his touch. He lowered his hand and bit back the quiver in his chin. As soon as they were all off the ship, he could better assess the damage.

"Uncle Dimi, it's going to take time for everyone to climb into your longboats. Can you take this first group and start the process? Adefa and I will be right behind you."

Dimitri finished unlocking the shackles on a young boy. He glanced up at Mick. "I can. We have only two boats. It'll be a tight squeeze with about twenty in each." He pointed a finger at him. "You'd better make sure you get your butt into one."

He handed the keys to Raidan to continue releasing prisoners.

Mick licked his lips, tasting the lavender and dill. "What about you?" he asked. "How many came over with you? How will the others get off the ship?"

Dimitri began corralling those who'd been freed from their restraints, grouping them so they would stay together. "One problem at a time, Mick." He spoke while he worked. "Let's just get everyone out of here."

As good a plan as any.

Daegan helped a man who favoured his right leg, and Dimitri instructed the teenage girl to stick close to a middle-aged woman. Mick didn't feel right letting Aira go from his sight. He wanted so badly to wrap his arms around her and comfort her. "Aira, can you manage with them? I'll help my grandfather here and will catch up with you on the shore. I'll come find you."

Aira barely met his eye. Her long hair, which he'd rarely ever seen out of its bun and cap, hung in front of her face, shielding her tears. Her head dipped in what Mick suspected was meant to be a nod. Without thinking, he rested a hand on her shoulder and she flinched. He retreated, fighting back his own tears. *What have they done to you?*

The man supporting her straightened and held her close to his side. Mick stood back and out of the way as Dimitri led the group out. He fought the desire to go with Aira to make sure she got safely away. But he wasn't leaving until each prisoner had been freed.

Raidan took over to release the last of the captives. He moved slowly and Mick noticed he kept wincing. Was this a new injury inflicted on him by Riggs and his men, or was he still recovering from the incident with Beiron?

"Here, Adefa. Let me."

Raidan handed the keys over and stretched his back. He organized this second group in a similar fashion to the first group. The youngest among them was a little girl of maybe nine. Riggs was abducting children as well as adults? Mick's blood boiled.

He freed the last prisoner, and the girl joined the nearly two dozen liberated Karthans. They clung close together as they made their way out, Raidan leading the way to the first ladder.

Raidan went up first. When he was about halfway up, a shot rang out. He fell to the floor flat on his back, almost landing on an older man whose face was difficult to see past all the grime to know how much was bruised. A few of the freed prisoners screamed or yelped.

The gunshot resounded in the hollow space between the decks and it took Mick a few seconds to register that his grandfather had been shot. He scanned his body for where he'd been hit. He panicked when blood oozed through the fabric of Raidan's shirt near his collarbone.

Mick collapsed to the floor and rushed to pour his healing magic into his grandfather. "Adefa!" Something like a wall blocked him from his power, keeping him from accessing it. *That gel!* He growled. "It won't work. Adefa, you need to get up." Tears pooled in his eyes. "I can't make my magic work. We have to go. Get up!"

Raidan's eyes fluttered open and closed. His head lolled.

A woman gasped. Before Mick could look up, Riggs pounced down the steps of the ladder and caught Mick from behind, grabbing a handful of hair and aiming a gun at his head. He shook him. "Everyone, get back!"

The prisoners shuffled back. Theérl slid down the ladder next. His dark skin glistened in the light of the sconces, and he flexed his biceps, holding his arms out to his sides. He grasped a whip in one hand. "Back up!" he barked.

Riggs bent to speak into Mick's ear.

"You cost me half of my slaves and Collectors. You're going to make all that up to me." To Theérl, he said, "Get them back to the hold. Make sure they stay there. I'll send for men to help."

The old man who Raidan had nearly fallen on top of stepped forward. "You have no right!" He directed his finger at Riggs. Brave man, but without the backing and support of others, he'd not get far. Theérl snapped the whip and lashed the man's face. The man cried out and cradled his eye with a hand.

Mick floundered in Riggs's hold. Riggs lifted him to his feet by his hair, tilting his head all the way back. "You're coming with me." He ascended the stairs, pulling Mick along with him. Mick's scalp throbbed in his grasp as he was forced to go along with him, leaving Raidan lying on the floor, unconscious.

As soon as they were on the next deck, Riggs replaced the gun to the side of Mick's head. "All this just for you? Even the Witch came on your behalf. I'll tell you what. If I get the Witch out of all this, I might even consider giving you a more comfortable accommodation than the cage I've set aside for you. It's the same one I used for the girl. By the way, did you like my surprise?"

Mick dug his nails into the hand that was gripping his hair. The seaweed outside blocked the light from the portholes on this level too. The ship vibrated. It was a wonder it hadn't broken yet with all its creaking and groaning.

Riggs gave Mick another shake. "What did you think of her tally? I told her, 'One for every time it could have been him.'"

Mick gritted his teeth and dug his heels into the floor. Riggs smacked his head with the gun, making him slump.

Riggs continued to drag him. "Don't worry," he said, his breath hot in Mick's ear. "I was gentle."

From someplace deep within, Mick screamed.

Glass smashed from the porthole behind them, and a piece of seaweed flopped into the ship's interior. It crept across the floor, trailing water. Riggs backed up, dragging Mick with him by the shirt. He looped an arm around his neck and aimed his gun at the seaweed as it inched toward them. He fired twice, hitting it both times. Mick's ears rang, but not only that—a stabbing pain took his breath away. The pain was not restricted to one place on his body. It shook his very being, and as the seaweed writhed and shrank back against the bulkhead, that feeling of fatigue weighed in his gut—as if his magic had an invisible tether uniting him with the plant life and they strained to connect.

Another two lengths of seaweed burst through the porthole.

"Argh! Enough of this!" Riggs hauled Mick along.

Mick's power might be impeded now, but the effects of the gel would wear off and he'd be himself again. Until then, he wasn't completely forsaken. Those whispers—the voices, the waters that were as much alive as he was—they fought for him to stay, to be in Kartha, where he belonged.

"You know," he said as he scratched Riggs's arm at his throat. "There's something else you don't know about my power."

"Oh, yeah?" Riggs yanked him along. "And what's that?"

"That when you come against me, you get more than you bargained for. My magic is one with Kartha." Mick tried to kick behind himself to knock Riggs's legs.

Riggs fired a shot from his gun right beside Mick's ear. Mick heard a high-pitched ringing resonate in his head, masking all other sounds. He couldn't even hear his own scream, nor did he realize how close they were to the next ladder.

"…you hear me?" Riggs shouted in his deaf ear. "Quit your squirming or I'll put another bullet in you."

"Hey!" a woman's voice called out. She sounded far away. Or was that just Mick's hearing? "You know who I am?" she said in a menacing tone.

Riggs turned to face the woman, taking Mick that way with him. Dimitri's words came to Mick then, and only now sunk in. *Laila was here.* How, didn't matter. She was here, and the gleam in her eye toward Riggs encouraged Mick.

Riggs kicked the back of Mick knees, dropping him to the floor. He then pressed the barrel of the gun to Mick's shoulder. "I know who you are, Witch," he said to Laila. "You cost me a lot of money too."

Outside, the seaweed continued to creep up the hull of the ship. The glass on the portholes was still intact at this end.

"That's the least of your concerns, Tormin," Laila said. "Your days of trafficking are over."

"Ha! Not today. Make one move, and I'll shoot him. He'll heal, but the bullet will be trapped in him. If I aim it just right, maybe I can get it lodged in his heart." Riggs backed up, dragging Mick with him. He was going to have a hard time bringing him up the ladder while maintaining his aim.

Mick eyed the seaweed outside. "You're forgetting what I told you, Riggs. You try to take me, Kartha fights back."

Then, as if he could telepathically communicate with the plant life, Mick called to it in his mind, bidding it to come. The whole ship groaned as seaweed smashed through every porthole on the deck. Dozens of strands of seaweed lunged inside, sliding, making their way toward them, water saturating the deck. Even though they heeded Mick's call, all he could do to guide them was project his feelings toward Riggs.

Riggs's eyes bulged. He aimed his gun at the seaweed again and fired as many shots as he had left. He hit a few tentacles—each one's pain felt by Mick—but they outnumbered the bullets and kept coming.

Riggs abandoned Mick and scrambled to the ladder. As he started climbing, more seaweed met him from above. He cried out and fell, landing on his backside. The seaweed skirted Mick and Laila, heading straight for Riggs.

Even though Mick couldn't tap into his magic, he could feel the pool within him reaching out, trying to attune his senses and power to the seaweed, trying to connect and ground him to Kartha. The hindering wall may have blocked him, but the seaweed could sense him nonetheless.

Riggs scrambled to his feet, but the seaweed twirled around his ankles, tripping him. He toppled, landing hard on his side. Laila took careful steps over the many lengths of seaweed so she could stand over him. He pulled himself with his arms, scurrying to get away. Laila planted her foot on his lower back, dropping him to the floor. She bent over him and yanked his wrists behind him. Once she had him so that he wasn't going anywhere, she glanced at Mick. "I've got this. Did Dimitri find you?"

Mick's heart jolted as he remembered about Adefa. He turned and, in his hurry to get to him, ran down the ship without giving her an answer.

When Mick got to the ladder where Raidan had fallen, his tension let up at the sight of his grandfather, awake and sitting up, supported by Dimitri behind him, who had a rag pressed to the wound. The bullet had hit just under the collar-bone. Theérl lay prone on the floor a few feet away, a man and woman restraining him, while another two people ushered the liberated Karthans up the ladder.

Mick blinked twice, not understanding what had happened. "Where are the others?"

Dimitri let all his tension go, looking equally as relieved to see Mick as he was to see them. "Royl got control of the situation on the upper deck, thanks to a bit of help from some aquatic plant-life." He smirked and shrugged. It was quite unbelievable, but so were a lot of things about this country. "After they got a handle on things, Royl delegated a few Warriors to take the first half of the prisoners ashore. They're all going to be fine."

Mick withheld a response. *Fine* was a relative word. Aira didn't look anything close to fine, but she was alive. She was safe. And Mick would ensure she stayed that way.

"You were taking too long," Dimitri continued, "so I came back for you and found Raidan like this and the others stowed away. This one tried to get the jump on me." He nodded toward Theérl and laughed. His laughter jostled Raidan, who grimaced and smacked his brother. Dimitri stilled. "Sorry, Raidan. Anyway, that one got what he had coming to him. They're in the charge of the Warriors now and will be brought to Litlen to stand trial."

Mick didn't know what he wanted to do more: cry, scream, sleep, or dance. He wanted to do all of those things at once.

When Laila found them at the bottom of the ladder, she grinned at Raidan. "The world keeps throwing fire at you, and yet, you prevail. Are you going to live?"

"He'll live," Dimitri said.

Mick slouched, feeling the adrenaline wear off. Now that he wasn't fighting for his life and for those he loved, he struggled to resist the exhaustion that overwhelmed him. He sank to the floor next to his great-uncle and grandfather. Although Raidan had lost a lot of blood and was in incredible pain—he'd make it, even without Mick's healing power. He'd manage until they could get him to shore, and then, when the gel wore off and Mick could use his ability again, he'd heal him.

For now, Mick leaned back against the angled ladder and relished this moment.

Riggs couldn't hurt anyone else now. Kartha was safe. No more sickness, no more curse, and no reason why Mick couldn't go home.

# Chapter 60

Mick found Aira sitting alone on the beach. Uncle Dimi had tipped him off that she'd come this way, and he'd left immediately to find her, resisting fatigue. However much gel Ighur had given him, it had yet to work its way through him, but this couldn't wait.

Riggs had been taken into custody by Litlen's Warriors along with his Collectors. Laila, Adefa, and Uncle Dimi worked to reunite families with their abducted loved ones. A process that could take days. Mick didn't mind. His feet were back on Karthan soil, and he was right where he should be. But something told him Aira wouldn't be inclined to stay

She sat in the sand, her legs drawn to her chest. A gentle wind swept her hair away from her face. She'd been given fresh clothes and had cleaned up a bit, but she still looked like a ghost of the woman he knew. A shawl covered her neck and shoulders. Mick tried not to think about what Riggs had told him about the cuts on her throat.

Aira flinched when he sat down next to her. Mick said nothing, nor did he touch her. He removed his shoes and stockings, then squished his feet in the soft sand, resting his elbows over his knees.

They sat for a long time before he sensed her tension ease gradually. Words couldn't change the course of events, nor would they take back whatever she'd endured at the hands of Riggs. If only they could.

Mick offered his hand and was relieved when Aira accepted it. Her hand was so frail and small. Not unlike Vidia's, except Vidia always held his hand with a firm sureness. Aira let hers sit loosely in his as she looked out at the sea and the low sun shimmering over its surface. Mick applied a small bit of pressure to her hand, affirming what he didn't have the courage to say aloud: *I'm sorry. I wish I could take back the things that happened. I love you.*

Tears fell from his eyes. He loved her very much, but his love for her would never become more. Kartha was where he belonged and where he would remain. Aira desired a life in Iptin. She'd said as much when they'd last spoken. Their lives were not on the same path, though they had been for a time. He didn't need to hear her say it to know that this was where they would part ways.

He lowered his head, not sure if he could fathom what that meant just yet—nor if he were ready for that. She knew the depths of his heart and made him a better man. How did one just…say goodbye? His tears flowed freely and he sniffed.

Aira rested her head on his shoulder, and Mick could feel her tears soaking through his shirt. Under his nose, her hair had the subtle fragrance of honey. He breathed it in, wanting to keep her scent in his memories forever.

She'd not wanted to come here, and yet here she was. And under circumstances that Mick imagined would haunt her for the rest of her life. Would she ever think fondly of Kartha? Or come back to visit under better circumstances?

Mick wiped his eyes, but it was futile.

Even if the gel had fully worn off, this was a kind of wound he couldn't just make go away. He sniffed again, and, for fear of his voice cracking, he whispered, "I wish I could heal your hurt." He didn't think she'd heard, but she let out a sob, followed by a bark of a laugh, then proceeded to weep against his chest.

Clouds floated across the sky, and the sun rays flared out from behind them. Mick wrapped his arm around Aira's shoulders and cried with her. He cried until he had no more tears. His weariness wore on him. He missed her smile and the way her cheeks dimpled. The way she snorted when she giggled and how her eyes would light up every time they greeted each other in the mornings before work. For as much as he'd missed her and loved her, she'd been right about him. He would have never settled until he came to Kartha. This sense of calm at having fulfilled this purpose—he'd never known peace until now. For the first time in his life, his mind and body were unified in stillness from the constant nagging feeling of incompleteness. Now he had a lifetime of catching up to do.

Mick's back ached. He shifted his weight, and Aira breathed in a long, shaky breath, stretching her own muscles out. She looked at him at last, and behind the pain in her eyes, was the same woman who laughed often and would readily impart wisdom. Although she didn't smile now, that woman was not gone.

Mick grazed his thumb across her bruised wrist. "If you stick around long enough, I can at least take care of this."

Aira's gaze fell to their hands, then wandered. "I'm taking the first ship to Ectarin tomorrow morning. I have to go home, Mick. When the Governor's men found me, they took me when no one else was around. My family have no idea what's happened. They still don't know where I am."

Mick knew she had to go, but still, he wished she'd stay. "I understand," he said.

Gentle dunes rose up behind them, eventually joining with grassy ridges. The coast extended down either side of the long beach. To their right, ships' sails stood out on the vast sea as the vessels glided into the harbour. Mick and Aira were far enough away, that the waves pounding the shore quashed any city noises.

Aira linked her arm into his and rested her cheek against his chest, holding him. "Did you find what you were looking for?" Her voice barely carried over the sweeping waves.

More tears came to him unbidden. Before returning to Litlen, he was really going to have to get a handle on his emotions. But for now, he let them come.

Aira leaned back and peered up at him. In the same way she'd been changed, had he? When she looked at him, did she see a shadow of the man he'd been?

*I'm still me.*

Except, not entirely. For all his gain, he felt loss too. Did he find what he was looking for? Yes, in a sense. He didn't realize finding it would mean leaving Aira behind. When he'd dreamt about going to Kartha, the prospect of it being long-term had occurred to him, but he'd not known just how rooted he was to this place. How had he survived so many years separated from this country?

He pulled Aira in closer, and she buried her face into his chest. He kissed her head. "I found the piece of myself I'd been missing. But I feel like I've lost another in the process." He bit his lip. "I don't want you to go, Aira. Not forever."

Aira drew away from him. She resumed her knee-drawn position while staring at her fists. Sand flowed from her hand in a steady stream, back onto the beach. "I know, Mick. I need time, that's all. I just need to feel safe. I'll feel better when I'm back home with my family." She met his gaze, then looked away. Her chin quivered. "We'll see each other again. Just give me some time."

What had Adefa said? Something about the heart not healing the same as the body? This wasn't something that would just disappear like a cut to the skin. This wound cut deeper and had no shortcuts to the healing process.

Mick pushed himself up and rose, brushing sand off his clothes. His muscles protested after sitting awhile. He extended his hands, and Aira accepted his help to stand.

"Take all that you need," he said. He reached toward her, hoping she'd allow him past her defences. She didn't flinch this time, but when he cupped her cheek, she closed her eyes and new tears streaked onto his hand.

"You're strong, Aira. And I'm here for you always." She leaned into his touch and grasped his hand. She would heal from this.

As would he.

# Chapter 61

A week after the defeat of Riggs and his crew, the roads were still not completely dry from the storm.

The journey back to Litlen had been uneventful. Unfortunately, this would be a shorter visit than Laila had hoped. Now that Governor Riggs was in the custody of Litlen's Warriors, they'd accomplished the first step of putting a stop to any future arrangements between him and his buyers. But now came the real task: tearing down his business little by little. It would be difficult to track down his contacts, but her crew relished the challenge. They'd be thorough.

She arrived outside of her mother's home. Royl had told her he'd arrive shortly after her, but she didn't have to wait. Her timing was perfect, as her brother walked up the road on his way toward her.

This was only to be a brief stop this evening, as Dimitri had asked her to come for dinner at Raidan and Ida's home.

Now that he was no longer bound to the Weldafire Stone, leaving the country wouldn't affect him the same as it had in the past, and he'd decided he would go with her to help begin the process of dismantling Riggs's business operations. Once she had the crew all filled in, Jude would take charge of the job.

Laila had another quest that had been on her mind for a long time. She'd heard rumours surrounding the disappearance of the *Crescent Cradle*, and certain facts just didn't add up. She intended to fill in the missing pieces and learn what became of Ilan and his company—if for no other reason than to bring closure to Daegan and his family.

Royl strode up the road, carrying a bouquet of eshuair flowers. Of all the plants in Kartha, why were these her mother's favourite?

"Are those for me, Royl? Oh, you shouldn't have." Laila laughed.

"Ah, Tsarioc. If I gave you flowers, I can count on them winding up in some concoction for an ailment I've never heard of." Royl kissed her cheeks, then entered the house.

Laila followed him inside, grinning. "You're not wrong."

At the kitchen counter, Royl poured her a cup of water. "But I love that about you," he said. "You know how to get the most value out of everything."

"If there's value to be had, I will find it." She took a sip of her drink. "Do you think you're ready to hear about all of my most recent adventures?"

Royl went about setting the flowers in a vase. "I don't know. Am I going to like what I hear?"

"Nope. Definitely not."

It had taken Royl years to come to terms with her insistence on putting herself in harm's way. If she were being honest, it took her a long time as well to realize she would never be okay with sitting cozy with a blind eye to the world and all that went on around them. Not when she had so much to offer to make it a better place. Having Royl on her side was freeing. Just knowing he was here for her, even if he didn't like what she did, encouraged her.

He sighed and shook his head, smiling. "I wouldn't expect anything less from you."

Freya called from her bedroom. "Is that you, Royl?"

Royl winked at Laila. "It's me, Mom." Their mother mustn't have heard that Laila was back. Laila smirked at her brother.

"Who are you talking to?" Freya called.

Her bedroom door clicked open, and a moment later she poked her head into the kitchen from the hallway. When Laila had been little, she used to envy Royl for inheriting their mother's looks. Freya had beautiful dark hair, dark eyelashes, and dark circles that made a halo around the green in her eyes. A smile filled her face, and she threw her arms out wide to wrap them around her daughter in a hug.

"Laila! I had a feeling you'd be back soon. Did you just get in?"

Laila shared a look with Royl. If by that their mother meant arrived in Litlen, then Laila supposed that technically she did. Not counting all this time she'd already been in Kartha. "I did, but I can't stay too long."

Royl clapped his hands together. "Ah, I knew you'd already have your next grand adventure planned. When will you finally decide to stick around and settle?"

Now that Dimitri was going to be joining her, who said settling meant one had to stay in one place? Laila shrugged. "I don't know." She made her way to the sitting room and nudged Royl with her elbow on her way past him. "It's a big world out there, Royl. And adventure awaits!"

# Chapter 62

The aromatic scent of yujin dressing pervaded the kitchen. Mick wrinkled his nose, undecided if he liked its coppery fragrance. He put it aside and opted to use a pepper oil instead, measuring out a small portion and adding it to the salad he was putting together. His grandparents' kitchen wasn't anywhere close in size to the one he was used to working in, but at least there was an oven.

A small fireplace took up space on the outside wall. Herbs were sealed in jars, lined in a row on a narrow upper shelf above the counter. He'd been eager to try a variety of new plants, herbs, and spices native only to Kartha, but his excitement turned into apprehension when the first few he'd tried were not what he'd expected. They were either they too bland, or too salty, or too bitter. These new flavours would take some getting used to.

The kitchen window let in the late afternoon light. A week had passed since his near departure from Kartha. It felt longer.

After leaving Hywreath, Mick had travelled back to Elefthan first with Daegan, Uncle Dimi, Adefa, and a company of Warriors. Laila and her brother had gone straight on to Litlen and would catch up with them all later. Along the journey, Dimitri and Daegan had been able to move past their feud and were on track to a fresh start. Mick had been right. The look on Vidia's face upon seeing her uncle safe and unharmed absolved him of Mick's grievances against him. Daegan had made peace with Waylan and Vidia—not least by calling off Vidia's marriage—and had sent for his other nephew to return to Elefthan, telling him to pack for a long-term stay. Supposedly Elefthan had been Daegan's home long before he'd settled in his ancestor's Keep.

Mick's stay in Elefthan had been brief while Adema was still at home and eager to see them. Adrik and Kameron had bid him farewell with the promise of a conversation down the road regarding the events since his arrival and his unique abilities. The time would come for that.

Mick mixed the dressing in with the salad and nodded to the oven. "Hey, can you take the bread out of the oven?" he asked Vidia. It was strange cooking with someone who wasn't Aira. And even more so when he realized just how inexperienced Vidia was in the kitchen.

Mick had received word that Aira had arrived safely home. Upon her departure, he'd managed to keep it together to see her off, but as soon as she had gone, he couldn't hold back the onslaught of emotions that he couldn't seem to shake now that he'd opened the floodgates. She'd left him with a simple kiss and a "goodbye for now."

Vidia removed the bread and set it down on a towel. Mick had already diced and cooked the steak, chopped and steamed the vegetables, and boiled the broth that made up the meat pie dish he was preparing. All that was left to do was to let the flavours blend.

He rinsed his hands, and Vidia handed him a towel to dry them. "Is this really what you used to do all day?" she asked.

Mick scratched behind his ear. "It is. I miss this. But…it appears I'm now out of a job."

"I'm sure Elefthan could use your expertise in their locameen. I can put in a good word for you if you'd like."

When Vidia had climbed out from the trench in the Gap, she and Boone had been quickly swept away by the Elefthan valients who'd come to help. She then managed to catch up with her brother and was able to help clean up in the aftermath of the battle in Elefthan. When Mick finally did show up at the camp, Vidia and Boone didn't hesitate when he asked them to return to Litlen with him.

Boone entered the kitchen. "Aren't you two cute?" He searched around the floor and counters. Mick had his lower back perched against the counter and his arms crossed. He raised a brow. "Did you lose something?"

Boone's face lit up, and he pointed to a crate tucked under an open cupboard. "Ah. That."

Mick bent to pick it up. He peeked in at the silverware and handed it to his friend, who raised it up and shook it. The cutlery jangled inside. Grinning at the sound of it, Boone did it again, then adjusted it in his arms to get a better hold on the crate.

"The table is set up outside," Boone said. "Your dad didn't think the dining area would be enough room for all of us."

"He's probably right." There were nine of them in total—his parents and grandparents, Vidia, Boone, Mick himself, Uncle Dimi, and, to Boone's great excitement, Laila. The dining room seated only four. It was a beautiful evening anyway, and Mick couldn't get enough of the fresh air in this place.

"How are your nerves?" Mick asked him. Boone had come to Litlen in hopes of meeting his hero and had experienced far more adventure than he could have hoped for. But for all his trouble, he was finally about to receive the payoff. Mick could understand his enthrallment with Laila. She was pretty amazing.

Boone shivered all over. "On edge. But hey, be cool, okay? She's just a person, right?" He did a little dance in place, jingling the silverware in his excitement. He left the kitchen, shaking it all the way outside and giggling like a child.

A feeling of fullness flooded Mick's heart.

Enveloped in the rich aromas of beef and onion, Mick determined the food was ready. He and Vidia carried it out to the table that had been set. Laila walked up the hill from the stable, and Boone was anything but cool, but he hid it well. Laila took his fervour in stride.

Once they'd all had their fill of dinner and finished off the rhubarb cake Mick had baked for dessert, Ida, Willa, and Vidia cleared off the table and wiped it down. Mick helped Dimitri with the dishes. By the time everyone was settled in their seats around the table again, the sun was out of sight over the horizon beyond the cliff's edge.

The conversation shifted from one topic to the next—Boone shared stories about his life in Xihngrahv with his seven siblings, Vidia talked about how she looked forward to resettling back in Elefthan, and Dimitri spoke of taking off with Laila on some sort of quest for a while, whatever that meant.

Mick eased back into his chair, considering what might come next for himself.

Coming to Kartha had always been his dream—the only thing he ever knew he *really* wanted. Now that he was here, that sense of impending danger was gone, as were the jitters and the feeling of some incomplete mission needing to be fulfilled.

He gazed up at the dark hues of blue in the sky. A few of the brighter stars were already visible. He could get used to nights like this. The gel that had suppressed his magic had taken days to fully wear off, but now that it had, his power never felt so complete. Adefa and Uncle Dimi had only shared with him bits and pieces of their roles as the Guardians of the Weldafire Stone so far. Mick was starting to understand the history, but he still didn't quite grasp what it all meant. Right now, he was surrounded by his family, and that was all that mattered.

The pink and white flowers that crept up the vines in front of the house gave off a subtle white glow. As the evening grew, Kartha came alive. The plants' colours and luminescence reminded Mick again of the aurora lights he'd seen many times in the prairie skies of Iptin.

Two butterflies floated around the table. Every time they fluttered their wings, a flash of neon revealed their colourful pattern. One landed on Mick's hand, resting on the table. Over the past few days, all kinds of creatures and insects had been acting strange around him. Critters such as this butterfly, as well as birds and small animals always seemed to be present wherever he went. Plants grew more vibrantly, and even the wind moved in sync with him.

A gentle breeze swished his hair off his forehead. He closed his eyes and smiled, sensing the wholeness in the land and in himself.

The conversation grew quiet around the table, and Mick opened his eyes to see everyone watching him. He'd zoned out and missed half the discussion. Were they talking about him? His cheeks burned.

"What? Is something the matter?"

Cassian smiled, showing all teeth. "No, Mick. Nothing is the matter." He chuckled. "Everything is as it should be." He rested a firm hand on Mick's shoulder and squeezed.

Peace overwhelmed Mick, and it was too much to contain. He let it flow from his hand and into the butterfly. The butterfly took off, floating away, glowing brighter as it joined its partner in their dance.

It was a wonder he hadn't talked himself into coming to Kartha sooner. To this place that called to him—spoke his name, fought for him. This place that made him whole.

Mick could have cried for how full his heart was. Instead, he let out a laugh. "It's good to be home."

# Acknowledgements

Always to begin, I thank God for creating in me a wild imagination to concoct stories and have the means and opportunity to write them and publish. I'm grateful that I've not only been able to publish one book, but now two!

My family—as ever—so patient with me. I've learned to pull back on my ramblings, even though you never complain or grumble. I love you all.

Despite what people say about writing being a lonely business, I have to disagree. I've had such amazing support and help from many others, including the Tw/X #writingcommunity and Nicole Whisler's Facebook group and all you lovely people I sprint with.

Nicole at Whisler Edits—your input is invaluable. With your help, I've learned so much, and am better equipped with tips and tricks for future writing. As always, my stories are stronger thanks to your insights.

I can't forget my amazing beta readers who offered very useful feedback. You're all amazing.

Who doesn't love a map in a fantasy novel? Thank you, Daniel Schmelling, for the map of Iptin Province and of Kartha. You did wonderful work on them both and I'm grateful for what you do.

Thank you Kevin Wilson for being the first person outside of family to read my very rough first version of Unbound when I'd first written it in screenplay format as a science fiction story. Your support and encouragement was exactly what I needed at that time to embolden me to continue this journey in doing the thing I love most. Your excitement about writing and pursuing this dream meant a lot to me then, and it still does today.

And of course, thank you, reader. Writing is one thing, but to be able to move forward with the work and publish is another, and it wouldn't be worth much if people didn't read our stories. So, thank you for taking the time to delve into Mick's story and adventure alongside him and Laila, and lose yourself in the country of Kartha. It's a joy to share this world that's existed in my imagination for years, and to let people in to see the beauty and feel the magic as I have.

Thank you.

# About the Author

There was never a time that Trinity hasn't loved writing. Songwriting, screenwriting—filling out a simple form—give her a pen and she's in her element.

In her younger years, movies and books were her escape. And when there was nothing on the go, she would imagine her own worlds. When her stories could no longer be contained by her thoughts alone, she began writing them down. Hundreds of pages of idea excerpts littered her notebooks.

Later, after pursuing courses in screenwriting and storytelling, she began to develop her ideas further. But it wasn't until 2020 that she got the inspiration to revamp her old ideas and write them into novels. Since then, she's found her passion, delving into these fictional worlds and bringing to life new characters.

Besides writing, Trinity enjoys reading, watching films, photography, and spending time with friends and family. She lives in Canada, with her husband and their three children.

# A note from the author

One thing about being a self-published author is that we start from the ground-up. Without agent representation (as there is in traditional publishing), it's up to me as the author to build a reader-base and spread the word about my work little by little.

Your contribution helps! Thank you for taking a chance and buying/reading my books. Another easy and accessible way that you can help to extend my limited reach is by going to sites like Goodreads and leaving a review. It doesn't have to be long or go into detail of anything. It can simply be a sentence, telling others whether or not you enjoyed the book. It all helps in the long run.

For your convenience, I've included the Goodreads link below where, and if you feel so inclined, please leave a review. Afterward, feel free to like and follow my social media pages (links for these are listed below). Thanks for your support.

GOODREADS PROFILE:

https://www.goodreads.com/author/show/45565748.Trinity_Cunningham

Social Media pages where you can follow and keep up to date with what's new:

https://www.facebook.com/TrinityCun

https://www.instagram.com/trinncun

https://www.twitter.com/trincun

www.ingramcontent.com/pod-product-compliance
Lightning Source LLC
Chambersburg PA
CBHW030922120726
47906CB00002B/440